DANCER OF THE DEAD

By

Edred Breedlove and Trish Breedlove

This book is a work of fiction. Places, events, and situations in this story are purely fictional. Any resemblance to actual persons, living or dead, is coincidental.

ISBN: 1-4107-6599-7 (e-book)
ISBN: 1-4107-6598-9 (Paperback)

Library of Congress Control Number: 2003094698

This book is printed on acid free paper.

Printed in the United States of America
Bloomington, IN

1stBooks - rev. 07/09/03

CHAPTER 1

The wind moved slowly down the hills and into the valley, lightly caressing the stones and the bark of the trees. It imperceptibly rustled what few leaves remained tightly clinging to otherwise bare branches. It crossed a small plain. Brown and flattened by recent snows, the grass remained unmoved and uninterested. Finding an ancient orchard, the breeze toyed with a wind chime hanging low on the branch of an old apple tree. It could turn the chime slightly but didn't have the force to elicit a sound. The wind carried no snow or rain in its wake. Neither did it carry the stirrings of an early, warm spring breeze. This was a whispering wind. The stones and the trees heard its message and became aware even if indifferently affected by its tale. The wind left the chime and moved on across stones now hewn flat, not by forces of nature, but by the hands of men. It wove around the boot of an old woman, standing without shivering, in the weak sunlight as she admired the beauty of a crystal clear February day. The wind caused the fringe of her long skirt to shimmy, as in a clockwise motion it danced upward across her body lightly lifting small wisps of her silver hair where it exposed her slightly reddened ear.

Crescent stood at the end of her sidewalk of Bedford Limestone. She could almost taste spring in the air, although she knew she was only fooling herself with the mental placebo. Winter had yet to relinquish its grasp on the land.

1

"Mrrrr" her cat spoke as it wound itself between her feet.

"Yes, Trinket. Persephone will be rising from the underworld soon and her mother will once more smile upon the Earth and bless all with her bounty."

Trinket rolled over once but found the limestone too cold to continue. She turned back to the house and beckoned Crescent to follow to where she knew the warm wood stove would provide a preferable lay down spot at its hearth.

"I'll come in a moment, dear." Crescent always felt cabin fever by this time of year. She longed to be starting seeds and tending the soil. Once the anticipation of the Yule celebration was over she saw no more reason for the cold of winter to continue.

"I should move to a warmer climate." She spoke as she had for many years, knowing all the while she would never leave her valley for good.

She was taking in a deep cool breath when the wind caressed her face. She smiled brightly as her hair spiraled before her eyes. Just as suddenly her smile froze. Her features drooped and a cold steely fire seemed to light behind her eyes. Her hair lowered, and her skirt tassels ceased their dance as the whispering wind moved on in search of others with the gift to hear.

Trinket returned to Crescent's feet and she gently picked the cat up as she began walking toward the house. Trinket purred in anticipation of warm milk and a possible tummy rub.

"You'll be needing to stay close to the house for awhile, dear Trinket. Not that that's any problem for you this time of year." She opened the heavy door and crossed the living room floor into the kitchen where she placed the cat on an old worn table. The house, having been closed for the winter, smelled heavily of the dried herbs and fruits Crescent had harvested in the fall. She shook the ashes down in the wood stove before adding another log and set a kettle on before getting Trinket her milk.

"There are changes coming and we must prepare." The cat jumped to the floor to enjoy the milk as Crescent sat down at the table and opened an old carved wooden box. She removed a deck of Tarot cards and cleared her mind as she methodically shuffled and lay out a Celtic cross spread, cards face down on the table. "Knowledge is power, Trinket, so we must see who, and what, is in store." Trinket

2

cocked her head to the side as Crescent spoke, as if listening intently. She nodded, licked her paw, and returned her attention to the last bit of milk in the bowl.

After years of study and experience, Crescent always trusted her intuition—and the wisdom of the cards. So often, while reading for others, she would interpret a card and surprise even herself with what she said. So helpful were these intuitive flashes of spoken word, it became a habit to speak out loud during a reading, even when she was alone. Of course, Trinket was there, but she seemed more interested in cleaning her fur after her snack, than curious about the cards.

Crescent turned over the center card, the first she had dealt, indicating the forces at work in the current situation: the Eight of Wands. "Yes, here are the changes the East wind whispered to me. Wands are change and the accompanying growth, yet I felt a sense of impending danger on the wind. Change is usually only traumatic to those who fight it. I've long since learned the futility of fighting change. Why would the wind whisper of these changes to me?"

Trinket finished with her bath, meowed to announce her ascent and jumped onto the table. She looked at the reading, then at Crescent. Lying down, she placed her head upon her front paws. "Thank you Trinket," Crescent murmured, "I always appreciate your cat magick augmenting mine! Funny, I never noticed how the wands, traveling through the air, are divided into two sets of four. Fours are foundations. Foundations will be sundered; these changes will be deep. Many changes are in the offing; some will be positive, some negative. Now they are at their beginnings, but to the untrained, their onset will seem swift and unexpected. The number eight indicates strength. This is not strength given, but strength needed. All my senses tell me strength will be sorely needed. But it will be found. Balance in everything." She paused.

When nothing else seemed forthcoming about the first card, Crescent turned her attention to the second one, which she had placed sideways across the first. This card told of the forces at work that would oppose the energies of the first. "The Universe in all its glory contains both the light and the dark," she said, turning the second card. "The three of Pentacles. Yet another of the changes to come. There will be an apprentice, and this person will be crucial in determining the outcome of future events. Hardworking, eager, in need of spiritual solace." Crescent was deeper into the state of being the Tarot always brought her: a place of magick, intuition, and knowing. As she briefly closed her eyes, she had a swift impression of a young woman with short red hair and expressive eyes. "Diana. Into troubled times walks the one who may be my apprentice."

Crescent turned the third card, below the other two, to learn of the energy surrounding the foundation of the current situation. It was Temperance, one of Crescent's meditation favorites. It was the fourteenth card of the Major Arcana that consisted of 22 Cards. The philosophy behind the cards, and the wisdom contained within their symbolic language, never ceased to amaze her. In numerical sequence, the Major Arcana showed the development of consciousness from fledgling individual in The Fool (0) to the integrated community symbolized by The World (21). She reviewed what her Grandmother had taught her so long ago: "The Magician, High Priestess, Empress, Emperor, Hierophant, Lovers, and Chariot: these cards exemplify personality traits. Strength, The Hermit, Wheel of Fortune, Justice, The Hanged Man, Death, and Temperance: these show Spiritual influences and relate to cause & effect. The Devil, The Tower, The Star, The Moon, The Sun, Judgment, and The World: these relate to the higher energies, the complex, powerful forces of existence."

Returning from her reverie, Crescent again looked at the card. An Angel standing with one foot in clear water and the other on solid ground was pouring water from one goblet to another. It reminded Crescent of the necessity of walking in balance by keeping one foot in each world: the material world and the spiritual world. It also reminded her of the spiritual truth 'as above, so below' and its equally true opposite, 'as below, so above.' Looking at the card, you couldn't tell if the water was flowing from the upper goblet into the lower, the lower into the upper, or both at the same time, which was what she always believed.

"Many years of Temperance, of walking in balance, support this foundation, yet foundations may still sunder. Care must be taken to be very aware. We can not afford to overlook anything important. We must see what is really there and not depend on old ways of seeing or believing." Partially aware that she had switched from the singular to the plural, Crescent turned over the next card.

The Sun, another Major Arcana card, was in the place that symbolized the immediate past. "Higher forces are at work, Trinket. We are coming from a time of illumination and balance, and that is what we will draw on during the challenges to be. The sun is low on the horizon. In this reading, I do not see its life-giving rays and warmth; I see the promise of the night to come."

Crescent shivered, and Trinket tanked up as a chill breeze sneaked past the wood stove from the crack under the back door.

At the top of the layout, showing a possible future, was the four of Pentacles. "There will be a grace period before we must meet the challenge. It will appear to be a time of abundance, yet there is a wall, an obstruction, behind everything. There was a wall in The Sun card, too. Hmm. Well, if we can't see over or around it, I guess we'll just have to climb over it or dig under it! Being prepared and having a positive state of mind is half the battle."

The next card, also of a possibility for the future, was the Two of Wands. "Yes, we will have a period of contemplation while we wait to learn what challenges we must meet. People will work together, and will be prepared for the challenges as long as they don't get too complacent. But that's always the case, isn't it, Trinket?"

To the right of the equal armed, or Celtic, cross that was formed by the reading so far, was a line of four cards. At the bottom, was the card that would show Crescent her fears. So many times, the fear card was one that looked really good, which had confused her until she realized people fear getting what they desire. "What if it doesn't make me happy, or isn't what I hoped it would be, then what?" But she had never been one to wonder "What if," and if she felt like doing something, as long as it didn't hurt anyone, she did it. As with the majority of readings she did for herself, Crescent's fear was a valid one, the Seven of Swords.

"Well that pretty much says it all. I'm getting on in years and I do fear having to do everything myself. Not like I do many things I don't like to do, but the amount of work hasn't decreased with my energy levels! Maybe I will take on this apprentice."

The next card showed other people's opinions. It seemed to be the least pertinent position of the layout to Crescent, but many people put a lot of stock in what others thought. She always included it out of respect for the efficacy of the rest of the layout. "Another sword! Strife. But, it's in the opinion position; that's not as bad as if it was in a possible future space or was the Outcome. The Five of Swords, in the 'other people's opinions' space. This one is hazy since I don't really know all the details of our situation. It looks as if there will be loss, and those affected will have the compassion and assistance of those who survive the storm."

"Next up: the Hope card. It's the nine of swords. Well, at least it wasn't the ten! At some point, it appears I will wish my hands were tied and things weren't left up to me. Fits in with the fear card. So, let's see what the Outcome is, Trinket dear." The cat stood up, stretched, yawned, then turned her back to the cards to jump down and lie by the wood stove, as if to say, "Outcomes are only new beginnings."

Crescent laughed. "You're right, Trinket. We humans put so much importance on outcomes, on the results of our labors and manipulations. Maybe you do have the right idea, living in the moment. I'm still looking at the last card, though!"

"The Hanged Man indicates a sacrifice will have to be made. We're definitely not talking a win-win situation. There will be losses before anything is gained."

Looking at the full layout, Crescent noted there had been three Major Arcana out of ten cards in the layout, indicating some higher forces were at work in the situation. "This is not a mundane circumstance mainly determined by individuals—the Major Arcana cards attested to that, as did the total absence of Court cards. There were no kings, queens, pages, or knights. Three of the remaining cards were Swords, indicating conflict and unrest. Two were Pentacles indicating industriousness and financial matters. The other two were Wands and indicated change. There were no Cups. We must remember to work from a place of love, compassion, and understanding in the days to come. A world without love is, indeed, a frightening place."

CHAPTER 2

Kratel was disturbed by the strange feelings that were even now causing his body to shake with an eerie, almost morbid, sense of fear and curiosity. In all his memory, he could not recall a time when there was a lack of food. Eating was something always taken for granted, like breathing. When you needed air, you simply inhaled and it was there. When you were hungry you merely focused your will and sang and food came. Now the food was taking longer to arrive and the portions were getting smaller and smaller.

Kratel knelt beside the pool that welled up in the niche where he lived. He dipped his hand into the cold water and drank. The liquid felt good upon his hand; he had injured his finger on a large stone a couple days earlier. He flexed his claws beneath the surface. The pain was still there but endurable. He ran his damp hand along the unruly fur of his forearm and flattened the white hair down.

"The tunnels must be blocked," Kratel thought. "That is the only logical conclusion. Only the smaller food is able to squeeze through at this time. That is why it is taking longer. The larger food will continue to work at opening the passageways until they are once more passable." Kratel decided, "It's just a matter of biding my time by nibbling on the small food until the bigger portions make their way down."

"But what if the big food takes too long to arrive?" Kratel's thoughts continued to nag. "Is it possible to starve to death?" This was a question he had never before considered. "How long could I go without water? Food? Air?" Water and air were still in plentiful supply. The tiniest passage would allow them access. The food, however, was another matter.

Perhaps going up the tunnel to be closer to the food when it finally broke through the blockage would be a more reasonable solution. Kratel's compulsive nature took over. "Yes, it's decided then—but how far up?" Kratel had traversed the upward passageways before but never with a goal in mind and always remaining within an easy journey back to his comfortable and safe dwelling niches. There are some things that are not too pleasant to run into in the less traveled passages. "How far do the tunnels go? Are they infinite?" The blockage would be somewhere ahead, though. "I'll travel until I reach the blockage, that's what I'll do. It will be better than waiting to starve to death, however long that could take."

Kratel crossed the stone floor and climbed onto the ledge that served as his sleeping quarters. He fluffed his bedding furs in preparation for his return. Tying on his belt pouch and loincloth, he gathered a glow-stone and a few of the other possessions he liked to carry when he journeyed.

Finally, he filled a water-skin from the pool, climbed through the access hole to his small chambers, and entered the tunnel which eventually led upward through the larger caverns.

CHAPTER 3

The mist was irritating to drive in. Chris always disliked the way it gathered on the windshield. Not thick enough to require the wipers to be on all the time, just congealing enough so you had to turn them on for a couple of swipes and then back off again when they started that dry scrape across the glass. But then, that was pretty much his attitude toward everything. 'If it's going to rain, it should rain!' Chris had shouted at the clouds often enough that he was, very likely, responsible for flooding in many of the low-lying areas around which he lived. When he bought a tool, clothes, appliance, or anything, he always bought the best product he could afford. "If you're going to buy a hammer, get a good one!" Unfortunately, Chris also managed to get caught up in his own opinion of how things should be. He often forgot things, such as the fact that his 'better than average' car had an intermittent wiper switch that would occasionally make the swipe at the mist for him, if he would only turn it on.

Diana was vaguely aware of Chris's inner struggle as she watched the landscape moving alongside the highway. She would have liked to have had enough time to take some back roads, but their departure from New York had come about so badly they were already many hours behind schedule, as if time really made a difference in a burg like Bedford, Indiana, anyway.

She and Billy, Chris's agent, had tried to dissuade him from making such a dramatic life style change. She could hear Billy now telling Chris, "Man, don't you know you can't go back home? New York is your home now. Your music is in you, not where you are or aren't. Everybody has a dry spell." Billy had shrugged and said, "Take a vacation, get some new insights and inspirations. Then you'll come back and write your ass off. Man, if a songwriter moved every time they had a writers block, Hell, they'd own half of the property in the country."

Diana turned her attention from her memory of Billy's words and the side window to look over at her husband. Although he was currently frowning at the weather conditions she still found pleasure in admiring his profile. His long blonde hair, as usual, was out of place and in need of combing. His strong hand swiped at the occasional errant strands that fell across his face. Pale blue eyes narrowed as he strove to see through the mist that once again gathered on the windshield. Diana also liked the muscular bulge of his arms moving beneath his shirt as he guided the car along the freeway. Even though most of Chris's work kept him in a chair as he composed or worked in the studio, he never let his body get too far out of shape. At five foot eleven, and one hundred eighty-five pounds he looked a little stocky, due mainly to his undisciplined eating habits. He worked hard at the gym and played tennis regularly to keep his muscles taut and to compensate for his caloric input.

"You know, Chris, I wonder if we're doing the right thing…"

"For God's sake, Di, isn't it a little late to be hashing this out again?" Chris interrupted. "We have talked and we've talked about this move, and we both agreed to give it a try. And now that we're actually doing it, you want to reopen the discussion?"

Diana wanted to shwap Chris upside his head. If he hadn't been driving, she probably would have done just that.

"If you would let me finish my sentences before jumping down my throat," she said icily, "I was saying it may not be the right thing to do in pushing ourselves so hard on the road to keep an appointment with the real estate agent! We could stop for a bite, you could phone him, and reschedule to meet in the morning. That way we could slow down, get a motel for the night and meet the agent tomorrow. At least in a motel I could have some maneuvering room for when you try to bite my head off."

Chris smiled. "I guess I have been a bit of a bear lately, huh? Sorry, Babe. I'll tell you what! You pick the place we stop to eat, and I'll phone the Realtor and call ahead for a room."

"Good," Diana said, "at least with some food in you my head will have a better chance of survival for the rest of the trip."

A few miles later, a Cracker Barrel restaurant allowed them time to eat the breakfast they had missed earlier while trying to escape from New York.

"You know, Hon," Diana said while stretching like a well-fed cat, "there's something delightfully decadent about eating breakfast at six p.m."

Chris enjoyed watching the lean muscles of her body as she stretched her long legs beneath the table. Giving birth to two children had rounded her figure from her skinny high school days. Chris, however, found her to be more attractive in a voluptuous, womanly, way. Her breasts and hips were fuller than when she and Chris had first met and Chris had to admit that he liked them that way.

Noticing the red lipstick on the rim of her coffee cup, Diana decided it was time to recheck her makeup. At 36 she still had a youthful complexion and could get away with minimal amounts when necessary, although she always felt a bit naked in public without eye shadow and mascara. Her green eyes stared back at her as she peered into the compact mirror from her purse. Deftly as a sculptor, she applied gloss to her lips and a touch of powder to her petite upturned nose. She ran her fingers through her short-cropped red hair as the final gesture and returned the compact to her purse.

"It reminds me of the old days of eating breakfast at three a.m. after playing music all night in a sleazy bar, then going home to bed while everyone else in the world was getting up." Chris said, as they stood and began walking toward the register to pay the tab. He brushed biscuit crumbs from his jeans as he walked behind Diana, admiring the sway of her skirt as she moved. She seldom wore jeans even though she had the long legs and figure to do it well. She preferred the long, flowing peasant-style skirts, especially the silk ones.

"It's been a lot of years since you've performed on stage," Di said while admiring a gnome statue behind the counter. "Do you ever miss it? The glamour and excitement?" she asked, holding open the door as Chris passed through. Diana took his hand as they crossed the parking lot.

"Not at all. Like Jim Morrison said. 'Man, we've done the Sullivan show.' My true love of music was always in the writing, not the performing." As she slid into the car seat next to him, Chris gently caressed the back of her neck and once more found himself lost in those sea green eyes. "You're all the glamour and excitement I need. And once we get settled in our new home, I'll be able to relax enough to start writing again."

As long as you're happy, I'm happy. Now back to that glamour and excitement thing," Diana purred. "How much further is it to the motel? And before you say you're tired from driving, remember, tomorrow Dad arrives at our new home with our two lovely children. No more evenings alone for a long while."

"Put down the landing gear, stewardess, we'll be arriving shortly."

As much as Diana enjoyed her makeup in public, she relished removing it from her skin in a hot shower. Especially this shower, because she didn't have to wash or fold the towels and washrags. The new soap and shampoos were not used up by someone else and she didn't have to scrub the tile before or after.

"Heaven." She spoke into the showerhead as if into a microphone. "Hotel showers are absolute heaven. Plenty of hot water, too! How could it get better than this?"

As she allowed the cascading water to wash over her face, she was unaware of the hands that reached through from either side of the shower curtain. She involuntarily jumped in surprise as encircling arms grasped the small of her back.

She turned in recognition and thrust her breasts into the clinging folds of the curtain. Her dark areolas and nipples stood out in wet relief on Chris's face.

"Who is it?" Di feigned innocence.

"Norman Bates," Chris responded playfully while continuing to slide both hands slowly up and down her wet spine.

"Well, Norman, are you going to be a mama's boy and hide behind the curtain all night, or will you come in and get me like a man?"

12

The plastic curtain sounded like separating Velcro as Chris peeled the clinging folds from Di's body. The water temperature was hotter than he would have liked but even so he stepped over the rim of the tub, joining her in the cavalcade of steaming water.

"Anyone would have to be Psycho to pass up a challenge like that."

As he moved into Diana's embrace he felt the hot droplets of water as they splashed across his back and trickled slowly across his buttocks. Diana's fingernails traced small furrows across his skin, bringing the already sensitive nerve endings even more alive. She moaned softly as his tongue chased a wayward drop of water down her neck and across her shoulder.

Chris marveled at the steam rising from Diana's breast. He lowered his head to suckle, but was stopped by Di's soapy hands.

Without a word, she rinsed the perfumed lather from her skin, lightly stepped out of the tub, and, leaving a trail of water and steam, headed off into the bedroom.

Chris watched her pink feet leave moist imprints in the carpet as she stepped through the door. He quickly turned off the shower and pursued her, leaving his own vapor trail in his wake.

The rest of the trip was much more relaxed. Once out of Pennsylvania and into Ohio, the speed limit increased from 55 to 65, which meant Chris could do 70 with less fear of getting a ticket. The spring scenery changed dramatically from rolling mountains to rolling hills, from flat land to bottomland, and back to rolling hills again as they entered southern Indiana.

"It's going to be great having a house again, instead of an apartment," Chris said. "Just think, we'll have more room inside and out! We'll have our own woods to walk in. No more city park picnics for us! And now you can apply those gardening techniques you've acquired from reading all those magazines over the years. If you can handle turning the soil as well as you turned those pages, we'll be up to our ears in rutabagas by midsummer."

"As if you would know a rutabaga from a Winnebago, Mr. Connoisseur of Fast Foods. If I hadn't put golden arches in the dining room and told you we were eating McStirfry with McTofu, you would have died of malnutrition long ago," Diana chided.

13

"Yeah, and with all those preservatives in me, I could have hung around for a long time and nobody would have known I was dead. Hey! Maybe that's what I need to get my writing back on track. Everyone knows dead poets sell better than live ones. You could contact Mel, my publisher, and tell him I passed away from Falafel poisoning, but you had some tapes I had recorded and you could keep sending them in."

"So," Diana said, "you'd literally become a ghost writer?"

"Or maybe," Chris added, "you could get a medium to contact me on the other side and I could continue writing from beyond."

"With an ego the size of yours, we had better forget the medium and get an extra large."

"Ouch," winced Chris, "no more puns. You win. I'll stay alive."

"Who said that was the way I wanted you?"

"Look," Chris said, nodding at the city limit sign of the town Highway 37 allowed them to bypass, Oolitic. "Next stop is Bedford; another ten miles until our new home."

"Ooh, Oolitic." Diana thought. "Bedford, the Limestone Capitol of the World. How did a nice city girl like me wind up in a place like this?"

"Okay, Hon, take a deep breath, it's new start time! Man, does this feel right, or what?"

"Or what," Diana muttered, "Definitely, or what."

The road that led to the house wasn't exactly a gravel road, but calling it paved was stretching the truth in the other direction. It was probably paved about a hundred years ago, around the time their "new" house was built. All of the original paving was now buried under several layers of patching. The driveway, which they were about to turn onto, appeared to be in much better shape than the road. Suddenly Chris slammed on the brakes. Diana was saved from banging her head on the windshield by her seat belt, which she always wore. She even had Chris in the habit, after all those years of refusing to drive the car unless everyone in it was strapped in.

"Sorry," Chris said, putting the car in park and opening his door.

"What is it, Chris? What's the matter?"

Diana opened her door and cautiously got out. Chris was leaning over the hood looking at the ground or something on the ground, in front of the car.

"What is it? Did you hit something?" Diana asked again.

"No, *I* didn't hit it. But something obviously did."

Diana walked to the front of the car and saw the raccoon that Chris had braked so hard to avoid running over.

"Is it dead?" Di asked, holding her stomach with one hand and her mouth with the other.

"Looks like it. It must have gotten hit on the road and knocked onto our driveway. I'll get a branch out of the woods and move it off the road for now, and come back and bury it later."

Diana looked around as Chris stepped into the brush in search of a substantial limb to move twenty or so pounds of dead raccoon. The house, from where they stood, wasn't visible. The drive curved to the right about thirty feet further on and disappeared into the trees. Diana had only seen pictures of the house. The closing had been done through lawyers and real estate agents. She knew it was secluded from the road, but the trees and undergrowth were much thicker than she had envisioned. Once again she was reminded that she was a city girl, used to nature as a manicured and maintained park - with trees properly spaced, and grass and hedges allowed to grow only so high. Seclusion she thought she was ready to deal with, but shoving dead animals off the drive in order to reach the house seemed a little much.

A sudden crash in the bushes beside her startled her from her reverie as a large antlered beast came pushing through the growth, heading directly for her. "How big do deer or moose get?" she thought, as she turned and ran for the safety of the car. "Chris! Chris!" she screamed. Di didn't realize she had walked so far away from where they stopped. An enraged bellow and thump behind her told her that the beast had surged free of the entangling growth and was now upon the road behind her. Five more steps and she'd reach the door, two more seconds to swing around it and slam it shut. How fast can a moose run anyhow? "Chris!" the name was barely audible upon her lips as the burst of speed robbed her of breath. There! - The touch of metal upon her hand, she nearly shot past the door opening, she was moving so fast. She slammed the door so hard she thought the glass would break.

15

"Just my luck," she thought, "break all land speed records getting away only to be gored to death through an open window." All thoughts of safety suddenly vanished as the shadow of the creature's horned head passed over the front of the car at the same time she saw the driver's side door standing wide open where Chris had gotten out.

Where the Hell was he? She flung herself across the seat, her right breast laying on the horn as she reached out for the door. "EEYaah!" Chris screamed, from right in front of the car.

"Oh my God! It's attacking Chris!" She began trying to reopen the door even before it had closed all the way. She pulled one of her shoes off as she rolled from the car. It was the only weapon she could think of to defend herself with. Why wasn't she wearing a pair of those stiletto-heeled 'fuck me' pumps?

"What the Hell are you blowing the horn about? You trying to give me a fucking heart attack?" Chris yelled. He was standing in front of the car holding a large tree limb that looked amazingly like a pair of antlers.

"You could have helped me drag this thing out of the bushes instead of running back to the car like that. What's with you anyway? And what's with the shoe?"

Diana didn't know whether to scream or laugh. She figured throwing the shoe at Chris's head was the only logical thing to do. So she did.

Maneuvering the animal off the road with a branch was no easy task, as Chris was finding out. He felt like some macabre puppet master trying to manipulate an uncooperative marionette. "A regular dancer of the dead," he thought. "Just like in the dives where I played with the band before finally cracking the big time. All the same people, night after night, sitting there in those smoke-filled rooms, lost in their own thoughts and conversations. Trying to drink away today or tomorrow, whichever one held the fear. Seeking the best oblivion that would remove the thoughts from their minds so they could relax a bit before taking on reality once again. Just like Liza Minelli said, "Reality is the thing we try to rise above." And rise they did, as soon as the music started. Each one seemed to dance to their individual, particular, beat. Some moving fast, in time with the snare drum. Others doing a slow bump and grind to the bass guitar. A few trying fancy steps to the dance rhythms of the guitar. But no matter

16

what set the pace, they still danced. They rose from the mists of their rum and beer, their wine and whiskey, even the ones who had begun drinking hours before the band began. They still came like lemmings to the dance floor, unable and unwilling to resist the piper's call. The music animated them. Seduced by the alluring rhythms, the 'dead-to-the-world' people danced. Their spirits filled with the motivating melodies flesh could not deny. They danced. The dead danced. And there, at center stage, stood Chris, the dancer of the dead, just as surely as he now danced the dead raccoon off the road and into the bushes.

CHAPTER 4

"The photos of the house didn't do it justice," Diana thought, as they rounded the bend and the hundred-plus year old home came into view. And home it was, just as it was love at first sight for Diana. She had such a profound sense of homecoming that she knew beyond doubt that this was where she belonged. The limestone walls spoke more of man's hands than handiwork; here was craftsmanship beyond just doing a job. The building was more a labor of love than labor for pay. Porches invited cool summer shade with drinks and languid conversations. The driveway paralleled the front, eastern face of the house, then swung out to the north, looping back to the portico on the north side of the house. From here, they could see the outbuildings and the site for the planned greenhouse—empty now but silently calling for projects and potting soil. Her hands ached to get into the earth. She would have a real garden, not just flowerpots and window boxes on the fire escape, but real space to cultivate, landscape, and expand. She would plant fields of lavender, and dig a pond out back. She would create a water garden just like in the magazines.

"Di." Chris's voice jarred her from her thoughts. "Look. Here comes Mr. Tremble, the real estate agent, with the keys. Now we can go inside."

Chris was walking around the car to stand beside her on the front lawn. She had been so taken by the first sight of their new home and the location of her future greenhouse, she hadn't realized she'd gotten out of the car and walked over to the front of the house.

Mr. Tremble pulled his station wagon behind their car and stopped.

"Gee, Hon, looks like we're going to miss parking down the block and then running for the front door of the apartment to keep our groceries dry." Diana said sarcastically.

"You mean Tofu isn't supposed to taste like that?"

"Like what?" asked Di.

"Exactly!" Chris said.

"Huh?" Mr. Tremble asked, adjusting his hat as he walked up behind the couple.

"Private joke." Chris and Diana both said at the same time and burst into laughter.

Mr. Tremble laughed right along with them, even though he didn't understand what he was laughing about. He did know, however, that he was making a pretty healthy chunk of commission from this sale. So if they wanted to stand on the lawn and laugh like loons until the cows came home, it was all right with him.

"Can we see the inside now?" Diana was finally able to ask, as she wiped the tears from her eyes.

"Anytime you're ready," obliged the agent. He fished in the pocket of his navy blue blazer and finally came up with two sets of keys. "One set for the mister and one for the missus. All of the locks have been keyed alike, just as you requested, and you now hold the only keys."

Limestone steps led to the porch, which ran the length of the front of the house and wrapped around the south side. The corner was rounded like a gazebo. The columns and rails were carved limestone and the ceiling was a beautifully stained wooden bead board. Diana could hardly wait to shop for the proper wicker furniture and, of course, a swing.

She also immediately fell in love with the large double front doors with their leaded beveled glass and stained glass transom windows. The key turned with a solid clunk and the group stepped through the threshold and into the foyer. The room was about ten feet by eight with a built-in bookcase on either side of the door and a red-veined marble floor.

An open doorway straight ahead led directly out of the foyer and into a hallway. To the right, a curving staircase disappeared upward to the second floor. On the left was a wall with two sets of pocket doors. The first set opened into a spacious living room. A large picture window looked out onto the front porch and a huge fireplace dominated the other exterior wall. One painting still hung upon the wall. The only other possession the room contained was the old Oriental rug that covered a large portion of the hardwood floor.

The second room was a library, accessible from the living room and the hall. Every wall was floor to ceiling bookcases except for the slightly more modest fireplace. Many books still adorned the shelves and both Di and Chris had to restrain their avid curiosity and reading desires until they got a little more settled in.

They exited into the hall and saw that the right side of the hall held small closets and cubbyholes under the staircase. Diana could picture the children playing in those small spaces when the weather precluded them going outside. The hall finally ended in a tee that opened into the largest kitchen Diana had ever seen, filled with cabinets, cupboards, pantries and doors. There was a double basin sink, plus a second sink built in an island, for washing vegetables. A cast-iron pot rack hung above the island, waiting for Chris and Di's favorite pots and pans, and the new copper pots Di had already decided to order. The floor was covered with Mexican quarry tiles. A side-by-side refrigerator/freezer and a large Aga stove completed the fantasy kitchen. It was wonderful. A back porch opened out the rear door. A bathroom was to the right.

A door that stood beside the door to the hall opened into a spacious dining room with a crystal chandelier, and a door leading to the portico, but no table as of yet.

On the left-hand kitchen wall stood two more doors. One led to a room that once was the servant's quarters and the other led to the small, narrow rear stairs to the second floor. A door from the bathroom led down to the five rooms of the basement.

The ten foot ceilings, oak and cherry woodwork, transoms and beautifully maintained old wallpaper designs made them feel as if they had stepped back in time to an era with more grace and manners than currently existed.

Chris started to ask Di what she thought so far, but when he saw the tears streaming from her eyes he knew that she was in love with their new home. At last he felt certain they had made the right choice in coming here. Now they *both* knew, 'This was home.'

The rest of the day was spent in exploring their new home, once Chris had finally gotten rid of Mr. Tremble.

Upstairs, at the front of the house, over the living room and library, was the spacious master bedroom. At the back, over the kitchen, were two smaller rooms perfect for the kids. Over the downstairs bathroom, was the upstairs bath. They'd all have to share—no private master bath, but there were more than enough compensations to make that seem trivial. On the north side they would create a guestroom for Chris's business contacts and friends they hoped would come visit from New York.

Later, a short walk in the woods provided enough ground-fall branches to build a small fire in the living room fireplace.

"Think how much nicer this room will be when we have furniture." Chris spoke, hugging Diana a little closer.

"I think it's just fine. The sparseness means less clutter to clean and maintain, although a sofa would be nice." Diana said while adjusting her bottom. "These old carpets do tend to get a bit uncomfortable to sit on after awhile."

"Are you sure you don't want to get another motel, just for the night?" Chris asked.

"No. The rollaway cot that was left here will be just fine for tonight. Now that we're here, I love it so much I don't want to leave."

"Should we bring the cot down here in front of the fire?"

"No, the fire's almost gone and I don't want to hunt for more wood in the dark. Do you?"

"Come on then, let's go on up." Chris stood and reached down to help Di up from the floor. "We'll just have to come up with ways to keep each other warm."

"We could always start the furnace." Diana thought, but she kept her mouth shut as they headed up the stairs to their room.

CHAPTER 5

How long Kratel had been traveling would be difficult to tell. He had slept some and eaten (not much) and had stopped to rest and drink several times. He had even checked his reflection in the last phosphorescent pool to see if he had begun to waste away from malnutrition. As his face shimmered in the silvery water, he thought he could detect a gauntness to his round cheeks and a hollowness beneath his very large gray eyes. He stood erect to his full nearly three-foot height and rubbed his hand across the white fur of his belly. He adjusted his loincloth and considered pulling his belt tighter by another notch before proceeding onward in his quest.

He nervously twisted the end of his pointed left ear as he paused in consideration. After having traveled what he considered to be quite a distance, he wondered how much further he must go.

In his subterranean world where no sun or moon ever shines, time, as a measured commodity, has no meaning. No calendars or clocks mark time's passage. There are only spaces between events. And space from this moment on has taken on a new meaning for him.

Kratel had been in some very large caverns, nothing, however, on the scale of this one. He found himself standing upon a vaster threshold than any cavern he could ever imagine. His eyesight was very well developed for night vision. He could see quite clearly by the light of the phosphorus pools and fungus found throughout his underground home. In the areas where it was difficult to encourage the growth of natural light, Kratel would illuminate the spaces with the cold stones that he mined. He would speak spells over them, until they began to glow with a light much brighter than the phosphorus. But even without light, Kratel's radar sense enabled him to move freely in the dark. His special song for telling the depth of pits or the distance of cavern walls had never failed him, until now.

When he sang upward toward the points of light upon the cavern ceiling, his voice did not return. How far away were they? And the air! Why the air was moving all around him!

As his vision began to adjust to the vastness around, he could discern shapes moving upon a rock ledge about twenty meters above him. They seemed to stand stationary in one spot and wave around in a viscous manner. The dots of light on the ceiling behind them seemed to wink on and off as his view of them was interrupted by the sinuous dance. Kratel wondered if their movement was causing the air to move.

After carefully observing for several minutes, his curiosity got the better of his fear. He began climbing up out of the basin and cautiously approached the weaving apparitions upon the stone crest. Even the rocks began to take on an unnatural feel. They seemed to have square cut angles and hard line corners and symmetrical grooves gouged into them, as if someone had deliberately shaped them into large blocks and stacked them up. But who or what has the power?

Kratel now knew that he had entered more than just another large cavern. If a blind fish from the underground lake had emerged from the water and suddenly found itself in one of the main chasms of the caverns, it would have felt no more like it had entered a new and alien environment than Kratel felt right at this very moment. The tall waving creatures seemed to be related to the moss and fungi that grew in his subterranean home, except their massive stalks were very hard, almost stone-like and totally inedible, unlike Kratel's favorite mushrooms. And the tops! Instead of being capped like a mushroom, they were more like moss but extremely tasteless as Kratel discovered after sampling one of the smaller plants. And not only were they massive but they seemed veritably endless. The various shapes and sizes grew as far as he could see. Owing to the fact that they were inedible and totally useless there evidently was nothing to check their growth and progress.

Kratel had emerged from the basin that led down to the caverns and wandered among the leafy giants for a long time. The sounds of the nightlife of the living forest were all around him. Never before had he experienced such a cacophony of sound. Everything moved and buzzed, hummed and screeched. Everything was ALIVE! All of the creatures, the plants, even the air was alive with movement. Kratel had seen many of the creatures before, but then they had been without life. They were just food. He had never even thought of them as having been alive.

They were food. You hungered, you sang, they came, you fed. It was all so simple, there was no need to contemplate anything so abstract as the thought that the food might have had a life of its own at one time. But Kratel had more to think about than just the food, even though he was still extremely hungry. He was also lost. He was so mind-blasted by the change of environment that his wanderings had gotten him completely disoriented, something which had never occurred in the caverns. His sense of direction always led him back to familiar territory. But now his senses were so overloaded with sensory input that he could barely think straight let alone navigate straight back home. Nothing to be done, he decided, but keep moving until he found some way to reenter the cavern. Once underground he was confident that he could relocate his home.

The spongy forest carpet finally let out onto a long expanse of solid ground. Although it was not stone, it was still enough like stone to make Kratel feel a little more comfortable in his journeying. At least it was hard enough for the forest things not to grow through, which made walking an easier task. Sitting down for a moment on the road, Kratel again realized how hungry he was. Experimentally, he tried his food song and was immediately rewarded as a large furry form lumbered out of the undergrowth and made its way down the road to where Kratel hungrily awaited.

But once again it seemed that his hunger would have to wait, for there was a new event taking place in this ever increasingly strange world and Kratel wasn't sure what was happening.

The night sounds that had become acceptable background noise were now decreasing. Kratel could sense the night creatures departing, heading for secret lairs and burrows. The call of the crickets and frogs was being replaced by bird song. Even the darkness seemed to be receding. But wait, not only did it seem to be retreating, it was retreating! Everything was growing painfully clearer. What could be the cause of this sudden infusion of light? What source was so brilliantly huge that could dispel such a vast amount of darkness? Kratel wasn't sure if he wanted to find out. The light seemed to be rising in that one particular direction so Kratel began hurrying away in the other. Fortunately the road ran in the direction he was traveling otherwise he would have to fight the undergrowth. It was second nature for him to manipulate the shambling beast into following him. He wasn't sure where he would take shelter from this new dilemma or how long he would have to stay in hiding, but at least he would have sustenance for a while.

Kratel was now traveling blind in the intense light of the dawn. He used his manipulative abilities to have the dead raccoon walk beside him so he could hold on to its fur much like a Seeing Eye dog. His radar sense kept him from running into things and his sensitive feet kept him on the road but none of this helped him to find shelter in this alien environment. Lack of food and water was beginning to take their toll on him and the ever-warming spring air was becoming intolerable as the daylight continued to intensify. The sun had yet to rise above the trees and hills so Kratel was only experiencing the diffused light of early dawn. But it was enough to blind and confuse his delicate senses. He was nearly ready to crawl into the thin brush along the road when his radar detected the house.

He didn't recognize it as a dwelling as such, but he could tell that it had a hollow interior by the echo of the vibrations he was bouncing off of it. He was ready to go over to it and explore when his feet suddenly encountered a familiar feeling. Stone. He had stepped off the road and onto the limestone walk that ran along the side of the house. Although the house gave promise of shelter, the stone gave hope of leading to an opening through which he could return to his underground home. As he followed the walk to the rear of the house, he came upon the tool shed. Here too, was a smaller version of the structure with the hollow interior. The door stood slightly open, and the cool darkness and the earthen floor felt like an irresistible invitation. The first actual ray of the sun ripping through the tree branches was enough to decide Kratel on his course of action. He rushed past the opening, closely followed by the lurching animal. The movement through the doorway caused the door to swing shut with a slam and click that immediately sealed out the light. Kratel picked his way past the mysterious objects that littered the shed's interior. He sank down to the earthen floor against the rear wall. As soon as his vision returned, he made a quick meal from the raccoon and allowed the wave of exhaustion to wash over him and carry him into sleep.

CHAPTER 6

Diana woke early the next morning, went straight to the kitchen and loaded up the Mr. Coffee with Lion Kona, her favorite coffee. She semi-trusted the moving van people with almost all her other possessions, but getting up in the morning without Kona was a hardship she refused to endure. So she loaded the coffee machine, coffee, grinder and filters into the trunk before leaving New York. Having Kona the next morning at the motel after that marvelous shower nearly made the whole moving experience worthwhile.

"The moving van," Diana thought, "should be arriving by noon. If there's a shovel out in the tool shed I could go give that poor raccoon a decent burial, then wake up Chris to have coffee on the veranda before the van gets here or Dad arrives with the kids."

She quietly sneaked back into the bedroom, trying not to awaken her sleeping husband. Even though they had each brought along an overnight bag, Diana hadn't packed anything appropriate for woodland excursions. She quickly dressed in Chris's clothes and left the room.

She was glad Chris liked flannel shirts as she quietly closed the kitchen door. She had used her own belt to keep the jeans up. And even though she couldn't wear his shoes, his cotton socks were warmer then her hose.

The limestone walk leading from the back door of the house to the tool shed was crisscrossed with thin wet trails. "Glad I put my shoes on," Diana said out loud to no one. Shoes were necessary in the city because of broken bottles and smoldering cigarette butts; out here, however, it seems they are needed to avoid snail and worm slime.

The door on the shed had faded green paint on its wooden surface, just like the doors in the *Country Living* magazine. Diana was thrilled. "I'll have to make certain Chris doesn't try to paint it," she spoke again, but this time realized that she wasn't speaking just to herself.

"Hello there, what's your name?" Diana knelt down and tried coaxing the orange cat that was winding itself back and forth across the corner of the shed. "Come on, I won't hurt you." The cat watched her warily like it was ready to dart for shelter at the first unfriendly motion on Diana's part. It didn't run, but it wouldn't approach within ear-scratching distance either.

"All right then," Diana spoke as she rose to her feet once more. "Hang out for a while and I'll get you some half and half as soon as I'm done playing mortician. We don't have milk yet, but I grabbed the good stuff for the Kona."

Diana's key turned the lock on the shed easily. It was smart of Chris to have all the new locks keyed alike so they only had to carry one key to open everything. "Gee, no lights!" Luckily the morning sun was shining through the open door and the interior was lit enough for her to spot a long-handled shovel leaning in the corner. The cat had followed her into the shed but when she reached for the shovel it turned around and lit out around the doorway as if expecting her to lash out and try to bash its furry head in.

"You poor thing." Diana sympathized, "what a rough life you must have had." The cat obviously wanted affection but was afraid to let anyone get within arms' reach. "We'll work on your paranoia just as soon as we deal with Mr. Raccoon."

As Diana returned to the task of getting the shovel, the door, which she had neglected to prop open, suddenly closed. Her annoyance at the disorientation she felt standing there in the darkness gave way to fear as she felt the unmistakable brush of animal fur against her bare leg.

"Cat? Is that you, cat?"

Surely the cat had come back in and bumped the door closed. Which way is the door? It's only six paces away, but which direction. Again she felt the furry contact upon her leg but this time it was accompanied by a sharp pinch behind the knee. "Ouch!" Diana lashed out with her foot and had the satisfaction of booting the offending cat solidly across the floor. The elation was short lived, however, as the shrill howl of surprise and anger washed over her in the stygian darkness of the tool shed. She felt the sound as strongly as she heard it. She was compelled to move toward the source, as the howl became a keening melody, a melody she almost remembered. A primal tune buried deep in the memory of her cells countered a racial memory telling her to run! Run! Run—for this song means death. Diana was resisting the feeling to move toward the song, even though she felt "Pulled" in that direction. She felt the coercion in her hair and fingernails, also in her teeth, and an almost itchy persistence in the outer layer of her skin. But her mind fought back. "No!" she would not move! If something wanted her, it would damn well have to come and get her where she stood! She thought as she raised the shovel to strike in anticipation that the thought would soon become the deed.

Her world suddenly became one of sight again as the darkness was split by the sunlight coming in through the door. And that was not all that was coming in. Ten pounds of fighting orange tom cat shot into the shed. Distracted by the spitting entrance of the cat, Di noticed that the eerie tune had ended. She spun to look in the direction that she had felt compelled to go but nothing was there. The cat was also staring at that side of the shed. Its ears laid back, and its tail bushed out larger than its body. Di saw the door starting to swing shut once again.

"Oh no you don't!" She leaped across the shed floor and grabbed the door while continuing to keep a good grip on the shovel. As she stepped back out into the full sunlight of the back yard, she closed her eyes and shuddered as if trying to shake off the memory, the way a retriever shakes off water. She reopened her eyes to find the cat sitting on the stone walk washing itself as though nothing out of the ordinary had happened.

"Well," Di spoke to the cat, "maybe this is your normal morning routine but it sure isn't mine! Anyway, I guess you earned a can of tuna along with your cream."

The cat turned and walked up to the back porch and sat down as if to say, "I'll be right here. As soon as you've finished the rest of your business you may feed me."

The walk down the driveway to the road was invigorating. Birds flew and sang in the tree-lined drive and a chipmunk quickly scurried into a downed tree. Diana saw it only because she happened to be looking in that direction as it ran. The sun had risen only an hour before and the new leaves on the trees mottled the road with their shadows.

"This part of the drive is going to be pretty dense when the trees and plants are in full foliage this summer," Diana thought. "Here's the place where we stopped the car, so the 'coon should be off the road right there."

Using the shovel to push the underbrush aside, she stepped off the drive and across a small culvert. The branch Chris had used to move the dead animal was right there, but no sign of the raccoon. Thoughts of wolves dragging the carcass off to feed popped into her head, but there was no sign that anything as big as that 'coon had been dragged away. And it was too big to be carried. "Besides," she spoke aloud; "there are no wolves in this area or any animals large enough to have removed the raccoon." And then, for the second time today she realized that she wasn't alone, and this time it wasn't a cat.

The fear she felt when she first looked up and saw someone standing in the woods with her quickly dissipated as she saw the face, wearing the most open and sincere smile that had ever been bestowed upon her. The greens and browns of her dress blended so well with the foliage it was no wonder Diana hadn't seen her approaching. The brown of her shoes, bag, and walking stick only enhanced the natural woodland feel of her appearance. Her eyes were as blue as the sky and her hair seemed to fight the constraints of the braids. "It must have been like golden wheat when she was younger," Diana thought. Although she couldn't have said how old she thought the lady was. Her appearance seemed to almost fluctuate. One moment she seemed wispy as a willow and the next as solid as an oak. Older, whatever that is, was Di's best guess.

"I'm sorry, I didn't mean to startle you. I often cut through this section of land to get off the road a bit. You can't get through this part in the summer you know. The brambles are too thick. This time of year, though, it's nice to walk amongst all the new growth and smell the fresh starts pushing up from the earth. See, right there, that's wild ginger. And there are some May Apples just poking out from under the leaves. Just the plant shoots. Of course, it's too early for the actual fruit. There's also poison ivy to watch out for, like the batch over on that tree. If you do happen to get into it, there's a nice patch of jewelweed just across the road, down by the stream. You just squeeze the juice from the leaves or the stem and rub it on the rash. It clears it up and stops the itch pretty quickly. You do like plants, don't you dear?"

"Oh, yes." Diana stammered, taken aback by the running commentary. "I'm planning a garden back behind the house as soon as we get settled in."

"You're the one who bought the Hudson place? Why, we're neighbors then, and I guess I'm trespassing on your property."

"Not at all. Trespassing, that is. My husband, Chris, and I just arrived yesterday. You're the first neighbor that we've met, not counting Mr. Tremble, the real estate agent."

"Oh, he's no neighbor. He doesn't even live in Bedford. He lives over in Bloomington. Actually, I'm your only neighbor on both sides. My house is north of yours, on the drive just before you reach this one. And, where your land stops on the other side, my land starts back up again. My grandparents sold off twenty acres to the Hudson's back in 1878. They cleared it off some and built the house that you just bought."

"Has your property to the south of here been cleared or is it still woods?" Diana asked.

"About sixty acres or so were cleared for the house and the farm land."

"I thought you said your house was to the north of us?"

"It is, now. The original house my great grandparents built stood just off the road to the south. There was a terrible fire when I was a child and the house burnt to the ground. My parents built a new house to the north of the Hudson place. That's where I live now."

"Do you still farm the land where the old house stood?"

31

"No, but I do have a nice garden, which is exactly where I'm heading now. The rain shed was left untouched by the fire and the herb and vegetable gardens were behind that. I had Rowan convert it into a potting shed with a fireplace so I could have a comfortable place to work without carrying everything back to the new house."

"Rowan?" Diana asked.

"He is one of the local handymen around. He's quite good with growing things and is a very talented artist. I have several of his paintings and woodcarvings. He's also quite pleasing to look at." Diana saw a trace of blush cross the lady's face after the last comment. "I can't recall his given name but once you meet him you'll understand why he chose to be known by the name of a tree. I'll send him around to your place as soon as I can track him down. He will be a great help to you in getting your own garden together or doing any repair work you might need."

"Would you like to see the work he did on the rain shed and my garden?"

"I'd love to, but I need to get back to the house. The moving van will be arriving and I still don't know where all the closets and cupboard spaces are. Unpacking is the worst part of moving don't you think?"

"I wouldn't know dear. I've only moved once and that was after the fire, and I was only four at the time. Although I can imagine how difficult it must be. I'll be on my way now, you come by and visit as soon as you're settled, or if you need anything. You can find me either at the house or at the rain shed."

"All right, thank you," said Diana. "I'll take a rain check on the garden for now."

"Oh, a punster, I'll have to sharpen my wits or a hickory switch, whichever seems to be most effective." The Lady laughed as she began picking her way between the trees.

"She walks like she's dancing with the woods," Di thought, "moving without disturbing a leaf or a twig. Wait," Di shouted, "what's your name?"

"Crescent Ryan, Diana. My given name is Crescent."

As her voice traveled back, she blended into the greenery and was gone from sight.

"Crescent, like the moon." Diana thought as she clumsily stepped back onto the drive. "What a lovely name. She called me 'Diana', but I don't remember telling her my name? Guess I did though, I'm sure I heard her say it."

Chris waved to Diana through the kitchen window. She waved back and motioned to the shed with the shovel, indicating she would be in as soon as she returned the unused digging implement to its undeserved resting place. Chris nodded and held up two cups of coffee as he turned away from the window.

The shed was still dark. Di felt a little apprehensive about entering such unfamiliar territory so she leaned the shovel inside to the left of the door.

"Maybe Rowan can run electricity to the shed for us." Di thought as she began walking up the steps to the house.

Chris was sitting in the kitchen at the butcher-block table they'd found in the basement and carried up to the kitchen the afternoon before. He was in his bathrobe, since Di had absconded with his clothes. She was struck by how natural he looked sitting there, as if he had taken his morning coffee in that spot for years. Diana sat in Chris's lap, partly because she loved to be close to him, partly because there was only one chair until their furniture arrived to augment what they had found in the house.

"I thought you would at least have breakfast before you started digging the garden. Are you compulsive or what?" Chris asked.

"I was out meeting the neighbors. Mister lazy bones, slug!"

"With a shovel?" Chris raised his eyebrows!

"I was going to bury the raccoon that was on the road yesterday," Diana explained. "But when I got there it was gone."

"Are you sure that you found the right spot?" Chris asked.

"The branch you used to move it off the road was right where you dropped it." Diana said, enjoying the first taste of coffee that morning. "But," she continued, "there was no sign of the 'coon and the ground showed no marks that would indicate it was dragged away."

"There shouldn't be any animals around here large enough to carry off something that size, without dragging it." Chris pondered. "I wonder if some person might have taken it?"

"What on earth would anyone want with road kill?" Di wrinkled her face in disgust. "It would surely be unsafe to eat. Who knows how long it was dead? Besides, do people eat raccoon anyway? Ugh! Bleah!"

"Gee. You look just like Bill the Cat when you do that." Chris chided. "No, I doubt anyone is desperate enough to eat that particular 'coon, although fresh raccoon meat is edible. More than likely someone wanted it for the pelt even though the time of year is wrong for fur, a free pelt that size and relatively undamaged must be worth something to somebody."

"What do you mean, wrong time of year?" Di asked. "Isn't 'coon fur in the spring still 'coon fur in the summer?"

"The fur is pretty much the same except that in the winter fur-bearing animals have thicker, more luxurious coats to protect them from the weather. Some actually turn white to camouflage with the snow. In the spring they begin shedding, so the fur isn't worth as much. That's why you always see the trappers in the movies plowing through the snow to check their traps. In the old days trapping wasn't illegal in the summer, it was just unprofitable except for food."

"Where did you meet this neighbor that you mentioned? Is it possible that he took it?" Chris wondered.

"First off, 'He' was a She. Although I did meet her in the same spot, I was there first and I doubt that she would have been able to take it without a truck."

"What was she doing there in our woods anyway?"

"Just cutting through to get off the road. Her property connects ours on both sides. I told her it was all right to cut through there. Do you mind?" Di added as an afterthought.

"No. That spot is far enough from the house so it shouldn't be a problem. It's always better to get along with the neighbors without starting a feud over boundaries the first day we move in. But, if she cuts through, then the chances are that someone else will also and that's probably who took the 'coon. This property stood vacant for a while before we bought it. The sooner it looks lived in again the safer we will be from trespassers. If the trespassing becomes a bother after people realize we've moved in, we can always put up signs and fences where its necessary."

"Speaking of trespassers." Diana said, pointing out the window. "There's a motley looking bunch coming right up the drive to the house." As Chris turned to look, Diana was already out the door. She was running across the yard by the time that he saw the car.

The car barely had enough time to stop before the doors flew open and two figures blurred their feet through the grass as they each rushed to be the first to embrace their mother—who was moving equally as fast toward them. Being children, their mouths, of course, were moving even faster than their feet—asking a million questions without waiting for an answer.

Chris walked over to the car and opened the driver's side door as Diana's father slowly emerged from behind the wheel.

'Hi, Nate. Have a safe drive down?" Chris asked, shaking the old man's hand. "Did you try to drive faster than the speed of sound to escape those kid's constant yammering?"

"Not at all, Chris." Nate ran his hands down his legs trying to press the wrinkles out of his gray slacks. "By the time you reach my age you learn tolerance and patience when dealing with the energetic voice of youth. Of course being able to turn down the volume on my hearing aid every now and then didn't hurt."

Chris knew that Nate didn't have, nor need, a hearing aid. His eyesight may have weakened some over the years but his ears were as sharp as ever.

"What are you guys laughing at?" Diana asked as she untangled herself from the kids.

"Dad!" They shouted in unison and suddenly Chris was the center of a whirling vortex of gangly elbows and bandaged knees.

"Calm down, calm down." Chris said, bear hugging the kids into tighter circles of gyrating activity. "You'd think we hadn't seen you in three years instead of three days!"

"Man! Look how big this place is," Alexander said. "Is it really all ours, the woods and everything? I can't wait to see my room!"

"A cat!" Jerrica squealed. "We have a cat!"

The big orange cat Diana had met earlier came walking around the house to see what all the commotion was at his once quiet abode. He took one look at the kids, turned tail and bolted for the barn with two charging dervishes hot on his trail screaming "A cat! We have a cat!"

"Dad, we really appreciate you watching the kids these past days while we tied up all the loose ends of moving." Diana said as she pulled Alex and Jerrica's suitcases from the back of the wagon.

"No problem at all, Di. Besides, it's the least I could do after agreeing to move in here with you and Chris. I'm still not sure it's a good idea. Young couples, like you, need your privacy without an old coot like me hanging around all the time."

"Privacy!" Chris chimed in. "We just moved out of a two-bedroom apartment in New York. Between the two kids and the paper-thin walls, this place is like a haven of solitude. Di, can you give me a hand opening the car-top carrier?"

"We couldn't leave you in that retirement home in Connecticut." Diana said, sitting down the cases and standing in the open door of the car to reach the tie-down straps. "It's a fifteen-hour drive from here. Besides, you promised to help keep an eye on the kids while Chris worked on his music and I start my classes on Herbology and Bioregionalism. So, you'll more than earn your keep."

"Let's get all of your things into your room now so we can be ready for the moving van as soon as it arrives. The room at the back of the house, right off the kitchen will make a perfect bedroom for you. There's plenty of space and you won't have to go up and down the stairs to get to your room." Chris explained. "The kids each have their own rooms upstairs, at the back of the house. Diana and I will have the front upstairs bedroom."

"Say, nice room." Nate said, stepping out of the kitchen and into the back room. "It even has its own door to the outside. Looks like it might have been a large pantry or mud room before it was converted to a bedroom."

"Yeah, you can tell that the closet was built in later. The style of trim and baseboard is different from the rest of the room. You can go ahead and put away as much of your things in there as will fit...until the van arrives with your dresser and bed."

"What's this?" Diana asked, nudging something with the toe of her shoe. "It looks like a ring set into the floor."

"Well, what do you know," Nate said, inspecting the ring. "It's a trap door. Do you know if it leads down to the basement or maybe a root cellar?"

"We haven't had time to do much exploring." Chris replied as he entered the room. He had dressed in the spare pants and T-shirt he brought along. "I guess this house will give up its secrets to us slowly."

"Do you happen to have an extra pair of socks with you Nate? Mine seems to have been borrowed and I didn't pack a spare pair."

As Nate opened his valise to retrieve the socks, Chris knelt down to examine the trap door. "Uh! Well I can't seem to budge the door from this side." Chris released the ring and stood up rubbing his back. "It's either barred from the other side or it's swollen shut from lack of use. We can try to find it from the basement later. Seems safe enough to walk on." Chris said while stomping soundly upon the floor. "I don't guess we have to worry about you falling through."

Jerrica and Alex came into the kitchen looking dejected. "Mom, Dad, we lost the cat by the barn. We hunted all over but we couldn't find it!" Alex exclaimed.

Diana walked back into the kitchen and sat at the table, hugging the kids once more, as much to be reassured of their presence as to comfort their sadness over the rejection they had received from the cat. Chris sat beside her and began pulling on the borrowed socks and his shoes.

"We thought we heard it moving in that other little building," injected Jerrica, "but it was too dark to see."

"That's the tool shed," Diana told the kids. "Stay out of there until we get some lights on inside. There are several sharp tools inside and you could hurt yourselves in the dark. "Besides," she added, "we live in the country now. There are wild animals around here that might hide in a dark building and attack you if you cornered them."

Di remembered the scraping noises she had heard in the tool shed and shuddered.

"Wild animals!" Alex said, eyes as wide as saucers. "You mean like wolves and bears?"

"No wolves or bears have been seen in these parts for a long time." Chris said coming into the kitchen to stand behind Diana "But there are plenty of opossums and raccoons. Even a squirrel or a rabbit will bite and scratch to defend itself."

"And don't forget about snakes." Grandpa called from the next room. "Most of the snakes around here are harmless but there are copperheads and timber rattlers, both of which are quite poisonous."

"Maybe you shouldn't go outside without an adult." Diana said, suddenly becoming nervous about this new aspect of country living that she hadn't thought about. All these dark buildings and dense woods with animals and serpents hiding in them waiting to bite and rend her children.

"Now Diana, don't over-react." Chris squeezed her shoulders as he spoke. "As much noise as the kids make any animal will be long gone before they get anywhere near them. We'll have them play close to the house for a while and stay out of the out buildings. Got that guys?" Chris directed this last part at the kids. "Besides, either you, me, or Nate will be around at all times. The kids will be well supervised and perfectly safe."

All thought of the difficulties of adjusting from city life to country life was suddenly put on hold as the conversation was interrupted by the rumbling arrival of the moving van and the reality of settling into their new environment began in earnest.

Many boxes and tables later a very exhausted Chris and Diana fell into their own bed in their own bedroom and refused to look at the things still in need of unpacking.

"I'm glad no one has thought of furnishings for the ceiling." Chris said while kicking his shoes off, over the end of the bed. "I can lie back and stare at it and say 'look, here is one great expanse in a room that we don't have to try and fill. Here, at least, is an area that is completely done.'"

"Like I always say," Diana added, while her own shoes dropped like stones from her feet, "One should always focus on the positive aspects of things accomplished instead of dwelling on all the things that didn't get done. You know though, if you moved the ceiling light about two feet over, we could probably get that big mirror that's in the living room to hang right over the bed."

"Eat pillow and die, bitch!" Chris yelled, finding enough reserve energy to wallop Di over the head with his feather pillow before collapsing back onto the mattress sans pillow.

Diana rolled over and sat on Chris's stomach, holding the pillow inches above his face. "The only reason I stay with you is because you continually broaden my horizons. Why, before I met you, I never thought of the word 'Bitch' as a term of endearment." Gently, Di lifted Chris's head and placed his pillow beneath it and then nuzzled down putting her nose in his left ear.

CHAPTER 7

Kratel had not been asleep long when the slamming door of the house brought him immediately awake. He could hear the approaching footsteps of something much larger than the animal he had found along the roadside. He assumed it would be approaching the entrance that he had used to get into the shed and so he began desperately searching for another way out. No other door or window seemed available, and then he saw a large rectangular slab of stone on the earthen floor in the far corner. The stone looked unnatural in its position and therefore may have been placed there to cover an opening or so Kratel desperately hoped, for the large creature had stopped directly outside the door.

Kratel attempted to lift the stone but the weight proved too great for his exhausted strength. Bracing his feet against the shed wall, he attempted to slide the slab aside. There! He was relieved to feel the stone's movement even though ever so slightly. He still didn't know if this was an exit from the shed, but it seemed his only hope. Another muscle-straining shove and, yes, there was a hole beneath the stone. Just a couple more pushes and he would have the access he needed. Bracing for another shove, Kratel suddenly was frozen into immobility. Never in all his life had he heard anything like it. The call of the frogs, insects and other night creatures had been strange to his ears. Even the songs of the birds at dawn were fascinating in their eerie timbred beauty. But this, this awesome thing standing mere yards away was intoning with a voice the likes of which were beyond imagining. Why, Kratel mused, it almost seems to have a cadence of communication. It obviously has a more complex vocabulary than the repetitive droning of the other creatures he had encountered.

His introspective reverie was quickly interrupted by the grating sound of the shed door being unlocked. His sense of wonder was suddenly surpassed by his sense of self-preservation. The rush of adrenaline gave him all the strength needed to move the stone aside as his radar instantly informed him as to the depth of the hole. Even as the sunlight flooded in, he was diving into the earth feeling the relief of being once more back in his own element no matter how shallow.

He had only gone a few yards when he remembered the raccoon he had left behind. He hadn't eaten much before sleep overcame him. The thought of losing such a prize without knowing when he could replace it was most unsettling.

After straining his ears for sounds of pursuit, and hearing none, Kratel made his way slowly and quietly back to the tunnel opening in the shed floor.

He stayed far enough back from the hole so that the diffused light coming down wouldn't impair his night vision if he had to make a hasty retreat down the dark tunnel.

He could hear the creature moving about up above him. It didn't sound as if it were moving in an agitated or disturbed manner, so he didn't think that his presence had been detected. Again he heard the eerie singsong voice. He was certain that it had to be speech no matter how alien sounding the words were.

Abruptly the light was diminished in the shed and the voice sounded on the verge of fear. Of course! Kratel suddenly understood. This creature had entered his haven in full light. It lived above ground and actually preferred the intensity that was so painful to him. With the light out, the creature was, as strange as it seemed, blind.

Realizing that this could be his only chance to retrieve his food, Kratel emerged from the floor opening and called to the raccoon. As it moved across the floor to him, it brushed into the leg of the other creature which yelped in fear, jumped aside and began chattering once more to the darkness.

41

It was blind in the dark. And it was gigantic! Kratel had seen humans only as food until today. As with all the other food sources, he had never acquainted them with having a life force of their own. He had also never seen one standing erect. By the time they crawled down through the caverns to the depths Kratel normally preferred to stay, most vestiges of humanity were gone.

And now, before him stood a walking, fully conscious being. The fact that he had been feeding off of its kind and never once entertained the concept of it having individual vitality made Kratel wonder what other avenues of his existence had been so callously taken for granted.

Kratel had unconsciously walked over to the giant. Unthinking of the repercussions, He reached out to touch, almost apologetically, this being with whom he had shared communion, albeit one sided, for his entire life.

Again the creature screamed and jumped. This unexpected reaction frightened Kratel also and his fingers involuntarily closed on the being's flesh in a pinching grip. With a speed belying its size, it lashed out with one of its lower appendages, kicking Kratel soundly in the chest, sending him reeling across the floor and stopping inches from the hole through which the raccoon had recently disappeared. Turning in his direction, searching with blind eyes it brandished a large weapon menacingly in his direction.

A howl of rage hissed between Kratel's teeth. To have his gesture of friendship so violently rejected after all the things he had so recently endured was the breaking point of his already stretched-to-the-limit nerves. With all of his will he began his keening call to the food. If it wanted to behave like a beast, he would show it who was the master and who the fodder. He could feel the tenuous web of his song reaching out and snaring the giant. Down, he sang, crawl to me as the lowly thing you are.

But, the creature stood still. He could feel his hold upon it, yet it had the strength to resist. Its will was defying his? This was totally unacceptable! Food refused to come to the Call? Kratel reached deep within himself. He sent his consciousness deep within the earth for grounding support. He called to himself the strength of stone. He would crush this ones will within the walls of granite.

Before he had the chance to focus the force of his calling, the outside portal once more was opened and another being, very similar to the raccoon, entered, intent on forcing his own will into the fight.

Kratel knew he could not combat both creatures and the blinding light. As the large giant turned its head toward the light, Kratel released his song and once more dove into the safety of the earth. This time, with his food lumbering ahead of him, he continued down the passage until it dead-ended into an earthen wall. Trapped!

If the creatures pursued him now, he had nowhere to go. He paused, silently mastering his rapid breathing and heart rate. With his own body once more in control, he began checking the passage for pursuit. He could detect none. The creatures obviously disliked the darkness. Down here they would be dysfunctional and he could easily overcome them. In his flight he had most likely missed a turnoff or an access tunnel. It could have been in the ceiling or even partially blocked. He would have to retrace his steps and find the way to go deeper into the earth.

Once again, however, he found himself at the mercy of exhaustion. What little sleep he attained did nothing to compensate for the amount of energy he had expended. Sinking to the floor, intending to rest only momentarily, Kratel was soon in a deep sleep. He dreamed of phosphorous pools and prehistoric fish that were trying to communicate something of vast importance if he could only understand their strange, burbling voices.

CHAPTER 8

Di was the one to sleep in today. She hadn't even heard Chris get out of bed. Putting on her robe, she went downstairs to find Nate sitting at the table, coffee cup in hand.

"Morning, Dad." Di gave the old man a kiss on top of the head. Although his hair was now white instead of his boyish red, he still had a full head of it.

No Kona this morning unless she wanted to dump out the pot of Maxwell House that Nate had brewed. She may have inherited his red hair, but the taste genes definitely went somewhere else. Di loved exotically flavored dishes smothered in herbs and sauce, whereas Nate ate only basic foods and no gravy of any sort. Di could tell that mealtime was going to get even more complicated with Dad's bland taste added to the kid's dislike of everything that wasn't pizza.

"Kids still asleep?" Di asked after her first slug of coffee. At least he makes it strong.

"Yeah, guess the ride wore them out. Chris went into town for a few things. He should be back soon. He left about forty-five minutes ago. Want me to make some breakfast?"

"We don't have any eggs or bacon until we can get to the store today. I think we have some cream of wheat but that's getting dangerously close to gravy isn't it?" Diana teased inquisitively.

"I didn't say that I was going to eat anything that I fixed, but if you want to be a smart-ass, you can forage for yourself. There's

Captain Crunch and half and half, and if you can't figure which one goes in the bowl first, I'll see if I can unpack a cookbook or two."

"This sludge you call coffee will be enough for now. Darn," Di said, looking out the window. "It's raining again. I was going to take the empty boxes out and burn them, now if we take them out of the house they'll get wet."

"I can store them in the tool shed until it dries out." Nate suggested.

"No!" Diana said a little too emphatically, remembering her frightening experience of yesterday. "I mean, the light's bad in there and it would be difficult to tell where to stack them. How about if we just fold them up and put them in the basement for the time being."

"All right by me." Nate said, eyeing her suspiciously over his coffee cup. "If I can get the trap door open in my room, we can just drop them straight down and then pick them up in a day or so when the weather breaks. I was looking at it this morning and it appears to be nailed down rather than locked. I have a hammer and a flat bar in my toolbox. I'll see about getting it open first thing."

"Why were you checking out the trap door so early in the morning, Dad?" This time it was Diana's turn to look suspicious. "And don't give me that 'I was just curious' bit. I know you too well."

"I thought I heard something last night." Nate confessed sheepishly, almost as if he feared being called a scaredy cat.

"Heard what kind of something?" Di was becoming a little frightened herself.

"Nothing to worry about, I'm sure. But, there was a scratching noise like an animal was trying to claw through."

"An animal!" Di shook, thinking of something the size of that raccoon tearing its way into their house.

"Calm down, Diana. This house has stood empty for quite some time. A rat or even an opossum in the basement is hardly unheard of. We'll get the door open and set some traps. If it's a rat, we'll catch it, and if it's an opossum it'll move away now that there are people living here again. Chris is getting some bait and traps. We'll take care of the mice, you've got plenty of other things to keep you busy—and I hear two of them getting out of bed now."

Nate was glad of the distraction of the children. Diana was always able to tell when someone was holding something back or telling a half-truth. And the truth was that whatever was on the other side of the trap door was big. It had hit the door a couple of times damn near hard enough to de-nail it itself without a hammer. Nate was thankful for the heavy construction of the floor panels. The way it was, he hardly slept last night. Tonight would be better though. Along with the traps, Chris was picking up some shells for his gun. He didn't want to tell Diana that and he sure as Hell didn't want to open the door until Chris got back. He would have to put her off until Chris returned. I wonder why she was so set against putting the boxes in the tool shed. It would have been easier and a lot less frightening.

CHAPTER 9

Chris parked next to the limestone building of the hardware store. Memories flooded in of the many times he and his father and uncles had parked in the very same spot and walked through the wooden screen door into Mr. Hensley's store. The screen door was still there, but the inner door was also closed due to the coolness of the air. It was like stepping back through time to enter the shop with all of the familiar racks and displays. Basic hardware, Chris noted, has changed very little over the years. The nuts, bolts, hooks, and clamps are like the alligators of evolution, continuing to look and function in the same manner regardless of the years and changes going on around them.

"Wood clamps and Coelacanths" mused Chris "maybe there's a song title there?"

"Can I help you find something?" An old man in a red flannel shirt walked around the counter looking as if he, too, had been inventoried and stocked in the store along with the rest of the goods.

Shaken from his reverie, Chris realized he had been standing there with a slack jaw and an idiotic grin. The store clerk probably thought he was a cracker from out of the sticks that had never seen the inside of such a plush establishment.

"Sorry. Guess I was daydreaming." Chris said sheepishly.

"I need to pick up a few things. Do you have electric cable to go outside between a house and a shed?"

"Yeah, I've got it for sale by the foot. How much do you need?"

"About seventy-five feet should do. I'll also need some conduit pipe, a switch and box, and a light fixture."

"You probably ought to get a weather head where it attaches to the shed. If you're going to all the trouble to put a light in, you might as well hook up some outlets while you're at it. Just make sure you know what you're doing and have enough amps to handle anything you plug in. Now, what else?"

"Let's see." Chris said, checking his list. "About six sets of hooks and wire to hang pictures on the wall, a couple of pounds of nails-various sizes- and, do you carry traps?"

"Traps?" The old man raised an eyebrow. "You don't look like a trapper to me. What are you fixin' to snare?"

"I don't know exactly." Chris said, rubbing his chin. "Something's in the basement scratching around."

"Well, I have these kind here," he said, pulling a vicious looking trap from behind a faucet display. It had jaw-like teeth that pulled apart to reveal a circle in the center of the deadly maul. "You just open it like this, and put your bait in the center. Anything this side of a Doberman will lose its head when it pokes its nose onto the button."

"I didn't exactly want to *kill* it, just get rid of it." Chris had trouble looking away from a device whose only function was mutilation and death. "Do you have any type of cage trap that would catch it without hurting it, so that I could turn it loose elsewhere?"

"I've got a couple in the back. But you need to be real careful. A caged animal is scared and dangerous. Even a rabbit will bite and claw to escape."

"I've heard that somewhere."

"And there are laws against releasing wild animals," the old man continued, "so if you catch it and get caught turning it loose, you could get in trouble. And you also need to get far away from your house before turning it loose, otherwise it'll come back, and you won't catch it so easily next time."

"Thanks for the advice, I'll be careful with the cages. You might as well give me a couple of rat traps just in case it isn't anything worse than a rat. I didn't hear the thing scratching, myself,

I'm only going on what my father-in-law said he heard. His hearing is good, and he doesn't usually exaggerate things out of proportion, but I may as well cover all the bases."

"Not many young folk listen to what us old timers have to say. It's a smart man that takes time to listen to the voice of experience. Where did you say the house is that has the beast in the basement?"

"I didn't say yet. It's the old Hudson house. Out off of Spider Creek."

"I know that place right enough. I pass by there every now and then." The flannel-shirted clerk's eyes clouded over momentarily like an old memory had passed behind them. "You must be Mr. Lane, the new owner."

"That's right. But call me Chris. How did you know my name anyhow? I know you're not Mister Henley, I still remember him from my childhood, and I don't recall having met you before, Mr.?"

"Bing. Folks just call me Bing. I came to work here after Mr. Henley, Sr., passed away about eight years ago. His son took over the place but he has no interest in it. He doesn't even care enough to sell the place. He has an accountant and a bookkeeper keeping an eye on everything that goes on here. But what I wonder is who's watching them? I guess as long as Mr. Henley can go to the bank once a month and draw off the profit from this place, that's all that matters to him."

"That real-estate agent from Bloomington sent his man in here to pick up some locks and keys and a few other things to get your new house ready for your arrival. A real talkative fella he was too. Knew your name, said you were moving here from New York City. Said as how you were a songwriter and that you was born here and figured you was coming back to retire. Said he was a songwriter too, but never got the lucky breaks that you did."

"Really? What was his name?"

"I don't recollect that he ever gave it. Knew all about you though. Stood right there and sung me a couple of your songs while I made them keys for the locks. Nice voice too. Why, he even knew your wife and kid's names and described their looks to me."

"That a fact." Chris was becoming a little uneasy about what felt like an invasion to his privacy. But, after all, this is a small town. And people talk. Hell, all of that information could have been looked up from his various interviews with *Rolling Stone, Billboard,* or *People* magazines just to name a few.

"I guess he was a Gabby kind of guy." Chris said lightly, "to stand around talking about me and singing my songs with so much work waiting to be done."

"Well, he did have to kill some time while I made the keys he wanted. I'm not as fast as I used to be and making five keys exactly alike takes a bit of time to do it right. Especially on this old machine we got. But would young Mr. Henley consider updating our equipment? Not if the President himself came in and wanted a key to the Mayor's private shitter. No sir, he wouldn't, and no mistake."

"Excuse me, Bing, but did you say *five* keys were made for my house?"

"Yeah. That's right. Made 'em myself, so I should know."

"The real-estate agent handed over two key rings, 'one for the mister and one for the missus'. The agent said we now had the only keys, but there were two keys on my ring and two on my wife's set. That only adds up to four keys. Who has the fifth one?"

Bing could see that Chris's concern was making him angry. He was probably paranoid from living in That God-awful City and trying to raise two kids and watch over his pretty wife. Be enough to make any man skittish.

"Hell, Chris, I wouldn't worry over it. Most people around here don't even lock their doors at night. This ain't the big city, son. I'll bet if you called that real-estate man, you'd find he was probably hanging onto a spare. Just in case you ever needed him to keep an eye on the place or something."

"Look, I'll go get your trap cages for you. Help yourself to a piece of candy. You'll adjust to the slower pace here once you've had time to settle in some. Is there anything else I can get for you while I'm back here?"

"Yes," Chris said evenly. "A box of thirty-eight cal., a box of forty five-magnum slugs and some shotgun shells. Make those deer slugs. One never knows how big a varmint is that's creeping around in your cellar."

CHAPTER 10

Nate was hanging the last of his clothes in the closet when Diana came in with another empty box.

"Well, between you and me this makes five more empty boxes. I had a thought though. Maybe Bedford has a recycling plant that would take the boxes? By tomorrow we'll have enough to make a trip out there worthwhile."

"If Bedford doesn't," Nate said, turning around from the closet, "Bloomington probably does. Being an ecology-minded college town and all."

"Unfortunately I just realized that we don't have a phone book to go with our new phones."

"You could always call information." Nate suggested.

"How about if I just borrow your car to run into town? I could pick up some groceries and find out where some of the local places are that we might need. I could even go to the Phone Company and pick us up a book."

"Sounds like you're just sick of unpacking. But if you want to run out for a while it's all right by me," Nate said while fishing in his pocket for the keys. "You can leave the kids here if you like."

"That would help me to go faster. There are still a lot of boxes to unpack."

"Chris should be returning any time. You might even pass him on the road. Say, do you even remember how to get to town?"

51

"Yes, I think so. Anyway how lost can you get around Tinytown, U.S.A.? I'll just keep driving until I pop out somewhere. Now is there anything special that you want from the store?"

"Just make sure and get the essentials. Cheese Whiz, Maxwell House, Wonder Bread, Bologna—You know."

"Yes, Dad, how well I know."

Kissing her Father on top of the head, Diana grabbed her jacket from the back of the kitchen chair. She held it over her head for protection from the rain as she ran to the car and climbed in. She was relieved that they were able to leave the vehicles unlocked. It made it easier to get in when the weather was bad. Leaving an unlocked car parked in New York was tantamount to destruction. She popped an old Creedence tape into the car stereo and turned around in the drive as Fogerty asked, "Who'll stop the rain?"

Diana turned into the driveway leading to Crescent's house almost before she had the thought to do so. She had been so intrigued by the sudden appearance and departure in their first meeting, that she had to make sure that Crescent was real and not just her overactive imagination acting up again. Although she hadn't had a visitation for many years now, her Shrink had said that as long as her adult mind could tell the difference between her Fantasy friends and her real companions that she could end therapy and consider herself cured.

Sometimes she missed the little folk. Call them pixies or Elves or whatever. They had, for some reason only they knew, taken pity on the poor lonely child and appeared and disappeared throughout her adolescent life. They always disappeared when anyone else came around only to resurface at some of the most inopportune moments.

They had warned her never to tell a soul about them, but one day while being teased at school for being unpopular, she had blurted out about her own special friends. Who needed classmate bozos for friends anyway?

The ensuing argument brought in the teachers. The teachers called in the parents and brought about the discussion that psychoanalysis might not be too far out of the question for such a bright young girl with a bright future. A future that would be bright except for the annoying touch of whimsy that gives her such a disregard for reality.

And so the sessions began. And as the walls of reality were built one by one, her special friends stopped coming, one by one.

She knew now, of course, that they had all been figments created by her desire for acceptance and popularity. But it didn't make her not miss them, for all their lack of corporal substantiality.

Chris was the first person she had met that, upon finding out about her early sessions with the shrink, didn't scoff at her personal form of psychoses.

Chris had remained silent for a moment when she had first gotten the nerve to tell him. She was about to accept his silence as reproach or even rejection, when he began to speak ever so gently.

"If I told someone that I had a melody in my head and it came around from time to time and it sang to me in a voice that only I could hear, people wouldn't call me crazy. And you know why?"

"Why?" Diana had asked meekly, still fearing that he was calling her crazy in a round about way. Even though the tone of his voice wasn't saying it.

"It's because I can take my own special head song Imp and with the help of modern technology in the form of tape recorders, synthesizers, and various other instruments, give shape and dimension to what once was only ethereal. I can give it a solidity that any Joe or Jill on the street can hear or even feel and see if touching the cassette counts."

"The Imp or Imps that visit you are not so easily transported into the mundane laps of those who disbelieve what they can't, or choose not to, believe in."

"That was when I fell in love with him," Diana thought, wiping a tear from her eye. "Now stop acting like a suck puppy. There is Crescent's house and there is Crescent as real as you or me," Di said with relief.

Crescent was standing on her front porch looking every bit as at home as she had that day in the woods. It must be nice, Di thought, to be so comfortable in your lifestyle that you seem to be a part of your environment rather than just taking up space in the surroundings you happen to be in at the time.

As a child, Diana had moved around a lot with her parents. She then traveled alone, seeing the world for a year after graduating college. She was twenty-two when she married Chris. Their first two years were spent on the road promoting Chris's songs. Shortly before Jerrica was born, they decided to settle down in New York. The eleven years they lived in New York was the most stable home life she had ever known. Even then, she knew it wasn't a permanent situation, although she never would have guessed they would come here to finally try to sink in roots.

Crescent was motioning her to come on up as she shut off the car and stepped out onto the soft earth. The rain and warm weather gave the ground that mushy, slidy feeling. Di tried to stay on the grass until she reached the sidewalk leading up to the porch. She felt so graceless remembering how surely, yet delicately, Crescent had moved. Di could walk in high heels with the best of the New York society girls. So why did she feel so awkward around Crescent?

"Diana, so good to see you." The wind was moving the sleeves of her billowing white blouse, but her long hair was braided back and only moved when her head turned. "I've just taken the teapot off the stove, so you're right on time."

Crescent held open the screen door for Diana to enter, all the while making sure the two cats at the doorway didn't escape outside. The smell of the house was wonderful as Diana crossed the threshold. There was lavender and other Herbs hanging from the beams in the ceiling. There were Herbal wreaths, potpourris, nosegays and pomanders everywhere. Beautiful bottles and jars containing oils and herbal vinegar lined the shelves and bookcases around the room. And the books: it was like a small library. Mostly hardbacks some looked very old, judging from their covers, which you are never supposed to do (and Diana nearly always did.)

"Your house is wonderful!" Di finally managed to say. "I feel like I've stepped right into one of the country magazines." Di suddenly realized she must seem very rude gawking so blatantly at someone's possessions when she hardly knew her. But when she looked back at Crescent, she was beaming.

"I don't have many visitors who haven't already seen my place a thousand times. It's nice to have a fresh face come in and admire things." Crescent walked into the living room, followed by the cats, who had opted for her attention since escape to the outside was impossible at the moment. She sat down on the sofa and poured tea into two heavy looking pottery mugs.

"Sit down, sit down." Di wasn't sure if Crescent was speaking to her or the pacing cats, so she sat down on the other end of the sofa. The cats did likewise.

"I'm out of cream, but here is fresh goats' milk." Crescent indicated the cream pitcher as she spoke. "And there is honey for sweetener, although I do have sugar if you prefer."

"Honey will be fine," Di said, sidestepping the goat milk. "These mugs are wonderful. Did you make them?"

"No, I have friends who are potters and sculptors. I have many of their pieces around the house. It's like functional artwork."

"I would be too afraid of breaking them to use them." Diana said, carefully holding onto the mug in fear the word became the deed.

"The very fragility of their nature is part of the beauty of their existence. I feel it is much more fulfilling to enjoy something to its fullest potential for a short while rather than safeguard its longevity while denying the true function it was created for. By allowing a cup to be a cup, no matter how delicate its structure, I will have a greater respect for its being no matter how transient its stay upon this plane. As a cup that is."

"What do you mean 'as a cup'?" Diana asked as Crescent took a moment to sip from her tea.

"It exists for us as a cup only so long as it is able to function as a cup. Once it is broken, it can no longer act as a container of liquids and ceases to be a cup, in our opinion, and therefore ends its incarnation on our worldly plane as a cup."

"You mean like reincarnation? Once it dies as a cup it comes back as something else? Like a soup ladle maybe?"

Crescent laughed her musical laugh. It sounded to Diana the way a wind chime might sound if left deep in the woods to favor an errant wanderer with a brief lilting melody when S/He, the wind and the chime came together at the right moment.

"You almost GROK it my dear. I'll continue if I may? I do get carried away in a stimulating conversation and the Lady knows that I haven't had one for quite awhile. So please stop me if I get too boring or long winded."

"Please, go on." Di was truly fascinated. How is it that someone with such a rural background could speak with such introspective eloquence at one moment and then switch back to Bedfordian colloquialisms without breaking stride? And GROK? Where had she heard that word before?"

"Let me freshen your tea." Crescent poured. "Now where were we?"

"Reincarnation." Di directed, distractedly adding goats' milk to her tea.

"Yes, well, reincarnation is the transference of the spirit from one corporal being to another. What the cup is experiencing is more of a MEincarnation."

"ZOOM" Diana said slumping back on the sofa and waving her hand above her head. "That one went right over. Do you think you could simplify the explanation so that a college grad could understand?"

"When someone dies," Crescent continued, "only the body has experienced death. The spirit—or soul if you prefer—lives on. It either moves onto another plane or dimension of existence or it continues to hang around in this world for reasons of its own. But of course, it has no body or corporate form as the psychics say. Depending on its abilities, such as how many incarnations this particular being has been through and how much it has learned about manipulating its surroundings through the psychic plane, is how much we are able to experience its effects on the physical aspects of our world. Your own psychic abilities determine, of course, how much of the beings actual presence you are able to perceive. Some people feel them as cold spots. Others seem to sense their presence through eerie feelings but nothing they can put their finger on. Some can hear them speak, others perceive them as an aura. The really attuned cannot only see and hear them but can converse with and sometimes coerce them."

"But what about the cup? I still don't understand how it can reincarnate? It doesn't even have a soul!"

"Well, dear, I believe that everything around us is manifested from the one creative life force. That's where the theory of MEincarnation comes in. Let us say the cup began as a lump of clay. We could go back further in its existence but this point will do nicely. One day the clay is taken up, shaped into the form of a mug, fired and glazed in a kiln. Now the Spirit of the cup wasn't changed. However, its entire physical structure has been. Its corporate form has been changed rather than its spiritual persona. The 'ME' that it was as clay is now the 'ME' as a cup."

"That's where you get MEincarnation. A totally new aspect of something through physical change." Di was so elated at finally grasping the concept that she was nearly petting all the fur off the cat in her lap.

"Very good" Crescent said, beaming like a proud tutor at her star student.

"But wait!" Diana thought for a moment before proceeding. "You said that when the cup broke and could no longer function as a cup that it was no longer a cup because of its inability to perform as such. And so another MEincarnation would occur?"

"That's correct."

"But what if the cup had only cracked a little at the top and a small chip had come off, and you were a person without tolerance for imperfection. You could not bring yourself to drink from a fractured vessel. In your eyes, the cup no longer functioned as a cup and therefore was no longer a cup, however, upon being discarded it was found by someone who had no problem drinking from the unbroken side. The object continued to be a cup and the MEincarnation only took place for the person who threw the cup out and not in the eyes of the new user or to the cup itself."

"Diana, you are very insightful. As you see, perspective is everything. More goats milk dear?"

Diana absently glanced at her watch and couldn't believe the time. "Oh my goodness!" she exclaimed. "It's nearly eleven o'clock!" Could an hour and a half really have gone by so quickly? The kids were probably starving and Chris was almost certainly back from his errands. They were sure to be expecting her back with groceries any time and she hadn't even gone yet.

"I've got to run, Crescent. I only stopped by on my way to the store to see if you needed anything from town. I didn't mean to stay so long. Is there anything that I can pick up for you?"

"I'm pretty much stocked up on everything that I need right now." Crescent returned from the kitchen where she had deposited the tea ware in the sink. She was carrying a brown box. As she re-entered the living room, she handed it to Diana. "I've put a few things together for you that you might need while you settle into your new home. There's another box outside on the porch also."

"You shouldn't have gone to all the trouble," Diana said, unable to see into the box because the top was taped closed. Her curiosity bell was ringing loudly in her ears.

"It's nothing really, just a few odds and ends from the garden and such." Crescent opened the door for Diana but this time one of the cats was too fast and darted out the door like a shot.

"Trinket." Crescent called to the cat as she stepped out onto the porch behind Diana. Trinket had already crossed the porch and was heading down the stairs to take advantage of the newly rain-less day. "Trinket. You hear me." She said a little louder and her voice took on a firm tone. The cat paused at the lower step and turned to regard her owner. Diana figured the cat would bolt any second and be gone for the rest of the day until hunger set in. Instead, Trinket sauntered back across the porch and went into the house as Crescent held the door open. "Thank you, Trinket. It's for your own good you know."

Di smiled to hear her talk to the cat as if it were a person. It was really odd behavior for a cat that usually had its own mind about its business and total disregard to any human's wants.

"They do hate being confined to the house, especially in such nice weather." Crescent explained as she closed the door, lifted the other box and followed Di to her car. "I'd suggest that you keep your pets inside for a while also, just for safety's sake."

"Not to worry, Crescent, we don't have any pets." Diana spoke with a grunt while hefting the box into the trunk.

"Those orange and white hairs on your jacket tell a different tale." Crescent said handing over the second box and nodding at Di's shoulder.

"Oh, that's not my cat." Di said brushing ineffectually at the hair. "It's a stray that just wandered up. It's probably moved on now looking for another handout somewhere else."

"People don't own cats, cats own people." Crescent spoke the old saw with a twinkle in her eye. "Remember how we spoke about things hanging around past their time? This time there was an edge of seriousness in her voice. A cat won't stay in a place that's bad. Their senses are much more attuned to things than ours are but their curiosity outweighs their sense of preservation. So you've got to keep track of them at times." Crescent went on ignoring Diana's denial of owning a cat. "Just keep him fed and he'll stay inside without too much objection. Awareness is the key, Diana. Stay receptive to the changes of moods and vibrations and you'll be all right."

Diana wasn't sure if she meant the cat's moods or her own, but didn't have the time to ask. She still had to get to the store. She figured she could stop at a fast food place to feed everyone as soon as she got home. As much as she disliked the thought she was sure everyone else in the household would be tickled pink. As she got in the car and started the engine Crescent leaned down by the window so she hit the button lowering the glass.

"Watch the children too, please. Its all right in the daytime but make sure that they're in well before sunset. And don't let them play near the quarry or the caves. Even in the daylight."

Diana was beginning to take exception to this turn in the conversation. Was Crescent questioning her ability to adequately watch out for her own children?

"I'm not trying to interfere into the way you handle your family. I've raised no children of my own, so I'm sure you're far better at natural motherhood then I could hope to be. I also am not intending on frightening you, dear. I've enjoyed your company too much to scare you off with the prattling of some old woman. But I'd be negligent in my own mind if I didn't try to keep you and yours safe, even if I sound paranoid in the speaking. We are going to be great friends you and I. I hope my concern hasn't offended you."

Diana's anger was quickly assuaged by Crescent's sincerity. If Crescent said to stay aware, then aware she would be.

"No offense taken." Di said lightly. She put the car in reverse and began backing toward the road. "I expect you over for supper tomorrow night, though. And I won't hear any objections, be ready by three p.m. sharp, I'm coming to pick you up. Bye."

Crescent slowly lowered her waving hand as Diana's car disappeared out of the drive. Her cheerful smile filled with sadness as Di's parting words echoed in her mind. "Be ready by three p.m. sharp, I'm coming to pick you up."

This was nearly word for word the last thing she remembered her dear sweet Jonathan saying to her. How long ago had that been?

Memories rushed around her like phantoms as she walked back into the house. Even the familiar surroundings seemed strange and alien at this moment.

Layers of age peeled away like the dried skins of an onion as she mentally returned to the first and only day she ever fell in love.

It was a remarkable spring day. Winter had released its grip early in the year. The warmth of the sun was unseasonable yet totally welcome after the cold snows that seemed to hold on forever, especially to a young girl of sixteen who disliked being cooped up inside a house for months and longed to return to her true love, the garden.

She was there now, feeling the damp soil which still held the winters chill not far down beneath the surface. She realized she was jumping the gun a bit with some of the seeds she was planting. There was still plenty of time for a frost or a late snow to come through and destroy the tender sprouts she was forcing. But she felt sure that it was alright; besides, her weather casting skills were very keen and she would know if she needed to cover the plants if winter did decide to pay a last visit before departing.

Her burrowing fingers felt the vibration in the earth before she heard the familiar sound of a vehicle pulling into the gravel drive. She stood and wiped the loam from her hands onto the blue work apron that covered her homespun dress. The old farm truck rounded the curve as she turned. She knew something had to be wrong for someone to be driving so hard, especially on such a warm day.

There were three men in the truck, none of whom Crescent recognized. The one driving was visibly shaken; the other two were in the flatbed. One was obviously unconscious or dead; the other was holding a cloth compress to the stricken man's head and trying to soften the ride of the bouncing wooden bed.

"We're looking for Mrs. Silvernail," the driver managed to stammer. "We rode from Mitchell to Doc Banner's house but he weren't home. The man at the drygoods store gave us directions to Mrs. Silvernail's. Said she was a healer, but weren't nobody home there either."

Crescent walked to the rear of the large green truck as the driver spoke. The other man offered her a hand up as she climbed into the bed.

"Do you know Mrs. Silvernail? Do you know where we can find her?"

Crescent silenced the man with a gesture as she gently removed the compress from the stricken man's brow. He was still alive, but an angry gash ran just below his hairline. She held back his long dark hair, matted now with blood, and examined the wound.

"Fetch some water and a clean cloth from the rain shed there," she instructed the driver.

"But Mrs. Silvernail...?"

"Is unavailable." Crescent cut him off. "She is my grandmother; what she knows, I know. Now do my bidding, or this man's death will be on your hands!"

"Is he going to die?" The man holding up the injured man seemed to go pale with the thought of being so close to a soon to be corpse.

"Not if I can help it." Crescent looked at the man for the first time and realized that he was no more than a boy, probably just a little younger than she was, and very frightened. The older man returned with the cloth and water. Crescent cleaned the wound, which set it freely bleeding again. She worked as quickly as her Grandmother had shown her, then instructed the young boy to once again hold pressure to the wound.

"He has lost a lot of blood. I'm going to make a poultice from my herbs to stave off infection, and then we will take him to the house and stitch the wound. I have potions there for pain in case he revives during the suturing."

The driver looked worried as Crescent passed him and headed into the rain shed in search of the things she needed. "I wish I had some fresh Comfrey root," she spoke aloud. "But it's too early in the year. Last years stock dried well and will be fine." She meticulously filled a basket with everything she would need, then returned to the farm truck.

"Drive us back to the house as gently as you can," she called to the driver who had already climbed into the cab. "When we get to the house you should see to your radiator, it appears to be overworked." Crescent gestured to the steam beginning to rise beneath the hood. "What's your name?" She asked of the boy holding the injured man.

61

"Jim." He answered without looking up from the compress he applied.

"Jim and I will take care of our friend here." She felt a wave of relief wash away from the driver as he turned the truck back toward the house.

"And what's his name?" Crescent asked of Jim as she sat down next to him on the jostling truck bed and once again moved the dark locks from the unconscious man's face.

"Jonathan Tender." Jim finally looked up and saw Crescent for the first time. Her manner made him believe she was older but now he saw the youth in her face, and fear for his friend once again wavered momentarily across his features. "He's our new Preacher. We're building the new church in Mitchell. It won't be finished for a couple more weeks, but he showed up anyway, a few days ago, and began building it along with the rest of us. Pa says that if he preaches as hard as he works, that there won't be a sinner left in Indiana by this time next year."

Jim looked solemnly down at the Preacher's face, and then his eyes followed Crescent's hand upon Jonathan's brow back up her arm to her face once more. "Are you a Witch?"

His bold question elicited a gasp from the other man, who believed such concepts shouldn't even be thought, let alone spoken.

"People have called me and my family that, Jim, but don't fear for your Minister. I'm interested in his life now, not his immortal soul."

The wooden sideboards wavered and groaned as the truck stopped outside the house where the agitated driver was more than relieved to deposit his human burden into someone else's hands even if that person was a witch.

Crescent was amazed at the way Jim followed her instructions for preparing healing salves and poultices. Reverend Jonathan only roused once into semi-consciousness as Crescent was finishing the suturing. He smiled weakly at her and said "Angel" before lapsing back into stupor. Only after Crescent was sure she and Jim had done all they could for their patient, did she allow them both the opportunity relax on the sofa and drink some of the rose hip tea Jim had brewed previously.

"Have you had experience with healing people, Jim?" Crescent asked, after inhaling the relaxing tea aroma.

"No, never before tonight." Jim stammered almost embarrassed, as if he thought she could read his thoughts. "Not people," he continued, "but I've been helping Mr. Best over at the veterinary clinic. I like working with animals. If my Pa would let Mr. Best take me on as an apprentice, then I could work with him all the time."

"Do you think your Pa would allow that, and is it what you really want?"

Jim couldn't look directly at Crescent at the moment, he felt as if she could see deep into his heart and knew his innermost dreams. "I think it's the only thing I've ever really wanted to do." He carefully set the cup down on the table and slowly lifted his eyes to meet Crescent's.

"My Pa needs my help with the farm, since I'm next to the oldest, but he's also good to me and my brothers and sisters. I think after this year's harvest he'll see clear to cut me loose.

My younger brother will be old enough to take over my chores by next year's planting. At least, I hope he'll see it that way."

"What you need is a charm!" Crescent was up and moving before he could protest.

He heard her ransacking in the next room until a cry of "ah-ha" brought her back to plop gracefully on the couch much too close to Jim for his own comfort.

"Here." She proffered her closed hand to Jim but he was unable to reach his own hand out for the gift. What if she dropped a severed finger or a spider into his palm?

Crescent realized that her exuberance and way of dealing with things were different and frightening to Jim. She slowly turned her hand palm up and showed Jim the octahedron stone composed of fluorite.

"It's a natural formation." She explained, while once again proffering the gift. "Its vibrational energies help manifest dreams into realities. You should carry it with you as close to your skin as possible, especially at night when you dream."

Jim held the stone between his thumb and index finger, marveling at the play of light through its purplish and yellow depths. "Are you sure you can part with it?"

"Sure, I have more. I traded some herb vinegar and oils for them to a tinker from Arkansas. He claimed that you couldn't dig potatoes out there without unearthing a shovel full of them."

"Crescent, you've done so much with the Reverend and food for us and now givin' me gifts…I'm ashamed to have nothing to give back."

"Maybe not right now you don't, but, Jim, somewhere down the road of your life you're going to meet up with someone or maybe an animal that needs your help, and you're going to pass the help on from me to them. That's what you're giving me right now—your promise to do that."

Jim looked deep into the gemstone once more and then met Crescent's eyes and nodded once with a smile that split his face.

"It's going to be dark in a few more hours, you and your driver friend should head back to Mitchell. I'll sit with the Preacher for tonight. He's going to need a couple of days before he can take another bouncy truck ride."

"Gary can take the truck back and let folks know that the Preacher's alright, but if it's all the same to you I'd just as soon stick close until he's up and about. I can sleep in the chair at the foot of his bed, and since there's still daylight left, I can haul in some firewood and water to help pay back a little."

"I'll pack Gary some food for his trip back. You go tell him that Mitchell will have its preacher back in three days and for everyone to mind their scriptures until he returns."

Gary was standing next to the green truck that he already had pointing in the direction home. He had drawn water from the pump and added it to the radiator once it had cooled enough to open. He took the proffered bag of fruit and cakes as if it contained snakes and lit out as soon as goodbye was said.

"Do you really think Jonathan's going to be back in three days?" Jim asked candidly of Crescent.

"By the time Gary finishes embellishing the story of what really occurred with how I called up the demons of Hell to seal the Preacher's wound with fire from the pit and demanded death to back up a step from his mortal frame, how could I possibly not have him up and about in that time? A Witch does have her reputation to think of." And with a cackling laugh that ended in a young girl's tinkling giggle, Crescent bounded up the porch steps to take another look at her new charge. "My, but he is handsome for a preacher," she thought, "and those eyes, when he opened them. Oh yes, those eyes could most surely look upon me again."

Jim wasn't sure if the morning sun coming through the windows had woken him, or if it was the wonderful smell of a great country breakfast. Crescent had, evidently, arose before him (if she even slept at all) and was preparing an early morning repast.

Jim quietly slipped out the front door and relieved himself in the bushes before washing his neck and hands at the pump. As his sense of smell awoke he realized he was wearing the same flannel shirt he had been working in the past couple of days. He looked to make sure no one was around to see him before he peeled off his clothes and took a quick 'whore bath', as his brother referred to it. He pulled on his trousers and rinsed out his shirt. As he was wringing the last of the water from it Crescent came into view from around the azalea bush—which, of course, gave no cover at all at this time of year.

"Don't you dare put that wet thing back on!" Crescent scolded as Jim turned his back to her and began trying to unwind, and climb back into, the wet flannel at the same time. "I'll not be nursing two of you back to health! Now you march in the house out of this chill and I'll get you one of my Grandfather's shirts and no buts about it."

Crescent went back inside and quickly emerged with a towel, which she tossed to Jim. "Dry your hair and hang that shirt on the line before you come in." And then, gratefully to Jim, she disappeared once again into the house.

Jim obediently, if not reluctantly, hung up his shirt as he was told. When he cautiously entered the house, Crescent was nowhere to be seen. A fresh shirt was, however, hanging on the back of a dining room chair where a large plateful of steaming food and a hot mug of tea were obviously set out for him as well.

Quickly donning the shirt, he sat down at the table. He tried to be polite and wait on Crescent's return, but what if she had already eaten? It would be a worse insult to let this sausage gravy and biscuits get cold. Once he started, he couldn't very well not eat some of the eggs, ham and grits since she had gone to all this trouble. "Say, isn't that hot apple butter and fresh baked bread?" He asked himself between swallows.

"Looks like the chill air didn't freeze your appetite none," Crescent laughed as she joined him at the table. "No, don't stop, I was only teasing. My Grandparents have been away for six days now, and I haven't had anyone around to share a meal with for awhile. Everything's alright isn't it?"

"It's great." Jim said after swallowing his last mouthful. "Why, a meal like this almost makes it worth hitting the Preacher in the head." Jim's face went pale as if he thought his words would get him struck down on the very spot.

"I didn't mean that the way it came out," he stammered. "I just meant that it was real nice of you after all the trouble we've been."

"It's okay, Jim. I'm sure that in a couple of weeks you'll say the same thing over a meal and Reverend Jonathan will laugh right along with you. There was no meanness in what you said, just bad timing." Crescent walked to the stove and returned with the steaming teapot. "I'm sorry we don't have coffee, would you care for more tea?"

"I should check on the Reverend first." Jim began to rise.

"I just left him; he's sleeping fine. He regained consciousness in the night and we talked for awhile. Outside of a headache he seemed to have his senses together. I gave him some doctored up broth to help him recover quicker from the blood loss and something to ease the pain and help him sleep. He'll probably come around again soon, so take your time with your breakfast and tell me how the accident happened. It was an accident, wasn't it?"

Crescent's way of speaking her mind was so disarming to Jim. He was never quite sure if she was putting him on or being serious.

"Of course it was an accident." Jim answered a little rougher than he meant too. "But it was still my fault all the same. I was shaping the timber for the rafters in the new church that we are building. It was past noon and I was hot and hungry and a bit mad. You see, Mr. Best came by the farm early that morning on his way to the Jenning's horse farm. One of their racing mares was throwing a foal and Mr. Best asked if I'd like to help with the delivery. I was all excited but Pa said no, that I had promised to work on the church, and that was what I had to do. Like I said, I had been drawing, planing, and shaping the timbers all morning and thinking some pretty bad thoughts about all that work for what? Another building that people only used on Sundays or during a wedding or a funeral? It wasn't fair! I grabbed up the beam I had been working on and tossed it toward the truck. I was blind mad. I had been out by the tree line all day by myself. I didn't see that the Reverend had come walking up and was standing between the truck bed and me. I only saw him for a moment, standing there with a cup of water in his hand, before the beam that I had tossed took him square in the forehead. I couldn't believe it for a minute. He just collapsed like the life had gone out of him. I came to my senses and checked for a pulse like Mr. Best showed me, only on animals. He was still alive; I was relieved. Then the cut on his head started to bleed. Lord, I never knew anyone could bleed so much. I had a bandana on so I grabbed it and put pressure on the wound. Everything Mr. Best had shown me so far on animals was coming back to me. Gary was just coming across the field to fetch the Reverend and me for lunch, I waved him on and he came running. We got the Preacher into the back. Thank goodness I hadn't fully loaded it, and that Gary had come back just then. I can't drive yet.

Jim paused to finish his tea. "The rest you pretty much know. We went to Dr. Banner's house and then to the Jenning's farm, but Mr. Best was already gone. When we stopped at the store they told us how to find you. Or rather, your grandma, but I guess you worked out just fine."

"I didn't do anything greater than you did. You focused on all the things you learned to heal and save lives. No matter whether it was animal or human, you kept him alive until you came to me. Otherwise he would have bled to death right there in the shadow of his new church. I just did what others have shown me to bring folks and animals back on the road to wellness."

Jim quietly studied his shoes as his logical mind wrestled with his guilt. A low moan from the next room brought them both out of personal reflection as they scurried into the adjoining bedroom.

"Parson!" Jim called enthusiastically as they entered to find Jonathan sitting up in bed and holding his head.

"Jim? Where is this? Where are we?"

"We're in Bedford at the Silvernail's house."

"I don't believe I know any Silvernails. Jonathan made an effort to sit but the pain forced him back down. He inquired of Crescent. "What happened to me?"

"Here, drink this first." Crescent offered Jonathan a glass of water. "This is my Grandparent's house. They are away visiting relatives. As for your head, you should be more careful in the future when you walk up on someone who is working. You gave poor Jim here quite a fright. If it wasn't for his quick thinking, you'd be exchanging how-de-do's with your Savior right now instead of us."

"Crescent, please." Jim pleaded. He couldn't believe she would say such things right to a man of the cloth.

"No need to be modest, Jim." Crescent could feel his blush on the back of her neck. "When a man owes his life to another, that's a considerable debt to be beholden to. A good man like Reverend Jonathan here deserves to know which of his flock he should be observant of so he may better tend to their needs. "Don't you agree, Reverend?"

"No! No!" Jim started, but Jonathan cut him off.

"The young lady is correct, son. My carelessness nearly cost me my life. I thank you, and if there is anything I may ever do to repay you, you must never hesitate to ask."

"Jim, I need you to run up to the rain shed and fetch me some more Comfrey. It's clearly labeled in a canning jar on the rear shelf."

"Yes ma'am, I'll be right back, Parson." Jim hurried out the door, relieved to be out of that room. "There's no telling what she'll say next!" He spoke aloud as he kicked a chunk of limestone down the road. "Why, here I was ready to beg forgiveness from the Parson and she turns it around and has him apologizing to me for ramming *his head* into *my board*. She even had me coming out a hero." Jim stopped, the dust settled, the limestone chunk came to rest on the roadside. "A hero." His indignation settled, his smile broadened, his stride increased. "Local boy saves Minister's life. Yeah, I kinda like that." Jim kicked the limestone off into the field and sprinted toward the rain shed.

"Do you have any pain or discomfort other than your head?" Crescent asked as she raised pillows behind Jonathan's back and eased him down onto them."

"No, just a little nausea and total exhaustion."

"You lost a lot of blood. I'll fetch you a tonic and some broth. Do you think you can keep it down?" Crescent had placed her hand upon Jonathan's brow to see if he was feverish.

"Will I live, Doc?"

Crescent had to back up a step. "I could get lost forever if I looked into those eyes too long," she thought. "Yes, you seem to be healthy enough. Probably hard-headed like most Irish Kentuckians," she replied out loud, and hurriedly left the room before Jonathan could answer.

She returned bearing a silver tray laden with a steaming bowl, large glass of milk and a mysterious brown bottle.

"Take a spoonful of this, then wash it down with the goat's milk while your broth cools." Crescent instructed, once more finding control in her nurturing format.

"What's in the bottle? Will it taste bad? Did a Doctor give it to you?"

"It's good for what ails you, yes, and no, now shut up and take it."

Jonathan was making an awful face before the elixir ever touched his lips. It actually wasn't bad, as Crescent had laced the concoction with honey. He lifted the goat's milk from the tray and gulped half of the contents.

"Slow down, the milk is cold, you'll give yourself a headache."

"Too late." Jonathan said, smiling a toothy milk mustache smile.

"I guess I owe you my life, too." Jonathan spoke softly between spoonfuls of broth.

"You owe me nothing," Crescent replied. "May I?" She indicated a corner on the foot of the bed.

"Please, sit down, after all, it's your bed."

"It's my grandparent's bed," she corrected. "My Great Grandfather carved the post, head- and foot-boards from an oak that had toppled in a storm. The underside is laced with hemp rope. The feather mattress is new. Grandma and I just made it last winter. The quilt has been in our family for many years."

"It's beautiful, so much stitchery, and such detail on the plants. And the writing stitches, why this one is German, but that one appears to be Dutch, and this one is definitely in Italian. Who created this quilt?"

"No one person." Crescent lightly smoothed a wrinkle from a patch containing lavender. "Many hands over many years put their wisdom into the making, several of the people never even met. The Herbs are stitched in exact detail to the living plant. The words give details on the medicinal nature of each one."

"It's lovely but not very reliable as a source of information, I'm afraid; after all, who could read all of those languages? Some even appear to be runes."

"My Grandmother for one, and I for another," Crescent answered matter-of-factly. "I come from a long line of Healers, Wise-women, Midwives. We are called many things. This quilt, along with other cherished possessions of my family, was passed along from one generation to the next, to the one chosen to carry the legacy."

"And that one is you?" Jonathan asked, as he finished his bowl and reached again for the milk.

"I'm the one now, although my mother was the rightful one before me. She passed away before my Grandmother bestowed the gifts upon her."

"So I am in the hands of the current Wise-woman of Bedford?"

"No, not completely. My Grandmother did begin my training in the ways very early on. There was no one else, you see? My Grandmother feared that she would pass on to the Summerland without leaving a properly initiated heir. There was much more to learn than the names of all the plants and the writings on this one quilt."

"The responsibility of such a tradition must weigh heavily upon those small shoulders."

"It's a good and proud calling. I have many ancestors to call upon when I need strength. And speaking of gaining strength, you should lie back and rest now, that you may regain yours."

"You're right, I do feel weary still."

"One more thing before Jim returns. Jim is a natural healer, although his interest lies in animal husbandry. Mr. Best has offered to apprentice him, but Jim's father is reluctant. You must speak to Jim's father and persuade him to relinquish Jim from his family duties so he may follow the path of his rightful calling. Everyone in the community would benefit from having a Veterinarian in town. Possibly even the church could help with a scholarship to college. Not too much to ask to enhance an ability which saved the life of one of their own Ministers now is it?"

"Your Grandmother may hold the official title as 'Wise Woman' but you, dear Crescent, are Heir Apparent." Jonathan closed his eyes and snuggled beneath the quilt. "If it's within my abilities then we shall have a new Veterinarian, this much, at least, I owe you both."

When Jim returned, Crescent said nothing of Jonathan's promise to her. She imparted to Jim as much of her healing lore as she could over the next couple of days as they ministered to Jonathan, who rapidly regained his strength. The day Gary returned with a car instead of the old truck to fetch the men home was met with sadness on the part of them all.

"Jim, be sure that the Parson changes the bandage and uses the salve you prepared every day. We don't want infection undoing all our hard work." Crescent spoke as she handed Jim a parcel of concoctions through the passenger side window; Jonathan had stretched out in the large back seat.

Jonathan said thank you to Crescent with the shake of her hand but he held onto her a long time as he asked, "When is it that your Grandparents will return?"

"In another four days," she managed to answer. The heat of his palm and the depth of his eyes were nearly overpowering her senses. "If he doesn't release me soon, I shall fall faint," she thought, even though she wanted him to go on holding her for as long as he would.

Jonathan released her hand and draped his arm across his forehead. Gary, who was once again anxious to be on their way, started the motor and revved it slightly as a hint. "I shall return next week to pay my respects and gratitude for the use of their home and the pleasure of being in the care of their lovely Granddaughter. Farewell, Crescent, thank you again."

Crescent felt as if her feet had rooted to the Earth, where she continued to stand long after the vehicle had departed from view. Finally forcing herself from the spot, she moved across the lawn and porch and entered the house. It was early morning, and she realized there were so many chores that needed to be done. She had fallen behind over the last couple of days as she tended to Jonathan. "Jonathan." She spoke his name, and the sound of it was musical to her ears. The house seemed very lonely. She had never felt alone before even when her Grandparents left her to tend for herself as they sometimes did. She was always self-sufficient. She had her studies and her plants to entertain and comfort her. Why then did she now feel incomplete? She entered her Grandparent's bedroom with the intention of making the bed and straightening the room in preparation of their return. Instead, she found herself crawling beneath the quilt, clothes and all, as she buried her face in the pillow. Yes, it still smelled of Jonathan's presence. She breathed deeply and inhaled the essence of him deep within her lungs. How long she held her breath she did not know, for she was soon asleep, dreaming of plunging naked into eyes where souls fall deep and secrets keep, where she would await tomorrow.

After the church was finished, Jonathan returned as promised. Crescent found him even more handsome than before as he arrived looking so tall and impressive in his black Minister's coat. Her Grandparents welcomed him warmly into their home. After a fine meal and exchange of pleasantries, Crescent took Jonathan to the front porch, where they sipped tea on the porch swing.

"Your Grandparents are wonderful, but I expected no less from people who could raise such a charming Granddaughter."

Crescent sat quietly, unable for the first time to know how to respond. She stared up into the night sky at her namesake. "Sister Moon, please help me," she silently pleaded.

"Crescent?" Jonathan had set aside their drinks and was once more holding her hand. "I would like to ask your, and your Grandparent's, permission to call on you. Would that be acceptable to you?"

Crescent swallowed a lump in her throat that felt as if she had swallowed the very moon to which she had prayed. "Jonathan," she finally whispered, "there is nothing that would please me more, but you know nothing about me."

"I know that you are kind, beautiful, caring, and easily the most wonderful person I have ever met. And I think that I've fallen in love with you."

Crescent's heart had turned into a wild bird, which was trying to escape from her breast. It took all of her inner strength to calm herself so that she could think and say correctly what she knew she must. "Jonathan, I believe that I also love you." She had to place her fingers upon his lips to stop him, so that she might finish. "I don't think you have an accurate idea of what I am, what my family are. You see us as a quaint family that farms a little and takes pride in helping others with old time healing practices. But it is much more complicated than just a way of living. Jonathan, we are connected to the very spirit of the Earth and all of nature from which we draw our power. We are interwoven with all that we serve and that serve us."

"Crescent, I have vowed to uphold spirituality, how can you possibly think that I don't understand commitments to things other than earthly ones?"

"But, Jonathan, your religion is based on the life of one individual, Jesus Christ. You surrender your lives to him and accept no form of spirituality other than His."

"Are you trying to tell me that you haven't accepted Jesus as your Savior?"

"I'm trying to tell you more than that, Jonathan. Not only do I not believe that Jesus is the one and true Savior of mankind; I never will believe it. It's not that we are anti-Christian, it is more that we believe in a pre-Christian religion. I would not expect you to renounce your God in order to have me. I gladly respect your right to worship in the way you choose. But I fear that you, and especially those who follow you, will not accept the fact that your betrothed is a Heathen."

"You surely cannot mean that you are an atheist?" Jonathan paced the porch. The wooden floorboards creaked along with the crickets in the still night air. "I cannot be mistaken in seeing a spiritual love that shines so deeply within your heart."

"Jonathan, an atheist is someone who does not believe in a greater spiritual force outside of their realm of existence. I am not an atheist; I just do not believe in your God as being the one and only."

"And never will?" Jonathan asked downheartedly without speaking the implied "not even for me?"

"No, Jonathan, I will not live a lie, no matter how happy that life could be. If you accept me, you accept me totally and completely for what I am and what I have dedicated my life to be. No less than I would accept you as well as your commitments without trying to change you to fit my mold."

"Crescent, I do accept you for all your being, but I would be going against my vows and all that I believe if I did nothing to show you the path to Christianity and save your soul for eternity. I feel that I know you, but I am not sure of what you think you are?"

"A Witch, my beloved Minister, you are asking to court and convert a Witch."

Jonathan's mind was struck as dumb as from the blow he had received from Jim. Surely his human form could not withstand the battle of the inner conflict which raged between his heart, mind, and soul. He made his good-byes and left hurriedly to pray, meditate and seek council on the difficult situation he found himself floundering in. "All are precious in the sight of the Lord." "Suffer not a Witch to live amongst you." "All are precious...Suffer not...All...A Witch...All!!!" His mind was on a treadmill. He was on his knees at the altar of his new church without an awareness of the journey spent in getting there. All night he prayed, with no answer in sight as the dawning sun broke through the stained glass windows and cheerfully colored the empty pews.

Jonathan's brother, Bing, arrived a few weeks later. Jonathan had been in correspondence with his brother about the delicate situation in which he found himself. Bing was the only family member Jonathon felt he could confide in. Their father was a very strict Pastor and Jonathan already knew what his council would be. Bing, however, had not followed the calling and could hopefully be a little more objective.

"It's good to see you again, brother." Jonathan helped Bing carry his things into the spare room in Jonathan's house. To say that the home was modestly furnished would be a gross understatement.

Jonathan had lived in his father's house up to the time that he entered the church rectory to complete his ordination. This house and church were the first places of his own and therefore he had acquired very few personal belongings. He had spent all his energy and money helping furnish the church, which left very little for his own personal comforts.

Bing was smaller in stature than his brother. He also lacked Jonathan's looks as well as his intelligence. He dressed in overalls and flannel shirts as opposed to his brother's dress shirts and creased pants. Bing was against Jonathan's involvement with Crescent. He figured that he could talk his brother into his senses once he arrived. But in the time that passed during their last letter correspondence, Jonathan had already made up his mind.

"I have it all figured out, Bing, and that's that. I'm going over to Crescent's house this afternoon and ask her to marry me. The only condition that I shall make upon her is that we have a church wedding and that she allows me to instruct her in the ways of Jesus. I'll not pound her into submission, but rather let the word of God soften her heart into acceptance."

"And what if she don't accept Jesus as her one and only Savior? How long do you think folks would tolerate their preacher being married to a daughter of Satan?"

"Don't call her that, Bing." Jonathan's eyes flashed as he turned on his brother. He grasped the iron railings of the bed in Bing's room and the entire frame shook from his agitation. She is a good and caring young woman. She has been brought up in ways that are different from ours but there is no evil in her soul. We spoke on the subject and she told me that the idea of a Witch selling her soul to the Devil in exchange for power was pure myth. She worships no demons, only the natural forces of nature, which you and I agree are but different manifestations of God. When she realizes this fact there will be no difficulty in her wanting to serve Jesus and to go on nurturing people in his name."

"Make yourself at home, Bing." Jonathan's shoes echoed on the wooden floor as he crossed the small room. I'm going to Crescent's now to see if she will accept my proposal. You can stay as long as you like. If you like it here, I can take you into town and see about finding you a job. It would be nice to have family living nearby."

As soon as Jonathon was headed down the road, out of sight, Bing slipped out the door to walk the two miles into the town of Mitchell. He found a telegraph station where he immediately dispatched a wire to his and Jonathan's father urging him to come to Mitchell as fast as he could as Jonathan's life depended upon it. He couldn't go into detail in the message, as he knew that the wagging tongues of a small town could do as much damage as if he let his foolhardy brother marry that Witch. He looked around the town as he headed back to the house. No hurry now, nothing to do until father got here and put things to right. "Not a bad looking little town," he thought, "maybe I could get a job and settle down here. It could be quite peaceful once my brother gets straightened out."

Jonathan didn't bother stopping at the house; he knew that this time of day he would find Crescent at the rain shed. As he pulled his car through the wooden gate, he saw her kneeling in the garden. Her red hair had fallen out of her braids and was hanging in thick folds, touching the Earth where she was tending her plants. She knew he was there but waited until he was standing behind her and spoke her name before she stood to face him. Her face streaked with mud and standing barefoot in a dirty smock, she was the loveliest girl he had ever seen. Jonathan gently took both of her hands in his and knelt in the fresh turned dirt to offer his proposal of marriage.

"Jonathan, I know as sure as I breathe that I will never convert, so you must not hold hope in your heart, even though I will gladly listen to you speak of the faith you so love. And I also know that the people of your faith will soon hold no love for either of us if we marry. You must be prepared to lose all if you gain me."

"It is a chance I am willing to accept, but before you judge my parishioners you must first meet them and see if they wrongly accuse you. We are dedicating the church tomorrow night and everyone will be there before the Sunday services the day after. Come to the dedication. I will not ask you to attend services but you must come to the dedication of my life work. Be ready by three p.m. sharp, I'm coming to pick you up."

Crescent started at a sound, then realized it was she making the noise, by crying. She had been lost in a reverie triggered by

Diana's words. What a strange day that had been, she mused as she dried her eyes on her apron and went back inside. That was also the day her Grandmother had told her to prepare for the initiation ceremony where she would have her rite of passage and take up the mantle as the acknowledged wise woman of their clan. She was stepping down and all duties and responsibilities would fall to Crescent as a Wiccan High Priestess.

Crescent had already declined to hive off and start her own Coven. She preferred to work as a Solitary; however, she would officiate as needed at gatherings and ceremonies. And now all of these years later how many Handfastings, Wiccanings, and rites of passage had she performed? "Too many to count this night," she thought. But why was she so caught up in dwelling on the past today? "Because it's nearly time to do another rite of passage. I am getting old, I have no children of my own to train to the calling and have not yet selected any other heir." Or had she?

CHAPTER 11

Chris didn't wait to get home to call the real-estate office. He loaded the hardware into the car and walked across the street to the pay phone outside the drugstore. He had the agent's card in his wallet next to his calling card, which he found that he didn't need since Bloomington was a local call.

"Top Home Real Estate, how may I help you?"

Chris wasn't sure if the voice on the other end of the line was real or a machine. "Hi, this is Chris Lane." (Chris always said 'hi' to machines.) "I need to speak to Mr. Tremble."

"Please hold, I'll see if he is available."

Chris looked around at the various buildings that could be seen from the phone booth. Most were made of limestone. The rest were constructed of brick or wood framing. Something seemed oddly missing from the structures. Perhaps it was just a memory from his childhood that was no longer there.

"Chris? Bill Tremble here. What can I do for you?"

"Graffiti!" Chris said aloud. The sudden voice on the line made Chris realize what was missing.

"What?" Mr. Tremble sounded shocked. "Someone has vandalized your property?"

"No, no. The buildings downtown have no graffiti painted on them."

"Well of course not, Mr. Lane. But I do appreciate you calling and letting me know. One can't be too well informed in the real-estate business." Bill was speaking slowly as if talking to an imbecile in need of patronizing.

"That's not why I called." Chris spoke quickly, maneuvering the conversation back on track and taking control. "How many keys did you have made for my property?"

"Why, four keys were made. Just as you requested."

"And you no longer have one of the keys, correct?"

"Of course not, Chris. I gave you the two key rings with two keys on each. Now that adds up to four in my book. Why are you asking? Did something happen?"

"No, not yet." Chris thought. "It's just that I was in the Hardware store and Bing, the guy who works there, insisted that he made five keys for the handyman you sent over."

"Look, Chris. I don't know Bing personally. But I'm willing to bet that the mistake lies in his counting abilities and not in some devious subterfuge."

"I'm not convinced, Bill, Bing seemed to take his hardware very seriously. If he says he stood there and made five keys, I believe he did. Now what I would like for you to do," Chris kept talking so Mr. Tremble had no room to interrupt, "is to call your man. What was his name?"

"Graves, Steve Graves."

"Fine." Chris kept going. "Call Mr. Graves and ask him about the missing key. I expect a phone call back tonight and the key in my possession immediately so that this infraction to my privacy is resolved without further altercations."

"What a God Damn paranoid son of a bitch you are!" Bill thought. What he said aloud was, "I understand how your peace of mind must be disturbed. Why don't you go home and relax and I'll take care of everything? I'm sure there is nothing to worry about."

As Chris hung up the phone he thought, "that's the second person to tell me there was nothing to worry about. You know, that kind of makes me worried."

Steve Graves pulled into the driveway of his house, stopped by the side door and shut off his truck. He only had a couple of small jobs today, which he finished early so he could take the rest of the afternoon off. "Maybe I'll get my guitar out and play some," he thought as he unlocked the side door and walked into the kitchen. He hadn't felt like playing for a long time. Today, however, was different. Today he felt inspired again.

He walked through the house to the front door. Opening it, he reached out and got the mail from the box. The small stack contained nothing of interest. He dropped the assortment of junk mail and bills on a side table. He noticed the blinking light on his answering machine. If it was an emergency repair job, he'd have to shelve the guitar for another day. If he listened to the message that is.

Of course he could listen and not return the call until later, claiming that he had just gotten in and received the message.

He hit the rewind-play button and pulled the sweatshirt over his head. His wavy black hair pretty much always fell back into place. He stretched his muscular arms and back and tossed the shirt toward the clothes hamper as he went back into the kitchen for a beer. He had a cleaning woman come in a couple of times a week so his place was always clean and tidy. Not like when Becky was here. His marriage had lasted two miserable years. Becky was a lousy cook and a worse housekeeper. Finally, they had enough of each other and went separate ways. Steve kept the house and Becky took the car. That was the last he had seen or heard of her and glad of it.

The answering machine beeped and began playing the first message. He grabbed a Twinkie to go with the beer and went back to the living room.

The first call was the lumberyard saying the windows he had ordered for the Carson job were in. Next was Ted and was he interested in watching the game on his big screen TV on Monday night. Last was Bill from Top Home and would Steve call him right away.

The other messages he could pass off but Bill gave him a lot of work and he didn't want to miss anything that might be big.

He ate one Twinkie and gulped half the beer as he punched the dial on the phone for Bill's office.

He had never actually been in Bill's office and therefore never seen the person or machine that answered the phones there, but he was always glad when he got past them to Bill. That voice gave him the creeps.

"Steve." Bill said coming right to the point. "You know the keys that were made for the Lane house? Did you have an extra one made for some reason?"

"The Lane house? Which one is that? I've made keys for a lot of locks lately."

"You know, the one in Bedford on Spider Creek Road. Lane wanted all the locks keyed alike, remember?"

"Oh yeah. I know the one. I installed the locks on all the doors to the house and outbuildings just like you said. Keyed alike, just like you said. And had four keys made to fit them, just like you said. After that I turned them over to you. Didn't one of them work? I tried all four keys in one lock to make sure they worked. I also tried each lock as I installed it. But I didn't try every key in every lock."

"That's not the problem. The hardware guy said he made five keys and gave them all to you. He told this to the Lane guy and now they think there is an extra key that either you or I have. And I damn well know that I don't have it."

"I've done work for you for a lot of years, Bill. I've worked for a lot of other folks around here too! I've never had one complaint about my conduct or my work. I have a good reputation around here and I don't like the implications I'm hearing."

"Look, Steve. If you say you don't have the key then I believe you. I'll find another way to appease this Lane guy. Just go on about your business and don't give it another thought. I'll call as soon as I need another job done. Thanks."

"Damn!" Bill said as he hung up the phone.

"Damn!" Steve said as he did the same. "Stupid!" Steve said, as he slammed his empty beer can into the trash. "Stupid!" He shouted as he took a cold one from the fridge. "Stupid! Stupid! Stupid!" He reiterated as he stormed into his study, slamming the key down on the desk.

So close once again and now to be tripped up by a stupid key! He should have thought to have the four keys made at the hardware store and then gone to another place to have the fifth one made. Who would have thought that he would get caught so quickly? After he'd gotten to Chris, yeah then they could track the key to him but by then

81

it would have been all over and it wouldn't have mattered. But he hadn't even used it yet. How could they be on to him already?

He hadn't even completely thought out how he was going to get to Chris. He had considered going through his wife or possibly through his kids. But now it didn't matter. Now they were aware of him. Now he had to strike fast and straight at Chris. Because now he was only going to get one shot and it had to count. No cat and mouse games, no slow insinuation. Just bam! One shot and that would end it once and for all.

Chris probably didn't even remember Steve. Steve remembered him, however. He remembered how his band was going to win the Battle of the Bands competition until Chris put together a band and dazzled all the judges. He remembered how he was sure to get a music scholarship to I.U. except Chris had won the scholarship while he had to swing a student loan. Then there was the songwriting competition the radio station sponsored. He worked his ass off saving enough money to make a professional studio demo of his song. Again Chris won the contest. And he did it with a lousy two track home recording.

Oh, yes. He remembered Chris all right. He had followed his career ever since he left Bedford. He bought all the magazines with music articles. Watched and videotaped all the Grammy award nominations. And bought all the Albums that had Chris's songs on them. He even had copies of the commercials and movie soundtracks that Chris had done.

Yes, he followed, plotted and schemed as his own musical talent withered away from lack of use. And how could you use it when you had to work every day just to make ends meet. Pay bills. Buy food. Fix a door here, a roof there. When was there time to sit down and be creative? Especially when your hands were so swollen from hammering all day that you couldn't even flex your fingers let alone run scales on an instrument.

Yes, he tracked Chris. Steve even lived his life vicariously through him, as Chris traveled all around the world. And all the while a gut feeling told Steve that Chris would come back someday. Return to the town that bore him. And Steve would be waiting. Waiting with a key to let him into all the safe, private spaces in Chris's life. But the stupid key had been discovered.

No matter. Steve knew what he had to do. Strike hard and fast while the iron was hot. No second chances and no more second places. Once and for all it would be over. And Steve was willing to pay the price for the attempt. Successful or not.

CHAPTER 12

"Hi, Nate, got that trap door open yet?" Chris asked as he walked in the back door and sat his hardware goody bag down on the table. "Where's Di?" he asked looking through the doorway into the next room.

"Thought I'd wait on you to get back just in case we needed some of the stuff you went to buy. And Diana went into town to the store. I'm surprised you didn't pass each other on the road. Did you get a trap?"

"Sure did." Chris said, as he pulled a small mousetrap out of the bag. "You think this will be big enough to handle your basement beastie?"

Nate was dumbfounded to think his concern over the noise that he'd heard in the cellar wasn't being taken seriously, until he saw the grin on Chris's face and knew he was being put on.

"Sorry." Chris said laughing out loud now. "I have a couple of big traps out in the car. I just couldn't resist seeing your face when you saw the mousetrap."

"All right." Nate said, still a little miffed by the joke, "but we'll see who laughs when we get the door open. Tell you what. You go in first with your mouse trap and I'll nail the trap door shut so it doesn't escape."

"Pass." said Chris. "Unruffle your feathers old man! If I didn't believe you heard something I wouldn't have spent the money

84

on those expensive traps. Pour me a cup of that coffee and I'll haul in the traps and the other things, then we can settle this once and for all. By the way, where are the kids?"

"Over by the barn. They're still trying to make friends with that old barn cat. That thing's as wild as a mountain lion. You ought to get them a kitten from the pet store so they'll give it up on trying to make a pet out of the un-pettable."

"Now that we've got the space maybe even a dog wouldn't be a bad idea. I'll run it by Di when she gets home. In the meantime, having the kids chase that cat will keep them out of our way until we can corral your critter. Get your hammer and gun. I'll be right back."

Chris saw Jerrica running in the field just behind the barn, her white legs flashing in the spring sun. It felt a little too cool for shorts but Jerri was a smart girl. She had enough sense to come in for long pants if she got cold. She saw Chris and waved but kept on going toward whatever destination she had in mind. Watching her run in that almost awkward gait that is reserved for the young, Chris thought of a colt galloping in the meadow. The warm wind blew her blond hair back like a mane. He was suddenly aware of the cycle of change that would one day take place. He could hardly believe that she was twelve already. "Why," he thought, "she will be a teenager on her next birthday!" He thought of how his children would become the parents and he and Di would take Nate's place as the Elder family members.

The girl in the clover would one day be the mother,
And in a time of her own, would call to her the crone.
As the boy in the glen would one day be a man,
Until the gray in his hair called the grandfather there.

The words seemed to appear in his head from out of nowhere. Chris wasn't worried about writing them down. He never forgot a line or melody once his imp began singing it in his head. He'd just keep bouncing it around in there until it finished itself and then he'd write it down and compose the music to go with it. The muse was back. And sooner than he expected. He was sure the move was what he needed—and watching the children play. He was sure that it was the best for them also. Now all they had to do was settle this basement beastie's hash and all would be right with the world.

Nate had placed a small carpet over the trap door; now he had it rolled back and several of the nails already removed by the time Chris returned. Chris walked around the door and picked the handgun up from the bed where Nate had apparently just placed it.

"It's loaded." Nate answered Chris' silent question. "Keep it handy, I think that's the last nail and she ought to lift up easy now." Nate stood up and put the flat bar aside. He picked up a large flashlight and took the pull ring in his other hand. "Take the safety off and if anything this side of a fruit-fly comes out of there, shoot it! Oh, and one more thing."

"What's that, Nate?" Chris asked.

"Try not to shoot me!" And with that he switched on the flashlight and yanked open the door.

Both men tensed as the door opened easily this time. Nothing rushed out, however, and no sound was heard from below.

"Shine the light further down. Where does it go?"

Chris was peering over the edge of the opening, gun at the ready. The drop was about eight or nine feet to what looked like a solid earth floor. The walls also seemed to be hard packed dirt. The room below seemed to be about ten feet by ten. There was an old wooden ladder going down from the top of the trap opening.

"I can't see anything moving from here," Nate said. "Guess we have to climb down there to find out for sure."

"I don't see any reason to go down, Nate. It's just an old root cellar that hasn't been used in years. Besides," Chris continued, "that wooden ladder is rotten more likely than not. We can get a real ladder and go exploring some other time."

"I'm not spending another night in this room until I find out what made all the racket last night." Nate had laid the door back flat on the floor and eased one foot over the edge to test the strength of the ladder. "Seems sturdy enough for me. You coming?" and with that he began his descent.

"Hold on, Nate, you should let me go first." But Nate was already halfway down and not turning back. Chris waited for him to reach the bottom and began feeling his own way down the ladder.

"At least you could shine the light on this damn thing so I could see where I was stepping."

"Sorry." Nate said, swinging the beam over to illuminate Chris' feet. "Get down here will you? There's a tunnel about four feet high going back into the wall opposite the ladder. You brought the gun down with you didn't you?"

This last part sounded more like a plea than a question. Chris showed him the gun and he immediately swung the beam around to light up the passageway that he had discovered. They both froze as a pair of eyes stared back at them from the tunnel's dimly lit passage. Nate stepped back and bumped into Chris and as he jumped a second time the flashlight slipped from his hand and hit the ground.

"Jesus Christ." Chris yelled. "Get the light back over there! Hurry! I can't see where it is!"

Nate grabbed the flash from the ground. Luckily it hadn't gone out. He swung it around toward the tunnel once more and they saw the animal still frozen in its beam. Chris had the gun up and was ready to fire when he noticed just how still the creature was. He waited a moment, allowing his eyes to better adjust to the darkness. Yes, just as he thought as he could now distinguish the animal better in the wavering light beam.

"This poor thing is already dead." Chris lowered his gun and walked toward the tunnel.

"You sure?" Nate approached slowly while continuing to train the light on the beast. "Well I guess it is," he said, finally getting close enough to see the state of decay the raccoon was in.

"I guess that solves the mystery of the noises. Let's see if this tunnel goes anywhere. Here, give me the light and you take the gun." Chris spoke, putting the safety catch back on before handing the gun over. He took the light and ducked into the tunnel as he stepped over the dead raccoon. The tunnel continued on, remaining the same height and around five to six feet in width. His shuffling gait took him to where the tunnel ended once more in an earthen wall. The light showed him another opening in the ceiling. He didn't need a ladder to reach this one though, as the ceiling was lower. The access hole was partially blocked by a large slab of limestone. Chris attempted to move the stone but was unable to get the leverage to budge it. The opening was just big enough for him to get his head and one arm through so he pushed the flashlight through first and then stuck in his head to see what was there.

"What is it?" Nate seemed a bit nervous standing behind Chris in the total darkness while the light was projecting through the hole in the roof. He kept thinking that he heard the dead raccoon creeping up on them out of the blackness. "What do you see?" he demanded. "Where are we?"

"Looks like the tool shed." Chris answered, bringing the light back into the tunnel. "The hole opens up into the corner of the tool shed. Maybe it was part of the Underground Railroad that got slaves out during the Civil War. Or maybe somebody just wanted a way out in case of an emergency. Let's head on back. I think we have seen all there is from here."

Chris motioned back up the tunnel with the light and they began walking back to the ladder.

"I'll take the 'coon out for a decent burial before it starts smelling things up down here. Luckily the ground's cold enough that it didn't rot too quickly. Seems like it's been dead a few days. It must have crawled in through the shed and came down here to die. Looks like it was hurt pretty badly. We can push the limestone block back over the opening in the shed and nothing else will be able to get into the tunnel. You can put a bolt or a lock on the door in your room though if it will make you more comfortable."

They reached the ladder and Nate scraped some loose dirt from the soles of his shoes before he began climbing back up.

"You'd think the tunnel floor would be hard packed after all these years. Throw one of the packing boxes down and I'll load the critter up and take him on out while I'm down here." Chris called up to Nate.

Nate found an adequately sized box with a good bottom and dropped it down the hole to Chris. A couple of minutes later Chris pushed the stylized coffin out of the opening and climbed out behind it. Nate closed the trap door as Chris hefted the box and headed for the kitchen door.

"You know it feels like I'm starting to make a career out of this raccoon disposal thing." For a moment it entered Chris's head that this could be the same raccoon as the one by the roadside. But no, he dismissed the thought. That 'coon was definitely dead on the spot. "No way it could have crawled back in here to die," he thought as he backed out the kitchen door with his burden.

Nate walked over to the trap door and knelt down. Maybe Chris was satisfied that the case was closed but he wasn't. "Too many loose ends," he thought. "Like how could an animal with such extensive damage climb a ladder and pummel the bottom of a trap door? And if this animal had been dead several days, how did it make all that noise last night? And lastly, how did it get into a shed that had no windows, limestone walls, a solid roof and a very heavy locked door? No," Nate thought as he began to re-nail the trap door shut, "I don't think that it's all over."

CHAPTER 13

Once again Kratel's sleep was interrupted by the sound of the large being. This time, however, it was moving around directly overhead. "Of course," Kratel admonished himself, "this is the creature's dwelling. It would know the entrances and exits from the tunnel." How could he have been so stupid to let himself become trapped?

The groan of protesting wood told Kratel that they were forcing the door he had unsuccessfully attempted to open. Wait a second? Why had he just thought of 'They' forcing the door rather than it? He listened more intently and discovered the muffled voices. Yes, positively. His subconscious mind had detected two distinct voices and neither sounded like the creature he had previously encountered. These voices had a much deeper resonance.

Kratel began pacing furiously in the tiny room. He had inadvertently stumbled into the dwelling of a whole nest of the giants and they knew where he was and were coming for him.

Both entrances to the tunnel were of no use to him and his previous search had discovered no other avenue of escape. Therefore, another means of egress must be created.

Kratel, on his own, was good at tunneling. His natural abilities with Earth and stone helped him access the easiest direction of least resistance. Time, however, was against him. So he stilled his mind and reached out with his song. He Searched desperately for aid in his quest. There, contact! A large mammal was back down the tunnel toward the shed. Its burrow had been behind the shed many feet below ground level. It was large for its kind, and old, and had not survived the last hard winter. It had died in its sleep as it hibernated. The cold had kept the creature from deterioration and all of its digging apparatus was intact.

Kratel ran down the tunnel in the direction of the shed, even as the groundhog began burrowing toward him. He stopped at the nearest point where the tunnels could intersect. Kratel dived furiously into the spot from his side, being as careful as he could to keep the freshly dug earth level and stamped down on the earthen floor of the tunnel. He was trying to make sure that the giants didn't discover his new exit any sooner than possible…if at all. He was counting heavily on their night blindness to buy him enough time to ensure escape.

He was keeping the hole as small as possible, but it was still a gaping hole as visible as phosphorescence to his eyes. He was several feet into the ground when he heard the creak and groan of the trap door coming open.

The groundhog was still about thirty feet away. The distance was too great, and if they caught him in this tiny cul-de-sac he was doomed for certain.

Kratel had been keeping his senses tuned not only toward the trap door and the approaching groundhog, but also toward the shed in case something approached from that side as well. He had detected no motion there, which was odd if they were trying to cut him off. With an effort he stopped his own tunneling. Fear made it hard to be rational. He crawled back to the main tunnel and over to the hole leading back into the shed. He listened intently but heard nothing. The sounds from the other end told quite a different story. The beings were even now descending into the tiny room.

Kratel leaped back into the shed and began searching. He didn't know exactly what it was he was looking for but he needed something to hide the entrance to the tunnel he was creating.

There! He spotted what he needed in the corner, leaning against the wall. Kratel had no idea what a metal trash can lid was, or what it was originally designed to do. But, it suited his purpose fine. Grabbing it like a life preserver, which in a way it was, Kratel dropped back into the tunnel and hurried to his new opening.

The voices at the other end were very loud and agitated. So Kratel didn't have to worry overtly about making too much noise. He quickly removed dirt from around the opening of his tunnel until the diameter matched that of the lid. Taking the excess earth he pressed it into the interior of the lid, packing it tightly with as much force as he could muster.

The voices were growing closer. He could hear the approaching footsteps of the giants. There appeared to be beams of light preceding them. The dancing light moved back and forth against the cavern walls. How advanced where these beings to utilize mobile light sources even as Kratel sometimes did?

No time for pondering now. Kratel lifted the lid by the conveniently placed handle in the center of its circle. He moved carefully as he backed into his freshly dug space. He pulled the lid into place over the opening and twisted it a half turn. He hoped the earth he packed into its rim would stay in place. If it fell out, the beam of light would reflect off the lid's metallic surface like a beacon. Kratel tightly gripped the handle and with a supreme mental effort lowered his breathing and heart rate. Even his body temperature dropped. No telling what senses these creatures had in place of their lack of night vision. Kratel became still as stone. He even ended the song that allowed him to remain in contact with the groundhog, which immediately discontinued burrowing. It was a mere ten feet away, but the giants were now directly outside his opening. If they saw his place of concealment now, the groundhog might as well be on the other side of the earth, for all the good that it would do him.

Kratel slowly opened his eyes and listened intently for sounds of movement on the other side of the wall. Hearing nothing, he gently released his aching grip upon the trash can lid and rubbed the circulation into his lead weight arms. The lid stayed in place so he left it there. Summoning the groundhog to once more begin its burrowing, he began the same. The stiffness of the trance soon left his body as the vigorous digging loosened his muscles once more. His sonar told him where the larger stones lay in his path as he efficiently went around them or undermined the smaller ones that fell onto his tunnel floor. He was glad he no longer needed to be careful of packing the dirt to avoid discovery. Kratel made excellent time.

He actually enjoyed tunneling and under less stressful conditions he would have blissfully dug until exhaustion overtook him.

He did not feel that he could afford the luxury of mindlessness at this time and so kept his every sense alert for danger until finally reaching the point where he and the groundhog intersected.

He stepped back, letting the groundhog finish the last couple of feet of earth. He laughed as the wall suddenly collapsed and the animal and the dirt came rolling into his tunnel.

Leaping into the recently vacated hole, Kratel began racing forward. The groundhog uncomplainingly turned and began retracing its course back to its burrow.

The den delighted Kratel. It was dry and cozy yet had enough room to move about. Its best feature though, was that it had more than one exit. Never again was he going to be cornered so helplessly.

Kratel went up what appeared to be the main shaft. Nearing the entrance he noted that the light was still upon the surface world, although it was shady here where the tunnel emerged from beneath an old stump about five meters from the rear of the barn.

Kratel could barely tolerate the dim light even if he kept his eyes shut. He was forced to rely on his other senses and occasional squinting.

He reentered the Den and explored the other tunnels. There were three in all, not counting the one he had just recently dug. From this Den he now had three escape routes to the surface, and an access tunnel to the giant's house and storage shed. He felt safer than he had since leaving his own cavern.

He thought about what he wished to accomplish now that sanctuary was secured. Food and water were a priority although not an immediate one. There seemed to be no lack of food in the area. The giants were the next things to enter his mind. He had, after all, invaded their space. He was not certain if they were vicious even though they were definitely large enough to do damage if angered. He would monitor the giants for a while and after careful study of their behavior would then decide if another attempt at contact would be prudent. But there were so many of them and only one Kratel. If he were going to attempt contact he would need to cover his back in case things went bad.

He stopped and set out his call for food in all directions. Almost immediately he made contact at several points. He would continue to call during the time that the light held the land. At dark he would go as close to the giant's house as he dared and watch their movements and habits.

He sent the groundhog deeper into the tunnel to enlarge a spot for the other animals. As they arrived, they could help with the space development. If things went well, he would have a plentiful food supply to share. If not, he had an army of the dead at his command.

Calling for food was as second nature to Kratel as breathing. And so he went about his other business even taking a long nap as the animals continued to sporadically appear in the shafts before making their way to the chamber below which was growing by extreme proportions.

Kratel continued to climb to the entrance periodically to check on the sun's progress. Having no time sense, he was trying to attune himself to the duration periods of the night and day. Once he knew how long he could stay away in the dark, he could begin working on his main concern. He needed to find his way back to the entrance of his own caverns.

He knew that he had traveled far that night before the light caught him unaware. What he didn't know was how long it had been dark before he had emerged. Would there be enough time to go there and return before running out of dark? This was, of course, assuming that he could find the caves. He had a good home sense below ground but this above ground movement was quite confusing.

Finally, on one of his excursions up, twilight was falling. He found this half-light tolerable. In the darker shadows beneath the barn, crickets began their evening song. Taking note, Kratel attuned his hearing to the vibrational rate of the insects. If they began their chirruping every time at dusk, then Kratel would know exactly when he could emerge without having to continuously check the openings. Luckily, he did walk over to check one of the other openings to his Den one more time. He saw a large animal trying to squirm down the too small hole. He immediately stopped the animal's attempt at progress into the underworld.

The creature was taller than he was. It stood on four spindly legs that appeared to be much more suited to aboveground running than to burrowing. Kratel hadn't considered the possible attention that hundreds of animals making a cross-country trek directly to this spot would attract. He sent the deer off to hide in the brush while he contemplated this new dilemma.

The next tunnel entrance over was further back in the wooded area. No paths crossed near it so if he enlarged the opening to accommodate the larger animals it should go unnoticed. Of course, opening the tunnel to this size would also allow the giants access to his Den. For now though, he saw no other way. He would have to take the risk that he would not be discovered.

He was also going to have to cease calling in the daytime. That was when the giants were active. He would spend his dark time calling food as well as monitoring the giants.

He called the creatures up from the depths below his den and had them begin enlarging the opening and shaft that he deemed the safest. If they only enlarged the shaft leading to the newly enlarged holding room, then the tunnel leading to his own personal space and the other two access shafts would still allow him escape routes that the giants could not pass through.

Having delegated the duties, Kratel began making his way carefully around behind the barn. He meant to approach the house from this angle on the opposite side of the barn where his entrance was located. If he was spotted, he didn't want them finding his burrow too quickly.

The dusk was gradually losing ground to the nighttime as Kratel saw the rear of the house from his approach on the north side of the barn. He stood in the darker shade of a very large lilac bush. He had a good view of the giant's home structure from here. When full darkness fell, he thought, he could move in a little closer.

Patience was not one of his stronger attributes and the slow waiting would be hard, he realized. Just then, movement from an area about twenty meters southwest of the house caught his attention.

There was a low rectangular stone wall around an area that contained dried varieties of the strange vegetation that grew so abundantly on the surface world. The area seemed to have been cultivated by the giants. The plantings seemed to be in neat rows of similar looking species.

The motion that had attracted Kratel's attention to the area was one of the giants. It had been sitting upon the wall so still that until it moved, Kratel had not noticed its presence.

A cold shiver of fear ran down Kratel's spine. Had he not been cautious upon his approach, the giant probably would have noticed him before he saw it.

Fortunately he was still the observer in this current situation and he made a mental vow to keep it this way.

The giant stood from the wall and walked a few paces (large strides for Kratel) into the cultivated area. Looking up into the darkening sky the creature heaved a sigh and turned toward the house.

It's almost as if it regrets leaving this place for the dwelling, Kratel mused. The graceful movements of the giant seemed oddly familiar to Kratel. Of course! This was the first giant that he had encountered in the small structure that was closer to their dwelling place. This is the one that had struck him.

He felt no anger toward the giant, understanding now that its weak eyes had rendered it blind in the darkness. "I had obviously frightened it. And it sure frightened me."

Kratel had learned his lesson from that harrowing encounter: No more recklessness. He would not risk another attempt at communication until he had determined, if ever, that it could be accomplished with mutual safety.

The giantess, For Kratel was sure that it was female, had walked up the stone steps to the dwelling and stopped, just as she reached the entrance. She turned in Kratel's direction and raised her hands to her mouth.

He had been seen after all. The creature had calmly attained the safety of the dwelling before calling the alarm. Kratel's heart hammered in his chest. He was just about to flee when the giant's voice once again caressed his ears.

The giantess called, but this was no call of fear or a cry for help. The melodic voice carried over the fields and through the woods. Kratel was entranced. He could not understand her words but the lilting voice was so captivatingly gentle.

"Jerrriiicaaa!, Alexaaanderrr, Come iiin nowww. It's getting laaate."

Kratel suddenly heard the approach of at least two more of the giants. He could feel the vibration of their thunderous footfalls as well as hear them as they raced up toward the house from the south side of the barn.

Kratel attempted to shrink further into the Lilac bush, being very glad that he chose to be on the opposite side of the barn, even if by pure chance.

As the two new giants lunged into his view his jaw nearly hit the ground.

"Why, they are no larger than I am!" Kratel was astounded! How could anything of his size make so much noise in its passing, even if there were two of them?

"Offspring! How stupid of me!" Kratel mentally slapped himself. The giantess was obviously the mother of these smaller, however louder, giants. The one with the long hair stopped and took the hand of the giantess as the other, which Kratel noticed was almost a head shorter, raced on past. He flung open the entrance barricade and entered the dwelling with little, if any, diminished speed.

Light suddenly erupted from the crystalline rectangle in the wall next to the doorway. The mother giant and child stood, for a moment, bathed in radiance. Silently, they entered their dwelling and once more closed the barricade.

Kratel sat down heavily and attempted to sort out this new turn of events. Unprecedented occurrences seem to continually permeate his ever changing universe with the sole purpose of dashing to bits any preconceived notion Kratel might have entertained of the order, rhyme and reason of his heretofore happy existence.

The second story of the dwelling suddenly gave off the same illumination through similar crystal rectangles. These rectangles must have been fashioned by the giants to allow visual connection to the outside parameters of their dwelling. It also, however, allowed Kratel to see in. He perceived shapes moving within the second level room through which the light poured.

Moving with caution, Kratel advanced upon the house. He regretted leaving the relative safety of the bush. There was no cover between the barn and the house. The storage shed was off to his right about thirty feet back from the house. Two large oak trees grew side by side about twenty feet from the house. Even so, the larger branches actually touched the house up near the eaves.

The darkness was now complete and Kratel felt relatively sure that the giants could not see his stealthy approach without their lights. He gained the trunk of the oak without incident. The lower rectangle still glowed but Kratel had no way of looking in without climbing up and putting his face in it. Not only would this action leave him blinded by the light, it would also illuminate him for anyone to see.

He studied the branches of the mighty trees and found a very large one that reached to within ten feet of the house on a level with the window. Although Kratel had never climbed a tree before, he spent his entire life climbing through tunnels, up fissure cracks and rock walls. His climbing abilities were every bit as honed as his tunneling techniques.

Finding finger- and toeholds in the bark, he gained the first branches with an ease a squirrel would have appreciated. Still moving on all fours, more to escape detection than for balance, he moved out onto the wide branch that gave him the advantageous view he hoped for.

His view into the house gave him more than he had hoped for. Both children were in this cubicle section of the dwelling. They moved among the strange artifacts in the room with such familiarity, Kratel surmised this was their own private quarters.

He watched them move little figurines and flip through rectangular objects that were bound on one side. These extremely flat surfaces seemed to have drawings on them but Kratel was too far away to distinguish the images.

The girl set aside her image rectangle and crossed the floor to a black square box. She depressed a small section in the corner with her finger and suddenly the face of the box lit up with an eerie green light. Almost immediately the room was suddenly filled with loud cacophonous sound. Kratel was glad that he still maintained a tight hold on the tree limb, the sound was so startling that he was nearly unseated.

The girl child seemed to be taken unaware by the sudden noise for she began gyrating around the room waving her arms and spastically stomping her feet.

After a few moments Kratel began to be concerned over the length of her reaction. Could she be having some form of seizure that the sound initiated? And why wasn't the other child rushing to her aid or summoning help rather than lying there swaying his feet in time with the voluminous rhythms?

Rhythms? Yes, Kratel noted, the tones and beats had a definite pattern. And so, now that he noticed, did the movements of the girl child. Why, she was dancing. And this box was creating the music (by a very extreme limit of his knowledge of what music should sound like.)

Again Kratel was amazed at the abilities of the giants. They built massive dwellings, created artificial light sources and could even generate music out of the air without instruments other than that glowing black box! What else were they capable of? He must learn all that he could about these enigmatic beings no matter what the personal risk. Any creature this advanced must be capable of reason. I must simply remove the element of fear from our next encounter and reason must win out.

Kratel began his subsonic call/song as he carefully climbed back across the branch and down the tree to the ground. He lifted a few lightweight stones from the ground and then waited a moment for the deer to emerge from the woods.

Forgotten was his vow to observe the giants for a while before attempting contact. The advent of the children and the music allowed him the space to rationalize his eagerness to the point of immediate action.

Unsure of the strength of the crystal viewing rectangles, Kratel carefully tossed a small pebble up to make contact with its flat surface. There was a small 'tick' sound as the stone made contact. It was too slight a sound to be heard in the room over the droning of the box.

Kratel used a little more force and a couple of slightly larger stones as he flung them upward one after the other. 'Tick. Tick.' Definitely louder contact this time, for the music in the room halted.

'Tick. Tick.' Kratel let fly two more gravel attention-getters. Two faces suddenly appeared in the window looking puzzled. Kratel peered up from behind the tree. He was in the shadows. The deer, however, was standing in the wash of light that projected from the house.

Again Kratel began his song. This time he sang in the decibel range of the tones that had issued from the black box. He wasn't sure what the hearing range of the giants was but they could definitely hear in this zone of sound.

His voice was incredible; as well it should be since it was his primary source for obtaining nourishment. He did intricate melodies utilizing a rich concert of hums, ahhs, and oohs. By mixing in some whistling trills, he easily filled a four-octave range, as only a being with three sets of vocal chords can do.

The children were less interested in Kratel's minstrel articulations as they were of the deer, which was delicately dancing on the lawn. Their eyes bulged and their mouths formed O's as the great doe stood on hind legs and did a parody of Jerrica's dance while Kratel attempted to recreate the music he had heard at that time.

Kratel was watching their faces in the window when suddenly they vanished from sight. Puzzled, Kratel stopped the music and the dance and wondered if he had still managed to frighten them somehow?

The deer was a gentle and familiar creature of their world, Kratel reasoned. The music was also done in a range of familiarity with tones and inflections based upon those he heard issuing from the black box. Dance was the third familiar aspect of the scenario. Nothing should have been frighteningly unfamiliar about the scene! Kratel had even stayed hidden so the music appeared from the very air as in their normal fashion. How had he failed? What caused them to run off?

Kratel got his answer as the back door opened and the two children emerged. They were obviously holding themselves in check as they slowly descended the stairs and tried to quietly cross the lawn to where the deer stood.

Kratel edged back against the tree, even though the children's eyes were only for the deer. His first thought was that their cautious approach was out of fear and that they would turn and flee to the house at the slightest provocation. That was not the case, however, as it became obvious that they wanted to attain the closest proximity to the deer before they frightened it into fleeing.

"This is awesome!" Alex said in an excited whisper. "How did it learn to dance like that? Where did it come from?"

"Maybe it got lost from a circus." Jerrica answered. "I've heard of dancing bears, so why not dancing deer?"

"Yeah, but what about that weird music? It sure ain't carrying a ghetto-blaster. Where did the music come from?"

"I don't know." Jerrica began looking around for an answer but it was so dark that she couldn't see far. "Look how still it's been standing since we got here. I don't think it's blinked once."

"Blinked? Jerr, I don't think it's even breathed." Alex held his left arm out and waved his hand back and forth. The deer didn't even twitch a response to his movement. "Boo!" He said, flinging both hands at the deer.

"I don't think it's real." Jerrica finally said. "Remember all those Animatrons we saw at Disney World last year? Maybe this is a robot like them. I can't believe that a real live deer could be taught to dance like that anyway."

"Yeah. Nothing even human could dance like that. It danced just like you. Hey, maybe that's it. Maybe Dad is working on a music project that lets robot animals make their own music and dance to it and he watched you dance and programmed this deer to imitate you."

"Wow!" Jerrica exclaimed, overlooking the insult to her dancing. "It would have a soundboard in it to reproduce the music. You wouldn't even have to carry it. It would walk along with you and play your favorite songs."

Their animated gestures and the rise in their voice levels affected no response from the animal, which they took to be an affirmation that the deer was mechanical.

Kratel watched the children's verbal exchange with interest. While their attention was fully on the deer, he was allowed a close range observation point without them realizing that they were being watched.

"There is just one thing that I don't understand, Jerr."

"Yeah, what's that?"

"Well, if Dad was going to make an animal that acted like you, then why did he pick a deer? It would be more realistic to use a pig or a skunk. Ha! Haaa!"

Jerrica swung her foot to kick him in the rump but he was already moving out of range.

"Maybe even a three legged hippo to recreate some of your fancy dance steps."

Jerrica looked down at the ground for a pinecone or some other missile. Alex recognized the sign of having struck a nerve in his sister and dove for cover behind the large oak tree and stopped dead in his tracks as he found himself mere inches away and face to face with Kratel.

"Jerrica." Alex's voice was a trembling whisper on the night air. "Juh. Juh. Jerrica!"

"What now?" Jerrica gave up her search for something to hurl at her brother and walked over to the big tree in hope of getting within kicking distance again.

"Jerr! It's, it's…"

"It's what? What is it?" "A couple more steps and I'll have him in my reach." Jerrica thought as she continued to question Alex on what he was looking at. "What are you trying to pull now?"

"It's an Elf." Alex whispered.

"An Elf? Where's an Elf?"

"Shhh!" Alex admonished. He held his finger to his lips as he shushed his sister but never once turned his face away from the great tree.

"I couldn't miss now if I only had one leg." Jerrica took a final step behind Alex and was about to deliver the butt kick of the century when her eyes fell on the form standing against the tree trunk and all thoughts of righteous retribution vanished.

"Oh my God!" she gasped. "It's another Animatron, Alex. It has to be!"

"No." Alex shook his head. "This one moves. And not jerky like those Disney presidents! I think its real Jerr."

So saying, Alex waved his hands in the air and cried "Boo!" the same way he had done to the deer.

Kratel was startled by this sudden gesture. Even so, he had seen the boy child do this once before and so returned the gesture hoping that doing so was the appropriate response.

"Boo!" Kratel yelled back at Alex and advanced a step while waving his arms. "Boo!" He cried again at Jerrica. Once more offering the opened handed arm swing gesture that seemed to be their greeting.

The children jumped back mildly frightened until they realized that Kratel had perfectly imitated Alex's voice and the fear dissolved into amusement.

"He sounded just like you!" Jerrica said in amazement. "Do it again", she asked of Kratel while pointing at her brother.

Kratel was not sure what the young female was asking of him. He was a perfect mimic, but he had only parroted the word back to the children. He had no idea of its meaning.

"Again!" repeated Jerrica, once more pointing to her brother so that the Elf would understand her.

"Again!" Kratel improvised. "Again! Again!" He repeated although this time he copied Jerrica's voice.

"Cool," Alex said, impressed. "He can probably imitate anybody's voice. Hi!" He spoke to Kratel. "I'm Alex Lane and this is my sister Jerrica. What's your name? Where are you from?"

Kratel was unsure how to respond. He was much relieved to find the children so non-aggressive and unfrightened, though they seemed wary of him, which was understandable given the circumstances of their meeting. He had not expected a direct encounter so soon and was totally unprepared as to what to do next. He could not continue repeating their words back at them without understanding their meaning. He could very easily commit some unforgivable breech of etiquette in their culture and ruin any further communication without even realizing what he had said.

Control of the situation was slipping from Kratel's hands as Alex continued to approach while talking non stop as only the very young can, seemingly uncaring or unnoticing that Kratel had not responded to his last barrage of questions.

"I told you he was real." Alex said back to his sister who still hadn't recaptured her poise enough to close her mouth after hearing her own voice come from so unlikely a source. "Are you an Elf or a Hobbit or what?" he asked, gazing unabashed at Kratel's long pointed ears and large round eyes. "Your face looks like an Elf but you have hair all over your toes like a Hobbit." Alex considered. "Are you a Halfling? Can you do magic?"

Kratel decided that some form of gesture was expected of him. He closed his eyes and placed the palm of his left hand on the right side of his chest and did a half bow. "I am Kratel. The echo of my cavern repeats as true as my words now. I am in awe of the variety and the beauty of your world and selves. I intend no harm and wish only the freedom to observe until I return to my own world beneath yours. Kratel, I am."

Having finished his speech, Kratel stood erect, opened his eyes and removed his hand from his breast and placed it upon Alex's chest.

Alex had quit talking when Kratel began his gesture. Although neither he nor Jerrica could understand a word that was spoken, the timbrel beauty of his songlike voice conveyed the heart of the message.

Alex looked at the hand resting upon his chest. Four fingers and a thumb just like his although the skin was covered with a fine white fur down to the first knuckle. The exposed skin was very pale, almost to luminescence and the retractable fingernails were more like hooked claws. They were wider than a cat's and much to Alex's relief' were now pulled in.

The hand was cooler than Alex's own body temperature but there seemed to be a pulsating energy coming from the touch and coursing along Alex's nerve endings and connecting him to the earth through his feet. No, wait. The energy was moving up from the ground and toward the hand. No. It was moving both directions at the same time. It was a pleasant feeling. It made him feel part of the earth and everything around. Not like someone just passing through.

"Alex! You all right?" Jerrica asked, putting her hand upon her brother's shoulder.

Alex hadn't realized that he had closed his eyes until he re-opened them at his sister's touch. He looked down at his chest and was amazed to see the hand of the Elf no longer upon him. He could still feel the connection. As a matter of fact Kratel was no longer standing in front of him at all. He had moved around the great oak and he and the deer were heading toward the woods.

"Wait!" Alex called. "Will you come back again?"

Kratel pointed to the moon hanging low on the horizon, soon to be out of sight. Then he traced its path back across the sky to where it had emerged just after dark. Although Kratel had lived his entire life without the moon, it didn't take him long to make the connection between its planetary path and the intolerable arrival of the sun's light.

"Tomorrow night." Jerrica said. "You'll return tomorrow night when the moon rises."

Kratel smiled and quietly disappeared as he turned into the shadows.

"Wow." Alex let out his breath when he realized that he hadn't breathed for some time. "No one's going to believe this."

"Then we had better not tell anyone. Not yet, anyway" Jerrica added. "Promise?"

"Promise!" agreed Alex. "Let's get to bed, Sis. I'm whooped."

Still holding his shoulder, Jerrica steered Alex back into the house, up the stairs and into his bed. He was asleep as soon as he hit the pillow.

Morpheus was not so kind to Jerr that night, however. She couldn't shut the events of the evening out of her mind. Each time she closed her eyes and snuggled down she would suddenly realize that she was staring out the window at the moon. The worlds of Fantasy and Reality had collided right before her eyes and now she was afraid to sleep because she was no longer sure which side she would wake up in.

CHAPTER 14

The next day would have been intolerably long for Jerrica and Alex if there wasn't so much newness around them to be discovered. They spent some of the early morning continuing to unpack their things and set up their rooms. When they were sure no one was around they talked about the Elf in the back yard.

"I'm tired of working, Jerr. Let's get a drink and go outside for a while?"

"O.K., but I've got dibs on the red pop. There's only one left."

"No problem, I prefer Coke anyway."

Diana was in the kitchen preparing lunch as they passed through on their way outside. The cat saw them as they passed the barn and immediately followed them in hopes of spare food tidbits. Jerrica had named the cat Joey but Alex wanted to name him Butterscotch, and everyone from time to time called him by his other, physically descriptive name, Bighead.

Jerrica sat down on the stone wall and dumped out the contents of the satchel she was carrying. Bighead sniffed at the books that fell out. He soon realized no food was forthcoming, so he decided that he would let Alex rub his stomach instead.

"What's with the books, Sis?" Alex asked, hefting one to look at the title. "Lord of the Rings," he read aloud. "What gives?"

"I couldn't sleep last night so I did some research on Elves to see if we could understand exactly what we're dealing with."

"Wow, good thinking, Sis. Did you find out anything? Is there a picture of him?" Alex began rummaging through the books looking at the covers. Along with getting no food, Butterscotch Joey now was no longer receiving tummy rubs. The cat decided he'd had enough of this party and left the barn in search of better offerings.

"Well, from what I could find, I don't think he is an Elf. He just doesn't quite fit the descriptions. He's not a fairy either. Too big, and no wings. His size, big eyes and fur make him sound more like a Hobbit, although I'm not sure if Hobbits really exist or were just made up by Mr. Tolkein in his story. I couldn't find them in any of the other books."

"Here's a Troll that looks a lot like him, only meaner, and its nose is much bigger and warty. Maybe he's a friendly Troll."

"Oh yeah, like a Troll would be nice to someone he wasn't planning to eat I suppose." Jerrica jibed as she removed the book from Alex's hands. "I'm not sure what he is." Jerrica stated looking helplessly at all the books. "The difference between Elves, Dwarves, Hobbits, Trolls, Goblins and the like gets a little fuzzy. But there is one thing I found that they all have in common."

"What's that?" Alex was suddenly captivated by the age difference between himself and his sister and her superior knowledge of the world of Fey.

"It doesn't matter if they are wood Elves or water Nymphs, the one thing they aren't is human. They live in a different world than ours—kind of like another dimension that sometimes overlaps ours. And during those times they can enter our world and we can enter theirs."

"You mean we could go into a faerie tale world for real if he shows us the way?"

"Yes, I guess so. But if we were over there and the worlds would, "Jerrica searched for the right word, "un-overlap, then we would be trapped there until the worlds crossed again."

"Gosh, Jerr, how often do you suppose they cross each other?"

"The books don't say, maybe every day or every year or maybe a hundred or a thousand years."

"Well I ain't going." Alex crushed his Coke can in punctuation to his words and tossed it in the air. "We can visit with him in our back yard, but I ain't leaving with him to go anywhere."

"Don't eat anything he offers you either. That's how they sometimes get control of you—by feeding you something from their world and then you have to go and stay whether you want to or not."

Alex was thoughtful for a moment, then said, "What if we gave him something to eat from our world, like a Bit-o-Honey or a Reese' Cup? Would he be stuck in our world then?"

"I don't know, but that may not be something we need to worry about."

"Why not?" Alex asked.

"What if the worlds have already un-overlapped. He might already be stuck here until the next chance to cross over. That could be why he came to see us. He might need our help to stay alive until he can get home."

"Maybe we should fix him a survival pack just in case he is stuck here."

"A survival pack?" Jerrica questioned. "And like what would you put in it?"

"You've still got that Girl-Scout backpack from when you went to camp last year. You said you were never going back so we could load it up with stuff and give it to him."

"Stuff? You mean like insect repellent and flashlights?"

"Yeah, and Bic lighters, a pocket knife, and a compass."

"Maybe you're not so dumb after all." Jerrica said, rising, and brushing off her clothes. "We have a lot of those things, but we're going to have to raid the kitchen and the workshop for some other things he might need. Come on, and don't leave your Coke can on the ground. It needs to be recycled," Jerrica reminded Alex.

"What if we get caught taking the stuff?" Alex was getting nervous as they approached the house.

"We say that we want to camp out in the yard and we ask to use the pup tent."

"And what if he doesn't show up?"

"Then we camp out in the yard tonight and put everything back tomorrow and forget about it all."

As Jerrica reached for the door, the knob was suddenly pulled from her hand. She nearly screamed as her mother stepped out onto the back steps.

"There you are! I was just going to call you to come in for lunch."

"Mom, we want to camp out in the back yard tonight. Can we?" Alex pleaded with his mother.

"We could build a campfire and roast hotdogs and marshmallows." Jerrica added. "I already checked the weather and it's not supposed to rain." Jerrica crossed her fingers behind her back as she told the little white lie.

"I don't know." Diana was thinking of Crescent's warning about keeping the kids in after dark. "Maybe later in the year when it's warmer."

"We can dress warm, Mom. Besides, we have sleeping bags and we'll keep a light close by the tent. Aw, come on Mom, how about it?"

"Please." Alex added.

The sun was behind the trees, in another hour it would be dark. Chris had enthusiastically helped the kids set up a campsite after he had asked them what they were looking for in his toolbox. He had even offered to camp out with them but they had talked him out of it. So he supervised the building of the fire and the setting up of the tent and did sit down and roast hotdogs over the fire with them.

Jerrica and Alex were, surprisingly, having a good time even though the tenseness of their prearranged meeting continued to intrude on their merriment. After the grownups finally went into the house, Jerrica removed the research books from beneath her sleeping bag and began pouring over them once more. She read only what she felt to be pertinent information out loud to Alex.

It had been dark for some time when the glow from the kitchen windows finally went out. Fifteen minutes later, the light in Nate's room followed it. Alex took a flashlight and crept from the tent to the front of the house. He reported to Jerrica that the living room light was out but their parent's bedroom was still lit.

"It doesn't matter." Jerr spoke knowingly. "They can't see the back yard from their room anyway and unless they hear something, I don't think they'll come back down to check on us again until morning."

Alex had been speaking to Jerrica through the tent flap. He turned, and picking up the bucket of water, dowsed the campfire.

"Why did you do that?" Jerrica came out of the tent and watched the steam drift off into the starlit sky.

"If someone does look out the window, do you want them to see us standing hand in hand around a campfire with a Troll?"

"He's not a Troll!" Jerr knew he was right about the fire but wouldn't admit it. "I said I didn't think he was an Elf, but that doesn't mean he's a Troll!"

"We can argue about what he is later, 'cause whatever he is, he's coming."

"How do you know that? Are you trying to scare me by acting weird? Well it won't work!"

"No Jerr, honest, it's like, you know, when he touched me yesterday? I could still feel his hand on me, even after he removed it. I can feel him 'here' even though he's not 'here' yet. But he will be soon. Coming right through there!"

Alex pointed to a dark spot of undergrowth, right at the edge of the woods off from the barn. Jerrica's eyes were riveted to the spot. She hadn't realized how dark it had gotten, and now, with the fire gone, the stars were their only limited illumination.

She had left her flashlight in the tent and even though Alex held his, it was not turned on. Many of the frightening stories of the horrible end that people met when dealing with the folks of Faery kept playing in her mind. She felt rooted to the earth, unable to tear her eyes from the point of appearance that Alex had indicated. Alex, too, stood still and quiet, which was most unlike him.

Many minutes went by as both children stood still as statues. If either of their parents had been watching they would not have believed their kids capable of such prolonged silence and inactivity, at least not while awake.

Finally, after a few moments more, Jerrica could no longer contain herself. Alex's little joke was out of place in such a strange setting and she was about to tell him so, when the bush she was continuing to stare at suddenly, almost imperceptibly, moved. Before she could gasp, Kratel emerged exactly from where Alex had indicated and with a most graceful walk approached the two children he had most recently become acquainted with.

As Kratel neared, Jerrica remembered the bow he had made with his hand upon his chest. When Kratel stopped a couple of paces from her, Jerrica imitated his greeting of last night. It appeared to them that Kratel smiled, and then he threw up his hands and in Alex's voice called "Boo! Boo!"

Both children jumped, then began to laugh hysterically all the while trying to shush each other so as not to disturb the adults in the house. Once under control, Jerrica indicated for Kratel to wait and then she entered the tent.

Kratel walked over and felt the fabric of the Nylon tent. He could not conceive of what manner of beast such skin could have come from. When Jerrica unexpectedly turned on the flashlight, Kratel winced and turned as if to dart back toward the woods. Alex, however, reached out and took hold of Kratel's shoulder and indicated the light was not harmful. After the initial fear, Kratel realized that he could tolerate the green diffused light emanating from the tent's skin.

"Jerrica." Alex spoke softly. "Be sure to turn the light off before pulling the tent flap back. I think the light hurts his eyes."

"Okay, Alex. Got it! I'm coming out now." The light went out and Jerrica emerged holding the stuffed backpack. "Here," she said proffering the bundle, "it's for you."

Kratel moved forward and took the pack. It was made of the same skin as that which made their portable dwelling. He had watched Jerrica operate the zipper on the tent door flap and now he duplicated the operation on the packs' zipper. Sszzzitt! The zipper sound seemed huge in the quiet of the night. Kratel smiled and did a perfect imitation of the sound. "Sszzzitt!" He said, pulling a box of raisins from the pack.

They spent the better part of the next hour demonstrating to Kratel how to operate the things in his survival pack. There were two cans of Vienna sausage in his pack but when they showed him how to open one he immediately devoured all the sausages and then opened the other can and finished them off too!

"Jerr, you show him how to wear the backpack and I'll sneak in the kitchen pantry for more Vienna sausages. But don't you eat them all at once!" Alex said, shaking his finger at Kratel who answered by making the sound of the sausage lid popping off and in Alex's voice said "All at once!"

The kitchen door was left unlocked in case the kids needed in for any reason. Alex opened the door as quietly as possible. He crossed the kitchen to the pantry and used his flashlight to find three more cans of sausage. There was also a can of sardines, so he grabbed that too!

When he returned to the campsite, Jerrica had the backpack on Kratel, who was trying to reach for the tins in Alex's hands.

"Oh, no! These are for the survival pack." He took Kratel's arm and turned him around so he could place the tins in the zippered compartments. "Shit, Jerr, did you feel his arm? It feels like he has steel cables instead of muscles! If he really didn't want me to turn him around and put this sausage in the pack, I don't think I could budge him with a truck!"

"Alex, I want to learn his name. If he has one." Jerrica placed her palm against her chest and said "Jerrica, Jerrica." Then she placed her hand upon Alex's chest and repeated "Alex, Alex." She then turned and placed her hand upon the creature's chest. She widened her eyes and looked into his large eyes expectantly. His eyes seemed to light up and a huge smile split his face although his pointed teeth did make his smile a little unnerving. He placed his hand upon Jerrica's chest and in her voice said "Jerrica!" He then turned to Alex and with the same gesture but with Alex's voice he said "Alex!" And then turning so that he could face them both at once he placed his hand upon his chest and in his own voice said "Kratel!" and did his small bow.

He realized from listening to the children's speech patterns that they were incapable of pronouncing his real name...the process required three sets of vocal chords acting at once. So he modified the sound of his name to fit their limited vocal abilities. He pronounced his name using only the Root note rather than the full chord. The children heard his name spoken as Kratel.

"Kratel, wow, dude." Alex said, and bowed.

"Kratel," Jerrica said, and also bowed.

Kratel looked toward the east at the sky and then indicated he would be leaving soon.

"The light of the sun must be too much for him." Jerrica guessed.

"Kratel?" Jerrica asked, his name sounding strange on her tongue. "Before you leave would you make the animals dance again?"

Although Kratel understood very few of the words she spoke, he was able to understand the pantomime dance that she performed. He took a deep breath, closed his eyes and let his voice rise to fill the little glen of the back yard. His song caused shivers of pleasure to coarse through Jerrica and Alex's veins as once more they felt the pull upon their own flesh and hair and even their teeth and nails.

Soon, the call was rewarded by the appearance of a small chipmunk that quickly emerged from the brush and began whirling in quick movements to the melody. To the squealing delight of the children he was joined by the appearance of several more of the seldom seen denizens of the woods. Jerrica and Alex joined in the dance as they were encircled by the arrival of rabbits and groundhogs, frogs and birds, all moving to the distinct idiom designated by their forms but locked in an uncanny rhythm created by Kratel's unique vocal capabilities.

The Children danced until exhaustion overtook them and they collapsed laughing to the ground. Kratel opened the dancing circle and one by one directed the animals off into the woods. He followed the last one into the brush; his backpack swaying to the rhythms he created. Wearily, Jerrica helped Alex to stand. They waved goodbye, then thankfully crawled into the tent and the warmth of their sleeping bags. They were fast asleep by the time Steve and his probing flashlight emerged from the woods.

CHAPTER 15

Steve sat bolt upright in bed. The ringing of his alarm clock had shattered a frightening dream that began fading back into the mists where dreams go even as he wiped the last vestiges of sleep from his eyes. He remembered being in a department store, and all of the mannequins had Chris's face. He had rushed wildly in the dream searching for an exit. When he finally found a door leading to the street, he stopped. Just before leaving the store he gazed through the glass at all the people passing by. Walking, driving, bicycling. They all had Chris's face, every man, woman, and child. And then he saw his own reflection in the window of the door, and he, too, was an exact image of Chris. That was when he awoke, sweating and gasping for air. Many nights he had awakened from this same dream, but tonight was different. Tonight was the last time he would dream that particular dream. Tonight he was going to pay Chris a visit and settle things once and for all. It was eleven o'clock p.m., exactly the time Steve wished to arise. He was sure everyone would be asleep in Chris's household when he arrived there. He had planned so carefully, he thought to himself as he dressed in his work clothes. There was no sense arousing suspicion if anyone did see him. Many times he had received calls in the night for emergency repairs of busted water pipes and broken windows. Anyone seeing him leave would assume it was another such call.

Steve turned the light off in his bedroom, walked down the short hallway to the kitchen, crossed over to the table, picked up his wallet and slid it into the left hip pocket of his jeans. He then picked up his key ring and checked one more time that along with his truck and house keys was the key that would fit every lock on Chris's property. Not that it had to open every lock. It only had to open the one Steve had decided was the most appropriate one. Lastly he picked up the small package. It rested like the culmination of his entire existence, right here in the palm of one hand. He gently carried it out the back door and placed it on the seat of the truck as he climbed in and started up the engine. It was not unusually warm, but Steve rolled down the window and let the night air in to cool his sweating brow. Everything was planned like clockwork. Nothing would go wrong, Steve assured himself. He swung the truck out onto the street and turned on his headlights.

He cursed as only one headlight came on. No time to fix it now. He didn't care if the whole truck quit working. He'd walk over if he had to. Just so long as the package worked and Steve knew that it would. He had very carefully and painstakingly assembled it himself. He had tested it and then set it so that there would be no delay time. As soon as Chris touched it—Boom!—right in the face. That was why he had decided to place it in the studio Chris was building. He was sure no one else would inadvertently intercept this package that was meant for Chris and Chris alone.

His plan was not to drive up to the house. No, he couldn't chance the truck engine waking someone. If he was caught in the act, the whole plan could backfire. Instead, he pulled off the road and turned up the drive leading to the old drive-in theater. The place had been closed for years. A 'For Sale' sign hung on the post that also held a chain, which stretched low across the drive. The chain was intended to keep trespassers out. Steve had come by earlier in the week with a pair of bolt cutters and removed the lock. He had replaced it with a similar looking lock with the exception that he possessed a key for this one.

Turning off the one headlight, Steve slid out the door but left the truck running, after removing the new lock, Steve drove the truck just inside the posts and then refastened the chain.

He now drove through the bumpy rows of the theater parking lot. Speaker posts stood like a metal forest. The bare posts were devoid of speakers due to vandals. Now mute, they stood before the giant white screen, like penitents waiting for their God to once more cast its magnificent Technicolor light amongst them that they might shout his spoken word to all the people assembled there. The vehicles arrived faithfully every Friday and Saturday night as the sun went down, the people gladly paying their tithes at the admission booths and rushing into the concession stand to accept their sacraments before the Great Silver God. Their devotion made his Image come to life and gathered the full attention of all. All but the few young couples that felt unworthy of the images and so hid themselves in the back seats where they sought to comfort each other's lack of piety amidst their moaning, and rending of clothing.

Steve knew, as he drove toward the back, that the Drive-in was a dinosaur: extinct, except for the skeletal remains. There would be no resurrection, no second coming, soon. Cable TV and video rentals had stolen away the faithful flock, writing *'Finis'* to an era that was as American as apple pie. But at least, Steve thought, it did have its day. It had its moment in the sun, so to speak, and that was the thing that he found so unfair. He never had his moment, his day. But his time had come, one way or another; tonight he meant to put things right. After this night he would be noticed. Oh yes, indeed.

He pulled onto the dirt access road that ran behind the last row and followed it until he came to the fence that bordered the woods behind the theater. Here he turned the truck engine off. Many times, before he had learned to drive, he and his friends would sneak into the theater from over this fence. He didn't even need the large flashlight yet. His feet remembered the path all too well. He did, however, keep a firm grip on the package. From time to time his hand would move to his pocket to reaffirm that the key ring was still in his possession. After walking a few yards into the woods, he switched on the light. He knew that the Quarry was still a long way ahead. He also knew that there was no one around who could possibly see the light. And he sure didn't want to trip and fall. Not now, not so close.

He felt the cool change in the air before he saw the rim of the limestone pit. Now this was where he had to watch his footing. If he fell, his body would be found broken on the giant limestone blocks that waited to catch him many meters below. And if he missed the stones and plunged instead into the dark green water, the fall from this height would send him down into the icy depths that never warmed. Hypothermia would lock his muscles in a death grip that would prevent him from ever reaching the surface. At least not face up.

Steve did not descend into the limestone pit. Instead, he walked the path around the rim until he had gained the other side. Here he took a smaller trail that led off into the woods. The path had not been used much and was a bit overgrown. When he was a child, these trails were the highways of the adolescent. All the kids walked them or rode bikes upon the hard-packed earth, which kept the vegetation at bay. An almost invisible path intersected the one Steve was using. This one, he remembered, led over through Sutter's farm and back through the pasture to the pond. He had spent many Springs fishing, Summers swimming, and Winters skating that pond.

The spiderwebs and thorns illuminated in his flash beam told him that it was no longer the popular place it had been. Kids today seem more intent on staying indoors, watching TV or playing Nintendo. Who needs to swim when Mario can do it for you in Water World?

Steve walked on by the little path. It was not his destination tonight either. "Other fish to fry, Steve, my man." His whispered voice sounded strange to his ears amidst the other night sounds of the woods. He made a silent promise to himself to come back soon and clear the path to Sutter's pond, where he could sit ankle deep in cool waters and daydream of prehistoric fish in languid pools while he recaptured the serenity of his youth.

For now though, he must push on. His mind, once more, focused on Chris. He walked like a ghost through the stygian night world. Nothing appeared to have changed since his childhood. Indeed, nature's world had changed little in twenty years. Various subtle, nearly imperceptible changes occurred here in the core of the woods. But on the fringe, where man's world intercepted, severe changes had occurred. Changes which Steve's mind had forgotten. Sutter's farm, for instance, had been sold to a real estate developer. The hill where he used to sled was now leveled; the excess dirt used to backfill the pond. Where cattle, oaks, crops, and kids once crisscrossed the land, now roads and cul-de-sacs intersect. The subdivision, now in its seventh year, sits waiting for the next grove of trees to give way, so it may continue its growth.

The moon, which occasionally joined Steve's flashlight in illuminating his path, decided to fully emerge as the last of the night clouds departed leaving the sky crisp and bright.

Although the moon wasn't full, it still aided his vision as, like the clouds, he finally departed the woods and emerged onto the cleared property of the old Hudson farm.

He extinguished his light and walked across the open field that ran behind the barn. He kept the barn between himself and the house, even though he knew it would take someone with the night vision of an owl to see his approach. It didn't matter anyway for the house was not his destination. The barn was where he intended to leave his little surprise.

He had helped prepare the barn for Chris's arrival, running new electrical conduits and scaling down the formerly giant room into smaller rooms surrounding the central control room. Yes, he had done his part in helping Chris build his dream recording studio. He hadn't returned after all the equipment and technical engineers had finished with it. But he still had the key. The one he used to go in and out as he did the dirty work of removing the years of filth and debris that accumulates in an old barn. Oh how he cleaned and hated and installed the new floor and thought of Chris with every nail he drove. And still he cleaned and built and hated and plotted and now! Now he felt a calm serenity that amazed him even as he cautiously peered around the corner of the barn before walking over and turning the key in the steel security door. He had purchased the door in town and installed it, just as he had installed the wiring for the security devices that would alarm the house, and police, to intruders. But not the intruders who knew of the second panel cleverly hidden outside the barn. The panel he had used to disable the system before opening the door.

Yes, he had indeed planned this time to a tee, and no mistake. He silently closed and locked the door before flipping on the interior lights. No windows to the outside existed in the barn anymore. Steve knew that the light would be as easily contained as would be any sound he made from here on out. The acoustic designers had seen to that.

As his eyes adjusted to the sudden glare that filled the room, Steve's heart nearly stopped at what he saw before him.

Like something from a movie, the old barn on the outside was an audio palace on the inside.

The main mixing console seemed to stretch endlessly before the window into the adjoining room. The high-tech levers and pan pots beckoned. It looked like something from Star Trek, 'Where no one has sung before'. Although Steve saw a twenty-four track open reel tape machine in the corner, he was sure that it would get less use than the new digital recorders and ADAT's that filled the racks. Two high-powered computers with hard disk recorders were prominent on the scene. The banks of MIDI gear, samplers and synthesizers made the crew of the Enterprise seem obsolete. Even though the main recording room was large enough to hold a fifty-piece orchestra, this fully automated virtual reality studio could be programmed and operated by one person.

Most of the gear he had only read about in Electronic Musician magazine and some of the things he had no idea what they were. But a mixing board was still a mixing board and regardless of everything else, Chris would come over and sit in this main seat before beginning any type of operation.

"So this is where I will attach my own little effect!" Steve said in a theatrically loud voice. "Lucky thirteen. That's the channel I'll wire it into."

So saying, he sat the device on the mixer board and happily hummed a Dire Straits song as he busied himself borrowing a patch chord here and toggling relays there.

He had completed his task in a little under an hour. He could have easily done it in half the time but he hadn't had this much fun playing with new gear in a long time. But time would soon start working against him and he didn't intend on letting his plans slip out of his control.

He did a final mental check of all his wiring and hookups as he turned out the lights and once more entered the world outside. He locked the door and reset the alarm. He wasn't going to take the chance of some thief in the night tripping his surprise too early.

He crossed the field and took one last look back toward the barn. Casually dropping the key to the Earth, he crossed over into the woods. The moon was again hiding behind the clouds. The dark enfolding woods had Steve fumbling with the switch to his flashlight before he had gone five steps. With some difficulty he finally located the path that would return him to his waiting vehicle. "Not that I need to hurry," Steve spoke to himself. "Once I get home, I will just settle in and wait for news on this evening's work. I have no more jobs scheduled and after tonight I may never have to fix another leaky pipe or patch a cracking wall. And that suits me just fine." Becoming aware of the visibility of his breath in the light beam, he shivered a little in the cooling night air.

The collecting dew made the trail around the quarry even more treacherous. Steve missed his step over an exposed sassafras root. His left foot arched a mud rainbow across the path as he came down hard, cracking his right knee on a slab of limestone.

Sitting there with his knee pulled up against his chest and the flashlight pointing at his face, he looked all the world like a bizarre caricature of a human tea pot with his steaming breath painfully hissing out between clenched teeth.

After a few moments the initial pain subsided and Steve was able to take inventory of his working parts. His knee seemed merely bruised but he decided to give it a couple of more minutes before attempting the hike up the hill.

He closed his eyes and turned off the light, breathing deeply of the cool dark air. Steve remembered how much he used to enjoy the night solitude of the woods. The calls of the nightlife, the frogs and birds, were singing just for him. He often escaped to the peace and quiet, away from the traffic. Yes, Steve thought, it's quiet. Too damned quiet! There was no back and forth calling of tree frogs or owls. Everything was still. "Dead still", Steve said out loud, wishing he had used different terminology even as he spoke.

"Maybe a little noise wouldn't be so bad after all". Steve again spoke. Rustling sounds in the underbrush made him wish, again, that he had chosen his words more carefully.

He raised his light to the bush and turned it on in one motion. He nearly screamed as he saw two red eyes staring back into his, not six feet away. Steve had grown up in these woods. The long gray snout and the grinning teeth of the opossum were immediately recognized. He knew the opossum would not attack a man, unless cornered. And it had the whole damn woods to turn around and run in. Yet Steve yelled and threw a golf ball size chunk of limestone at the creature. To his surprise, the thing didn't run. In fact, he had hit it dead on in the head and it hadn't even flinched. "Maybe I stunned it," he thought, but just then the beast began lumbering toward him. Its rolling gait was a little awkward and Steve noticed as he began to stand, that the opossum was missing its rear left leg. But it seemed to take no more notice of that than it did the rock.

Steve was a little frightened, but not yet terrified. He knew that he could easily outdistance the advancing creature. He reluctantly turned his beam away from the opossum to shine upon the path going up and around the yawning quarry hole. After taking a couple of steps up the slope, Steve's light caught the writhing motions of the bushes and ground ahead of him. Every branch and leaf seemed to be crawling with some type of insect. The ground was pulsating in a sickening flow. Not only bugs, Steve became aware, but mice, toads, even flopping birds. They all appeared to be moving downward, toward him.

Steve stopped, playing his beam all around. They seemed to be in every direction. Only the Opossum's un-solid footing on the slippery mud, saved Steve's ankle from receiving a terrible gash. The razor teeth closed on the air, directly behind his foot.

Steve saw the near miss from the corner of his eye and became immediately galvanized into action. Silence reigned no longer in the night. Steve tried to ignore the sounds of the breaking of small bones and the chitinous crunching of exoskeleton's as his work boots stamped upon the advancing horde making them one with the earth of the path.

Steve was now terrified as he received countless stings and bites. He slipped once again and screamed aloud at the prospect of falling face down into the pestilence that was attempting to swarm up his legs. Madly he swatted with his free hand and occasionally with the light. Fear of losing the path or dropping the light kept him rigidly pointing it forward, directly into the advancing faces of the relentless and seemingly endless horde that attacked him. He was unsure if tree branches or flying things grabbed at his face and hair as he ran this gruesome gauntlet.

Surely the branches helped to knock away some of the clinging vermin that were attached all too numerously to his body. As he whirled and spun madly into the night his waist and legs were suddenly grabbed by something that had the strength to halt his blind rush. It held him upright and scored his skin with deep fissures from its claws.

"Christ almighty!" Steve screamed. What in the name of heaven could be holding him in such a grip?

With every ounce of his remaining will, Steve had to fight against the very muscles of his neck to be able to bend his head downward to see the Hell-spawned beast that held him in its deadly grip. Fear made the recognition dawn painfully slow as Steve realized he was entangled in the barb wire fence that separated the woods from the drive-in lot. His truck and salvation were mere yards away.

The familiarity of the fence restored enough of Steve's sanity to realize that he needed to back up in order for the fence barbs to release him. He took two steps back and the crunch of something underfoot shot him forward. This time, however, he jumped headlong over the fence. His flight was cut short as a barb grabbed the cuff of his left trouser leg causing him to crash painfully upon his previously injured knee.

His fear made the pain all but unnoticeable as he limped toward the safety of his battered truck. His right eye was swollen nearly shut from the vicious sting he received during his insane flight for life. He continued to brush and swing at the clinging vermin that still held onto his clothes, even though their numbers had decreased after he left the forest edge.

Miraculously, he still maintained a hold on the flashlight that continued to work even after the battering it had taken on this unholy outing. Lost in thought, he was startled when a face appeared suddenly before him. He gasped in fear, only to realize that it was his own reflection in the truck's window. The cold metal of the door handle was like a tonic as he thumbed in the button and pulled upon his salvation. It took a moment for him to comprehend that this action did not open the door.

"Locked!" He spoke out loud. Locked!" He spoke as if he needed to give voice to the words of his predicament to fully comprehend the meaning of the situation. A fly buzzed by his ear, forcing him once again into action. He dug furiously into the left pocket of his jeans. And came up empty. No keys! He transferred the light to his other hand and inspected his right pocket. Some change, a wire nut, a guitar pick, but still no keys.

Frantically, like a smoker looking for a light, he meticulously checked each pocket of his pants, shirt and jacket, to no avail. The keys could have fallen out anywhere along his mad flight. And he sure as Hell wasn't going back to look for them.

Groping along the bed of the truck, he searched inside for the crowbar he always kept by the tailgate. "Got it!" He said, "but now what? Even if I bust out the window to get inside, I still won't be able to start the truck." And any opening that I can crawl through, all of those rodents and bugs can get through also! Think! Damn it, Steve, think!"

Even as Steve's hand closed upon the wrecking bar, a small hand gently lifted a set of keys from a barb of the fence that Steve had recently crossed.

"The Spare key!" Steve's moronic shout broke the silence of the night. He had forgotten about putting that magnetic box under the fender well of the truck. It contained a spare key, just in case of an emergency. And if the situation he now found himself in didn't constitute an emergency, then he didn't know what did.

Dropping to the ground, he pulled himself along the length of the truck. He had to leave the crow bar behind but he maintained the flashlight. His left leg was all but useless as he dragged himself along using the drive shaft and the exhaust pipe. Finally reaching the front axle, Steve searched frantically with his hands along the road crusted interior of the fender well. Where was it? What if it had jarred loose as he bounced over one too many pot holes or ditch ruts. "No wait, there it is." Steve felt the angular edges of the box and pulled for all he was worth. The box came loose and opened in the same motion. The key fell out and landed upon Steve's chest. Still holding the light, his free hand closed on the key and his good eye closed with tears of relief to feel the cold metal in his grasp.

He never saw the angular darting head of the snake as it struck from behind the tire. He only caught a quick glimpse of motion as it buried its fangs into his cheek. Ironically, it was the same tire that had recently ended the snake's life as Steve unknowingly drove across its back as he parked. Steve dropped the flashlight, which continued to shine, as he rolled and howled from beneath the truck. He pulled the copperhead from his flesh and hurled it into the night. Like a deflating toy, he sank to his knees. He could feel the venom burning through his veins as if he had been injected with tiny, writhing, fiery snakes beneath his skin.

He shook the tears from his good eye and looked up directly into the face of the creature that was controlling the movements of the attacking vermin. Steve's mind was very clear. He understood that this was the controlling force. For as the creature quit singing, all of the remaining insects dropped from his clothing. Steve hadn't been consciously aware of the creature's song, but now in retrospect, he realized that he had felt and sensed it on some subliminal level. From his kneeling position Steve was eye to eye with the…What is it anyway? The large luminous eyes and the oversized pointed ears suggested an elf or a troll.

"Why?" Steve finally managed to say. "Why?"

And the creature replied in an exact duplication of Steve's voice. "Why?"

Steve was impressed with the mimicking ability although he realized that his grasp on reality was fading. Something hard was digging into the palm of his hand. He unclenched his fingers and in the waning light of the flash beam he could make out the key.

"This is important," he thought, although he wasn't quite certain why. Oh, yes, the key. It fits all the locks at Chris's house. "But I'm finished with that now," he said. Slowly, he turned his hand over and once again a key fell to the Earth. A moment later Steve followed it. Face down in the last row of the Starlight Drive-In Steve raised his hand as if pointing out something and then lowered it to rest beside him. It was the last movement he would ever make.

At least, of his will.

CHAPTER 16

After an interminably long winter it was finally noticeable that Spring had arrived in Indiana. All the trees were sporting their new wardrobe, as were the mating birds. The cardinals and Indigo Bunting had incredibly vibrant colors. Diana was enthralled with it all. Her dream of being able to sculpt her environment into her ideal surroundings was finally within the realm of possibility. At Crescent's encouraging, she raided her potting shed and garden for cuttings, bulbs, and transplants. She dug into the Earth of her garden with reckless abandon. Crescent tried to warn her of the creeping plants that would try to take over, but Diana was consumed with the passion of giving life to every sprout.

Crescent arrived early on Wednesday morning. She found Diana, as expected, kneeling in the garden she had resurrected behind the house. At least she was always there when it wasn't raining hard enough to keep her inside. Crescent sat down quietly on the low stone wall that bordered the East end of the garden. She enjoyed the feel of the cool limestone on her legs as the sun warmed the back of her neck. The air was alive with the smell of freshly turned earth and the plants Diana had been handling. The combination of scents was a heady aroma that Crescent found nearly intoxicating. Crescent, at last, announced her presence with a laugh, as she said, "You'll see come next year."

"It'll be fine." Diana beamed, wiping soil from her cheek as she stood from her latest endeavor. "I'll grow order from this chaos yet. *Better Homes and Gardens* will storm our ramparts to get a picture of my garden for their spring cover. Hmm." She said. "What do you think? Will these three mint plants be enough or should I plant a fourth for balance?"

"You've much to learn about balance, Diana. But the way you put your heart and spirit into the growing you'll find your center soon. Come over here and sit down a moment."

Diana walked over to the corner of the garden where she kept the carafe of coffee. She poured Crescent a cup with a spot of honey and refreshed her own mug before joining Crescent on the wall.

"You'll have an espresso machine out here next." Crescent chided, even as she accepted the Kona from Diana. "I have always preferred teas in the morning to coffee but I must admit that this brew seems quite addictive."

"The first cup's always free." Di smiled impishly. "And there is your morning 'tease'."

"If I did pay you, then I would immediately fire you."

"Why?" Di asked.

"Bad coffee puns in the morning are grounds for dismissal."

"At last! It's BEAN a long time since I've had a worthy pun opponent. I'll have to FILTER your words with care, for I would GRIND my teeth in disappointment if I let a pun DRIP through unnoticed."

"No more! No more!" Crescent moaned. "I've SANKA to my knees in defeat. If you BREW up another pun I'm out of here in an INSTANT and I'll PERC-YOU-LATER."

Both women laughed until tears rolled down their faces. Diana's left trails through the smudges of Earth still upon her cheek.

"I'm done." Di promised, finally able to catch her breath and take a drink of the coffee that started the whole thing off.

Crescent sat her cup upon the wall. She removed a handkerchief from the folds of a scarf she had tied gypsy fashion around the waist of her dress. She gently held Diana's chin with her left hand and removed the dirt from her cheek with the kerchief in her right.

126

Diana had felt awkward in the beginning of their friendship whenever Crescent had offered such motherly tending. As she began to know the ways of the woman, however, she found her ministrations to be more nurturing than motherly. And she freely gave of this quality not only to Diana but anyone in need. She offered the same loving care to animals as well as the plants she tended.

"I wish I could be more like you."

"Why?" Crescent seemed taken by surprise. "A pretty young thing like you with so many good qualities of her own? Why on earth would you want to be like me?"

Diana was embarrassed. She hadn't realized that she had spoken out loud.

"It's just that you're so...Oh I don't know, comfortable, natural. You're such a part of your world. It's like you always know where you are and where you're going. People and things respond to you, even your garden. It's like when I work in my garden. It's me planting or sowing the seeds. But when you're in your garden, it's like you're a part of the environment. Like you and the plants and the Earth are so...So...?"

"Connected?" Crescent offered.

"That's it! Connected. There is no cut off point, no division between you and the things you tend. It's like you're all a part of a larger picture. I'd like to feel that. Rather than feeling like I'm always on the sidelines looking in. I want to be totally integrated with my surroundings. To feel part of, rather than apart from."

Diana grew suddenly quiet. She hadn't intended on saying all that she had. Crescent was also quiet. Diana felt she had probably embarrassed her new friend. But now that she had started, she found herself unwilling to stop.

"It's because you're a Wit...A Wiccan, isn't it?" Diana asked meekly. "You have knowledge on how to become one with things?"

"It's true." Crescent finally said after waiting to see if Diana was finished. "My training and honing of certain skills and senses allow me to connect, and move comfortably in situations others might find..." She hesitated looking for the right word. "Difficult."

"Is it possible for me to learn? I mean could you, would you instruct me in becoming Wiccan?"

127

"A moment ago you began to call me something other than Wiccan. You started to call me a Witch. Why did you stop and change the word?"

"The word felt awkward to use." Di explained. "Almost derogatory. I didn't want to insult you even though I've heard you use the term for yourself."

"So the name 'Witch' brings to mind pre-conceived images of old crones with long noses and chins with warts, eh? What else?"

"Oh, I don't know. I mean, you're nothing like that."

"Like what?" Crescent was adamant. "What other images come to mind at the word Witch? I am serious, Diana. This is important!"

Diana stopped her sheepish grin and replied as seriously as Crescent's newly adopted manner demanded.

"Pointed black hats and black clothes," she began, closing her eyes and letting childhood memories rush in. "Black cats, brooms, cauldrons, Halloween, spells, magic, potions, bats, black masses."

"What about selling your soul to the Devil by signing a contract in your own blood?" Crescent interjected in a serious tone.

Diana was startled from her reverie. She nearly expected to see Crescent leaning over her with a brown parchment and a sharp dagger in the offering.

Crescent, however, was still calmly sitting beside her on the stone. Anyone watching from a distance would have thought they were probably discussing what they were going to prepare for dinner that evening rather than the turn of topic that had suddenly arisen.

"You see, Diana." Crescent continued. "These are the things you must be willing to contend with if you would become Wiccan."

"You mean the Devil really wants to buy my soul?"

Crescent was unable to contain her laughter. "No, child. First off, Wiccans do not believe in the Christian demon known as Satan, or the Devil, if you prefer. He does not exist, nor has he ever existed, as part of our Religion. Therefore it would be ludicrous for a Witch to make a pact with some nonexistent being. I mean, what would be the point? Other than the one used to spill your blood. No, some of the things Wiccans have to deal with are the preconceived notions and lies about our lifestyle and religion."

"Contrary to popular belief, we do not eat our children, or anyone else's for that matter. Most of the Wiccans I know are vegetarian, actually. Nor do we engage in blood sacrifices. We are a life-affirming people and believe in harming none! Which includes yourself, by the way."

"So if Witches are so harmless, why were they feared and executed? Like during the Salem Witch trials?"

"Many reasons, Diana, such as possessions. And I don't mean people being possessed. I mean owning property. When the anti-Witch laws were passed, making it punishable by death to be a Witch, many people were falsely accused of Witchcraft in order for the state to take over their farmlands or businesses. After they were executed, of course. The Christian church was also trying to convert as many people as they could. They degraded the ways of the Old Religion and called the ceremonies sinful and blasphemous. Vicious rumors were started about the Pagan folk in order to sway and convert people to the new aspiring Christian beliefs."

"Also, the medical association was flexing its manly muscles and trying to coerce people away from the midwives and healers. They defamed the Witches' abilities by calling them uneducated and ignorant to the modern ways of medicine. They referred to their practices as superstitious mummery."

Crescent continued, "Today, however, science is finding out that there is merit to the Herbal remedies used by yesterday's healers."

"Well at least you don't have to fear Witch hunters today," Diana stated.

"It's true we are no longer burned at the stake. But, that doesn't mean the Witch hunters are gone. Prejudice and hatred still thrive against anyone different from what is considered 'the Norm'."

"Becoming a Wiccan, Diana, is like changing to any other religion. You must be totally willing to accept the guidelines and face the fact you will change as your outlook on life is altered. Many people you now call friends, including family members, will no longer associate with you. People will think you're strange at the least. And some will fear you."

"I thought you said Wiccans were harmless."

"I never said harmless, dear. I said we do not believe in harming others through our will to achieve a desired end. However, when necessary, we will defend ourselves and our kindred using whatever method it takes. We will then accept full responsibility for those actions."

"What I would like for you to do, Diana, is talk to your husband, children, and any other loved ones about this decision, for all will be affected by it. If you decide not to become Wiccan, I will still teach you all the things I know that you wish to learn with no strings attached. Except friendship and the promise to use your knowledge wisely and to help any who need."

"And if I decide to become Wiccan, will you teach me the full ways of The Craft?"

"There is a saying that when the student is ready, the teacher will appear. Yes, Diana, I will instruct you in the ways of Wicca. But it will be a year and a day of hard lessons before we do an initiation ceremony for you. There is one other thing dear, and you must do it now or I'll teach you nothing ever again."

"What is it?" Di asked, almost fearing the task Crescent was about to set for her.

"You will dig up all of the mint you planted in your garden and re-plant it down by the side of the barn. Or if you must have it in your garden, then plant it in a tub or bucket to keep the roots contained. And from now on, you will listen intently to my every instruction. If you disagree, that is perfectly acceptable, and we'll discuss it further. If you disobey, that is totally unforgivable because someone could then suffer serious harm at your hands, and at that point I would no longer be inclined to teach you or possibly even protect you."

Diana sat for a moment. Then stood and walked over to her garden. She picked up a spade and without a word began removing the plants she had so recently and laboriously installed in the Earth. When the last one was disinterred, she placed them in the wheelbarrow and began trundling them to the barn without looking back.

Crescent smiled and sipped her coffee. She already knew Diana's decision on becoming Wiccan as well as Diana did. The "year and a day" was a viable part of the training and they would see it through. She reached down and picked up a leaf of mint that had fallen off one of the plants. She swirled it in her coffee and began to follow Diana down to the barn.

"And sometimes," she thought, "when the teacher is ready the student will appear."

Diana set the wheelbarrow down beside the barn. She looked up as she heard the sound of an automobile pulling into the drive. Crescent was waving even as she turned, as if she knew the very sound of the rattling truck and the straining four cylinder Toyota engine as well as who it was transporting into their morning.

The small Toyota had a camper shell on its back that looked packed to the gills with who knew what kind of Brick-a-brack. It seemed to be loaded unevenly as it had a slight list to the passenger's side, although, Diana could see no passenger. As the truck rolled to a stop the driver slowly unfolded himself from the cab. His fluid movements were reminiscent of a cat languidly stretching and in no particular hurry to be anywhere. After a lifetime in New York City, that was a sight Diana seldom saw amongst its inhabitants. The truck had been painted all around with trees and brush and what looked like dancing people, although Diana couldn't quite make them out from the distance. Crescent moved in and gave a hug to the smiling driver who returned it with every bit as much enthusiasm. He was a tall young man, dressed only in knee length cut-off jeans. He was bare-chested and Diana wondered how anyone could have such a golden tan this early in the year. This man definitely did not look like the tanning bed type. He removed his straw hat as Crescent introduced him to Diana who was startled to suddenly realize she had unconsciously covered the distance between the barn and the house without realizing she had even moved.

"I at least hope I had my mouth closed as I walked up." Di silently berated herself.

"Rowan is one of my dearest friends; I've known him since he was first born. Actually his father and I delivered him. His father, Jim, was the local Veterinarian and had plenty of practice at delivering babies no matter how many legs or feet they had. Rowan here was so long at birth and came out so strong and magickal that I said he reminds me of a Rowan tree and the name stuck."

Diana extended her hand to shake but Rowan just sidestepped it. Before she could react he had her in a bear hug of an embrace. It was such an open show of friendship Di found herself hugging back as if she had known him all her life. He smelled wonderfully of wood chips and campfire smoke. Di realized if she didn't let loose first they might be standing there until dark.

"It's good to finally meet you, Rowan." The name seemed odd for Diana to say. "Crescent has spoken so fondly of you and I've seen so many of your paintings and carvings at her house. It's nice to finally see you in the flesh." Diana felt her face flush at her choice of words as she stood next to this bare-chested man. She found it difficult to keep her eyes away from the muscles that moved so wonderfully beneath his bronzed skin.

Rowan beamed at the praise and his smile brightened visibly. "I've brought a housewarming gift." He was suddenly in motion, opening the back of the camper shell and emerging, finally, with a large canvas. He sheepishly presented the painting to Diana.

The spirit of the artwork immediately captured Diana. It was a golden sunrise over a lake in the woods. All the trees were done in a dark tone with gentle strokes of light filtering here and there. A purplish hue pervaded the scene. What Diana felt was the most fascinating thing was that nearly all the trees and limbs contained figures and faces. Each seemed to be either sultrily rising with the dawn, or languidly returning to their rest, until next nightfall. Diana was unsure which interpretation was correct, but she did know the piece would go perfectly over the mantle in the library.

"Thank you Rowan, this is too kind! Look, Crescent, isn't it wonderful?"

"I admired this one as he painted it; I think he knew you were coming when he started it."

The back door of the house opened and Chris emerged. He looked very comfortable in jogging pants and an oversized sweater. However, the briefcase he carried looked very out of place. He passed by the tent where the children had spent the night. He caught up with Crescent, Di, and a stranger who must be Rowan.

Diana was carefully sitting down a large canvas painting. He thought he saw a disapproving look upon Crescent's face as she noticed the little pup tent. Crescent was becoming more and more of a household fixture and influence. Diana had discussed her interest in learning the practices of Wicca with him and the children. Chris did not consider himself either religious or superstitious so he had no conflict with Di adding another interest notch to her bedpost of life, no matter how far outside the norm it seemed to be. They lived so far from family and friends that any stigma that could be attached to his wife studying to become a witch was almost laughable. He cared more about Diana's happiness than what anyone else thought, anyway. If she wanted to learn about Wicca, fine by him. The kids were, for once, in total agreement on the matter. Jerrica wanted to know when she could start learning witchcraft and Alex wanted to become a warlock. Diana explained as Crescent had to her that "warlock" was a word made popular by movies and novels. Wiccan males and females were both known as witches in the modern Craft. The old Scottish word for warlock actually translated to "truce breaker," something no self respecting Wiccan would want to be known as.

"Chris, this is Rowan, Crescent's handyman friend." Chris's reverie was broken by Diana's introduction. "She asked him to come over to help with our projects. And look at the painting he gave us!"

"Nice to meet you." Chris transferred his briefcase to his left hand and extended his right hand to Rowan, who quickly shook it and then gave Chris a crushing hug and a resounding pat on the back. Chris, slightly shaken by Rowan's aggressive show of familiarity, found himself speaking quickly. "Thanks, that's a great piece of art! I've got a list of things that need to be done, if you'd like to look it over and…"

"Now hold on a minute, Chris." Di interrupted. "I saw him first and I need help with my garden projects. After all, you have your finished studio in the barn."

"Di, you agreed I could have the barn for my studio and in exchange we would get you a greenhouse later, when we could afford it."

"I changed my mind. I want the barn back for my planting projects!" She encircled Chris's neck with her arms and rubbed foreheads with him before giving him a kiss.

"Barn? I don't see a barn. Only this state-of-the-art recording studio where I am preparing to lock myself in and work mercilessly to create another hit song and then, maybe, if all of that happens, we can build you a greenhouse behind your garden."

"Sounds good as long as I get Rowan first." Di purred. "So why are you standing around out here? Get your ass in gear and get creative." She gave Chris another smooch and turned him around with a playful shove toward the barn door.

Chris pretended to stumble in the direction of the barn as he called back over his shoulder. "I'll be in the studio for a while and I have my new beeper with me." Chris had soon discovered that cell phones wouldn't work in their valley so far away from a tower. "The number is by the phone, in the study, if you need me for anything and don't feel like walking out here."

"I'll just go check on the children and then Crescent, Rowan and I will start our battle plans over some food. Want lunch?" Di asked.

"No, I'm fine, I had a couple of sandwiches and I have snacks in the barn. Studio." Chris corrected himself. "The kids have already eaten and they're in playing video games."

"Okay, then T.T.F.N. as Tigger would say." Diana turned and went happily about her chores, Crescent and Rowan in tow.

The move had been exhausting but exactly the change they all needed, Chris thought. Crescent was the perfect small town neighbor and Diana simply adored her. The kids seemed to adjust effortlessly to their new home and he was even excited about working once again in his new studio.

Chris stopped outside the studio door and pulled his keys from the pocket of his jeans. He looked up at a giant white cloud passing overhead in the deep blue sky. He closed his eyes, took a deep breath, and let it out slowly. At long last, feeling at peace with himself and his world, he unlocked the door and entered his new sanctum sanctorum.

He hit the master light switch and turned all the lights in the place on. He wanted to be able to control the intensity of the room's lighting so he could visually set the mood for the style of music he was invoking at the moment. He had some recessed lights as well as direct spots. Most of them had shields for colored gels.

But right at this moment he wanted to see everything as clearly as possible. He wanted full sensory input to the max. He hoped to wash away the few remaining fears that moving here would not overcome his writer's block in the high tech visualization of this studio he had created.

His mind was instantly distracted, although not in the way he had planned. Because the first thing he saw was a small package sitting right there on his mixing console, a package he knew wasn't there yesterday and one that he sure as Hell hadn't placed there.

Diana, of course, had access to the studio since her house key would also fit this lock. But this package wasn't her style. She would never leave a plain brown-wrapped box to be found as a surprise. A lone rose? Definitely. Ribbons and bows and bright colored paper? Of course. But never anything like this plain little thing.

Anger began coursing in Chris's veins. The missing key, he thought. The handyman who had the extra key made has been here in my private studio and carelessly left behind a taunting reminder of his presence. Chris reached for the package, without noticing the wires attached to its side.

"Maybe this contains just the evidence I need to make the police put you away, buddy!"

Chris's voice was suddenly lost in the startling force of sound that erupted from his monitor speakers.

"What the...?"

Chris ripped away the paper in his hand and revealed the miniature tape player that he held. He pressed the stop button and the music ceased.

"Well, I'll be a son of a bitch!" Chris exclaimed while turning the device over and examining the wire configuration.

"The Bastard wired it right into my console. He even had it set with a motion detection switch like on a car alarm so it would play the minute it was touched."

Chris thumbed the rewind button and then sat down and adjusted the volume before hitting the play button again.

This time the music began in a less startling vein. A classic Rock-A-Billy style guitar played the first two opening bars and then the vocals began. Chris listened to the whole song. He was about to turn the recorder off when a voice suddenly came from the monitor speakers and it was addressing him.

"Mr. Lane? Chris? I certainly hope it's you listening. I went to a whole lot of trouble to get this to you and make it work right. You probably don't remember me. My name is Steve Graves. We went to school together. I was a couple of grades ahead of you."

"I have always admired your work, even when you played around here before you got famous. I tried to be a successful songwriter also but I never quite made the grade. I never really quit trying and when I found out you were moving back here, well, I figured I'd give it one last make or break shot. The song, of course, is one that I wrote. If you think it might have possibilities or you would like to hear some others, my phone number and address are on the cassette."

"If, on the other hand, you want to have me arrested for breaking and entering, then you know where to find me and I'll confess and go along quietly. But I had to try."

"By the time you hear this, I would have destroyed the key, so you don't have to fear it being in my, or some other crazy's possession. If I hear nothing from you or the police then I'll assume you wish to have nothing to do with my music or me and I'll never bother you again. Sorry for any inconvenience."

Chris was stunned. He vaguely remembered Steve. He recalled that they had spoken once or twice of their mutual interest in music and had agreed that they should get together and 'Jam' but it never happened. And now all of the fear and anger Chris had built up over the missing key were displaced by empathy for the man who had recently broken into his studio.

Chris rewound the tape and listened to the song one more time. The recording quality, as well as the production, was poor. The song itself did have possibility. Chris's mind was already at work on instrumentation and harmonies as he picked up the phone and dialed the number on the cassette box. It seems that he wouldn't have to prosecute Mr. Graves after all. In fact, working with someone on a project right now could be very cathartic. After a couple of rings, the phone was answered by Steve's machine. Chris waited for the schpiel to end and then left his message.

"Mr. Graves? This is Chris Lane. I received your surprise package today. I don't think that we need to involve the police in this matter. If you would return my call, we can set up a meeting to discuss where we should go with our mutual interest."

Chris hung up the phone and then carefully disconnected the tape device Steve had left. Placing the bundle in a desk drawer, he rubbed his eyes and then set about putting his new studio through its paces.

Several hours later, Chris could barely keep his eyes open. He shut down all of his gear and then double checked the lock on the door, an old New York habit, and began walking toward the house. He was a bit surprised to find that it was dark out. Time always got away from him when he was in the studio. "At least I don't have a long drive home through New York Traffic," he gratefully thought.

He heard the unmistakable sound of tires on pavement and turned to see a police car pulling into the drive. The car beat him to the house by a couple of feet and the Sheriff exited the vehicle as Chris approached.

"Mr. Lane?" The officer asked, as he tilted his hat back.

"That's right, can I help you with something?" Chris hoped that this was just a social call.

"I'm Sheriff Dawson Dalton. Do you know this man?"

Sheriff Dawson handed Chris a photograph of a man, late thirties, long wavy black hair, rather muscular looking.

"No, sir. Can't say that I do. Why do you ask?"

"Are you in the habit of calling people that you don't know, Mr. Lane?" Dawson ignored Chris's question as he came back with another one of his own.

"Sheriff, I'm afraid I was just going to have a late supper and then go to bed. I'm extremely tired and you are making very little sense to me."

"It's early for someone from the city to be turning in so soon. Were you up late last night?"

"That's correct, Sheriff, and I would like to get some sleep now, so what is your point?"

"The man in the photo is Steve Graves, a local contractor. His truck was found not too far from here in the old drive-in lot. There were signs of a scuffle and it seems that no one has seen Mr. Graves since yesterday morning."

"I spoke with the real estate firm that uses Grave's services and Mr. Tremble informed me that you were very upset with Mr. Graves. We entered Mr. Graves' home and found a message from you on his answering machine. On it, you proposed a meeting between the two of you, 'without the police'. And so it's possible that you may have been the last one to see Mr. Graves."

"Do you still wish to deny that you know him?"

This weird turn of events left Chris dumbfounded. Being suspected of foul play of a man he hadn't seen in years was a bit overwhelming.

"Sheriff, I'm sorry I didn't recognize the man in the photograph. You see, I haven't seen Steve Graves since High School. There was no way I could recognize him from a recent picture. As for the phone message? We never had time for a meeting. I left that message not three hours ago. You said that his truck was found early this morning? Surely you can check the time on his machine and see that I tried to contact him well after his disappearance, and not prior to."

Sheriff Dalton studied Chris in silence a moment before speaking. "You think pretty fast for a man who's dead on his feet. I'm afraid, Mr. Lane, that Steve had one of the older models of answering machines. It just lumped all the messages on a tape and if the caller didn't state the time and date of the call then there is no way of knowing when it was placed."

Chris stared at the officer. "Are you charging me with something, Sheriff Dawson?"

Before the Sheriff could answer, the front door opened and Crescent came from the house. "Why, Dawson Dalton, it sure is nice of you to come pay your respects to the Lanes." Crescent attempted to disarm the official quality of the Sheriffs presence by not acknowledging his appellation. "It appears that living in the big city for so long has made Chris a bit slight on his hospitalities. I have coffee on the stove and a fresh baked pie. Why don't you let me send Mr. Lane off to get some sleep? Then you and I will have a sample."

Dalton was surprised to see Crescent come out of the house.

"I'm afraid I've been here visiting for so long over the last few days they think I'm part of the package and came with the house."

"You were here with Mr. Lane last night?" Dawson asked as they entered the front door.

"Why, yes, and wait until you meet his lovely wife. Why, you won't want to leave either. It's so nice to have good neighbors again."

"Sorry I didn't tell you sooner that I had an alibi, Sheriff, but like I said, I'm worn out. And I sure wasn't expecting to get cross-examined on my front lawn." Chris held open the wooden screen for the lawman. "Besides, and most importantly, you never asked!" And with a large yawn and a kiss on the cheek from Crescent, Chris headed up the stairs.

*   *   *

Diana met Crescent on a hill behind the Rain shed the next morning before dawn. She had bathed in the salts and oils Crescent had prepared for her the night before. She had lit the incense and placed crystals in her bath as she was instructed for the cleansing ritual. She had dressed in a simple white dress as instructed. Now, as the cool pre-dawn air raised bumps upon her bare arms, Crescent placed in her hands a beautifully carved crystal goblet. She couldn't see the carvings in the dim light but she could feel the deep etchings with her hands.

"This vessel contains purified spring water." Crescent informed her. "You will face the east and hold it up to the rising sun. As you focus on the east, allow wisdom, knowledge and enlightenment to radiate into the water in your goblet. 'Will' the rays of a new day to penetrate deep within your being and burn away the darkness of any illness, whether of body, mind or soul. Empty yourself of 'all' as the glass was empty before it was filled with the purified water. Let the sun's energy fill and purify you. When you feel the moment has reached its pinnacle, give thanks to the Watchtower, or Guardian, of the East and drink the water. Lower your arms and enjoy the pleasure of the vibrant energy you'll feel coursing within you and around you. Any water left within the Chalice you will pour upon the Earth, giving thanks to the earth mother, ancient spirits, or Gods of your choosing. At this time, you may also send out white light, healing energy to anyone you feel may need it. When you are finished, meet me at the rain shed, but take as much time as you need."

Crescent kissed Diana on the forehead, then turned and made her way down the path to the rain shed. Her ever-present teapot was steaming. She moved it away from the direct heat of the little woodstove but she did not immediately prepare a cup of the brew. Instead, she picked up a pouch she had been working on for Diana. She had hand punched and stitched the soft goatskin bag. It was about six inches deep and nine inches in circumference, with a long leather drawstring so Diana could tie it onto her belt. She had decorated it with beaded stones and feathers. One stone was carved with the Rune 'Dagaz' representing the eternal moment. The sun was beginning to filter in through the cracks of the shed's log walls. Crescent always loved this time of day and she cherished the beautiful display made by the shafts of light and shadows. She had even placed refracting crystals at strategic points so the interior of the room would suddenly burst forth in dancing rainbows. She had placed her favorite teacup at just the right angle from one such stone. Now it was time for her tea. She loved the idea of the cup catching rainbows before she filled it with tea. She realized it didn't make the tea taste any different but she so enjoyed the concept of drinking rainbows. Even if she manufactured them herself. Her Opal ring clicked on the ceramic mug as she lifted it. She placed another cup in the rainbow catching spot, for she knew Diana would be coming in soon. She had better prepare her something to eat also. Crescent knew from experience that Diana would be so energized from the morning ritual she would be unable to sit still and focus on any other lesson until she grounded some of that abundant energy. And one of the best grounding methods was solid food in your belly. Of course, this being Diana's first energy ritual, she might also need a Hematite necklace and earrings.

As predicted, a radiant Diana soon entered the door. She walked through the rainbows and light shafts, ducking the occasional low hanging herb that was drying, suspended from the overhead beams. Crescent smiled up from her worktable, which was now serving as a breakfast table.

"Sit down and join me. I've prepared a small meal; usually I'm the only one who eats out here so I don't stock much in the way

DANCER OF THE DEAD

of food and drink. Would you like to eat in silence or shall I continue to bend your ear as I normally do?"

"Oh please, I love it when you talk." Diana was hungrily eyeing the slices of home baked bread and preserves. She had fasted the night before as per Crescent's instructions and she could almost hear the cheese and fruit slices calling her name.

As Diana prepared her plate, Crescent filled her cup. "A purifying bath prior to any ritual helps allow you the space to attain the proper frame of mind needed to better focus upon the task you are about to perform. It gives you time to separate yourself from the shopping list, laundry and dishes and other chores we fill our heads with during everyday activities. When you do ritual, however, you create a separate space away from the mundane. You step into a space between, where Magick is tangible and reality is as you "Will" it."

"Doing the morning Sun ritual is impossible to do every day. You should strive to do it as often as your daily routine allows, especially if someone far away is in need of healing energy. It is the best time to focus and direct that energy to its greatest end. I will also show you some Tai Chi moves to go along with this way of starting your day. The Eastern religions are very big on energy gathering and directing. Tai Chi is a very empowering way to begin a morning."

Diana was overwhelmed by how great the blackberry preserves were as well as everything else. It was as if her tastebuds as well as her other senses were heightened. She washed down the last bite with her tea and gave a relaxed sigh.

"Crescent?" She asked. "How many different religions and practices do you incorporate into Wicca?"

"Wicca is as diversified as any other religion. If you stop someone on the Street and ask their religion they might answer 'Christian'. Now are they Baptist, Methodist, Catholic? All of these fall under the heading of Christianity. The same holds true of Muslims, Buddhists, and Wiccans. Some forms of Wicca are very traditional and the High Priests and Priestesses try to follow the practices that were handed down by their ancestors to their best and most accurate interpretation. Gardnerians are very traditional and Alexandrians are quite dogmatic about their Secret rituals."

"I can really only answer for myself, and I am Eclectic. I have spent my entire life gathering knowledge that I may use to help myself, and others in need. The more one knows, the more one can do. Wisdom and practical knowledge is universal; therefore, I turn to the universe in its entirety to draw upon for my religion."

"That seems like an awful lot to learn."

"Not if you learn it a step at a time and continue learning. Intuition is the path that allows you to walk between the sets of knowledge. And Diana, your intuition is strong." Crescent stood and cleared the surface of the table. She returned with a notebook and pen.

"I have prepared an outline for the lessons you will be receiving. This will give you a better focus on what is coming. Also, the Universe isn't so imposing when it is broken down into smaller, more digestible, bites. All the lessons are so interwoven that you will find you are working with several lessons at the same time. You can't apply a poultice for healing a wound if you don't know how to prepare the proper Herbs for the poultice. So your skill at recognizing, planting, harvesting and preparing Herbs will be ongoing throughout everything else."

"I have no problem with that." Di chimed in.

Crescent remembered Diana telling her about studying botany one semester at college, smiled at Diana's love for plants, and continued. "I will help you to create a good Witches garden. It will be your most powerful resource—other than yourself. You will grow specifics for medicinal, culinary, magickal, and aesthetic purposes, all of which are important. Recognizing plants and gathering from the wild is also important knowledge, for you never know where you will be when your abilities are needed. There are also many ways to prepare the same plant for different usage. The leaves may perform one function whereas the roots or seeds may be used in a different way. As well as the need dictating whether you prepare the plant into a salve, a poultice, tincture, or an infusion. If the product is to be imbibed, inhaled, or applied…So, you see, you must also learn the processes that allow for the cure."

"This is most intimidating." Diana confessed.

"As well it should be." Crescent nodded her head. "You must realize that it is not a light task to be accomplished in a year. It is a way of life with a lifetime's worth of learning. I am still a student of the Universe, as are we all. I can show you all I know, and along the way I will learn many things from you. But you will never hang a Diploma on the wall and say 'my education is complete' because it never will be."

Crescent allowed Diana a moment for it all to sink in before continuing. "Now shall we go on with the outline, or are you ready to run back home."

"Bring it on, Crescent, I'll earn my wings yet. Or is that a broom?"

"Diana, I wouldn't be surprised if you did learn to make one of those things fly. And if you ever do, you must teach me."

CHAPTER 17

The days quickly passed for the Lanes as they settled into their new surroundings, each in his or her own way. Diana was enwrapped in her new studies as well as their practical applications in planting the garden. Chris was still fine-tuning his studio, but the new music was swarming in his head like bees. Kratel paid regular visits to Jerrica and Alex, even though he didn't show up every night. As a matter of fact, the children hadn't seen him for the past three nights and they were beginning to worry.

"What if he went back to his own world and can't come back for another hundred years?"

Alex asked as Jerrica handed him another plate to dry.

"We don't know that he is from another world, so worrying about it is stupid." Jerrica scrubbed off the last pot and let out the dishwater as her brother finished drying and hung the pot on the ceiling rack. "Look, Jerr, if he doesn't show up tonight by ten o'clock, let's take flashlights and go look for him."

"And where do we go to look? We haven't been able to communicate with him very well so he sure hasn't told me where he stays."

"He always comes out of the woods at the same spot. We could see if maybe he's left a trail. Come on, Jerr, what if he's hurt or caught in a trap or something. He might need us."

"All right, it gets dark around seven thirty. We'll go to bed early and keep a watch out for him until ten. If he doesn't show, we'll scout around for an hour but no more. If we don't find him tonight, then we can start again in the morning and look around longer. Now leave me alone for awhile. I'm going to go read in the library."

"She's always got her nose in a book." Alex thought as he headed upstairs to find his Gameboy.

Jerrica spent the next couple of hours lost in a novel of far-off lands and strange places. She looked up as the Grandfather clock sounded the hour and decided it was time to get ready for her own adventure. Her Mother was also reading in the library and Jerr gave her a kiss and told her good night. For a moment she thought of telling her mother about her strange friend, Kratel, but at the last minute changed her mind. "No." She thought as she ascended the stairs to her bedroom. Parents always put their concern for your well being ahead of having fun. Not only might they forbid her and Alex from seeing Kratel in the future, but they might also feel obligated to report him to the authorities. The thought of Kratel locked up in a zoo or a laboratory made her shiver.

"And speaking of 'shivering', I'd better get out of this dress and into some jeans just in case we do go romping through the woods tonight."

Alex, of course, was always wearing jeans and a sweatshirt so he was ready to go. But he had to wait for Jerr to find her tennis shoes and flashlight. "Should we stay up here and keep watch out the window until ten or do you want to go on outside?" Alex asked when Jerr finally entered his room. It had been dark for nearly an hour but Kratel never showed up that early.

"Let's wait in here. Dad's out in the studio and Mom's in the library, so they are no problem, but Grandpa doesn't go to sleep until after nine so he's probably watching TV in his room.

It was nearly ten o'clock when Alex's elbow jarred Jerrica awake. She hadn't realized that she had dozed. "Look out by that tree. I think it's him."

Alex leaped off the bed, but Jerr grabbed his arm and stopped him short.

"Don't go thundering down the steps. If it is Kratel the last thing you want to do is wake up everyone in the house."

"Sorry, Jerr." Alex turned and quietly went down the rear stairs. They crossed the kitchen floor and stealthily opened the back door. It took a moment before their eyes adjusted to the lack of light. They didn't want to use their flashlights. Not only did it cause pain to Kratel, it might also give them away to anyone near a window.

"Kratel! Alex, it is him." Jerrica rushed to the little creature. He was difficult to hug while wearing the backpack they had given him, but both kids managed.

"Where have you been man? We thought you were gone for good."

"Gone for good." Kratel mimicked Alex with his own voice.

"We have got to get beyond this communication barrier." Jerrica sat down on a large rock and offered Kratel the can of Spam she had pilfered as they passed the pantry on the way out of the kitchen.

"Spam, Grundage!" Kratel called, overjoyed. He had picked up a few rudimentary words and phrases from the kid's language.

"Good to see ya, dude." Alex punched Kratel's arm.

"AlexDude." Kratel said it as one word. "Jerrica righteous babe." He spoke around mouthfuls of Spam.

"Tunes?" He asked, looking to see if they had brought out their portable disc player.

"We forgot the tunes. Hang on, I'll be right back." Alex dashed into the house to get the C.D. player and grab Kratel's favorite Disc: *Frampton Comes Alive*. Jerrica stood up when Alex returned so he could set the miniature boom box on the rock. He punched the play button but they knew to keep the volume low. Kratel was in full swing, imitating Frampton's vo-corder box and his guitar at the same time. A chorus line of animals emerged from the tree line and once again the party was on.

"This is why we don't get any further in our communications. It always turns into a Disco. Oh well, music is supposed to be the universal language." Jerrica joined in the captivating rhythm until her heart stopped. She slowly turned, for she was sure she had just heard the kitchen door shut.

"What the Hell?"

The dance suddenly halted as Jerrica turned to see her astounded Grandfather gaping at the now still collection of wildlife that encircled the children.

"It's all right Grandpa Nate, they…"

"Be quiet, Jerrica, you and Alex move very slowly and come over to me right now!"

Nate held his terrycloth robe closed with one hand and shakily extended the other for the kids to come and take. The glistening sweat on his brow and the timbre of his voice told of the fearful reaction to the scene in which he found the kids.

"But Gramps, you'll scare Kratel!" Alex pleaded.

Nate walked closer to the macabre circle. His distress was obvious in his face, even in the dark.

"You kids come here right now!" He angrily spoke. "Right now! Do you hear me?"

As they moved forward to obey, Kratel walked over and placed his hand on Alex's arm. He was terrified of the giant human that spoke so harshly. However, he didn't want to relinquish the only positive contact that he had with the giants.

Kratel fought his fear and began walking toward Nate. As he got within a few steps of the giant, he saw Nate's face grow pale as the human faltered back a step. Kratel understood now that the giants are as much afraid of him as he is of them. He had to reassure the Grandpa Nate that he intended no harm. He pulled himself up to his full height. He opened wide his mouth to expose his pointed teeth in an imitation of the smile performed by the children. He raised both hands above his head, palms outward and claws fully extended and walked toward Grandpa Nate yelling "Boo! Boo!" in his imitation of Alex's voice.

To his surprise, Grandpa Nate's face went even paler. Both hands now clutched frantically at the chest of his robe. Choked gurgling noises issued from the old giant's throat, his eyes rolled back, his legs buckled, and like a felled tree he toppled to the ground. He barely missed falling on Kratel.

Alex screamed and Jerrica leaped out of the circle of animals which now lay as still as Nate.

"Grandpa, Grandpa!" She called over and over as she shook the old man's shoulder. But no response came from the fallen Giant.

Kratel was stunned. Again he was caught off guard in a situation with the giants that he didn't understand. He saw lights appear through the windows of the house in response to the children's cries. He quietly dispersed the animals back to the woods and then turned back to the Jerrica child.

The pack upon his back suddenly felt like the weight of the world as he read the hurt and anger so openly and violently displayed in her green eyes. He was bewildered to find these emotions were turned directly at him.

"You killed him!" She accused. "Why did you kill my Grandpa? I hate you!"

Alex was unable to talk. Great tears and sobbing breaths wracked his small frame. The accusing anger was also present in his face. Alex bent down and picked a stone from the makeshift firepit, oblivious to the heat it still contained. With all his strength he threw it at the stunned Kratel. The rock caught him a glancing blow across his forehead. He was momentarily shocked by the impact and felt nothing until the blood clouded the vision in his left eye.

As if in a dream, he heard the screams of the female giant as she raced from the house.

"Dad, Dad!" She called. The other male giant was silently running closely beside her.

Another stone bounced off the backpack. Kratel turned to see Jerrica's face buried in the robe of the Grandpa and Alex bending to pick up a third stone. He could see the blisters forming on the boy child's hand. How could so much hate erupt so quickly from the joyous communion they were sharing? How could this be? Kratel felt his own anger beginning to rise. Without a backward glance he turned and ran into the enveloping woods. The stone bounced off an elm tree several feet away and as he headed for his lair he heard the mortal wail of the female and the male giant saying "Hold on, Dad, hold on! I'll call 911!"

Kratel furiously wiped the blood from his eyes. His pounding head only darkened his mood. How dare they attack him? What had he done other than offer peaceful trust? Was it his fault that the old one was too frail to accept one of his own kinds' greetings? No! Had he been harmful or shown disrespect to the children in any way? NO! NO! NO!

He could understand the pain and concern for their fallen loved one but it was not his fault! And to be attacked and treated like some mad, rabid beast was too much. If the humans wanted to act like he was a creature to be feared, then so be it! He would show them what it felt like to have the proffered hand bitten! Woe to the next giant to cross his path! Kratel's vision was again obscured by red but it was not the blood in his eyes this time, but the blood red anger behind them!

CHAPTER 18

Thelma's Restaurant was the kind of place that used to do a very good business until the new highway came through on the West Side of town. Now the new malls and all of the fast food restaurants get most of the business from travelers, leaving the downtown storeowners to rely on the local trade they had built up over the years. Or to sell out and relocate to where the traffic now passed through. It seemed to be a recurring theme throughout America. The businesses set up on the roadways that connected the commercial hearts of towns across the states, and so they prospered. Until the new super express highways cut across the country connecting city to city and bypassing the downtown sections of the small towns. The locals knew where Thelma's was, right on old State Road 37. It was where many of the folk went for an early, unhurried, breakfast before starting their workday. That was why Bill Garten was there. Not solely for the breakfast, but because he knew Sheriff Dawson would come in, regular as clockwork, and order the same breakfast he'd eaten for the last sixteen years. Bill also knew that if he conversed with Dawson before the Sheriff's mind shifted into work mode, he might be able to get some information as small talk, strictly off the record, of course.

At six thirty the Sheriff walked in and sat down at his favorite table by the window. He looked over the menu as the waitress brought coffee. Dalton then ordered his eggs and bacon the same as always. Bill waited until the waitress departed with the order, then picked up his cup and walked over to Dalton's table.

"Morning Dalton, mind if I join you?" Bill sat his cup down on the table across from the Sheriff.

"Looks to me like you already are." Dalton realized that his quiet breakfast wasn't going to be so quiet. He knew Bill well enough to know that he would get no peace from him. Until he let him get 'inside information' on the latest hot story that Bill had set his journalistic bulldog teeth into.

"How's your younger daughter looking for taking over her sister's place on the basketball team next semester?" Bill asked, trying to sound as casual as he could. "You know that Jean's graduation will be a feather in the old sports cap of whatever college she goes to, but she's leaving quite a hole in Bedford High's game. Is Nikki going to fill Jean's Nikies?" God! How could he talk like that? He sounded more like an aging sports caster than one of the local good ol' boys. He might as well have had a photographer snapping shots while he slammed a tape recorder on the table.

The waitress returned with Dalton's coffee and freshened up Bill's. The Sheriff stirred in sugar and cream and finally arrived at the desired color. He took a sip before answering.

"I don't think Nikki will even be trying out for any sports, let alone trying to pick up where her sister is leaving off. Nikki doesn't have the love of the game that Jean has. It's just as well. Jean is one of those one in a million athletes. Oh, she works hard don't get me wrong. But sports always came easy for her, a natural, as they say. Nikki would only burn herself out trying to compete. No, she'll have to find her own field to shine in, whatever she chooses to do."

The waitress had placed Dalton's breakfast in front of him. While speaking, he methodically covered every inch of everything on the plate with salt, pepper, and catsup.

"Now, what's really on your mind Bill? And please, if it's anything too upsetting could you bide your time until I've finished eating?"

"You're right, Sheriff." Might as well use the title now, Bill thought. "I don't think this will be too unsettling for you, just a couple of questions concerning disappearances."

"What? Who's missing? How do you news hounds find out about things before the Police Department?" Dawson was so agitated he was sloshing his coffee onto his eggs, which diluted the catsup, causing the yoke of one egg to poke through like a bulging eye. It looked very similar to Sheriff Dawson's eyes at this moment.

"Ease up there, Dalton. I didn't say '*someone*' is missing. What I was referring to was '*something*' that is missing." Bill went on quickly before the Sheriff could have another coronary. "Have you been receiving calls about missing pets?"

"Pets?" Dalton said between bites, having resumed his meal. "You mean like dogs? Cats? People call in all the time thinking that we've got nothing better to do than to track down their missing poodles. Occasionally we get the farmer who has lost a sheep or a pig. Why? What's up?" Sheriff Dawson knew that Bill wasn't a shadow chaser. If he was asking about missing pets, he had a reason. Especially if it got him up this early. He knew from past experience that Bill was a late riser, unless a story really warranted his extrication before noon.

"I know there are a certain amount of missing pets at any given time of the year." Bill continued. "I'll even give you that with the warming of the weather more people are letting their animals outside, unfettered, and so there are probably a higher percentage of missing pooches and whatnots right now than say a month ago. But even if you doubled or tripled the number of ads people placed in my paper for missing pets last month, it doesn't come anywhere near the amount of ads that I have sitting on my desk right now. And if you multiply this number by the number of people that may have lost a pet but didn't put in an ad? Well, the numbers look pretty out of proportion."

Dalton finished his breakfast and neatly stacked the silverware, napkins and sugar packets on his plate. He leaned back in his chair, reached for a cigarette in his shirt pocket, and then absentmindedly remembered that he had quit seven months ago.

"We file a report on every legitimate call that comes in. I had not, personally, checked the missing pet file, but if you would like to follow me to the station we can do that first thing."

"You know who's doing it!" Both men turned to the next booth to see Bing sitting there, obviously having listened to every word and now ready to expound upon his own theory as the men were getting ready to leave.

"It's those godless heathens stealing poor little animals to use in their bloody sacrifices, that's who."

"Poor little animals?" Bill thought, everyone knew that Bing was a self-proclaimed animal hater.

"Bing." Sheriff Dawson said, standing up and putting on his hat. "We've had this talk before. You keep on making these public accusations without proof and one day you're going to get sued for slander."

"What kind of proof do you need?" Bing was now up on his soapbox. "Let's go over to their land and look around for the missing animals! More than likely, we'll find their bones in a fire pit. And who knows if they're all animal bones?"

"That's enough, Bing." The Sheriff's tone said that he would hear no more, and Bill hoped that Bing had sense enough to shut up. "No one has made any accusations about foul play in the missing of a few strayed pets. Bill and I are just looking into the possibility that stricter leash law enforcement may have to be invoked if a larger than normal amount of animals are lost due to owner's negligence. And that's all! Do you understand me, Bing? That's all. If I hear any wild rumors, I'll know how to track them to their source. Do I make myself clear?"

"Maybe I can't prove what I say, and maybe I can. The Lord and I know my truths. We know when his creatures are abducted. We know who bought the biggest traps and cages, and The Lord and me, we know who they been mucky mucking around with. We seen her walking in his woods and dancing 'round his toadstools and instructing his wife in her foul heathen ways. Jesus collects full toll on trespassers, Sheriff. Just make sure you ain't running their escort service when they dead end at the gates of Hell."

Bing stood up as he was delivering his sermon and quickly spun on his heel and walked out the front door of the cafe as if they were the gates of heaven. Both Bill and the Sheriff had seen him worked up like this before and they both knew why.

What they never knew was what would set him off. This time it was lost animals, last time it was someone who came into his hardware store and mentioned that a solar eclipse was going to happen that week. Time before that someone asked if he sold herbs in his store. No matter what the catalyst it always came down to the same ending—The Pagans—and the one Bing perceived as their evil heart: Crescent.

There was a Pagan community settled on the outskirts of town. For the most part they were harmless, although they did tend to get a little loud with their drumming during some of the bigger Equinox and Solstice gatherings they held. The Sheriff had been called to quiet them down on occasion, but nothing ever got out of hand. When they came to town, they were most always friendly and went about their business the same as everyone else.

They always welcomed Bill or anyone else onto their land and invited them to attend their festivals freely. As a journalist investigating any story that might pertain to community activities, Bill had gone to a few gatherings. Everything he saw there attested to the fact that they were of a life-affirming order. They did no ritual sacrifice in which blood (animal or human) was spilt. Neither Bill nor the Sheriff believed that the missing animals, if there was any foul play, would be connected to the Pagans. No matter what Bing said.

After all, Bing's rage was only indirectly focused at the Pagans, and that was mostly due to their association with Crescent. Crescent, the Heathen Witch Bing believed cast a spell upon his saintly brother, and made him fall insanely in love with her.

In their youth, Bing's brother was the new minister of a recently built Baptist Church near Mitchell. He met Crescent and fell in love with her while she was nursing him back to health after a nearly fatal accident during the church's construction. He fought hard to convert Crescent and bring her into the fold where they could be properly wed and accepted by the community. Bing telegraphed their father, also a minister, who was living and practicing in Kentucky. He told him briefly of the brother's dire straits. The father quickly traveled to Mitchell and arrived unexpectedly, to Jonathan, at the dedication ceremony of the new building. Caught up in righteous indignation the Kentucky minister proceeded to rain down fire and brimstone upon the hapless couple. He promised eternal damnation to Crescent unless she repented her unholy ways right then and there. Crescent laughed, attesting that his conception of the Devil and Hell were his own devices and held no fear or command over her. She told her beloved she was fulfilled by her Religion and would never convert to Christianity, just as she would never try to convert him from his chosen path. If he wanted to live his life with her, he would have to accept her as she was. With that, she turned and left the Church where they had gathered for this final enactment. The son, realizing she meant what she said and would never convert, told his father that he would not choose to live without her.

The father, also believing that his son was under a spell, realized that if Jonathan joined her side it would only be a matter of time before he renounced his God and lost his immortal soul in the doing. So in the name of God, and believing it was better to save his son's soul than to save his body, he removed the heavy cross from the altar and struck down his son as he neared the Church doors, intent on joining his beloved Crescent.

Crescent was walking away from the Church, passing through a crowd of the parishioners who were gathering outside for the dedication of their new church. As she passed through the crowd she suddenly dropped to her knees as if felled from behind. "Jonathan" was the only sound that barely escaped from her mouth. She turned and rushed back to the Church. As she opened the heavy oak doors, her beloved Jonathan fell out onto the steps.

Crescent stepped over the body as if she knew that his spirit had already taken flight, and walked back into the church as people moved up to help their stricken minister. A human throat should never have uttered the cry that issued from the church. Time itself seemed to hold its breath. Finally, realizing that Jonathan was beyond help, they gently laid him down upon the grass beside the church. No one wanted to enter the church, and all seemed unsure of what to do when Crescent emerged.

She walked over to Jonathan's body and knelt, saying many words, but of all those gathered there, not a one could recount what it was she had said. Standing, crying freely, she told the people they should gather his body and bury him proudly after the faith he had dedicated his life to serving.

They asked after the father, who was still inside the church. "He is dead," she replied. "Do with him as you will."

"Did some madman enter and slay them both?" they asked. "No," she spoke. "The father has slain his son and paid the price of his transgression."

The father was found leaning against the pulpit, his dead eyes staring at unguessable horror. He was holding up the bloody crucifix as if to ward off some unspeakable terror. No mark was upon him. The coroner's verdict was that he had died of a massive heart seizure, most likely upon the realization of the act he had committed against his son.

Bing was at Jonathan's house preparing to leave for the ceremony. He didn't know that his father had arrived. When he was told of the death of his brother and father it seemed to totally unhinge Bing's mind. Regardless of the findings of the court, which absolved Crescent from any part of his brother's untimely demise, Bing never for a moment believed she was not guilty of the murder of both his brother and father. He swore never to rest until vengeance was his. And the Lord's, of course.

Anyway, that was the story as Bill recollected it. His mind had wandered back over the old case as he followed the Sheriff's car to the police station. It had happened five years before Bill had been born. But something that sensational never quit being a popular topic of conversation. Especially since so many key players were still living, and residing in the community. Bill was forty-five years old. So that would make it fifty years since Bing's brother and father had died. "What would fifty years of carrying hatred for another human being do to you?" Bill wondered as he steered his car into the space next to where Dalton parked. "Especially if the person you hated was someone who lived in the same community. Mere minutes apart at all times. Shopping the same stores. Running into each other time and again on the streets, in the mall, at the post office?" Bill could only imagine as he headed up the steps and through the double doors.

Sheriff Dawson was already at the front desk as Bill caught up with him.

"Morning, Bill," Sergeant Sterne said, smoothing imaginary hair back over a long since bald head, "still looking for the story of the century in our back yard?"

"Old habits die hard, Sergeant." Bill watched the hand come up and caress his pate again. "Some of us keep retracing the same old

156

familiar ground looking for something out of place that we may have missed. Don't you find this so?"

"Maybe reporters like you, or Detectives, but not old war horse desk jockeys like me. No, sir. A place for everything and everything in its place. That's how I run my ship. You won't find me searching for something that isn't there."

"Bill is interested in misplaced pets these days, Sergeant." Dalton interrupted Bill's mental battle with his unarmed opponent. "Do we have a log on missing pets over the last couple of weeks?"

"Do we ever. It's probably as thick as a Sears Roebuck catalog if you printed it out. Every time the phone rings lately I want to answer it 'City Pound' or 'lost and found.' And mostly lost! I don't think anyone has called back in to say that Fido or Miss Kitty has returned home."

"Its cause they ain't come home. And ain't going to either!"

"Bill was about to reenter the conversation when a man sitting on a bench against the wall beat him to it. He looked like water was a stranger to him, both for washing and drinking. He was fairly large. Probably six-foot one or two, and easily over two hundred pounds, Bill guessed. Although he couldn't figure how old the man was. He had those back woods weathered features of the folks that seldom come to town except when necessary. The long johns that could be seen through his unbuttoned flannel shirt were probably white once. "About the last time his hair had been introduced to a comb," Bill thought as the man stood and slowly walked over to the desk where they had stopped.

"What do you know about this, Clem?" Dalton turned from the desk and to Bill's surprise shook hands with the man.

"Only what I seen happen to my own, Dawson. That's why I came in. Hardware store ain't open yet. So, I figured to tell you about last night's goin's on. Chubby here," indicating the Sergeant with a jerk of a callused thumb, although Clem never looked away from Sheriff Dawson, "wanted me to fill out a form like I was his secretary or something."

The Sergeant started to protest but the Sheriff silenced him with an open hand gesture of his own.

"Come on into my office, Clem, and you can tell me about it. I'll write it down myself, if it needs to be done, so you won't have to waste your time on paper work."

Bill figured that Clem probably couldn't write and that the Sheriff knew it, too. His little speech was to help Clem save face instead of getting angry and clamming up.

"Hey, Sheriff," Bill interjected, "mind if I come along? I am the one who's got you looking at this particular can of worms. Besides, I can take shorthand and save you and Clem both the trouble."

"Clem, Bill here, is the Editor of the <u>Bedford Crier</u>. Anything you say in front of him is liable to wind up in print. I don't see anything so particular about the coincidental disappearances of animals that we need to keep a lid on the story. So, it's up to you if you want to talk about it in private or not."

Clem's gaze drifted over to Bill and he seemed to take on an air of righteous defiance. "My Ma always said you should never do anything that you would be ashamed to see in print in the papers. I've got nothing to hide, Mister. Although I do expect people to respect my privacy. If you promise not to print my address in your paper, then I reckon that I don't mind you getting the rest of the story."

"Hold my calls while we sort this out," Sheriff Dawson instructed the Sergeant. "Unless it's an emergency. And go ahead and print out the reports on missing animals over the last couple of weeks. Also, call the stations over in Mitchell and Oolitic and find out if they have an abnormally high incidence of reports. If those stations do, then go ahead and check with Bloomington and some of the other county offices. I want to know if this is local or how widespread it is."

The last part was said in retrospect, over his shoulder, as he led the way down the hall to his office.

Sheriff Dawson's office was small and tidy. He seated himself at his desk, with his back to the window, and offered chairs to Bill and Clem. One wall held personal photos of family, and high school and college team sports. A diploma and a couple of citations for outstanding work achievement were also displayed. He had a pen and a clean notebook already on his desk. Bill took a pad from his jacket pocket and noticed Clem looking around the room in search of something. Dawson reached inside the wastebasket beneath his desk and extracted a Folgers coffee can, which he offered to Clem. Bill had never seen the Sheriff with chewing tobacco, so he guessed that he must have enough locals coming into his office who chewed to warrant the can.

"Clem's full name is Richard C. Clemmons. He's also my cousin on my Mom's side. Now, you didn't lose any of your dogs did you?" The first part the Sheriff had directed to Bill 'just to keep the record straight.' He then moved the conversation right over to Clem to get things rolling.

"Lord, no, Dalt!" Clem seemed taken aback by the very notion. "I'd as easily lose my right arm as to lose my dogs." "It was my rabbits. I had about twenty in the pens back by the barn."

"How many are gone?"

"All of them. Not a one left."

"Not hide nor HARE," Bill thought, but said nothing, stifling his own humor.

"Why did you let the rabbits out of the pen?" Sheriff Dawson asked.

"I didn't, Dalt. The pens were trashed and all my rabbits gone."

"A fox or wild dog could have broken into your pens, grabbed one or two rabbits, and the others escaped in panic." Dawson offered, but Clem wasn't having any of it.

"I've lost animals to all kinds of varmints, including man. I know the traces and signs they leave behind. Shit! Don't you think I know how to find escaped animals even if they run off frightened? No, sir! I didn't find my rabbits 'cause they didn't run off. And they weren't carried off by something breaking into the cages, neither."

"Clem." Dalton stood up and walked over to look out the window. Then he turned around and leaned on his desk looking the big man in the eye. "You're not making any sense. Either something broke into your pens or it didn't. And either your rabbits got carried away or they ran away, or they are all still there. There are no other ways."

Clem grinned like a man about to put four aces on the table. "My cages weren't broke into—because they were broke out of. And judging from the amount of blood and fur left on the wire, those rabbits pretty much killed themselves getting out."

"So something spooked them and they destroyed your pen and themselves along with it. I've heard of that happening before."

"Yeah. But where are the rabbits? Weren't no tracks on the ground around the pens of anything big enough to carry them off. And no rabbit tracks showing where any survivors hopped away to safety. I live by my hunting, Dalt. You've been in the woods with me. I can read the signs like the back of my hand. There were drag marks like something dead was hauled across the yard and into the woods. Like twenty something's dead. But there weren't no tracks of anything that dragged them. It was like they dragged themselves."

"Clem." Dawson said after a moment's silence. "I think you should tell us the whole story about last night. With no interruptions." Bill was sure this part was directed at him.

"Bill will write down the events as you tell them. Just start at the time prior to your noticing anything out of the ordinary happening. No matter how unrelated it may seem. Would you like something to drink before you begin? Bill?"

Both men declined the offer, although Bill did pop a stick of gum in his mouth prior to opening his notebook and taking his pen from his pocket.

All set?" Dawson asked. "All right then, just relax and tell the story in your own words."

"As if I could tell it in somebody else's words." Clem jabbed. Then he got quiet and looked down at his shoes. The feeling was like he was looking inside his own mind and rewinding a movie back to the point where he would choose to begin his narrative.

CHAPTER 19

"The day was really hot, for this time of year. I got up earlier than usual to get the chores done before the heat set in. I worked in the shade as much as I could, but that old sun kept poking its nose in my business. So I kept moving to the opposite side of the house or barn. There's always plenty of something to do somewhere, so I just kept moving."

"By late afternoon I was back in the house setting on my sofa. I had the radio and the fan going and I had called it a day on the heavy work. I'd made myself my first drink of the day. Now," he looked directly at Bill, "Dalton knows that I'm a drinking man. But I wait until my workday's done. I've seen too many accidents happen - even to sober men who get careless or distracted. There ain't nothing more unforgiving than a John Deere tractor or combine. They are more than willing to chew you up and spit you out neat, just like you was any other kind of harvest." Clem emphasized this last part by spitting a wad of tobacco juice into the Folgers can.

"As I said, I had gotten up earlier than usual and somewhere around nightfall, the day and the whiskey caught up to me. I don't rightly know how long I had been asleep on the sofa. But I came awake real sudden like. I was kind of fuzzy headed and not quite clear about where I was or what had woke me. My mind may not have been fully awake yet but my body seemed to know that something was going on outside. I came up off of that couch and was out the front door and on the porch before I even thought about it."

"Now I don't know if it was the fresh air or the sound of my dogs that brought me around. Maybe both. But I sure came full awake real sudden like."

"My dogs are my only family that lives with me. We're real close. My hound named Blunder? Why, I had her mom and dad and their mom and dad. So I know her bark and bay like every word to a Hank Jr. song. And the ruckus her and her brood were putting up was like they was telling me that the gates of Hell had opened in the chicken coop and my old rooster, Bentwood, had turned into Satan himself."

"Like I said, my body was moving faster than my brain. I had jumped off the porch and ran to the dog kennel without thinking to grab a gun or a flashlight."

"When I got to the pen, I could see that the dogs were all right. But they were bristled up and fit to be tied. I tried to calm them down but they weren't havin' none of it. They were all staring, half-crazy like, over in the direction of the barn. That's where I keep my Rabbit pen, outside, in back of the barn. My dogs have let me know before whenever a fox or coyote was prowling around. Usually I would have just let Blunder or Stringer out to chase the varmint off. But as out of control as they were, I didn't think that I could let just one or two of them out without the rest rushing out on their heels. And I didn't want this whole wild-eyed pack howling up the countryside and pissing off my neighbors. Shit, if someone shot one of my dogs then I'd have to shoot them and then where would we be?"

"Now, its plenty dark down by the barn, so a while back I had Rowan help me rig a couple of lights in the back and on the side. The problem was that the switch to turn them on was back on the porch of the house, or inside the barn itself, which was blacker than a lawyer's heart. I knew I could find the switch in the barn by feel. I hoped that if I made enough noise I reckoned that I would scare off anything before I got there."

"By this time my brain began catching up to my body. As I got closer to the rabbits and further from the dogs, the sounds coming from the rabbit's pen made me wish I had gone back to the house for the light switch and the gun. I changed my strategy about making a lot of noise as I approached. And I felt a bit better when I grabbed the axe off the woodpile by the barn. I tell you, I was sweating bullets trying to get up the nerve to either walk around behind the barn in the dark or to reach my arm through that coal black barn doorway and feel around for the switch."

"About then, I heard a couple of those rabbits scream, and I knew that I didn't want no part of whatever was attacking them in the dark."

"I swung the barn door open and the hinges seemed to screech in sympathy to the tormented rabbits. I swear that stepping in the doorway and reaching blind in the dark was one of the hardest things that I ever did. But a man's gotta take care of his own. So I did it."

"Just before I touched the spot on the wall where the switch was, I felt something drop on my hand. Jumpy as I was gettin', it scared shit out of me. But I've had spiders and every other kind of crawling varmint jump on me at one time or another, so I shook it off and reached for the light switch again. And again it jumped back on my hand. Except this time there were a couple more. I was getting mad, so I shook my arm harder and stepped further into the barn. I held the axe near it's head and waved it back and forth in front of me to clear out any spider webs so I could get on with my business. Suddenly my hand and arm was covered with what felt like a million bugs swarming on my skin. I shook my arm and noticed for the first time that they were also covering my feet. I hadn't bothered to put my shoes on when I ran outside and now I was paying for it as I felt the unseen swarm began climbing up my pants legs."

"I was swatting and stomping like crazy. It's a wonder that I didn't do myself in the way I was swinging that axe around. It was awful. I could feel legs and wings, pinchers and stingers scuttling under my clothes and heading for my private parts. And the ones I slapped or stomped just seemed to crunch. Not like smashing a bug, but like crushing a jarfly's empty shell. You know, like the ones you find hanging on a tree? Anyway, when they got on my face and began digging through my beard, I guess I was damn near going crazy by that time. I had spun around so many times that I no longer knew where the door was. Swatting at my face and crotch, I took a step back and hit the wall. I felt something dig into my back between my shoulder blades. I guess I still had enough sanity left to recognize it as the light switch. I turned around like a drowning man reaching for a rope. I dropped the axe and grabbed that switch with both hands. When I flipped that toggle, I felt like I was ringing the doorbell to Heaven."

Clem had to pause for a moment and wipe the sweat from his brow. Evidently, the memory of the event was too fresh for him not to be shaken by the retelling.

"When the lights came on," he continued, "I was every bit as blinded by them as I was by the darkness. The difference was that all motion had stopped, except my pounding heart. Oh, the bugs were still there. I was picking them out of my beard and shaking them out of my pants. But they were no longer moving. Hell, they weren't even *alive*."

"The floor and walls all around me were covered with bug carcasses. Have you ever looked at the front of a car after a long drive in the country in the summer? You can see the grill, the headlights, and the radiator all covered with dead bugs of different types? Well, that's exactly what the inside of my barn looked like. Except these bugs had been swarming all over me just seconds before. And I don't think the light killed them. Stopped them maybe. I'm sure that most of those bugs had been dead for a while. They were little more than dried husks. But they had swarmed, and bugs of different kinds don't swarm together. Bees swarm. So do ants, locusts and butterflies. But not together. No sir, the only place you see them together is on the front of a car when driving selection puts them there. But you get them one at a time and not all in one big swarm."

"I walked back out of the barn and around the back. The lights had it as bright as day. The dogs had quit barking and everything was dead still. I mean to say, absolutely quiet. No frogs croaking, no living bugs chirruping. Not a night hunting bird or anything. It was like the entire woods held its breath to see what was going to happen next."

"The rabbits were gone. The cages destroyed, just like I said. Thousands of bugs, and bug parts, were laying everywhere around the cages: Wings, legs, bodies. But no rabbits. Now, I'll give you that those bugs could have killed the rabbits. Hell, I believe that they damn near killed me. And would have too, if I hadn't found the light switch when I did. But the bugs didn't carry them off. I heard the rabbits fighting for their lives the same time that I was fighting for mine. And when the lights came on the bugs dropped like flies, so to speak. Now, I've seen ants carry things larger than themselves, but it still takes quite a bit of time. And there wasn't enough time from when I hit the lights and walked around to the back for a pack of bugs, no matter how many, to have carried off all those rabbits without me seeing them."

"My guess is that something used all those bugs to attack me and my rabbits. And that the bugs were already dead when they attacked. Like little insect zombies. And once the bugs had killed the rabbits, whatever controlled the dead bugs now controlled the dead rabbits. It had them hop and crawl and drag themselves off into the woods."

Clem leaned back in his chair and looked each man directly in the eye before finishing. "And that's it. Drunk or sober that's my story. Exactly like I saw it happen. And here's all the bites and stings on my hands and face to prove it. If I was allergic or more of them things still had poison juices left in them, I'd probably still have dropped dead after turning on the lights."

"But," Bill interjected, finally breaking the silence Sheriff Dawson had placed upon him, "If something was controlling the insects as you suggest, then what purpose would it have in causing them to attack your rabbits? And why would it then abandon the bug army?"

"Food would be my guess." Clem suggested. "As I said, the bugs were dried up of juices. Nothing worth eating was left. So, the Bugs were exchanged for better eats."

"Or," Bill paused reflectively.

"Or what?" Asked Dalton and Clem simultaneously.

"Or as you infer, the insects were an army. The controller of that army may have sacrificed the small bugs for creatures of larger mass."

"Wait a minute!" Sheriff Dawson said, standing and throwing up his hands. "You mean we need to watch out for an army of killer bunnies? Get real!"

"If we are believing Clem's story of attacking swarms of deceased insects of different varieties, then we must seriously consider the possibility of roving mammals. "Not just rabbits, but also raccoons, opossums, and what about all of those unaccounted for pet dogs and cats?"

"Come on!" The Sheriff stood abruptly and reached for his hat. "We'll go check out Clem's place. And if we find nothing but an empty whiskey bottle then we've wasted an afternoon."

"And if we find more?" Bill asked.

"Then, we, my friend, have a serious problem on our hands."

CHAPTER 20

"Just hold on a minute, Dalt." Clem scratched at one of the numerous bites as he spoke. "I didn't come all the way into town just to talk to you and then head back home. I still need some things from over to the hardware store."

"Fine, Clem." Sheriff Dawson continued toward the door, and motioned for Clem and Bill to do the same. "Bill and I will head on out to your place. I've been there often enough to find the Rabbit cages without you. You can catch up to us as soon as you're finished in town. But mind you, Clem." The Sheriff paused with his hand on the doorknob. "Don't say a word of this to Bing. He's up on his soap box again and we don't need your account of supernatural goings-on adding fodder to his fire."

"Dalt," Clem drawled, "Bing has had a hate on for Miss Crescent for as long as we've known him. Ain't nothing I can say or do that's going to change that one bit."

"Just do what I ask you until we get this sorted out. Buy your goods and meet us at your place as quickly as possible with as little talk as possible. Can you handle that?" The Sheriff finally opened the door, allowing Clem and Bill to pass through into the hall.

"No problem, Sheriff." Bill noticed that this was the first time today Clem had addressed Dalton in his official capacity. "Hell, I'll probably even beat you guys there," Clem called back over his shoulder as he marched off down the hall and out the front door.

"Well, Sheriff, are you really buying this story of roving zombies?" Bill asked, now that Clem was gone.

"Not as such, Bill. I know that something happened out at Clem's place. He wouldn't come in here with a tall tale just to draw attention. But he drinks a little more than he should, so I wouldn't put too much stock in it being exactly the way that he told it."

"He won't keep a story like that to himself for long, you know. And it will grow with every telling. I should print something just to keep the public informed, if not warned."

"The gossip in this town can do more damage than anything you print, Bill. And true or not, I can see that you're fascinated enough to run with it. But I would still like you to run your copy by me before it hits the paper."

"As long as I get the exclusive from you when this story breaks. And..."

"And what?" Dalton was afraid to ask.

"I get to tag along until it does break. Then you have my word on it."

"Your word's been good in the past, Bill, come on." Sheriff Dawson said as they passed the front desk, "I only wish I felt as confident about Clem keeping quiet."

*   *   *

Bing was behind the counter opening a box of paintbrushes when he heard the creak of the front door opening and Clem's heavy steps on the complaining floor boards.

"Morning, Clem," Bing looked at him rather suspiciously as if something was up. "Kind of late in the month for you to be in town, ain't it?"

"So? What are you getting at?"

"Nothing at all, Clem." Bing tried to look all innocent-eyed. "It's just that for as long as I been working here you always came in on the first Wednesday of every month to get your stock. Why, I know people that see you in town and go home and flip their calendar pages over realizing that another month has passed. And here you are standing in my store and not only is it not Wednesday, but it's the middle of the month. So I have to ask myself, what's up?"

168

Bing's voice attracted the attention of the other two patrons of the hardware store. Although they seldom bought anything, Walt and Pete could almost always be found hanging out in the vicinity. Bing kind of inherited them after the barbershop next door closed down and moved up by the highway where higher priced hair was waiting to be cut.

"I just ran out of a few things and didn't want to wait." Clem explained seeming a bit miffed. "A man has a right to change his habits. Just like I can go somewhere else to spend my money if I get the notion."

"I hear there's a sale going on at that big store up by the highway." Pete offered, pointing with his cane.

"The highway is in the other direction you old fool." Walt interjected. He indicated the proper direction by thrusting his large stomach toward the back wall. His too small flannel shirt opened in ovals from button to button at this gesture.

"Sale, my ass." Bing quickly jumped in. "They mark everything up seventy-five percent and then offer a fifty percent off sale and fools like you think that they're getting a bargain. Besides Clem, you know your credit's good here no matter when you come in. I was just surprised to see you, that's all. Now what are those things that you need?"

"Let's see now." Clem scratched his elbow and looked up at the ceiling. "A twenty-five foot roll of chicken wire, a case of Raid. Can I get half of that for flying bugs and half for crawling? A half a dozen fly swatters, the brightest flashlight you've got, and do you carry those hats with the nets on them like bee keepers wear?"

"That's quite a list of things to run out of?" Bing said after a moment of stuttering. "You must have one Hell of a bug infestation problem." He turned around and took the fly swatters off the wall behind the counter. "All I have is the blue and green swatters. If you want red or yellow I can get them next week and hold them for you?"

"What you've got will be fine." Clem said, exasperated.

"I can make you a better deal with a pump up sprayer and a couple of gallons of all purpose killer than all those individual cans. And what about a roach motel or some fly paper?"

"Yeah, the sprayer, and maybe the fly paper but I don't think that they'll go for the motels."

"The roach motels work great." Pete added. "I got them in my house for the ants."

"Why didn't you buy ant motels instead of roach motels if you knew you had ants?" Walt asked.

"What's the difference? Ants can't read the box anyway."

"No motel's gonna work on these bugs cause they won't be interested."

"You saying that your bugs have higher standards then the rest of the world's bugs?" Bing asked while sitting a sprayer and a gallon container on the counter next to the flypaper and swatters.

"Maybe not higher, but different." Clem knew he should shut up now, but this was only the second time he had spoken to anyone about his narrow escape and he was still caught up about it.

"How so?" Bing asked, hooding his right eye and slightly turning his head to the right, he peered at Clem from the corner of his left eye. A gesture that said 'yes, go on, I'm listening. But I'm reserving judgement on your story until the end.'

Clem leaned his forearms on the counter and opened his hands as he spoke. "Until now, I thought that there were only two driving forces in a bugs' life. Food, he ticked off on his fingers, and sex. Now the swatters, spray or flypaper can catch these varmints no matter what their business is. But the motels have to attract them with either the scent of food or sex as the bait. But if you got a different kind of bug—one that no longer gives a hang about eating or getting laid—then you ain't going to lure them into no box."

"You said your bugs had something different on their minds," Pete spoke, leaning heavily on his cane while caught up in the telling, "if it ain't food or sex then what is it? What drives them?"

Clem bowed his head and clasped his hands together over the glass countertop that held a sundry of pocketknives, combs and fishing reels. He looked to be praying. He was as good a storyteller as he was a fisherman. As if he were using one of the Zebco's before him, he let the lure be taken and waited the proper moment to set the hook and ensure the catch.

"Death!" He waited another moment and let the word sink in. "These vicious little insects are only interested in killing."

A moment of silence held and then Walt found his voice. "Spiders kill. So do wasps and ants. They have to kill in order to eat."

"That's the point!" Clem rose up, pushing himself from the counter. "Number one." He lifted his hand from his tangle of beard and held up his index finger. "These bugs are not interested in eating, 'cause they are already dead themselves. He paused for that to sink in before holding up a second finger. "And number two. Spiders kill flies. Wasps kill spiders. These bugs aren't killing each other. Hell, they were fighting side by side. They killed my rabbits, and then they tried to kill me!"

With this, Clem rolled back his sleeves to show the numerous sting and bite wounds that welted his flesh.

"I heard of killer bees." Pete finally said, "but…"

"But nothing," Clem interrupted. "I'm telling you that these were bugs of all kinds, swarming together with the soul purpose of doing murder. Do you think I'd be in here spending my hard-earned money on this shit rather then a case of beer if I wasn't scared shitless about being at home tonight when it gets dark again? Do you think that Sheriff Dawson and that reporter from the paper would be out at my place right now if this wasn't some kind of life-threatening emergency that could affect the whole community? Last night it was my rabbits! What or who will it be tonight? Not me, by God. I'm telling you I ain't going down without a fight."

"Winston Churchill!" Walt finally broke the silence.

"What?" Clem asked.

"It's his cat." Pete explained. "He let him out two days ago and he hasn't come back."

"Winston Churchill," Walt said again, "I had a bad feeling that something happened to him." One of the buttons had blown off of his extended shirt and the others threatened to follow.

Clem watched the white button arch through the air and land spinning on the counter top. It slid across the glass and stopped against Bing's hand. The hand clenched the edge of the counter in a bloodless grip that made the knuckles stand out like pistons. Clem's gaze traveled up Bing's arm and he gasped in surprise at the feral expression that etched his features. Even as Clem watched, the hateful expression rippled into a sinister caricature of a gloating mask.

171

Bing's tightly drawn lips were all but invisible as they moved in short spastic rhythms. Clem thought Bing might be having a seizure and then he detected the rising volume in Bing's voice.

He was quoting scriptures. Clem had not been to church for a long time. And he sure didn't know the Bible all that well. But he had heard those passages before. No boy can grow up in the heart of the Bible Belt and not have the scriptures quoted to him. And he recognized this one as the one about plagues being brought down upon the sinners like a plague of locust and other creatures that creepeth and crawleth across the face of the Earth.

Just as suddenly, Bing stopped. Strangely, because Clem had never seen Bing touch another person, Bing reached out and gently placed his hand upon Clem's shoulder. Clem was glad he wasn't squeezing him as hard as he had the counter.

"Fear not, brother." Bing looked directly into Clem's eyes. "You need not face these demons from Hell alone and in the dark. For tonight is the Lords' night of retribution. It's the sign that the time has come for us to gird ourselves in the light of the holy and purge this community of the vile one that has too long dwelt amongst us."

Bing came around from behind the counter. He walked to the door and turned the open sign around to read 'closed.' "Nor do you need those things you sought to buy. The insects are not the enemy though they may be controlled by the fiend's treacherous hand. No, we will not stop the flow by standing in the torrent's path rather, shall we stem the tide by damming it at its source."

Too late, Clem realized that he should have listened to the Sheriff's warning. Bing was off the deep end and seemed Hell bent to take Clem along for the ride. "If it's all the same to you, Bing, I'd just as soon buy those things anyway."

CHAPTER 21

"Well", Bill spoke while watching the light filter through a wing that had recently been attached to a Cicada; "it looks as if the part of Clem's story about the insect horde was true." Bill released the wing, which helicoptered down to land amongst the plethora of insect skeletal remains that still littered the floor of the barn. "Are you going to gather up some of the exo-skeletons to take to the lab for analysis?"

Sheriff Dawson didn't even try to repress the look of disgust on his face as he wiped his hands upon his pant's leg. He too had been examining the bug carcasses.

"No, Bill. I don't see where it would do any good. Chemical analysis is expensive and time consuming. If we didn't know what to tell them to look for in the remains, the reports would only confer that we had discovered large quantities of dead bugs. And some bureaucrat would probably come looking for my ass for wasting taxpayers' money. Come on let's go back outside."

Bill didn't need to be asked twice. The chitinous remains were bad enough outside and extremely unnerving in the enclosed area of the barn.

Clem was sitting on his porch as the two men walked up from the barn. He had already downed a glass of whiskey and was now chasing it with a Bud. It wasn't unusual for him to be drinking this early in the day. But usually he enjoyed it. Right now he was trying to stave off the jitters from thinking about nightfall approaching.

"Beer's in the fridge." Clem's voice sounded hollow to his own ears as well as to the Sheriff's. Where was his usual boisterous manner? Bill thanked him and stepped inside to collect the cans for the Sheriff and himself.

"You're sure you didn't say anything to Bing while you were at his store?" Dalton studied Clem's eyes as the big man answered nervously.

"Like I told you, I just got what I needed and headed straight out here to meet up with you boys. I got no time for gossip. And as soon as you get out of my way I'm gonna rebuild my rabbit pen so I can get all of this business behind me.

"Are you sure it's over with?" Bill returned from the house and handed Dalton the procured beer. "I mean there wasn't any warning that it was going to happen last night. How can you be sure it won't happen again? Maybe even tonight."

What was left of the color in Clem's face drained away. He took a large pull from his can before answering. "I ain't got no more rabbits right now." Clem tossed the empty can aside. "I don't figure those bugs really wanted me. I think that they wanted the rabbits and that I just got in the way. Anyway it looks like most of them are dead for sure so there probably ain't enough left to do any harm. And like I said I'm gonna rebuild my rabbit pens. This time though I'm gonna make an outer wall that's electrified. It'll be like a giant bug zapper to anything that tries to get into them."

"I thought you said it looked like the rabbits were trying to get out? Not something trying to get in!"

"'Course they was trying to get out!" Clem looked at the men as if they had just escaped from a lunatic asylum. "You would too if you had a million bugs all over you."

"Calm down Clem," Dalton said. "I wasn't trying to rile you up. I was just getting around to asking if you want some company tonight just in case anything unusual occurs?"

"I appreciate it, Dalt, but I ain't exactly on my own. I got my dogs and a couple of them will be spending the night inside with me. Ain't nothing alive that's dumb enough to take on a man and his dogs on his own property. I'll be just fine."

Sheriff Dawson finished his beer and tossed the can to land beside of Clem's. "Your decision Clem. Here's my card with my pager number on it. You know my home phone and office number. Anything that gets slightly out of the normal and you get a hold of me at one of those numbers. Got me?"

"Sure thing Sheriff." Clem used Dawson's title again. "Now if you're all done, I'd like to clean up around here while its still light enough to see what I'm doing."

"Thanks for the beer," Bill said as he and the Sheriff headed toward the patrol car. "I'll stop back by in a day or two with a six-pack to return the favor."

"Sounds fine by me." Clem called back from the inside of his truck camper. He had walked over and begun pulling out the chicken wire he bought, even though Bing had insisted it wasn't necessary.

Bill opened the passenger side door of the car and poured the contents of the beer can onto the ground.

"It doesn't look like you drank much?" Sheriff Dawson observed.

"I didn't drink any. I don't care for this brand. Give me a dark beer or a good Ale any day."

Sheriff Dawson started the engine and when Bill got in and closed the door, began backing out the drive and onto the gravel road that led back to the highway and the station house.

"So why did you take the beer if you didn't want it?"

"Come now, Sheriff. You know that most people don't like to confide in reporters. A drinking buddy is another matter. I mean anybody that drinks the same brand and is even willing to buy can't be all bad. After a few rounds being a reporter becomes just another job. You would be amazed at the interviews I've gotten and the things I have had to eat and drink in order to be just one of the guys."

"The advantage of not wearing a uniform. I still can't get away with it though even when I'm off duty. People still treat me like a cop. Not Clem, he's family. Hell, he doesn't even think of me as a cop when he's standing in my office. People I went to high school with and ones that I knew before I joined the force though, they're the ones that only see the badge now. Some days I think it would be nice to be plain, old Dalton Dawson, grocery clerk. Or maybe run Dawson's Garage."

175

"There's still plenty of time to change careers. You're not too far over the hill. Look here," Bill pointed at the building set just off the road with a 'For Sale' sign in the front yard. "We could chuck our jobs, buy that place and open up a bait and tackle shop. We could be just Bill and Dalton. Not a Cop and Reporter, just a couple of the good ol' boys that hang out on the square, spit where they want, and live every day like it was the day before or the day after."

The car proceeded along in silence for a few miles. Both men lost in private thought. Finally they turned toward each other and in unison said. "Naah!"

"Hit the lights and siren on the way back would you Sheriff?"

"My pleasure Mister Reporter."

They both laughed as the car came to life and screamed down the road.

As soon as the car drove from sight, Clem stopped unloading the truck and returned to the porch. He sat down heavily on a weather worn wicker chair that had once been green. He had no motivation left to rebuild the rabbit pen right now. He sat looking at the yellow fly swatter he had taken from the truck. He thought of Bing, who right about now would be closing up shop. Clem wondered if Bing would even stop for something to eat before coming on out to his place?

Clem was afraid that Dawson would not leave before Bing arrived. He realized that it was too late to undo his going against the Sheriff's wishes and talking so much at the hardware store. He only hoped that by allowing Bing to come out to his place he could mellow him out a little. If he could get a few drinks in him and show him that the gates of Hell weren't really about to open in the back forty. Then maybe Dawson would never find out what a blabbermouth he had been and no harm done.

It was still a couple of hours before sunset. Clem went in and turned every light on in the house as well as outside. He made especially sure that the barn was well lit. Setting out some kerosene lanterns and candles, just in case of a power outage, he then double-checked the working of his new flashlights. He loaded up and primed the bug killer pump and had a flyswatter hanging, at least one in every room. Clem regretted that Bing didn't carry Beekeepers' hats and had to console himself that at least he was better prepared than last night. Tonight he wouldn't be caught off guard, he hoped.

Clipping a flashlight on his belt, Clem went outside to let the dogs out of the pen. He had just opened the kennel gate when he heard another car coming up the road.

He half hoped that Bing wouldn't come but he recognized the old Ford truck pulling in his driveway even before he saw the hardware sign painted on its door.

Sounder and Tracker bellowed and raced toward the truck. Bing cut the engine and got out of the cab even though the dogs were making their territorial growls. Bing's sights tonight were set on confronting the fiends of another world and no earthly attempt at intimidation could even attract his attention.

When Clem commanded the dogs, they went immediately to the porch. They realized that it was no fun antagonizing the oblivious and so gave up in hopes of better game like a field mouse or Rusty, Clem's tomcat.

Bing's eyes had a weird sheen to them. Clem wondered if he was on drugs. He was wearing a suit and carrying a King James Version of the Bible. Clem guessed that both had belonged to Bing's Father. Because neither one really seemed to quite fit him right.

"Good evening, Brother." Bing spoke in an oratory fashion after the revivalist ministers. Although it was not Bing's voice that caused Clem to start but rather the realization that indeed it was becoming evening. The sun was well below the tree line and dark clouds were moving in from the west, helping the twilight to quicken.

"We best be getting inside." Clem muttered as he headed toward the house. Bing, however, had other intentions, which he demonstrated by grabbing the sleeve of Clem's coat as he passed within range on his way to the door.

"Clem! Inside is exactly where we do not want to be. You told me that the attack came after dark. Do you want to be sitting inside your house waiting for them to easily find you and possibly succeed in finishing you off this time?"

"Now we don't know that they'll be back again." Clem sounded as if he were trying to assure himself as well as Bing. "Besides," he continued, "it won't be any safer out here in the yard if they do come back."

"Who said anything about waiting for them to make the move? No, Brother Clem, tonight we beard the lion in its den! We shall carry the fight to the demon's lair and drive it screaming back into the pit of Hell from whence it came."

With this Bing began marching toward the woods with Clem's reluctant sleeve in tow.

"Hold on, Damn it, hold up a minute!" Clem was visibly frightened. Just where do you think you're dragging me? I ain't going out in those woods tonight. Or maybe any other night. You didn't see the things that I saw or you wouldn't be so damn fired up to get yourself in the middle of those dark trees."

Bing paused in his egress and looked Clem up and down for a moment. He pulled back one of the too long jacket sleeves and pointed his Bible at Clem as if it were a gun.

"Clem, the Lord knows the truth and tonight the Lord is working through me. I don't believe that you have told all the truth. You've lived in these woods all of your life. I believe that it would take a lot more than bugs, no matter how many or aggressive, to make you afraid to enter your woods. You saw something else, didn't you? You saw something that wrenched the very nerve from your gut. What was it? What is it that you ain't telling?"

Sweat beaded up on Clem's face even though the night was cool. When some of the drops began to trickle down, he thought that the insect swarm was upon him again. He jumped, swatting at his brow and was embarrassed to find droplets of moisture rather then insect carcasses.

"Look at yourself boy!" Bing cajoled the big man. "Your nerves are shot. What is it you're holdin' back? Before God's own book of holy law, what did you see?"

Clem swallowed hard. He looked ready to drop to his knees like a penitent sinner. But he stood, although slightly bowed and week in the knees.

"It was just outside the doorway of the barn." Clem's voice went soft and his lips were rimmed in white. "I was spinning around fighting the bugs off. I didn't even know which way was up, let alone which way I was facing. When my hand closed on the light switch and I flipped it on I stopped dead in my tracks. It took me a moment to get my bearings. I was facing the barn door, not two steps from the outside. The bugs had all dropped like stones and my eyes were adjusting to the light. And then I realized that I was staring straight at this little creature that looked like it was right out of the twilight zone."

"Describe it!" Bing's entire body was vibrating inside that oversized suit. He hung on Clem's every word, totally mesmerized by the tale.

"Did you ever see Star Wars? Not the first one, but the second. The one where Luke crashes his space ship in the swamp?"

"Yes, Yes! Go on!"

"Well it looked kind of like Yoda. Only it weren't green; it was white like it had a fine fur all over its body except its face. It didn't seem to be as wrinkled as Yoda. More smooth. Although it had its hand over its eyes and my eyes weren't totally adjusted to the light. So I can't be real positive of details. It took off kind of quick too! If it had run at me instead of away there would have been no way I could have gotten out of its way, it was that fast."

"What else man? Think!" Bing encouraged. "What about its hands? Were they like claws or talons? How many fingers did it have? Was it naked? Male or female?"

"Uh! The hands." Bing had fired so many questions that Clem was having difficulty remembering. He closed his eyes trying to recapture a moment that he would, more than anything else, rather forget. "The hands were like human hands only smaller. Of course the whole thing was about half the size of a man. It had a belt with pouches and kind of a loincloth hanging down from that. I would guess that it was male although I never saw the works that would prove it."

"Pointed ears," Bing filled in, "fang-like teeth, and large dark eyes. A small scuttling caricature of the divine human form." Bing intoned.

"I, uh, only saw the ears. Its eyes were covered and its mouth was shut," Clem corrected to Bing's deaf ears. Bing was now seeing the creature in his own mind as a Hell-spawned Demon complete with cloven hoof and barbed tail.

"This is the Demon that controlled the swarm of dead vermin which attacked you. But though the creature controlled the swarm, it was in turn controlled by another, a human that gave away her humanity when she sold her soul to Satan. Yes, it is the Devil who is the ultimate puppet master of this bizarre stage and though we may be unable to wage a physical battle with the lord of lies himself, still we can sever the cords that bind our earthly counterpart to him."

"I don't understand?" Clem was afraid that he understood the gist of Bing's words all to well.

"If we remove Satan's human marionette then she can no longer summon the Demon who controls the legions of the dead."

Now Clem knew where it was Bing intended on going.

"Bing," Clem pleaded, "We've got no right or proof to go over to Miss Crescent's house. She's always been kindly toward me and everyone else around here. No one but you has ever spoken a hard word against her. Let's just go inside and have a drink and forget the whole thing?" Clem attempted to remove his sleeve from Bing's grip.

"You can't turn your back on Satan, Clem. He'll always pop up in front of you again and again until he finally trips you up and that is when he gets you! Bing released the coat and gestured with the Bible. "I'll make you a bargain. Let's take a walk over to her house. If we don't see anything odd in the way she's acting, then we will just return here with a how do you do."

"And if she does seem to know something about the strange goings on?" Clem asked, unsure of the second part of the bargain.

"The Lords' will is very clear on that point brother. Suffer not a Witch to live among you."

"We can't just take the law into our own hands Bing!" Clem was busy wringing his large callused hands as he spoke.

"Man's law or God's law, that's the choice you have to make. I'd rather risk this earthly body than my immortal soul. Now come, enough talk. Walk with me and lets finish this, once and for all."

"All right. But I'm not going unarmed." So saying, Clem left Bing standing and walked into the house. A moment later he reappeared. Carrying his shot gun in one hand and the bug sprayer in the other while a fly swatter hung at each hip as well as a flashlight, Clem looked ready to wage war against a very strange enemy. As he stepped off the porch, his five dogs appeared ready for the hunt.

Bing turned without a word and strode off in the direction of Crescent's house.

Darkness enfolded the small band as soon as they had gone a few steps into the forest. Normally Clem never turned on a light when he hunted, but every limb he bumped into made him jump until his normal woods sense failed him utterly. He soon had both lights going. Bing plunged on a step or two ahead, guided by some inner sight that directed him unerringly in the right direction. Even the dogs were unusually quiet as they rushed the bushes unsure of what type of animal Clem wished for them to flush.

Sounder's deep bellow halted man and dog alike. Something in the primeval tone of his bay raised the hackles on each neck.

"Where is he?" Bing finally broke the silence that followed Sounder's call.

"Up ahead." Clem barely whispered. "Maybe fifty feet or so. Hard to tell. Come on."

This time Clem led the way as Bing attempted to stay within the circles of light thrown by the jiggling lights on Clem's belt. The other dogs kept pace. An occasional whine told Clem where each one was.

Again Sounder howled. This time, however, Clem had just entered the clearing where the dog sat, head thrown back, and looking up at the base of an old hickory tree.

Bing grabbed one of the flashlights and aimed it up the tree as Sounder spoke again. This time, a couple of the other dogs joined in the song.

"There," Clem said. On that big branch, a little higher and to the left."

Bing brought the beam over and illuminated the source of the animal's consternation. "What is it?" Bing stammered, as two red eyes glared back from their perch. Bing was discovering that demons were more easily faced from a well-lit pulpit than in a dark forest.

"Raccoon. Big mother too!" Clem spoke calmly now. He was, after all, in his own element. He had hunted these woods since he could walk, and now that he was immersed in the rhythm of the hunt his fear dissipated.

"Shoot it!" Bing no longer seemed unhappy that Clem's lack of faith had led him to bring a weapon. "Blast the thing and let's get on with it."

Clem had raised the rifle and the 'coon was in his sights. Still, he hesitated. "Something's not right. A 'coon don't just set there unmoving and stare you down while you shoot it. Even the dogs know. Look at 'em just sitting there staring. Normally they would be all over each other trying to scrabble up the tree after it."

"If that 'coon has no more sense than to high tail it to cover, then we are doing it a favor by putting it out of its misery. Now shoot!" After a moment's hesitation, Bing added "Please?" He was obviously finding discomfort in the situation.

After another few seconds of waiting, Bing's nerves could take no more. He stepped forward and took hold of the shotgun by the stock. "If you won't shoot it then let me. This has wasted enough time."

The look in Clem's eyes told Bing that he had over stepped his boundary. His fingers released the gun as if too hot to touch. Slowly Clem returned his gaze to the treetop. He snugged the gun into his shoulder and expertly squeezed off a thunderous shot.

The animal pitched over backwards and tumbled to the ground below. The growling dogs scattered and warily circled the spot where the coon had landed.

"There that's…"

"They ain't rushing in." Clem cut Bing's words off. "Mark the dogs and hold your ground." Clem once again raised the gun and sited just as the 'coon suddenly became a blur of movement in the darkness. Bing screamed, unable to move from the path of the charging animal. Two of the dogs broke and headed for home. One, Clem wasn't sure which, was hot on the heels of the oblivious beast. All of these things appeared very clear and distinct to Clem as he pulled the trigger and fired a second round into the 'coon. Its right shoulder exploded from the impact and it was flung backward into the jaws of the rushing dog which gave it a savage shake and then tossed it aside and began circling warily.

"Blessed Jesus!" Now it was Bing's turn to be covered in sweat beads. "I didn't imagine that something could have survived such a fall after being shot. Let alone rise to attack so furiously. Thank the Lord. You've finished it now."

"It didn't survive the fall." Clem's voice was a monotone as he spoke. "It was dead before I fired the first shot."

"But how? That's not possible." This time Bing stopped himself from speaking as understanding hit home like a runaway truck. Even as realization dawned, he saw the mangled raccoon rise, once again and begin its undeterred assault. Just as surely as he understood that Clem was telling the truth about the dead attacking him in the barn. Bing also knew for certain that he was the target for this attack, not Clem, or his dogs.

Indignation cauterized the wounds fear had opened. With a screaming rush, Bing launched himself at the lumbering beast and kicked it soundly, elbow over appetite, into the brush.

Clem lowered his gun and whistled in amazement at the panting parson. "Bing, old buddy, I didn't know you had it in you. Why a kick like that would even put any football player's dick in the dirt." Clem fished a pint of whiskey out of his coat pocket and offered Bing the first drink. Bing wasted no time in wrenching away the cap and drinking his share off the bottom.

Handing the bottle back to the waiting Clem, he wiped his mouth on his sleeve and paused. A button on his jacket held his lower lip off to one side. His eyes darted from side to side and his lip slid loose of the button as he said. "Where are the dogs?"

Clem was about to claim his drink when he stopped mid tilt and surveyed the perimeter of their surroundings.

"Don't know." Clem answered. "They was here a minute ago. Sounder? Singer? Where are you boy?"

A rustle in the bushes brought both men around, training their lights on the undergrowth. "Come on out boy, it's all right."

The Bobcats' leap was swift. It took Clem by the arm before he had his gun half way up. The jaws closed on his wrist and the rifle fell from disobedient fingers as he heard the crunch and snap of bones. He slammed the animal to the ground and beat it over and over with his left fore arm. Finally the tenacious jaws opened and he was able to roll away from his feline adversary.

He held his mangled arm to his waist as he regained one foot and a knee beneath himself. The cat had also righted itself and was preparing to reengage its foe when it was suddenly set upon from its left side. Sounder rolled the teeth-baring cat onto its back. As the cat reached its lethal claws for the dog's eyes Singer moved in and tore open the animal's stomach.

The cat leaped erect and continued its attack, all the while tripping over its own intestines.

Clem found the silence of the carnage to be the most terrifying aspect. The cat took wound after wound in stride. The wary dogs struck again and again. They crushed the animals' spine and pulverized the bones of its hind legs and still it fought, dragging itself forward by its front claws. Ever striving to renew its attack upon Clem. The dogs had, by this time, gone totally over to savagery and soon nothing recognizable was left of the foreboding feline.

Clem fell heavily to the ground. He was losing blood swiftly from his severed wrist. Where was Bing? Why wasn't he helping to stop the bleeding? Clem looked around as best he could. He found no trace of the would-be preacher until he saw his Bible lying open upon the earth. Bing would never have left it if he had been given the choice.

Clem tied a clumsy tourniquet around his arm with a bandana and a stick. He felt very weak. He knew he couldn't defend himself if attacked again. "Now isn't that odd?" he thought. "Here I am the perfect target and they haven't made a second attempt yet."

Clem listened for a moment. Along with the dog's growls as they continued to savage the cat, he could hear the frogs and crickets calling in the distance. "They're gone!" Relief washed over him like a wave of snow. "But gone where? After Bing of course." He felt helpless. Hell he probably couldn't even get himself back home alive, let alone help anyone else. Sounder came over whining and licked Clem's ashen face.

"You guys came through." He patted the dog's head with his good arm. "Sounder, fetch the book, bring it here boy."

The dog moved around with its nose on the ground. It even passed over the book a couple of times until finally deciding this was the only thing around his master might want. Sounder picked up the Bible and carried it over to Clem's good hand.

"Good boy. Good Dog. Now smell it! You too, Singer. Smell it good! Now hunt! Go on; go find Bing. Hunt!"

Singer bellowed to the sky true to his name and took off running, unlike Sounder who quietly followed but stopped at the dense edge of growth and looked back at Clem. Clem had reclaimed his rifle and levered himself to his feet. "Go on boy. You can't help me now. I'll either make it home or I won't. Help Bing, boy. Go!"

This time Sounder did call. But it wasn't a cry of the happy hunt. It was the voice of a torn soul caught between duty and loyalty. With teeth bared, he soon caught up to Singer and together they set off in an attempt to be loyal to what they felt was their master's last command.

CHAPTER 22

Bill climbed out of Sheriff Dawson's car. He walked across the lot to a pay phone where he called his office to check his messages. After making a couple more calls, he walked over to where he left his own vehicle. Anyone who saw the middle aged, slightly overweight journalist in his wrinkled gray suit heading across the lot would never have guessed the auto he owned judging only on appearance. The four-wheel-drive truck was a pure macho machine. With its over sized tires, jacked up suspension, complete with chrome roll bars and a brace of halogen lights, you expected someone who looked like Arnold Schwartzenegger to climb in, instead of Bill, who looked more like the Volkswagen type.

Bill, however, knew that getting a story often meant getting to the story. That's why he bought a vehicle that could go anywhere a story might lead, no matter how rugged the terrain.

The engine roared to life and Bill punched up Badfinger on his C.D. player. As he headed down the road out of town, he fumbled in the glove box for spare batteries and blank cassettes for his portable recorder. Things were happening very fast and Bill wanted to get more information on the weird happenings at Clem's place. Bill knew the best place to get info on the weird and unexplainable.

Peter Ham was wailing out the last few bars of 'Without You' as Bill turned onto the gravel drive that led back through the woods to the Pagan community. "Or is that 'Witch's community?'" Bill mused to himself.

Evidently, no festivals were scheduled, as there was no one in the gatehouse. The gate, as always, stood open, so Bill continued onward.

Many different styles of dwellings were hidden amongst the trees on the land. You could find geodesic domes, mobile homes, straw bail houses and others just camped out in tents or an occasional yurt.

Bill parked in the gravel parking area, which now only contained a couple of other cars and trucks. He walked the trail back behind some of the shrines until he branched off the main path and took the one leading to Kyrra Elfin's home.

Bill met Kyrra several years before while doing a story on the then newly forming commune. He had learned many things from Kyrra, most of which he did not print. Bill had given them good press over the years, which helped to ease the concerns of the locals over having to share the area with a group definitely outside of the norm.

Bill admired Kyrra and respected his ways as Kyrra did Bill's. The two men became friends and often shared a bottle of scotch (Kyrra's favorite) by an open fire. Bill had stopped at a package store on the way and now carried the precious liquid in hand as he knocked upon the door.

"Come on in!" Kyrra called from behind the door. When Bill let himself in, he found Kyrra sitting naked in the next room staring at his computer screen. Bill had become used to the residents of the land's lack of attire on warm days and so wasn't surprised or shocked to see him sitting in the buff.

"Bill", Kyrra's smile split his weathered face. "By the Gods, it's good to see you again, been awhile". Kyrra spotted the paper sack with the unopened bottle. "Now why do I get the feeling this isn't just a social call?"

Bill sat the bottle down as Kyrra stood and gave him a welcoming hug. "I know I've been bad about coming around just to visit lately. And you're right, this isn't just a friendly visit. I've come across something I can't explain and I was hoping you would have some time to let me pick your brains a bit?"

Kyrra swiveled his lean brown body around in his chair, turned off the computer and materialized two yellow glass tumblers in one smooth move. "Inside or out, Bill? Got time for a fire or just bullshit on the couch?"

"Better make it the couch tonight but I could use a good fire session soon".

"How about a sweat lodge one day next week? Looks like you could use a good spiritual cleansing; your Aura looks a bit tarnished. Kyrra stood and led the way into the living room. Bill broke the seal on the bottle as they walked. Both men halted conversation momentarily as the fiery scotch found its way into their vitals.

"A sweat lodge sounds good." Bill finally answered the question. "How about if I free up Wednesday evening and we'll do it then? Say? Where's your wife, Starna, and the kids?"

"They left yesterday for Arkansas to visit her parents. I don't get along too well with the in-laws, so it usually works out better if I stay home during long visits. You know how it is?"

Kyrra poured the tumblers full again and then waited patiently for Bill to speak of whatever it was that brought him here this time.

"I'm not quite sure what it is that I want to ask you." Bill slowly turned the tumbler in his hands. With deliberate fascination he watched the amber liquid coat the glass.

"I know your belief system runs a very broad range," Bill hesitated, "Do you believe in Zombies?" Bill could think of no other way to broach the subject other than blurting it out. "I mean, do you think that they exist?"

"Like an animated corpse, night of the living dead, kinda thing?"

"Yes, sort of." Bill felt embarrassed by the subject. "Except maybe not strictly human corpses."

"You mean animated animal bodies?" Kyrra seemed nonplussed by the topic.

"And insects, yes!" Bill was a little easier with the conversation now that he realized the man he was talking to wasn't going to laugh at his questions.

"Wow." Kyrra took another hit of scotch before continuing. "The animation or 'zombification' is very big with the voodoo cults, also Santeria and many other tribal offshoots. Most religious and spiritual practices fear as well as revere their dead. They usually don't appreciate them coming back. Especially the in-laws!"

"However, to answer your question, Zombies in one form or another do exist in nearly every culture in the world. Even the Christians had Christ rolling back his tombstone and cavorting about mere days after his death. As to the Animals?" Well that one is quite prevalent among the American Indian tribes. Animal spirits, totems, and Manitous are found across the United States in every trading post and gas station. The Native American Culture has become very popular again."

"What about insects?" Bill asked again.

"I don't rightly recall any zombie bug legends off hand. Again, the Indians have their Spider Woman, the great weaver. And the Egyptians have scarabs all over their tombs. But I'm not sure if any of the insects were reanimated corpses. Although I don't see why Zombies would have to be limited to mammals. After all, The Christian God animated a lump of clay and Odin animated the first people from trees, so bugs don't seem so far fetched when compared in context, eh?"

"The thing I hear you saying over again is animated. Are you saying that Zombies have an outside force controlling their movements?"

"For the most part, yes. Although there is always the exceptional case of someone returning from the dead by the force of their will. But I would say true Zombieism requires a controlling will separate from the animated corpse. Especially if you're talking about Zombified animals and insects. I hardly think that a tick or a piss ant could muster up the will to return from the dead; and after all, why would they want to? Being what they are. YECK!"

There was a lull in the conversation as both men studied their glasses and their own thoughts. Finally Kyrra broke the silence.

"What is it that has you asking these questions Bill? Have you seen a zombie?"

"Not exactly, only the aftermath of what appeared to be an attacking hoard of dead insects." Bill related the account of what he had seen at Clem's place as well as the story he and the sheriff had been told by Clem.

"Well whoever is controlling these insects shouldn't be too difficult to track down. After all, there aren't many people in the area with the knowledge and skill to pull off mystical resurrections of that scale."

"And you, I assume, know who does and does not have the ability?"

"Yes and no." Kyrra sipped his drink. "I don't mean to sound vague but the ability to direct the action of merely one deceased being is quite a task. It would require complete concentration to maintain control. So someone who would put the time and energy into developing the skill to master the will of thousands of insects at the same time seems a bit excessive. After all, what would be the benefit that would motivate someone into spending years of life cultivating this particular ability? Not to mention the aspect of Free will."

"What kind of Free Will would a dead bug have anyway?"

"I wasn't exactly considering the insect's Free Will, although that too should be taken into account. I was talking more of the Free Will of the individual who would perpetrate such an act. You see most of the people who seriously work Magick believe in the Rede 'And it harms none, do as ye Will.' Now this statement isn't as simple as it appears. Harm, for instance, can take on many forms. In the case of zombies, the spirit may not be able to leave this plane of existence while someone else is manipulating its corporate form. Therefore, harm may be done to the being's spiritual evolutionary path. By interfering with another's Karma, you would also be doing harm to your own Karma."

"Like acquiring negative karmic brownie points?"

"Something like that. What goes around comes around as we say. Another point of the Rede is doing as you 'Will'. The word 'Will' is not to be confused with the word 'Want'. To do as you 'Want' would be to feed your own desires at the total disregard and expense of others. Will must designate conscious awareness in totality of the deeds which you perform."

"But just because you are aware of the harm you may cause, doesn't mean that you wouldn't do the deed anyway?" Kyrra added as an after thought. "To most of us, believing in Magick is also to believe in the karmic debt we acquire in the doing. We strive for spiritual peace and growth. Anything done that negatively affects

Karma is detrimental to the individual doing the working. To work Magick that affects another's Free Will is a most serious crime to the spirit of all parties involved."

"So you are saying that 'Black Magick' isn't done?"

"No, unfortunately it is done. The Magician, however, must be willing to accept the responsibility for his or her actions."

"The reward must be worth the price." Bill added.

"Exactly." Even something as innocent seeming as a love spell is a violation against a person's choice of who they would love. I would never carry the karmic debt involved by forcing someone to fall in love with another."

Kyrra fell into a long silence that Bill took to be the end of his speech.

"So are you saying it probably either wouldn't or couldn't be done by anyone around here, that you know of?"

"Not at all! What I was thinking was how I would go about doing it without expending so much time and energy. You see, according to legend, there are elemental and spiritual beings that innately have the ability to do just as you describe. So I would summon up such a being and bind it to my will. Then I could direct it to use its natural abilities to control the multitudes in the zombie hoard and I would merely be controlling one creature."

"I thought you said no one would want the Karma?"

"No one wants a hangover but it doesn't stop people from drinking too much." Kyrra winked as he took a sip of scotch. "And as you said, the reward must be worth the price. Who knows what reward our mysterious Necromancer has been promised? For some, the power alone would be worth the price. Revenge is also a very strong motivator."

Bill attempted to soak all of this in before he said, "so you would use a spiritual creature with an affinity for creating zombies, but how could you control such a creature?"

"As with most things there are several ways. A pact is one way. This of course is assuming that you have something that the being would be interested in. That old bit about bartering for souls is so much bat shit. An elemental would have no use that I can think of for something so trivial. And remember that these beings are very old, if not immortal, so what mundane artifact could possibly interest them?"

"Assuming the person has nothing worth trading for, what then?"

"The next way is a summoning ritual where you would bind the desired spirit with spells and incantations. Gargoyle spirits were captured in silver monocles made of amethyst glass. When done properly you would look through the glass and focus your will into the amethyst to activate its particular energy, depending on the type of Gargoyle that you had captured."

"And if you didn't do it properly?"

"The backlash would be devastating to the person evoking the powers. You see most any living thing does not take kindly to being confined and used against its will. So imagine something with the muscled strength of stone, razor sharp talons and teeth, and you have improperly contained it in a bauble and then have the audacity to put your eye up to the glass?"

"I get the picture." Bill said, wiping the sweat from his brow. "Must be the scotch making me warm," he thought.

"Ok, so it would take an extremely powerful magician who was very sure of their abilities, or very desperate, to try this avenue. Are there any other ways? Better yet. How would you do it?"

Kyrra allowed the fiery nectar to burn its way down his throat before answering. "Ah, now my friend you are learning the importance of properly framing a question. I would use a weapon that humans have mastered much to our advancement and disgrace, one that most Elementals or spirits have never encountered and are totally unaware of its existence. I speak of deceit."

"I would dupe the unsuspecting creature into doing my bidding through subtle psychic manipulations, thus making it think it was acting out of its own will. It would be unaware of outside control as it reacted to the stimulus of the environment it found itself in. An environment that I would have manipulated it into as well as the reaction which I was cultivating at the time."

"I'm sorry, I don't quite understand? Environment? Reaction?"

"I could lead it to someone's back door by enticing it along the way with butterflies and flowers and other things in need of inspection to satisfy the curiosity that I had fostered within its mind. Thus it is within the environment that I wished. Now someone hearing the noise outside comes to investigate. I manipulate the stimulus toward curiosity and change it into fear. The being sees the human for the first time and is terrified. A split second later I change the fear to anger. Thus an outraged elemental unleashes an army of the dead upon the hapless person and neither are aware that the scenario was manipulated by an unseen and therefore unattached third party."

"But having the ability to manipulate emotions seems to be a tremendous amount of power for someone to have."

"Not at all. Everyone has this ability to some degree. Like any other natural ability, there are those who are naturally adept and others who must work hard in order to use this talent."

"You make it sound like playing a piano rather than playing with emotions." Bill was rubbing his left cheek, which was beginning to tingle and soon would grow numb if he continued to imbibe the scotch. "Are you saying that even I have the ability to manipulate the emotions of others against their will?"

"Exactly, old friend, you do it every day. If you were walking down the street and approached someone you knew with a friendly greeting, a large smile on your face, an outstretched hand, and an open and sincere concern for their well being, chances are you would have placed this person in a relaxed state open to peaceful and harmonious suggestions. On the other hand, if you approach the same person with a menacing stride and an angry, accusing, demeanor then this person will immediately become defensive. So you see, the way your own psychic emanations were flowing toward this person as you approached, directly affected the emotional state and response of that person."

"Are you saying that I am responsible for the mental state of everyone that I come into contact with?"

"No, no. The only person's demeanor that you are responsible for is yourself. The way you, or anyone else, reacts to outside stimuli is totally up to you. If someone comes up to you brusquely and attempts to put you on the defensive you can always smile and walk away thus disarming their aggression in your refusal to play their game. Manipulation of emotions only works if you feed power into it thus allowing the other person control of the situation."

"Of course we are using the contingencies of one on one direct confrontational manipulation. The means that our secret friend may be using to manipulate the Elemental are much more devious. The subtle machinations could leave no room for the creature to even realize that someone else was creating its emotional responses."

"You mean that if you do not realize that you have an adversary then you would not attempt to fight them."

"Now you're getting it Bill!" Kyrra swirled the remainder of his drink before finishing it off.

"So if an Elemental or some such creature is on the loose, how do I find it?" Bill was still a couple of swigs from finishing his glass.

"I'm not so sure that you would want to, Bill." Kyrra's solemn voice sent a chill through Bill's spine despite the warmth of the scotch. "Your best chance is to discover who is controlling the creature and stopping them. Without the controller the elemental would probably return from whence it came and without the Elemental, no more zombie bugs. Comprende?"

Bill finished off his drink and stood to leave. "That's assuming that your theory on emotional and environmental control are factual." Bill felt the room shift slightly as he spoke. "I'm still not able to totally accept the thought that someone could psychically make me do something without my being aware that it wasn't my own idea."

"Whatever you say Bill." Kyrra stood and walked Bill to his truck. Bill climbed into the vehicle. As he put his hand on the ignition, Kyrra said. "Coming to see me tonight may have been your idea, but don't you find it a bit of a coincidence that I just ran out of scotch before you arrived, and now I have half a bottle? Goodnight Bill, thanks."

"Goodnight, Kyrra," Bill said dryly and slowly drove away.

CHAPTER 23

The sudden appearance of the cat terrified Bing so badly that he fell backwards over the brush as he attempted to move out of harm's way. The combination of fright and alcohol contributed to his disorientation in the dark woods. He regained his feet and took a few staggering steps in an attempt to aid Clem when he discovered that he could no longer see the man or his adversary.

Bing's breath was coming loudly to his own ears. He forced calm upon himself and tried to slow his breathing so he might hear the direction of the scuffle.

There! Off to the left. That was definitely Clem's voice. Bing turned his head in that direction to better insure his bearings and was immediately struck in the forehead.

"AHH!" He screamed, raising his hand to the welt forming on his skin only to have the heel of his hand attacked in a like manner.

"I've been stung!" Although stating the obvious didn't relieve the pain, crushing the offending bee between his fingers did, however, make him feel better.

Bing rubbed the welt on his face and the two on his hand. "Now which way to Clem?" He mentally questioned himself, but before he had time to reconnoiter, his thought process froze him solid. "A bee can only sting once, a bee can only sting once, A bee can…Oh my God!"

The sound of the approaching swarm was like a ghost train in the night. Bing remembered several of the local beekeepers coming into his store, complaining of a virus that had killed their entire colonies. The thought was fleeting, just as Bing was. Clem would have to take care of himself, wherever he was. Bing was having enough trouble avoiding low tree branches while swatting the swifter of the bees that were, time and again, finding their mark.

Bing's feet were suddenly treading air as his headlong flight took him across a ridge and over an embankment. He felt as if he were in free fall for eternity. Until the solid reality of mother Earth pulled him, once more, into the 'BE HERE NOW', state of awareness that only pain and surprise can achieve in one.

Realizing that he had suffered no additional damage, Bing crawled through the mud that he now found himself in. He fully immersed himself in the creek at whose edge he had landed. The cool humus was a soothing balm to the fiery welts upon his skin. The oblivious bees that swarmed in after him were gently washed down stream by the current.

Bing kept as much of his body and head immersed as he could, until he was certain the last of the creatures were gone. The creek was neither wide nor deep and so he easily, albeit soggily, made it to the other side without mishap.

Wearily he climbed the bank where he sat heavily on a large rock and wiped ineffectually at the mud-streaked water upon his face. Not since the death of his father and brother had he felt so lost and alone. A large splash in the creek brought Bing out of his commiserating and back to the fact that he wasn't yet out of the woods.

Once again fear gave strength to overtaxed muscles as Bing's legs carried him through the night in another race against death. But fatigue was setting in more quickly this time. Bing knew he was faltering and whatever was behind him would surely be his deliverance if he fell.

He began a prayer litany, which ended abruptly in a curse as he stumbled and nearly dropped to the ground. He grabbed a dogwood tree for support and as he strained his eyes into the night he saw, off in the distance, a glimmer of light between the trees. The crashing underbrush galvanized him into motion. No telling what refuge from the grave gave pursuit this time. The light was his only chance. The night wood was the world of death. The advantage here lay completely with his adversaries. Only attaining the light could tip the scales to his favor.

The brush of muscled fur nearly bowled him over as one of the dead creatures lunged at his leg and then disappeared into the undergrowth. He could see the shape of a building in the halo of light. A few more yards and he would be out of the trees and into the open. Again a blur of motion arched by and vanished into a sumac row.

Bing felt as if he were being herded by the unworldly demons rather then attacked. He could feel hot breath on his exposed calf as he broke through the edge of growth and pitched headlong onto manicured lawn. Bing rolled with the fall and regained his footing from the slathering jaws that glowed eerily in the artificial light emanating from the porch. He saw a second beast leap free of the forest and begin to circle as if to place Bing between it and its fellow Hell-spawn.

Bing wasn't about to be taken so easily. He faked as if to go left, and then ran for all he was worth toward the light and the shelter that it promised.

He once again outdistanced his attackers; safety was his. Then he stopped. Bing's legs buckled and his jaw dropped as his overtaxed body shut down. He refused to believe his eyes. For there, standing on the porch, holding open the door was Crescent. What he thought was the door to heaven, in reality, was the door to Hell. "I was right," he thought, "I was being herded."

"Come in." She called in a voice others would have found calm and soothing. "Bing! I know you can hear me. Stand up and come in! It's just a few more steps."

The creatures that were in pursuit rushed in and Bing prepared to die. Better a clean death under the sky than to knowingly enter her Witch's boudoir. Bing braced for the assault that never came. The furry creatures shot passed him and entered Crescent's house through the door she proffered to him. "Were those Clem's dogs? They must have met their death with Clem and then been sent out to herd me into her evil clutches."

Bing wondered if Clem might not be far behind, dead eyes stalking him if he reentered the woods.

"Bing!" Crescent was speaking again. "You must get up and come inside. Must I come out and drag you in?"

"Your foul flesh will only meet mine in a death battle, Witch!" Bing finally found his voice. "I realize now that you have no power over me. Otherwise you would have killed me long ago like poor Clem. Yes, Clem was a good man but he knew sin and that was your toehold. But I have stayed clean, a proper vessel of the Lord to do battle with ilk such as you."

"Bing!" Crescent was annoyed now. "You will do as I say. Come…"

"No!" Bing cut off her words and regained his feet. "I have seen what I came to see. You are positively in league with the Devil. I am going to walk back to my truck and return with a righteous flock to lay waste to you, and your evil surroundings, once and for all."

So saying, Bing turned without a backward glance and proceeded to say the Lord's Prayer as he strode toward the trees.

"The Lord is my Shepherd I shall not wan…"

The words were stolen from his mouth as a large crow swooped out of the woods. Silently it ripped across Bing's throat with beak and talon, its momentum adding force to its razor like appendages.

Bing turned back toward the house, futilely holding his severed jugular as he looked in disbelief for the one who had killed him. But she was no longer there.

CHAPTER 24

Crescent hadn't watched Bing die, although she had felt his astonished spirit leave his body. She'd found that it was always with an air of astonishment that people left this mortal realm, as if no one believed that they would ever die.

She didn't know exactly what the menace was, only that it was there, and someone was dead because of it. Crescent held up her hands, closed her eyes, and felt the energy of the Earth connect with the energy of the Universe, around and within her. She envisioned white light spreading outward from her fingertips.

"A sphere of protection surround this land, house, beings all around who live here, physical and astral. I thank you. Blessed Be!"

As she crossed the small, enclosed porch and entered the door into the main house, she felt the electrical current that always accompanied her Magickal workings.

So many of the old ways were no longer taught. The rites of passage that should be learned from birth to childhood, adolescent to teen, teen to adult, and then death to birth were no longer commonly known. The never-ending Circle of Life: The Christian churches took this away from the people, telling their flocks not to worry about it: we are here to intercede for you. "Well, where were the preachers and priests for poor old Bing as he met his fate, alone and bewildered, tossed headlong into the afterlife with no spiritual guidance to lead him?"

Crescent was busily opening cans of cat food for Sounder and Singer as she fumed along on one of her pet peeve tirades. The dogs sat obediently at her feet awaiting the repast.

"You poor fellows look done in." Crescent sat the bowls on the kitchen floor and the dogs fell to as if they hadn't eaten in days. Sounder had a hand carved wooden bowl while Singer was eating from a ceramic bowl with two blue rings.

"Finish your food and then rest up." Crescent told them. "I have a ways to travel yet tonight and it looks like you'll be keeping me company."

So saying, she crossed into the living room and sat in an overstuffed chair. There were two wicker suitcases beside the chair. She rested her foot on one as she picked the receiver up from the phone on the end table. She closed her eyes and took a deep breath as she dialed Diana's number. Crescent had never upgraded to a push button phone. She preferred the rotary dial although she had originally possessed a crank type on a party line. Two longs and one short. She would always remember her ring although that never stopped anyone else on the party line from listening in.

Diana had gone to bed around ten with the rest of the household, but was unable to drift off. The death of her father had greatly affected her in ways she was only beginning to realize. "How could such a thing happen after finally getting to a place where they all seemed to be so happy?" Could she really live here now, not only in a place where her father had died but where such strange goings-on threatened to continually unsettle her world? She knew sleep was necessary if she was to deal with all the arrangements for her father's funeral with a clear head, but every time she closed her eyes she thought of him alone in the funeral parlor and that was unbearable. After over an hour of tossing and turning, which kept waking Chris, she decided to go downstairs for some warm milk. "Maybe if I read for awhile I'll get tired," she thought.

She considered getting one of the books Crescent had lent her, but she knew better than to start in on one of those. Her study of Wicca had become so invigorating that she lost all track of time when absorbed in her studies and she knew she would never get back to bed. Besides, the thought of doing something she found pleasurable at this time was abhorrent. "No," what she needed was something dry and boring to make her eyes tired so she could sleep.

She was standing at the first book case in the library picking over titles when the phone rang and she nearly levitated off the carpet.

"Who could be calling this late?" She spoke aloud as her bare feet left the relative warmth of the library carpet for the hardwood floor of the hall. Di and Chris had decided not to put a phone in the library so whoever was in the room could remain undisturbed. "Like dashing down this cold hallway is undisturbing," she murmured, as she rushed to answer the phone before the second ring so no one else would be awakened, unless necessary. She snatched the receiver in mid-ring from the parlor table and tried not to sound out of breath as she answered.

"Lane residence, this is Diana!" She always answered the phone formally in case it was an important contact for Chris.

"Diana? It's Crescent, dear. Please listen and do exactly as I say. I haven't time for lengthy explanations so you must trust me."

"Of course I trust you." Diana was perplexed by Crescent's tone. "What's wrong that you would call so late? Are you all right?" Diana was becoming worried.

"I'm fine, but I'm going to be leaving my house for a short while. I must visit my sister. Remember how I told you that at times you were to follow my words as law or I would no longer be able to protect you?"

"Ye-yes," Diana stammered. "What is it? What do you need? When are you leaving?"

"I'm already packed and I'll be going as soon as I finish talking with you. Bad things are happening, Diana. Things I thought could possibly be controlled are getting out of hand. You and your family should leave tonight. Get as far and fast away from this area as you can and don't return until you hear from me again."

Diana was dumbstruck. "Leave? Now? In the middle of the night? Just like that? Walk upstairs, wake up Chris and say 'Honey, grab the kids, we're out of here?' Crescent, you can't be serious. What about my father's funeral? What is going on? You must tell me more!"

"I don't have time for a lot of details. Bing is dead and probably Clem too, seeing as how his dogs showed up here without

201

him. You and the kids are in danger from the same thing that killed your father!"

"Killed my…But dad died of a heart attack; he wasn't killed. And Bing from the hardware store? He's dead? And Clem, I don't know anyone named Clem. Crescent, I'm confused and scared. Is it that Steve guy Chris was talking about? Did he kill my Dad?"

The dogs had come in and briefly slept by Crescent's feet but now they were pacing and whining.

"I don't have time to talk further, Diana. As I love you, trust me. Take those you care for and run. Don't believe the things you may hear of me. Look with your heart as well as eyes. I'll return as soon as I can and set things right, but don't you come back until you hear from me, even if it means you never return. Blessed Be, Diana."

"Crescent! Crescent!" Diana realized that she was yelling into a dead phone. She dialed Crescent back but no one answered. She was so frightened. What should she do? Was her father really murdered? Chris! Even as she thought of waking him, her feet were already climbing the staircase toward their bedroom.

As she opened the door, she found Chris already awake and slipping his bare feet into slippers as he closed his robe.

"I heard the phone, what's up? What time is it?"

"After midnight," Diana sat on the bed, visibly shaken, so Chris sat beside her and held her hand waiting for her to continue.

"It was Crescent on the phone. She said we were in danger here and that we should leave tonight, now."

"What? In danger from what or who?"

"I don't know. She was vague." Tears began forming in Diana's eyes. "Oh Chris, she said that my father was murdered. She said the same person that killed him killed Bing and someone else. I can't remember the name."

"But Di. Your father had a bad heart. You know that. No one killed him. And I saw Bing this morning driving that old truck of his right up the road from the house. Look I've gone along with you on your commitment to learn Wicca from Crescent but you have to admit that this is asking a little too much. We can't just up and leave for an undetermined time on the say so of an old lady who practices a by-gone religion."

"Chris!" Diana had been leaning against him but now she sat bolt upright. "Crescent is as sound of mind and more than anyone I know. I trust her and if she says we are in danger then I at least will listen to her warning. She warned me to keep the kids inside and I didn't listen that time and now Dad is dead."

"Look, Chris spoke as he stood up from the bed, let me give Crescent a call and I'll see if she can be a little more specific."

"I tried calling her back already. She doesn't answer."

"Alright then," Chris was becoming exasperated, "how about if I phone the police station and see if they have any information about Bing being dead. At least we can narrow her story down a little. Is that O.K. with you?" Chris asked, for Diana had suddenly grown quiet.

"Call whoever you like." Diana walked to the bedroom doorway and then turned back in to face Chris. "I'm going to check on the kids and then pack a few necessities for over night. As I said, I trust Crescent and I'm not making the mistake of ignoring her requests again. Make your phone calls and then meet us in the car. We can sort all this out in a Motel in Bloomington. At least for tonight." She added meekly trying to sound like she wasn't totally usurping Chris' say so in the matter.

"Sounds fair enough." Chris knew her well enough to know when to go along. Especially when she developed that 'I won't back down' attitude. "Hell, probably couldn't sleep tonight anyway."

Di gave him her 'thanks Hon' look and proceeded to check on the kids. Chris had finished dialing the police office and his call was answered on the second ring.

"Yes, I received some news that a friend of mine may have been involved in an accident and I was wondering if you had any information?"

"One moment, Sir." An official sounding voice spoke in his ear. "What is your name please?"

Chris hadn't wanted to give his name but it was either that or hang up. "Chris Lane."

"And your address and phone number Mr. Lane?"

"10255 Route Five, Spider Creek Rd. Area code 812-555-6373"

"Thank you Mr. Lane. Now how may we help you?"

"I was inquiring if you had information about Bing…Chris realized that he didn't know Bing's last name. Time for a small town bluff. "You know? From over at the hardware store? Was he hurt in any way this evening?"

"Please hold for one moment while I verify your information."

Chris closed his eyes and rubbed his forehead. Why was all of this happening? The country life was supposed to be less hectic, but with all the mess of moving and then being in the middle of arranging Nate's funeral, and now this! Not to mention the added burden of getting his recording studio up and running. Oh shit! I forgot about working in the studio tomorrow! I can't leave tonight. Chris looked at his watch. I mean today, it's nearly two A.M."

"Mr. Lane?" The annoying voice had returned. "Sheriff Dawson is on a run in your area. He asked if you would remain at your home until he contacts you shortly".

"Fine, not like I'm going to get any sleep or anything. What donut shop did you say he was in?"

"I beg your pardon?"

"You said he was in my area? I was wondering exactly how far away that would be?"

"Sheriff Dawson is currently investigating a possible homicide at Crescent Ryan's house. He will be in touch with you as soon as he is finished there. Is there any other assistance that you require?"

"No thank you. This is more assistance than I had counted on to begin with."

CHAPTER 25

Sheriff Dawson hung his radio microphone back on its dashboard clip, leaned back in the seat and rubbed his eyes.

"Now how in the world did Chris Lane know about Bing's murder?" Dalton spoke to no one in particular, as he was alone in the vehicle. The other officers as well as the county coroner were setting up lights and taking samples and photographs over by the site of the crime.

Although there was no body present, there was enough blood soaking into the ground to have filled an adult's body. Bing's glasses had also been found just a few feet from the impression that was made when the body fell to the ground.

Sheriff Dawson got out of the car and walked back up to the rear porch of the house. He had knocked once and received no response when his deputy called him over to examine the bloody ground. The dispatch from the office interrupted that line of investigation so he decided to go back to square one and try the house again. Although he was sure no one was home.

He noticed muddy paw prints on the wooden porch floor. He didn't recall Crescent ever owning a dog. She was more of a cat person. Upon closer inspection he discovered one of the prints had six toes. One of Clem's dogs, was it Singer, had six toes. He remembered Clem remarking about it on more than one occasion.

After receiving no answer to his knock, Dalton tried the door and found it to be unlocked. He turned on his flashlight and drew his revolver from its holster. Nothing lit the interior of the home, except for the probing beam of Dalton's flashlight. He entered carefully, moving slowly. His well-honed senses detected no motion or noise from inside the house.

His beam found a light switch on the wall and the click was rewarded by light flooding down from an overhead fixture. The kitchen smelled heavily of herbs and candle wax and other aromas unidentifiable to the sheriffs untrained nose.

He located the phone in the adjacent living room. He didn't touch it. If Crescent had used this phone to call his office when she phoned in to report Bing's death, then he wanted the lab boys to get a good set of prints.

His dispatcher, Betty, said that Crescent had been cool as a cucumber when she reported the murder to her. Just stated that they would find Bing dead in her back yard and then hung up without going into details.

"Now why," Dalton pondered, "would someone commit a murder, phone in the deed to the police, and then disappear? If she had done the crime, the logical thing to do was dispose of the body, that is, if she had wanted to get away with the murder. On the other hand, she did report the crime." Of course, the Sheriff knew many criminals did exactly the same thing in an attempt to throw the blame away from them. "But then, why did she take off like a fugitive if she was trying to look innocent?"

"She may have been taken by force." Remembering the thousands of insect remains and the disappearing rabbits at Clem's place caused an involuntary shudder to run down his spine. Further investigation showed no sign of violence or bug body parts.

The thought that Clem's dogs may have been here worried at the sheriffs' mind. That and the fact Clem was heading over to the hardware store where Bing worked right after being attacked. And now, with Bing dead, it's possible that Clem's dogs and therefore, Clem may have been on the scene when it happened.

"Jackson," Sheriff Dawson called out the back door to one of the officers searching the grounds.

"Yes Sir Sheriff?" Jackson headed toward the house immediately.

Officer Jackson had the ability to arrive at a crime scene in the middle of the night, crawl around outside in the bushes and still look immaculate. He probably never had a hair out of place in all of his twenty-seven years of life. The part on the left side of his short brown hair was as sharp as the crease in his pants. His leather holster and shoes nearly glowed in the dark from polish.

"Take one of the other men and go check out my cousin, Clem's place." Dalton barked orders at Jackson because he knew that the officer lived for it. "If he doesn't answer the door? Look in the barn and surrounding area. He doesn't usually lock his door, but if you go inside, make plenty of noise. See that you don't sneak up and startle him and get yourselves shot."

"If we find him, do we bring him in?" Jackson cataloged the information given and was eager for more.

"No, he's not a suspect. I just want to make sure he is all right. If he's not too drunk, try to find out if he saw anything unusual tonight. Either way, find him or not, give me a call on the radio as soon as you've checked the place out."

"Sure thing sheriff, I'm on it." Officer Jackson spun on his heel and waved to his partner, who was at that moment shining his light under a gooseberry bush. "Yo! Robert! Let's roll!" Jackson was already sprinting to his car, all puffed up over the importance of the mission Sheriff Dawson had entrusted to him. "Man, I can already see that citation, or maybe even a promotion, when I pull off this assignment and neatly type up his report." Jackson loved assignments but even more he loved filing reports in little neat folders and stamping 'CASE CLOSED' on the cover.

He had personally bought the rubber stamp and pad that bore this legend. He was incredulous that the department hadn't owned such an important piece of equipment before he had hired on. And, he smiled knowingly at his own cleverness as he slid behind the wheel, he had kept a duplicate of every 'CASE CLOSED' file he had worked on in the last two years. "Yes," he put the car into drive and smoothly pulled out onto the road, "promotion time draws near, Robert. And when I drop my armload of file folders on the review board's desks next month, why, they might even make me chief of police! What do you think about that?"

Jackson watched with disapproval as Robert haphazardly brushed at the dirt clinging to his uniform. "He probably slept in those clothes." Jackson thought as his partner finally climbed in the car and closed the door.

"Great, Chief, just great!" Robert responded because he knew that although he, and most of his fellow officers, thought that Jackson was nuts, the possibility of Jackson getting promoted to a position of power did exist. And Robert wasn't about to 'piss off' someone who might be handing out his assignments in the future.

CHAPTER 26

Diana came down the rear stairs, herding the sleepy-eyed children with her suitcase. She sat the satchel down on the kitchen floor and turned to Chris as the kids immediately plopped onto chairs and laid their heads down upon the table.

"Well?" She inquired. "What's up?"

"Sheriff Dawson is over at Crescent's house now. They said he's investigating a homicide."

"Oh no!" Diana was suddenly worried. "Is Crescent all right?"

"They didn't say, but I'm sure she is. After all, she called here to say that there was trouble and that she was leaving, remember?"

"Okay, so if the police are there and she isn't, then the only thing to do is wait for her to contact us like she said she would."

"Right," Chris agreed. "The Sheriff said we should wait here until he arrives also."

"I didn't mean to wait here until Crescent contacted us. I just meant that we should wait for word from her that she's all right. I still mean to follow her warning to leave until she says that its safe!"

"But the Sheriff…"

"We can call the Sheriff from the motel. It's not like we're wanted for anything or that we're running away. We'll just get the kids safe, then phone the police and tell them where we are."

"All right." Chris gave in. "You get the kids in the car. I'll get dressed and grab my wallet. At least we can take it on the lam in comfort."

Di locked the back door and then with much persuasion and nudging, she managed to steer the recalcitrant siblings into the back seat of the car. She popped the suitcase into the trunk and climbed into the front passenger seat. Her night vision was poor and so Chris did most of the night driving when they traveled.

Chris was not far behind her. He was always able to dress and hit the door running or pace the house while Diana continued to get ready. But tonight she was glad of his expediency. She was forcing herself to remain calm even though she was growing more nervous with every moment that they remained.

Chris slid into the driver's seat and placed the key in the ignition. "Seat belt." Di reminded. Chris dutifully buckled up and then turned the key.

The engine spun about half a turn and then ground to a halt. The annoying 'URRR' sound usually reserved for cold winter mornings chilled Diana even in the summer heat.

"The battery can't be that low." Chris said, unbuckling his seat belt and opening the door.

"Where are you going? What are you going to do? Di was losing what little control of her nerves that was left.

"I'll just check under the hood. Maybe it's just a loose wire."

Chris popped the hood from the inside as he left the car. Diana lost sight of him as he disappeared beneath the raised hood. The entire car shook, waking the kids, as he forcefully slammed the hood back down. His face was pale in the darkness as he ran around the car and jerked open the front and back doors.

"Chris, what?"

"Get out!" He yelled. "Come on everybody, out of the car and into the house, now!"

Chris opened Diana's door and the rear one so violently that she was nearly flung from the car while holding onto the handle. Chris grabbed up his son and with Jerrica in tow he ran full tilt back onto the front porch.

"The keys! Oh God, I left the keys in the car!"

"Chris." Diana tried to sound calm as she realized her husband was very near hysterics. "Here, I have my keys."

Chris released Jerrica long enough to fumble open the door, he then leaned his full weight back onto the door, solidly closing it after everyone entered. He stayed there like a dead weight, still holding Alex in his arms.

"Daddy put me down." Alex squirmed in his father's grip until he was placed on the floor.

"Chris, what is it? Just because the car wouldn't start...Oh my! Your hands, you're bleeding. Did the car hurt you?"

"What?" Chris seemed dazed. "Oh, the blood. No Hon, it's all right, it isn't my blood. There was an animal in the car, up under the hood. It was all tangled in the fan belt, that's why the car wouldn't start."

"Oh how awful, no wonder that you were so upset."

"It wasn't just that". Chris spoke as they moved away from the children who were now sitting on the sofa. "I could see the thing in the light under the hood. It was mangled beyond telling what kind of a creature it was. But when I touched it in hope of untangling its remains from the car,..." Diana could see Chris's eyes glaze over in memory.

"It moved!" He finally completed. "I'm telling you that nothing that mutilated could possibly have been alive, and yet it moved. It almost seemed to be reaching out for me."

Diana ran her fingers through her hair as she watched Chris pace the floor. She knew she had to come up with some alternative to their predicament.

"Look Chris, it's very late and you haven't had much sleep. You've also been under a lot of stress. Why don't you call the police office back and tell them that we are calling a cab to take us to a motel? That way it won't seem like we are running from anything and it will give us the space to evaluate exactly what is happening and what we are up against."

"Look, Di," Chris started, when an unexpected knock on the front door made them both spin on their heels and face the door in silence. They were both frozen in place, unable to move when the knock came again, this time with a voice.

211

"Mr. Lane? It's Sheriff Dawson from the police department. Would you open the door please?"

Chris started across the oriental carpet for the door when Diana cautioned him.

"Look out the window before you open the door to make sure it really is the Sheriff."

Chris began to respond that they were becoming paranoid, but after a moment's consideration he decided maybe a bit of precaution wasn't out of place. He pulled back the blind that covered the window in the door and could plainly see the Sheriff standing on the threshold. He could also see the police cruiser sitting in the driveway with the headlights on. He realized how upset he must have been to not have heard the vehicle approach the house.

Chris turned the deadbolt latch and the doorknob at the same time and pulled open the old wooden door. The Sheriff removed his hat as he entered the house. He nodded at Diana and then his face froze as he looked at Chris.

"What is it?" Chris became concerned by the expression on the Sheriff's face.

"Mr. Lane?" Dalton pointed with the brim of his hat at Chris. "Is that blood on your hands?"

"What? Oh. Ah, yes it is." Chris ineffectually wiped at the accusatory stain.

"Is it your blood? Have you injured yourself?"

"No. No." Chris stammered in his haste to explain. "This is animal blood. There's something caught in the fan belt of our car and I tried to remove it." Chris looked to Di to corroborate his story.

"We were trying to leave." Di interjected. "But when the car wouldn't start, Chris raised the hood and found the dead animal."

"I see." Chris detected an air in the Sheriff's voice as if he didn't quite believe them. "Didn't the dispatcher at the station tell you I was on my way and for you to remain here until I arrived?"

"Well yes, but my wife was afraid of staying the night here. We were going to get a motel room and call you from there." Chris's voice sounded lame even in his own ears. Little wonder the Sheriff looked suspiciously at them.

"This is your home, Mrs. Lane? Now why would anyone be afraid of staying in their own home?"

Diana took a moment before answering. This was all sounding very flaky and she wanted to compose herself before speaking. She motioned for the Sheriff to come into the living room and close the door to the outside. She realized how tired she was feeling and sat down in the green leather chair beside the sofa.

"We received a phone call from our friend Crescent." She began. "She said that Bing from the hardware store and that another man, I can't remember his name, were killed tonight." She had to steady her voice to continue. "And that the same person who killed them had killed my father and that Chris, the kids and I could be in danger."

Diana suddenly realized the sofa on which the children had been sitting was now empty.

"Chris?" The nervousness was back in her voice. "Did you see the kids go upstairs or into the kitchen?"

"No, I didn't. They were just here a moment ago. I'll go check upstairs."

"Just a moment Mr. Lane." Sheriff Dawson spoke in his official, no nonsense voice. "I don't think you should be going off alone just yet."

"Now see here, Sheriff," Chris was becoming angry, "are you accusing me of something here in my own home?"

"I would just like to get some facts straight before you go waltzing off on your own."

"And what facts do you have that need straightening out?" Diana inquired.

"Well ma'am, the fact is that your husband knew Bing was dead even before we did. We haven't found Bing's body yet but there's enough blood and personal items belonging to Bing that we seriously suspect he was killed. Clem, on the other hand, is still a speculation. I have my men checking on him right now."

"Now I come over here to your place to find you admittedly trying to leave and your husband covered with blood."

"We told you that this is animal blood!"

"Maybe it is and maybe not. But the fact is I'm not letting you out of my sight until the coroner gets a sample to prove your story one way or another."

"Fine, Chris said exasperated, so I'm a suspect. But I still intend on checking on the whereabouts of my children, so would you care to accompany me to the kitchen?"

"Go on Mr. Lane, but if you feel the least bit froggy to me I'll drop you before you hit the ground. Do you understand?"

Before they could leave to walk down the hall to the kitchen, something thumped against the door causing them all to pause. A moment later it was followed by two more thumps.

"What the Hell?" Sheriff Dawson was becoming angry over the lack of control he seemed to have on the situation. "Everybody just stay put."

Sheriff Dawson walked calmly over to the front door but Diana noticed that he now had his hand on his pistol. He pulled aside the curtain just as a fourth and fifth bird flew against the glass.

Dalton's eyes were drawn down to the porch floor to the birds, which were trying to regain flight.

"Damn, something must have spooked their flock. It looks like they mistook your window for an opening."

"Guess again, Sheriff. Two of those birds are sparrows, one's a robin, the other's a starling and the other is a cardinal. Haven't you ever heard that only birds of a feather flock together?"

Two of the birds managed to launch themselves at the window again just as a swarm of insects began pelting the glass on the side of the house.

"My babies," Diana yelped and headed for the kitchen.

"Mrs. Lane, please let me go first." Dawson drew his gun but not to intimidate Diana. Rather, it was in anticipation of what might happen next.

Dalton passed Diana in the hallway and entered the kitchen followed by Chris who held tightly to Diana's hand. Chris fumbled on the wall for the light switch with his free hand but the Sheriff stopped him.

"The kids don't seem to be in the kitchen and I'd like to look out the back door without making myself a target."

Chris released the switch as Dalton walked slowly to the back door.

"Do you hear music?" Diana asked "A kind of weird humming melody?"

"Yes." Chris agreed. "It sort of makes my skin itch."

"The tool shed! Shit, Chris, I felt this same weird music when I had that freaky encounter with something in the tool shed."

"What encounter? I don't think you mentioned it to me?"

"Be quiet a minute and come over here." Sheriff Dawson ordered. "I think I just found your kids. Who is it they are talking too?"

Chris put his hand on the table so as not to bump into it and led Diana around it and the chairs in the dark kitchen.

"There." The Sheriff pointed out. "About ten feet from the back porch. Do either of you recognize that man?"

Diana eased past the Sheriff to look and nearly squeezed Chris's hand off. "Oh!!! OHH! MY GOD!!! It's my Father! Oh dear Goddess, CHRIS, it's Dad!"

"Is there something wrong with your father speaking to his Grandkids?" Dalton asked, picking up on Di's anxiety.

"Sheriff." Chris attempted to explain. Diana's father recently died of a heart attack. Our children are in the back yard talking to a dead man!"

Dawson turned from Chris to look into the yard once more. Jerrica stepped back while making a gesture. Her form had hidden Kratel until then. He suddenly became visible to all for the first time.

"Holy Fuck!" The Sheriff exploded. "What the Sam Hill is that?"

CHAPTER 27

Kratel casually tossed aside the bone he had been gnawing on for the last hour. His den, he noticed, was beginning to fill up with bones. He would have to do some house cleaning soon. That is, if he wished to continue to stay here.

The food was much more plentiful and he was beginning to develop a taste for freshly dead flesh as opposed to the 'dragged through tunnels' carrion he had grown up on. Still, he did miss his own dwelling caverns. How long had he lived in them? Kratel didn't even know how old he was. Time had no meaning beneath the Earth's crust. But here, with the passage of night and day every moment was placed in bold perspective before you.

Kratel had just recently entered his Den as the Sun arose to hold its blinding sway upon the surface. He knew he would never be able to tolerate its shining embrace. How long he had lived without even knowing of its existence, and now it regulated his movements as well as his sleeping habits.

His anger was no longer a throbbing wound which goaded him toward violence. His logic was once again in control of his emotions. He realized that the small 'humans', (as they called themselves) had reacted with their emotions following the death of a loved one. Kratel, unfortunately, was there to bear the brunt of their misplaced aggression. He was, after all, so close to having a working relationship with the 'Humans'.

Communication, that was the biggest downfall. What he needed was a go-between to explain to the children that the death of the large human wasn't any of Kratel's doing.

Kratel was aware of the thought patterns of the creatures he animated. Most were basic survival thoughts, Eat, Mate, Hide, Fight...and so on. Most of the creatures didn't even know they were dead. And insect thoughts were so chitinous that Kratel blocked them out totally.

Human thoughts, however, were so marvelously complex!

When Nate died that night, even though Kratel had not animated him, a link had been established between them. Once Kratel established this mental link, he could tell exactly where the body of the contact was. This ability enabled Kratel to know the location of food sources in the vast caverns underground. Kratel, therefore, knew that Nate's body had been removed to a place about fifteen miles from the house.

Kratel loosened the thong to his loincloth a bit and retrieved a scraping rock of Obsidian that he kept in his pouch to groom his fur.

"Now", he thought while running the edge of the stone along his arm, "I'll call the body of the giant human here. I can study its thought patterns while awaiting its arrival. Then I can use it to vocalize my thoughts to the children. It can tell them I had nothing to do with its death and I would like to try, one last time, for peaceful understanding before I return to the caverns." Kratel sighed as he thought of his own dwelling niche, where there would be time to digest the entire onslaught of information that he had been force-fed since he left. With the army of food he would be taking back with him, he could digest both physically and mentally for a long time.

And so decided, he sent out his tremulous call to the body of Nate, which now reposed in the Bentor and Flanders Mortuary awaiting burial service.

Nate's spirit was trying to adapt to this new existence of life on the 'other side'. He realized immediately, unlike some others, that he had died. His spirit had separated so fast from his body that even as he witnessed it falling to the ground (he couldn't exactly say 'saw' since he no longer had eyes) he was already spiraling off into a huge vortex of sounds and colors. Although that isn't exactly what he experienced either. Nate was discovering that the limitations of being able to only describe things from the viewpoint of the five senses was most difficult.

The other beings traveling the vortex with him were in various stages of conscious awareness. Some, as Nate already observed, thought they were sleeping or were disoriented and felt they would regain their bodies as soon as they 'woke up'.

Others had obviously been in the vortex for some time or they were very enlightened, having had glimpses of the other side while still in corporate form, and were better equipped to deal with life in the afterlife.

The enlightened ones attempted to console the distraught traveler who's erratic fighting of the spiral of the vortex caused tidal-like ripples of agitation to erupt in plasmic flashes imbued with the most dramatic colors and non-colors that Nate had ever seen or not seen.

Occasionally a spirit traveler would become so distraught they began a reverse spiral causing them to disappear from the vortex with a painful 'VEEE!' kind of noise, and the entire length of the vortex would go into a pulsating purple hue.

Even though Nate was unsure of his destination, he somehow felt that this 'going with the flow' was the proper way. Everything about it felt right and he seemed sure that all would eventually become clear.

Nate was passing sort of above and to the left of two beings who appeared to be enlightened ones. One was blue-green and the other a lovely rose hue. Nate contemplated spiraling over to these kindly spirits when a strange tickling-like sensation began right behind what used to be his right ear. He concentrated on the spot and soon a most distinct melody began to unfold in his mind. Now every thing he was currently experiencing had a very distinct unearthly quality to it. The 'Sights' and the 'Sounds' were not of corporal nature. But this melody was definitely Earthly. It had an undeniable physical manifestation.

Nate noticed that as he focused on the sound, his spiraling movement began to slow down. The rose-hued being also observed Nate's progress being impeded and began spiraling closer to him. It urged him to disregard the music and to rejoin the dance.

Nate wanted to do as the spirit suggested. The melody, however, was much too compelling. Something was definitely going on back on Earth and whatever it is, it involves Nate's body.

Nate placed his full attention on the music. His energy self slowed, stopped, and began a counterclockwise spiral. The other beings moved away, emitting waves of sorrow although none tried in any way to force his progress.

"I guess free will really counts here," Nate thought, as he suddenly erupted in a flash of color and the VEEE sound filled the Ether.

The vortex dissolved and Nate found himself floating in a large room directly over his ex-body. As he looked down upon himself, he saw the corpse twitch violently and then the eyes slowly opened.

Nate's metaphorical mouth opened as well, and his jaw hit the floor.

"That's impossible!" Nate thought. "You're...I mean, I'm, dead! I can't be getting up and running around like that."

After a moment's hesitation the corpse sat up. As its covering sheet slid slowly onto the checkered tile floor, it swung its legs over the edge of the gurney upon which it had been laid, proving to Nate it obviously was possible to get up and run around—because it was doing it with or without Nate's guidance.

The body scanned the room, getting its bearings and then began a stiff-legged walk toward the double doors at the room's end. "It's leaving without me! What do I do now?" Nate found that he could follow after simply by concentrating on moving in that direction. "That's a relief!" Nate thought. "I'd hate to think of spending eternity floating around in a morgue like a big fart cloud."

The doors swung open as the corpse passed through an electric eye beam and closed immediately behind it before Nate could pass through.

"Oh shit, I don't know if I have enough substance to trip an eye beam."

Nate swooped down to make sure he passed through the beam. Just as he feared, the doors remained closed. Nate reached an ectoplasmic hand toward the door handle and recoiled as if burnt as his hand passed through the solid wood.

"Of course, you Astral Asshole." Nate abused himself. "You're just like Casper the friendly fucking ghost!"

He projected himself forward and this time his entire being passed through the door. He found himself in a corridor, to the left a ramp led to an exit. Nate assumed it was probably back to where the hearses were kept. Straight ahead was a set of steps leading to the upstairs parlors and viewing rooms. And, of course, he saw his body just topping the stairs and opening the door.

"If anyone alive is up there, the screaming is going to start any second," Nate expected, "just as soon as they get a glimpse of my zombie self, risen from the grave! Or I guess that's 'graveless' since I haven't actually been buried yet."

Nate took off fast. He heard a 'glorp' sound and looked back to see an ectoplasmic version of his own head hanging in the space he just vacated. It instantly melted and fell to the floor with another glorpy sound.

"Wow!" Nate thought as he continued his chase. "I'll have to remember how I did that!"

Nate was surprised again as he topped the stairs and found the hallway full of people, none of whom were taking the slightest notice of the cadaver nonchalantly working its way through the crowd toward the exit.

Nate looked around at the gathered mourners of whoever was laying in the next room. They were all so internalized with thoughts of their own grief or greed (wondering what they stood to inherit) they were totally unaware that death was walking right in front of them.

As Nate-zombie approached the door, one of the ushers moved over to intercept.

"Surely he will recognize a cadaver even if it is walking!"

But the somber faced mortician only moved to open the door and see Necro-Nate out. Albeit not the way he should have.

"What's wrong with everyone?" Nate felt his mood growing icy. "Are we all so caught up in ourselves we can't even notice when the Macabre leers in our faces?"

He moved down the gray carpeted hall passing indiscriminately through tables, chairs and people alike. A thin layer of frosts appeared upon lampshades and suit collars. Everyone gasped as their steamy breath issued from their gaping mouths.

Nate sensed the commotion in his wake and turned back to look as a young man with hoarfrost eyebrows was shaking crystals from an elderly woman's shawl.

"Ha! I don't know how I did it but that sure brought them to full attention. Be here now!" Wasn't that something he had heard Crescent say?"

As he passed through the outer door, the mortician was still holding on to the metal handle. His stony face never changed expression as he called for some aid in removing his hand from the ice that had welded it to the door.

"All right Necro-Nate where be you?" Nate elevated his perception a bit to get a further view. "Ah, there he is walking down the sidewalk. Nate zoomed over, cautious not to drop any more ectoplasm and once again hovered over his own body.

"Say, I do look pretty good in that blue Sears suit. I only wore it out once. It would be a shame to bury something before it's at least got a little wear on it. I wonder if I can get back inside my old self and try to find out what is going on around here?"

Nate lowered his spirit form and linked back up with his physical self just like putting a piece in a puzzle. The shock was like ice water down the back, as suddenly, Nate was once again seeing and hearing and all the other senses through a physical body and not through spiritual conceptions.

"Alright, I'm back in. Let's try this baby out. Left hand, reach up and straighten my tie." Of course Nate didn't have to say it out loud like a command but his absurd humor was his way of dealing with these stressful events.

Nate's hand came up and caressed the silk of his tie. The tactile sensation was like a drug.

"O.K. so I'm back in control. There's a park across the street, if I sit undisturbed for a moment on a bench maybe I can think of what to do next."

Nate attempted to cross the street but his legs continued walking in the direction they were going when he entered his body.

"UH OH! Loss of control! Maybe I'd better just stop here a moment." Nate tried to stop the piston like pumping of his legs but to no avail.

"No go again! A little test then, I'll turn my head and stick out my tongue at that old biddy staring at me from that parked car."

As Nate passed the car, his head obediently turned and delivered a resounding raspberry to the mortified onlooker.

"All right, assessment time. I can still hear the music and I can damn well feel it in every joint of this body. Obviously that is what is animating and compelling me on. I have the ability to affect the motions of my previous body so long as I don't deviate from the course this controlling force has set. Therefore, the only logical thing to do is to sit back and enjoy the ride until I arrive at whatever destination my puppet master has planned. And with a little luck maybe it won't know that Necro-Nate is not alone in here and I can somehow throw a 'Spaniard in the works' to quote John Lennon. Say, maybe I can catch up with John after I get these physical problems in order. That is if I can figure out how to get back into the vortex".

Nate was continually amazed at the way he could just walk down the street in broad daylight and attract no attention. A car full of teenagers did drive by and yell 'Hey Gramps, get a horse!' Without thinking, Nate flipped them the bird and said something derogatory. He was immediately shocked by the hoarse (no pun intended) sound of his own voice.

He was thankful the car kept on going. He wasn't quite sure how Necro-Nate would have responded if the juveniles had attempted to impede his progress. Nate was quite sure that his destination was back home to Diana's new house. His body was making all the right turns to indicate this assumption was correct. He was fascinated by the fact that Necro never cut through anyone's yard, even if it was a more direct route. He also walked on the sidewalk and not in the street, and the really amazing thing was that he stopped for traffic lights and traffic.

"There must be some kind of muscle or cell memory that functions independently of the mind." Nate mused. "I was always cautious about traffic laws and people's property when I was alive and so I guess the memory is ingrained in the bones somehow. That might prove useful if whoever is holding the puppet strings doesn't realize he has total control."

Nate soon left the sidewalks and town behind as he continued onward on his unwavering journey. The houses became fewer and the woods thicker until eventually as he had surmised, he turned and began walking up the driveway toward home.

Night was falling, and Nate again was surprised as he walked past the house and along the side of the barn. He entered the underbrush beside the barn where he went a few yards more into the thicket and then stopped, or rather his body stopped. Nate was only along for the ride.

"What now?" Nate thought.

He was afraid to turn his head and look around the area. He didn't know if he could be seen by whatever was animating his corpse and he didn't want to give away the fact that his consciousness was still inside.

Darkness fell and Nate found himself nearly blind in the blackness of the woods.

"This waiting is driving me nuts and now I can't see a damn thing even if there were something to see. I wish I could just take off! Wait a minute? Maybe I can take off! I put this body on, I'll just take it back off for a moment and scout around."

Nate focused on his spirit self rising up from the corpse. As his conscious level left the confines of his body, he was able to perceive his surroundings in total clarity.

"Whew, that's better." Nate thought. "Now what is going on in this 'jumping spot', that old Necro was in such a hurry to get here?"

Nate surveyed the area and found a large opening in the Earth about six paces ahead of where his body had stopped. The compelling melody was emanating from there.

"Well I don't see Cerberus guarding the entrance. I wonder if I should poke my astral head in or wait a bit to see if anything comes out. I surely wasn't obliged to walk all this way just to stand here and miss my own funeral."

A flurry of movement at the tunnel entrance gave Nate pause in his consideration to enter. As he watched, a couple of field mice scurried out of the opening and darted off in the direction of the barn.

Nate realized that he had been doing the ectoplasmic equivalent to holding his breath. The relief of seeing only mice emerge was short lived as a larger, and obviously quite dead, body of a musk rat lumbered from the hole and paused by the entrance. It was soon joined by a couple of squirrels, a cat and various insects and reptiles all being road kill refugees.

The last to exit was the one Nate was waiting for. Its pale white body and fur nearly glowed in the darkness that surrounded this macabre scene. Its large eyes seemed to light up and its lips pulled back to expose sharp white canine teeth as it saw the body of Nate in the thicket.

Nate moved his etheric form back into the corpse; once again he became night blind. He didn't know how, or even if, he could harm this creature in his spiritual form, but with the element of surprise on his side he might be able to strike down this hell spawn by using his own body as a weapon.

Nate was startled to suddenly feel the touch of the creature's hand upon his arm. He nearly flinched from revulsion as sheer force of will held him immobile. The creature had closed the distance between them so quickly and quietly that Nate hadn't even detected its coming. He would only get one shot, he now knew, and it had to count.

The creature gripped his arm like steel and Nate felt a subtle change in the tune that it was intoning. The melody coursed through his veins like blood and began moving swiftly through his heart and lungs. Nate could feel the un-Earthly vibrations begin to invade his brain, rushing through synapses and cortex.

"My God!" Nate was unnerved. "It has control of my body! What is it trying to do with my brain?" Nate didn't know what Kratel was attempting, but he realized that this was his chance to strike. "Now while its full attention is on probing my skull and I know exactly where the little bastard is by its grip on my arm! Now I'll give him a taste of vengeance from beyond the grave. Die you albino maggot!"

Nate raised his unfettered arm although the blow never fell. Kratel's voice filled his head from the inside as well as falling on his ears and he realized exactly why Kratel had summoned his body from the morgue.

"Grandpa." Kratel spoke. "Sorry. I sorry I scare dead Grandpa."

Nate looked down at Kratel and finally saw him through eyes of understanding rather then eyes of fear. Kratel had been trying to communicate with us, the giants, and was unable to breech the communications gap with anyone except Jerrica and Alexander. "But now that I, Nate, am dead, Kratel is able to form a kind of mind meld. He can now channel his thoughts through my mind and translate them into English and speak through my voice."

Kratel still did not know that Nate's consciousness inhabited the body. Kratel's own mind and motives were there for Nate to see and he realized that Kratel was ready to return to his subterranean home and merely wished to communicate his peaceful intentions to the kids and possibly the older 'giants' as well.

Nate read the compassion Kratel felt over his death. He understood the fear of being thrust into an alien environment where it was "adapt or die." Nate no longer wished Kratel harm and did nothing to resist as Kratel's song compelled him to turn and walk toward the house to summon the family for Kratel's farewell message.

"And," Nate thought, "I can have the opportunity to say goodbye myself, something that very few are fortunate to be able to do."

CHAPTER 28

Sheriff Dawson opened the back door as quietly as he could while motioning the Lanes to remain inside. As he eased himself down the steps, he cautiously removed the safety latch from his gun. Even as fear knotted his gut into a braid, he continued his slow advance toward the unsuspecting group.

Kratel was the first to spot the Sheriff coming toward them. He saw the weapon in Dalton's hand and knew from contact with Nate's mind exactly what it was capable of.

Kratel stepped protectively in front of Jerrica and Alex and held his hands high in an empty-handed gesture.

"Go back into the house." Nate's raspy voice intoned. "This does not concern you. The children are in no harm."

Sheriff Dawson heard the words of the expressionless corpse and it was all he could do to keep his hand steady on the gun. As fearful as he was, there was no way he would turn tail and leave those kids to the mercy of these walking nightmares.

"Stand away from the children." The command in the Sheriffs voice made him feel better. "Kids, walk over here to me now!"

Sheriff Dawson had a dead bead on the small creature and even in the dim light he could see that neither it nor the corpse was armed.

Kratel sent a small swarm of insects before the giant's face hoping to distract him into lowering the weapon.

The arrival of the insects awakened the memory of Clem's tale in the sheriff with frigid horror. Dalton swept at the insect cloud with his left hand and once again advanced on the group; his gun sights never left Kratel.

The muskrat and squirrels moved forward within mere steps of the sheriff and stopped rigidly in his path.

Chris and Diana entered the macabre chess game and called to the children from the rear porch.

"Mom, Dad, please, everyone just wait!" Jerrica pleaded but made no move to join her parents.

Everyone remained motionless for a time as if time itself held still for the outcome of this bizarre scene.

A sudden blur and a large German Shepherd rushed from the bushes. It's massive jaws closed upon the sheriff's right knee.

Time was suddenly unleashed and everything began moving at once. Jerrica and Alex screamed and began running toward their parents who were also moving toward them across the rear lawn.

More creatures frightful and crawling began to assail the sheriff as his legs buckled and he was taken to the ground.

Kratel began backing up toward Nate in preparation of flight. Nate was the only un-moving thing on the whole lawn.

Pain was everywhere at once on Dalton's body. His right eye was full of blood, useless. He tried to stay upright but the force of the creatures along with the tendons they were severing was too much. He thumbed the hammer back on his gun and shifted to aim with his left eye even as he fell.

Kratel saw the motion and was about to turn and flee when the deafening sound of the revolver's explosion caused everything to seem to halt once more.

Dawson smiled as he fell the remainder of the way to the ground, satisfied that he had at least destroyed the thing that had killed him and plagued his community.

Alex and Jerrica had just reached their parents when the shot rang out. Once again they screamed in unison but only Jerrica was able to remove herself from her father's grasp as she rushed back toward Kratel and Grandpa.

Sheriff Dawson's marksmanship was not amiss. The magnum slug tore through the left side of Kratel's chest and out the back to go spinning off into the night. Kratel looked down momentarily at the gaping hole before his knees buckled and he collapsed to the soil.

As Kratel fell, so did the body of Grandpa. Nate's spirit was once again released to the vortex. Without Kratel, he could no longer animate the corpse. "Goodbye." He rasped as he fell. "Love you..." And then all was silent except for the sobbing children.

Diana and Chris finally got the children inside and closed the door on the brutal scene outside.

"I'll phone for the police," Chris spoke softly feeling overwhelmed and still unsure of exactly what had taken place.

"I'll make everyone some tea while we wait." Diana tried to think of what Crescent would do in this situation as she gently untangled herself from Alex and placed him on a wooden kitchen chair next to his sister.

"Jerrica?" Di asked. "You called the small creature by name and then ran to it when it was shot. What was it and how do you know it?" Diana spoke in low soothing tones while placing the tea and some herbs in a pot to simmer.

"Kratel was his name." Jerr said between sobs. "He called to me and Alex one night. He sang the most marvelous songs and dead things would get up and dance when he sang."

"He was our friend." Alex added. "But he couldn't speak very well."

"Is Kratel what Grandpa saw that frightened him into having a heart attack?" Di asked painfully.

"He didn't mean to kill Grandpa." Alex continued. "That's why he brought him back so that he could tell us himself."

"Kratel could speak our language and understand it easier through Grandpa's mind." Jerrica informed them. "He lives far from here in an underground cavern. He was just saying goodbye before going back there forever when that Cop showed up and killed him. Why did he have to kill him?"

Chris returned from the phone and joined the conversation. "He was trying to protect you and Alex at first. I'm afraid that Kratel started the actual violence by attacking him with those dead vermin."

"Kratel wasn't trying to hurt him. He was just putting things in his way to stop him." Jerrica turned to her mother. "Kratel wouldn't have hurt anyone on purpose."

The girl's sobs ended the conversation. As Diana held her close Chris put his hands on Di's shoulders and said, "The phone doesn't seem to be working. I tried the other ones in the house also, they're all dead." Chris regretted his choice of words as soon as he spoke them.

"Chris?" Diana asked. "What are we going to do? There are bodies in the back yard! No one is going to believe what happened here tonight, they'll think that we murdered the Sheriff!"

"I know, Hon. Look, the Sheriff left his car running out front. Turn off the tea and we can drive his car into town. I'll see if I can make the radio work so we can phone ahead for help. All we can do is tell the truth about what happened. Someone will have to believe us."

Diana nodded her agreement and walked to the stove still holding on to Jerrica. They walked down the hall to the foyer where Chris stood with the door open but even as they approached he slammed the heavy door shut.

"What's wrong?" Diana asked of Chris's pale face. "Isn't the car still there?"

"I looked out but I couldn't see the lights any more." Chris stammered. I thought maybe someone had driven it off but then I noticed I could still hear it running. I stepped out on the porch and peered through the darkness at the spot where the Sheriff had parked it."

"Was it moved? Is someone else here?" Di asked hopefully.

"No! It was still in the same spot. I could dimly make it out and occasionally get a glimpse of light from the headlights. Chris swallowed hard to continue. "It's covered! My God, Diana, its covered in dead bugs and animals!"

"Probably Kratel covered the lights with them before he died." Jerrica spoke again. "He couldn't stand bright light."

Diana looked hopefully to Chris for confirmation that this was the solution but all hope drained as she saw the shaking of his head.

"They're not just lying on the car, they are moving, right now as we speak."

"That's impossible! Kratel's dead!" Diana refused the concept. "There is no one to control them now. They are just bodies of animals piled up on a car."

The crash of the living room window ended all conversation as a large and very dead looking rat attempted to claw its way into the house even though it was impaled upon one of the glass slivers from the shattered window pane.

Chris jerked open the hall closet and removed their winter coats.

"Everyone hold one of these over your heads." Chris instructed. "We have to make a run for that car, it's our only chance of getting away from here."

"What if we run upstairs or to the basement and barricade ourselves in until help arrives?" Diana suggested fearing the run into the night through a writhing gauntlet of decomposing vermin. "That might be a safer move than rushing through those zombie beasts with the children."

The adjacent crash of windows throughout the house told them their home had been violated.

"I don't think we have enough time to seal off any room so bugs couldn't penetrate. And we don't have any idea as to when help will come." Chris's heart raced furiously. "We have to risk the car, Di. I'll go out first to draw their attention. Give me about thirty seconds to cross the lawn and get the doors open, then you and the kids run out. Hold onto each other real tight. If one falls the other two will drag them along until you get in the car, is that alright with you guys?"

The kids nodded their assent and Jerrica attempted a smile.

"Here I go, I'll be behind the wheel. When the last one gets in, I'm giving it the gas whether the door is closed or not, so hold on tight. I love you guys!" He quickly kissed all three as he thrust the door open and pelted toward the covered squad car.

Chris kicked small things out of his way, jumped over the larger and stepped soundly on the smallest. He felt various bodies ricochet off the heavy leather coat that protected his head. He fully understood the term 'The quick and the dead' for even though there seemed to be an army around him, they were indeed slow.

He managed to gain the car without mishap. He jerked open the door so violently, small bodies were hurled from the vehicle. He turned on the interior dome light to familiarize himself with the controls and then hit the windshield wipers in hopes of dislodging things and better perceive Diana and the kid's progress. He located and thumbed the power lock switch, which unlocked all the doors so they could use whichever they had to. Then he peered through the smeared windshield in search of his family.

Diana and the kids started across the porch as soon as she saw Chris open the car door. The children screamed as they were pummeled by a score of things hitting their coats. Diana kept a firm grip on both children as she hurried them forward as fast as they could go.

She focused her thoughts inward, ignoring the attackers upon her body when something unseen hurled itself from the rafters and struck Diana full upon the back of the head just as she was stepping off the porch onto the stairs.

She came down hard on one knee half way down the stairs and was again struck upon the side of the head by her unknown assailant. Her world went end over end as she tumbled the rest of the way down to the lawn. She had lost her hold on the children as well as she was losing her hold onto consciousness.

She fought hard with the darkness that was trying to engulf her in its consuming embrace. She knew if she succumbed, she might never awaken again. She fought for consciousness like a drowning person fights for air. The children needed her, where are the kids? She had lost her hold! She must get them to the car.

Full awareness came flooding back. She reached over her shoulders and grabbed two handfuls of fur and flung her assailant away, never knowing what kind of a creature it was. Something even larger was reaching beneath her sheltering coat and groping toward her face. She slapped violently at bare flesh and screamed as her coat was flung aside and she was grabbed painfully by the shoulders and jerked erect.

"Diana! It's me! Chris!"

Relief washed away the pain. It was Chris! He had come back for them.

"Where are the kids?" His words hit her like a bucket of ice water. "Diana, I don't see the kids! Jerrica! Alexander!" Chris called. "WHERE ARE YOU?"

Diana closed her eyes and shook her head to clear her vision. "Alex! Jerr!" She added to Chris's call but no reply came. She could see vague movement all around them as if they stood in the center of a ring that was growing ever smaller. To her dismay, none of the things she could see were her children.

"Chris! Oh Chris! I lost my hold on them! I wasn't dazed long, was I? They couldn't have gone far!" She told herself. "Where could they be?"

CHAPTER 29

When their mother was knocked from the porch, Jerr and Alex were pulled right along with her. Jerrica maintained her balance in a controlled run but Alex rolled down the stairs behind his mother, and finally stopped by the bush next to which Jerrica stood.

"My arm!" He cried. "Jerr, I hurt my arm!"

He had lost his coat in the fall. Jerrica covered Alex with her own and pulled him back into the shelter of the shrubbery in front of the porch.

"I want mom! Where's mom?" He cried.

"I don't know, Alex! It's so dark! Please quit crying; we don't want to attract anything's attention. Mom fell off the left side of the porch and we went off the right. Hold on to me real tight and we can crawl back out and find her."

"No Jerr. No!" Alex was terrified. "The dead things are out there! I can't go back."

"Alex, we have to! Mom might be hurt!" Jerrica considered the possibilities. "Do you want to wait here while I go look?"

"By myself? No way!"

"Then hang onto me and come on!"

Jerrica threw the protective coat over them once more as they crawled out of the shrubbery.

"Mom? Dad?" Alex called as they came out onto the lawn.

"Look over there by the corner of the house." Alex pointed. "There's someone standing there."

Jerrica felt something clawing its way up her leg. She managed not to scream as she kicked off the offending thing and pushed Alex in the direction of the figure.

The full moon was obscured by a thick cloud cover, which made the night pitch black. A warm wind began rising, allowing the clouds to thin as a gray haze settled over the landscape.

In this eerie partial light the kids rushed over to the person by the house. Their elation stopped short when they saw that it was neither of their parents.

"Grandpa!" Jerrica gasped. "But it can't be! You're dead! I mean Kratel's dead, and without him you're really dead! Aren't you?"

Nate held out his hands and the kids tentatively went to him. They huddled to his familiar side as he encircled them in his arms.

"Alex! Look!" Jerrica gasped. "It's Kratel. He's alive!"

Alex turned to look where his sister was pointing and there stood Kratel, not five feet from them. His chest and loincloth were covered with blood, but the bleeding appeared to have stopped.

"Please, Kratel." Jerrica implored. "Please stop attacking us with dead things. We didn't mean for you to get hurt."

"Yeah!" Alex added. "It was the sheriff that shot you, and you killed him back!" Alex began to sob again. "We wouldn't hurt you. You've got to believe us! Please make those things go away!"

"SSHHH!" Jerrica quieted Alex. "Listen, I thought I heard Mom call us!"

Nate's grip tightened on their shoulders.

"Ouch!" Jerrica moaned. "Grandpa, you're hurting us!"

"Kratel make him stop! Let us go to Mom and Dad! They might need us!"

"Don't hurt them, Kratel." Alex felt himself about to cry. "Let's all go talk to them. Kratel why don't you say something?"

"Alex, something's not right with Kratel."

"Wh...What do you mean?"

"Look at him, he's not moving. He's just standing there like one of those zombies. Like Grandpa is!"

"Jerr, I don't think he's breathing! Boo!" Alex tried weakly.

"Look, Alex! Look!" Jerrica was breathing hard. "It's another one! It's another Kratel!"

As the creature stepped into their range of vision, they saw that indeed it was of the same race as Kratel. They could also tell that it definitely was not Kratel!

This one was slightly taller although thinner of frame. It appeared to be older. Jerrica noticed a slight limp in its movements. The white fur on its chest had a more grizzled appearance. Its eyes were set closer together and they seemed to hold none of the curiosity or compassion that Kratel's did. Its loincloth was of a darker material than Kratel's and it wore two small pouches on either side rather then one large one.

Alex gulped! "I guess Kratel really is dead. And now this one is in control of him and Grandpa."

The jagged tooth sneer that crossed the creature's face told Jerrica quite clearly that it was also in control of them.

"No!" She shouted and made a move to break free. Grandpa, however, lifted them both from the ground and began a fast pace toward the woods, away from the house.

Jerrica tried to scream but Nate's arm tightly encircled her waist. She could barely draw enough air to breathe.

She squirmed to look back behind them and saw Kratel's body hastily keeping pace with the longer legged Nate. The new creature, which was now directing the show, limped along in the rear, followed by its ever-present army of dead vermin.

"At least we're moving away from Mom and Dad!" Jerrica thought. "They'll be safe from attack by these zombies. They can get help and come rescue us!"

"Unless!" She didn't like the thought that popped into her head, but she couldn't get rid of it. "Unless there are more creatures like Kratel out there. No! There just can't be!"

CHAPTER 30

Small plumes of white dust settled on the squad car as the tires crunched noisily on the gravel drive leading to Clem's house. As they pulled in behind Bing's truck, Robert and Jackson looked at each other, wondering how Sheriff Dawson had known that Bing had come from here.

Robert reached for the radio but Jackson stopped him.

"Who are you calling?"

"Sheriff Dawson. I was going to let him know we arrived and that the hardware store's truck is here."

Jackson sighed heavily. "The Sheriff knows that we're here and he probably knows that the truck is here. Lets do some investigating first and see if we can find something worth radioing in that he doesn't know."

Robert reluctantly placed the mike back in its clip on the dashboard, and opened the car door.

"Looks like all the lights in the house are on." Jackson pointed with his nightstick. "Lets go see who's home."

The officers cautiously approached the house. They had, after all, just left the scene of a probable murder and they were unsure of what they would find here.

After listening for a moment, Robert stood beside the rear door and peered into the well-lit kitchen. There was no indication, other than the lights, that anyone was home.

"Stay back and cover me." Robert instructed. "I'm going to knock." Robert tapped loudly on the window of the door. After receiving no response, he tried the knob.

"The door's unlocked." He informed Jackson. "I'll go in and check it out. Keep an eye on my back."

"Got ya!" Jackson took up stance in the doorway so he could see inside and out at the same time.

After several minutes search, Robert returned to the kitchen and holstered his gun.

"Nobody home and no apparent signs of a struggle." Robert reported. "The place is kind of a mess but it looks lived in rather than ransacked."

Officer Jackson seemed disappointed. "Let's check around the grounds before we write this place off. After all, he added, the other crime took place outside."

So saying he stepped off the porch and walked around the house. The Officers began splaying flashlight beams under the porch and in the bushes. Their diligent search, which included the barn and busted rabbit cages, turned up nothing worthy of a report.

Officer Jackson was visibly upset. After months of nothing but traffic violations and the occasional domestic squabble, here was a case he could sink his teeth into. And what happens? He gets sent away from the crime scene to check out a dilapidated farmhouse whose only crime appears to be using too much electricity to light a house no one is in!

"Look." Robert said attempting consolation. "Let's report to the Sheriff that all is clear over here. He'll probably request us back at the murder site to help wrap up things there."

Officer Jackson was still sulking.

"Tomorrow we can write our reports from our observations of two alleged crime scenes, which means we will have twice as much to report than anyone else."

Jackson brightened visibly. "You know we did discover Bing's truck here after all. And he is the alleged victim." That means that whoever lives here probably drove him over to Crescent's house, where he was attacked!"

"Or they walked over through the woods." Robert suggested. Which direction would that be from here?"

"Over this way I think?" They played their lights along the wooded edge adjacent to the barn until they discovered a small cleared path leading off into the darkness.

"Let's check it out for footprints. If we can find a clear print that matches Bing's from the crime scene then we may be on to something."

Officer Robert knelt a few feet inside the forest canopy. He moved his light slowly and ran his hand gently across the soil.

"This ground is pretty soft. We would probably do more harm than good by stumbling through here in the dark."

"I agree." Jackson nodded. "Lets go back to the car and report to Dawson. We can tell him of our deductions and request that we be allowed to follow up on our surmises at first light." Jackson turned his beam from the path and started to walk back to the car.

"Wait." Robert called. "I thought I heard something."

Jackson turned back as Robert stepped deeper into the path and probed the dark with his light.

"There it is again. Come on, just a little further in."

The path declined sharply about fifteen feet further and then took a turn to the left. Robert had paused and was listening intently as Jackson caught up to him.

"We're probably walking all over any tracks that could be used as evidence. What's that over there?" Jackson trained his light on a large tree and Robert added his to the spot. A large form had been leaning against the tree. As the lights illuminated it, it disinterred itself from the bark and moved toward the officers with a shambling gate.

Both men were shocked to see someone out in the woods and stood dumbfounded as the figure moved within a few feet of them.

"Are you guys gonna help me or are you just gonna stand there with your lights in my eyes and your chins on the ground?"

The officers blinked in embarrassment and then Robert went forward as Jackson held the much-needed light.

"Who are you?" Robert asked, helping the injured man up the path. "What happened?"

"Name's Clem." The man spoke while biting pain back as they continued to move. "This is my place." He paused for a moment considering how much of the story he should relate. "Damn Bobcat attacked me."

Clem had been using a tree limb as a makeshift crutch. He dropped it as the officer draped his good arm across his shoulders for support. Clem had used his belt and a smaller stick to tie a tourniquet around his injured wrist. He winced as the brush moved across it as they entered the clearing by the barn.

"Go look in the cabinet above the sink." Clem instructed Jackson. "There's a bottle of whiskey there."

"We need to get you to the hospital right away, Clem." Jackson protested.

Clem reached across Robert's shoulders and grabbed him by his right arm in a grip that meant business.

"I just walked my ass out of miles of woods with my hand tore clean off. I think I got time and earned a snort before we go. Please?" He added as an afterthought.

Jackson nodded and Clem released him. "Get him to the car. Robert." He acquiesced. "I'll get the bottle and catch up with you. "But just one shot, Clem!" He added trying to regain authority of the situation.

Robert leaned Clem against the car and took a couple of breaths before opening the rear door. Clem was no lightweight and Robert was winded by carrying him.

Jackson showed up with the bottle just as Clem sat down heavily on the seat. Clem took a healthy pull from the bottle and then handed it back to Jackson.

"Thanks. There have been times I thought I needed a drink before. But I do believe this time takes the cake."

Officer Robert helped Clem swing his legs in, then turned back to Jackson.

"Radio ahead that were bringing him in. I'll ride in the back in case the tourniquet needs adjusting."

Jackson shut the door and then hurried around the vehicle and climbed in the driver's side. He hit the lights and siren as he turned around in the yard. He had the radio mike in hand as they hit the pavement of the road.

"Unit five to base. Unit five to base. Priority call. Over." He released the button as he navigated the curvy road using as much speed as he dared.

After a couple of seconds of static he hit the mike again and repeated the call.

"What's up with the radio?" Robert asked, leaning over the seat.

"Don't know? Maybe the desk Sarge is taking a leak. I'll radio the hospital direct so they know we're coming."

He called the hospital and again there was no answer. "Maybe the Damn radio's busted? I can't seem to raise anybody. How's our boy doing?"

"He nearly passed out on that last turn. His pulse is steady though. I'd say he's tough enough to make it if we can get him some medical treatment soon."

"Tougher than you candy asses." Clem spoke up. "I thought you was gonna piss yourselves when I came up out of the woods."

The radio finally came to life before either of the officers could respond to Clem's jibe. "Unit five, Doctor Sandlor here, I've only got a second. All Hell's broken loose, all over town. What have you got?"

Officer Jackson was shocked by the disregard of radio protocol. He would have this person on the carpet just as soon as the emergency was over.

"Unit five to Hospital base. We have a Caucasian male, about forty-five years of age, arm severed at the wrist, presumably due to an animal attack. Our E.T.A. is approximately ten minutes, Over."

"Try to keep him conscious and the bleeding under control. Sign him in at the emergency desk and I'll get to him as soon as I can. I'm signing off now."

"Wait! Doctor!" Jackson yelled into the useless mike.

"What the Hell was that all about?" Robert asked as the radio once more lapsed into silence.

"Must be some calamity like an explosion at the chemical plant or a bad traffic pileup? A lot of people must be hurt if we have to put this guy in line. That still doesn't explain why we can't raise dispatch I'll…Shit!"

Robert grabbed Clem as the car suddenly power braked and began a sideways swerve. He heard the sickening impact as the rear quarter panel struck something. Jackson tried to correct the skid but the car fishtailed and spun around onto the shoulder facing the opposite direction they were traveling in before coming to a stop.

"Everybody alright back there?" Jackson asked. He had hit his head on the door window and was a little woozy himself.

"I'm O.K." Robert responded. "You still with us Clem?"

Clem's bravado seemed to have drained away along with the color in his face. He grimaced in pain as he attempted to regain a sitting position after having slid across the seat.

"I'm fine, except there's no feeling in my right hand. Shit, just get us out of here fast."

Jackson turned on the interior dome light and undid his seat belt. The goose egg on his forehead was obvious as he turned around to talk to Robert.

"I have to go check outside first. There was a woman standing right in the road. She didn't even try to move"

"No!" The veins in Clem's neck stood out from the exertion of him grabbing the back of the seat. "You can't go out there. You don't know what's going on. You've got to get us out of here now!"

Robert tried to calm Clem, fearing that he was slipping into shock.

"We have to check. She's probably hurt and needs medical attention like you. We can't just leave her. She could die."

"I saw her just before the car swerved." Clem's voice was hollow. "She was already dead." Clem swallowed hard wishing for another drink. "I wasn't alone out there in the woods. Bing from the hardware store and my dogs were with me. It wasn't just a Bobcat that attacked. It was a dead Bobcat and hundreds of other crawlin' and flyin' vermin. They were all over us and they were all dead, just like her!"

Jackson and Robert looked at each other, wondering if Clem was becoming delirious.

"She's out there, waiting for us to get out of the car. And she's not alone you can bet your candy cop ass on that. If they kill you, then you can become a zombie just like they are."

"Clem, I know my duty." Jackson opened the door as he spoke. "I'll assess the situation and be right back." He said to Robert.

"At least close the door." Clem yelled and then sat back with a sigh as the door thunked shut.

"Clem, listen to me." Again Robert attempted to console his agitated passenger. "You've lost a lot of blood and are probably in shock. Your mind can play tricks on you during traumatic times." Robert thought of getting Clem another drink but decided against it. "Try to relax and force yourself to be rational."

"There are no such things as zombies, people, animals or otherwise. A wild animal attacked you and Bing, and your mind is refusing to accept the loss of your hand. We will be at the Hospital soon and the Doctors will fix you up good as new. You've got to hang in there with me buddy. Okay?"

Before Clem could answer, Officer Jackson's scream split the night. It was immediately followed by shots from his revolver. The car rocked as Jackson fell heavily across the hood while trying desperately to dislodge what looked like a squirrel from his shoulder. He was kicking at some thing that was out of Robert's range of vision, beneath the car.

"Jesus!" Robert exclaimed and reached for the door handle. Before he could open it, the figure of a woman in a torn housedress slammed her fists into the glass attempting to break in.

Her hands slid down the door reaching for the handle. Clem, however, was faster and reached across Robert and slammed down the lock button. The woman resumed pounding on the glass and then started for the front door through which Jackson had left the car.

This time Robert moved. Diving headfirst over the seat, he hit the power lock button and locked all the doors at once. He stared in horror at the woman who had obviously been dead for some time.

He could see bone showing through her forehead and another sticking out of her left arm through a tear in her dress. Her left eye and many teeth were missing. None of these severities seemed to decrease her fervor of attempting to batter her way into the automobile.

"Where's Jackson? Clem did you see where Jackson went?" Robert looked frantically through the windshield into the dark night.

"He's gone. He got that thing off of his shoulder and then ran off down the road like the devil himself was on his heels. And maybe he was." Clem added as an afterthought.

Robert had managed to get his legs swung around under the dashboard and pulled the shift lever down into drive.

"Hold on Clem. We're getting out of here." Robert hit the gas pedal but the tires spun in the soft earth of the shoulder gaining no traction. The woman corpse, seeing that her prey was attempting to escape, redoubled her efforts to shatter the glass.

As she pummeled and rocked the car, she was joined by a score of dead and decomposing animals that threw themselves at the vehicle disregarding any damage that was afflicted upon them in the process.

Clem felt on the verge of losing consciousness. The pain, combined with the fear of all those things hitting the car, was more then a sane mind could bear. Abruptly the car leaped as a wheel found purchase. As it spun its wheels and lurched forward, the car and its obscene horde were, once again, on the pavement.

Robert stomped the gas and cut the wheel hard. The tires screamed in protest as the car did a donut in the middle of the road. Bodies and parts were flung into the night by the force of the turn. Rob straightened the wheel as the car came around to face the direction they had been previously heading.

The woman held on as long as she could as the vehicle burned rubber. She finally lost her grip on the side mirror and the car bumped sickeningly as she fell beneath the rear wheel.

Robert stopped the car a few yards down the road and shined its powerful spotlight back and forth in every direction. There was no sign of Officer Jackson anywhere.

"He's gone." Robert said resignedly to the fact. "No telling where he left the road."

"You sure as Hell ain't considering going out and looking for him, are you?"

"No, my first duty is to get you to safety. If Officer Jackson managed to escape, then I'll find him when I come back with help."

The car began to smoothly move forward once again. Clem leaned back and tried to relax and prayed that the rest of the trip would be uneventful. He was trying to ignore the intense pain of his severed arm. He heard a scraping sound against the rear glass. His throat locked as he imagined his own hand clinging to the rear of the car, trying to get in to squeeze the life from the rest of his body that they could be rejoined as a whole zombie. He glanced back, his need to see conquering his enervating fear. His stomach flipped, albeit in relief, as he stared into the face of a large bat clinging to the outside of the rear window.

He faced forward again and observed the white-knuckle grip Robert had on the steering wheel as he navigated the dark road. Clem closed his eyes, thinking that this was the longest night he had ever seen.

Jackson saw the body lying across the road opposite from where the car had stopped. He hurried over and knelt beside the woman and started to check for a pulse when his flashlight illuminated her face. He nearly gagged. This corpse had been dead for some time. The skin was mottled and decomposing. "Who in the world would be sick enough to stand something like this up in the middle of the road?" He asked the night.

The corpse's hand came up and slapped the light from Jackson's hand before he thought to react. It sat up and reached for him with grisly fingers. He stepped back to run for the car when something the size of a small dog attached itself to his leg. He kicked it away and was off balance as a squirrel hurled itself from a high branch and sent him tumbling backwards where he fell back onto the road.

He grabbed at the squirrel that was ripping into his flesh but before he could dislodge it, the woman's corpse dropped full upon him, filling his lungs with its fetid stench as it clawed for his eyes.

He screamed and rolled over, tossing the creature off. He rose to a kneeling position and fired point blank into the back of the prone aberration. Without waiting to discover the effect the bullets had, he rushed back for the safety of the car while still trying to dislodge the squirrel.

With great effort he removed the tenacious rodent from his shoulder. He also removed flesh and hair of his own along with it. His freedom was short lived as the creature on the ground grappled with his legs. He lost his balance again and slammed down hard upon the hood of the car.

Jackson kicked out with both feet, and sent the dog-thing back across the road. He rolled across the hood of the car and fell panting on the other side.

The flashlight that had been knocked from his hand had come to rest at the cars rear tire. The beam projected beneath the car. To Officer Jackson's horror, it illuminated several pair of feral eyes and gaping mauls that were moving in dead silence toward where he lay.

He didn't scream again, there was no use. All of his breath would be needed to either escape or fight. He saw the she-zombie beating against the car windows and realized that he could never make it inside the vehicle without several of the creatures entering also.

He leaped up and crushed the skull of something beneath his heel as his right ear was torn by a shadow that flew off before he recognized it. He spun with the blow and began running down the road. Unsure of the direction he was taking except that it was hopefully away, he ran. He had run every day of his life for the past sixteen years. He had always enjoyed running. Sometimes he ran on a track, other times on the street or through the park. Where wasn't important, only the running mattered.

It was never as important as it was now though. He ran as if his life depended on it, for it did. A large bird, owl or crow, appeared as if out of nowhere right before him. It slashed with wings and talons. Jackson covered his eyes and lowered his head and ran harder. His flailing right arm connected with a wing with a satisfying snap. He left his assailant floundering on the ground.

He was still moving, but not unscathed. The bird had opened a wound across his forehead and the blood mingled with the sweat of his exertion. He wiped the blood from his eyes as he fought off more attackers. They were clawing at his face and body from all directions.

He stopped, not knowing which way to turn and realized that he had left the road somewhere back. He had been fighting off tree branches that were snagging him as he ran.

He tried to quiet his own gasping breath to listen for sounds of approach. No sounds came to his ears, not the night calls of birds or crickets, nothing. Wait, there was something. Far away on the very fringe of hearing, a melody, familiar, frightening, compelling. It made his skin crawl, as it seemed to pull at his hair and teeth.

Wiping the blood once more from his eyes and covering his ears, Jackson began picking his way through the undergrowth.

A sense of direction was never something Jackson could brag about. As lost as he ever had been, he continued to move. The pain in his leg wound vied for attention against the one on his shoulder and face.

A steep incline finally gave way to a set of railroad tracks. Jackson had no idea which direction town lay so he began jogging between the rails in the way that seemed to slope downward.

His night vision was bad. Tripping continuously over roots and stones let Jackson know just how blind he was though the thinning clouds allowed the moon to lighten the landscape occasionally. Jackson lost track of the number of times he had fallen.

The last stumble, however, brought him up against a chain link gate. He must have gotten off of the main line and onto a spur track. The chained gate meant a factory of some sort that received and transported by way of rail.

Pulling and squeezing between the junction of the gates, Jackson finally managed to slide through even though he left some of his uniform behind on the twisted wire mesh.

The loading dock doors were down and no workers were visible as he approached the building the tracks had led him to. Rattling and pounding and ringing the bell brought no security guard to inspect the ruckus.

Sitting down on the dock, he rested his head in his hands. He was amazed to find that he was still holding onto his gun. After a few minutes his breathing was back to almost normal. He inspected his wounds as best he could and found nothing too severe. Of course if one of the creatures had opened an artery he would have been dead in the woods from blood loss by now.

The rattle of the gate brought his attention back to the situation at hand. He strained his eyes against the darkness and detected movement. Something was making its way up the spur line. A few poorly placed and shielded bulbs lighted the loading dock. Unfortunately they didn't cast a light very far away from the building itself. Actually, Officer Jackson was more visible to anyone else then they to him. He didn't care though. He found comfort in the light that surrounded him. At least anything would have to come into the light to get at him.

Finally he was able to make out what at first he took to be several children, walking along the rails. But as they neared the light's periphery his mind reeled. Two creatures, right out of a Tolkien novel, stood shielding their eyes against the minimal glare of the lights.

The song that Jackson had been ignoring began to rise with new strength. Realization dawned that the creatures were using this melody to control the action of the dead animals that attacked him. He could see more forms coming down the spur to join them. These things did not walk upright, however.

Jackson shook his head to clear his eyes. Was his vision failing totally? It seemed to be getting darker. Turning toward the nearest lamp, Jackson saw that it was swarming with insects. Not swarming in the way like moths and such flit around a bulb. These bugs were climbing right onto the bulb and clinging there even against its searing heat.

As the darkness encroached so too did the Gremlin-like creatures. Jackson realized he had to find a way into the building. In a sudden motion he fired his gun at the nearest Goblin and leaped to his feet. Before running around the side of the building, he looked back and saw the one creature leaning over the prone form of the other.

The knowledge of their vulnerability leant courage to his heart. He stopped his retreat and attempted to draw a bead on the creature still standing. The click of the empty chamber dropped his heart to his feet as he met the gaze of the remaining Ghoul and saw his own death wished for in those malicious eyes.

He thumbed open the barrel and dropped the spent cartridges on the ground as he ran. He reloaded in flight. The creature's malevolent gaze had robbed him of his nerve to stand there and reload and attempt to fire on the creature before its minions ripped him to shreds.

The side of the building contained no openings at all. No windows adorned its featureless expanse. A fox rushed up behind as

Jackson made for the building front. He stopped, turned, and fired two shots. The beast was flung back by the force. The first took off part of its skull; the second shattered its front shoulder.

Silently, the fox righted itself and began its attack anew except with a three-legged gait and only one eye. Jackson had already begun running. It appeared he could easily outrun his adversary and its hoard but they were tireless as well as relentless. Already this new exertion was wearing Jackson down even though he had taken a rest on the docks.

Weariness caused him to stumble as he rounded the building's edge but he maintained his footing and rushed to the door placed a few feet in from the edge. He pointed his gun at the shrubbery that grew on either side of the door but evidently nothing had beaten him to this spot to hide there.

He considered trying his key ring on the lock but the return of the fox and a few other tattered beasts made haste a prime directive. Shielding his eyes with his hand, he fired point blank into the one lock on the door.

Hot metal stung his protecting hand and the sound had nearly deafened him. He grabbed the twisted knob, oblivious to the bite of metal through his palm. The door budged half an inch and then hung on the partially shattered throw of the lock mechanism.

Jackson released the knob and with a bellow of rage kicked out at the door with all his remaining strength. The bolt snapped and Jackson flung himself through the aperture. Slamming the door behind himself, he felt the force of small bodies crashing into the now unlocked and unlockable door.

The darkness of the room was absolute. Jackson knew if he released the door to search for a light switch or piece of furniture to block the door, several of the beasts would be able to force their way in.

Turning his body around, Jackson placed his palms against the door and extended his legs into the room as far as possible. On the third swipe his foot encountered something solid about three feet to the left. Standing back upright, he placed his left foot at the base of the door and leaned over in the direction of the object. He waited until the pause between attacks on the door to take one hurried step in that direction. Grasping hands found the arm of a solid wooden chair, which he thankfully hauled over and firmly placed against the abused door.

Hoping the chair would momentarily hold, the frantic officer began blindly searching the walls until finally coming up with a light switch. The light seared his eyes as the room illuminated. Blinded by the light, this time, he threw himself back toward the chair and felt it had indeed been pushed open ever so slightly. Thrusting the door closed again, he squinted against the glare and found the desk that stood in the center of this reception room/office. Soon the desk added its weight to the chair as well as a potted plant and other furnishings.

The commonplace surroundings helped clear his mind and allow him to think. Phone! It was probably among the things that fell from the desk when he pushed it across the floor. Shaking hands pulled the receiver from the littered floor only to find silence. No dial tone sounded from the earpiece. Tracing the cord back, he found it had been pulled from the wall when the desk moved.

A business this size would have to have more than one phone! Forcing himself to calmly look around and assess the room was a real measure of control. Jackson didn't recognize the office and had no idea where he was. There were three doors from the room, which was about fifteen by twenty feet in dimension. It had normal office accoutrements. On the desk sat a computer, printer, and copier. There was a sofa over where the chair had been. Jackson stood and walked over to the door on the side by the sofa. If it was an adjoining office, it would have a phone.

Cautiously opening the door, he reached in and flipped the light switch. The face that stared back at him as he peered in was ghastly. It took a moment to realize this room was a restroom and the face in the mirror was his own.

Never in his life had he been this filthy. His face and hair were matted with dried blood and grease. His clothes were torn and ruined. He looked much like a zombie himself, with his face so pale. He quickly took his own pulse to make sure he was still among the living.

A thudding crash brought him out of his reverie. Rushing back into the office, he expected to find the door being forced but the attacks seemed to have subsided. Again came the clamorous thud.

This time, he realized it was coming from the area outside the third and untried door.

Maybe he was wrong about the place being empty. Or maybe a night shift had finally arrived. Still he retrieved his gun and reloaded before opening the door. The crash and thump came again as if people were moving large crates about. Walking over to the door he straightened what was left of his tie and cautiously turned the knob. Outside the office was a large hallway that led to the main confines of the building. The shapes, which were moving down the hall, caused Officer Jackson to break into laughter.

He closed the door, walked over, and sat down in the pile of papers and trays that had fallen from the desk. He lifted one from the floor and he rocked again with laughter as he read the letterhead. Now he knew where he was, and the reason for the Spur line, he was at the stockyard. The building he was in was the main slaughterhouse.

His nerveless fingers dropped the gun. Tears from hysterical laughter glazed over his eyes as he fumbled to retrieve it. Frantic fingers closed on a familiar object, but it was not the gun. He wiped his vision clear on his shirt tale and read the backward lettering on the rubber stamp.

"File closed." Officer Jackson spoke, his voice sounding far away. "File closed." He repeated.

He was still saying it when the hall door caved in.

CHAPTER 31

Chris and Diana stood very still, holding each other close. They listened for any sounds their children might make but nothing came to their straining ears. The whole world seemed to be holding its breath at this moment. There was absolute silence. "At least the attack seems to have subsided," Chris thought.

Diana carefully removed the protective coat from their heads and peered all around them into the darkness.

Vague shapes were visible all around them, even on the porch. Although none of them were moving, as yet, occasional crashes from inside the house told them that whatever had possessed the dead creatures to move was still active. They watched, mesmerized, as one by one the lights in the house were extinguished, either by something large enough to shatter the lamps and bulbs or by the wiring being chewed through.

"What do we do now Chris?" Diana asked as quietly as she could. "What do they want?"

"I don't know Di. But the next move seems to be theirs. I guess we just wait a moment longer."

"But the kids?" Diana's voice was desperate.

"We don't know where they are." Chris said bluntly. "Any direction we would run in could lead us further from them."

"Something's moving over there!" Diana nodded her head to indicate direction. "See Chris? It's coming closer."

Chris and Diana watched as the creature approached. It looked like the one the Sheriff had shot in the back yard. Although no wound or blood was evident.

"Over there, Di. By the sidewalk." Chris pointed. "There's another one."

"How many of those things are there? What are they?"

"That last one to arrive looks to be female. I guess it's possible for an entire colony of these things to exist." Chris shrugged his shoulders in the darkness. "But what they are and what they want is beyond me."

Four more of the beings stepped from the shadows and joined the ones that confronted Chris and Di. Chris felt himself awestruck at the sight, and then the unearthly creatures began to speak amongst themselves.

It was like nothing he or Diana had ever heard before. It had to be a language because of the way they gestured and waited for one to finish before another started. But such a melodic language as no one had ever heard before.

"Chris, they're talking to each other. How do they make those sounds? What are they saying? It's so frighteningly beautiful."

"They're speaking in polyphonics."

"You know that language? You can understand them?" Diana's voice sounded so dull by comparison that she could only speak in a whisper.

"No, I'm afraid I don't understand them." Chris explained. "Polyphonics isn't a language. It's playing, or in this case, speaking more than one sound or note at a time. We speak in monophonic, that is, one sound right after another in a linear fashion, because we only have one set of vocal chords. We are physically incapable of talking like that."

"How many vocal chords do they have?"

"I can hear at least three. Of course they may have more they're not using or some may operate on a higher frequency than we can hear so it's difficult to say."

"Well I don't care how many they have! If we don't get the kids back soon, I'll start pulling their vocal chords out through their noses!"

Diana's shout caused the conversation to cease. Chris thought it just as well for the debate seemed to be becoming overheated and Di and he were the main topic.

The female of the group turned from the others and slowly approached Diana. Her loincloth and belt pouches were similar to the others. Her hips, although small, were definitely rounder and her breasts were full and also covered with the fine white hair that adorned all of their bodies.

She spoke something in her melodious tongue and lightly ran her hand along Diana's bare, smooth arm.

Chris was proud of Diana in that she did not flinch from the touch. And he was even more surprised when she returned the gesture by caressing the furry arm of the female.

The She-creature quickly returned to the others and the heated debate began anew. With everyone talking at once it sounded as if Beethoven, Brahms and Mozart were having dueling orchestras all play different songs at the same time.

Finally, one of the males raised his voice above the rest and reached out and slapped another male hard in the face. Chris winced at the force of the blow and was amazed that the creature had remained erect.

This, however, ended the confrontation. The female moved over to the side of the one that had been struck and placed her arms around his shoulders. Then they walked off into the dark without a backward glance. One of the others said something and likewise walked away. Several of the dead animals moved off into the underbrush following in the direction of the departed creatures.

"This doesn't look good." Di said. "I think the ones that might have been on our side were just outvoted."

As the remaining creatures began to lift their voices in song, rather than conversation, Chris had to agree. For the dead animals and insects that stayed behind, began once more to arise. This time they were moving closer toward Diana and Chris rather than away.

"Do you have your keys?" Chris asked.

"Yes, in my pocket, why?"

"I'm going to rush our little friends here. I don't think they'll be expecting that. I want you to run to the studio. It has only one

253

door and is sealed pretty tight. The phone is on a separate line as well as the lights. Call for help as soon as you're locked in."

"I'm not leaving you out here alone!" Diana was appalled at the thought.

"It's not just me and you, Honey, it's also the kids and everyone else in the community." A snake darted in and Chris ground its head beneath his heel.

"No time to argue; if I can make it over after you're inside, you can open the door and let me in behind you. But call the cops first!"

Chris tensed to make his leap over the first line of animals when all motion stopped. The white furred creatures were looking puzzled and distracted. They were turning their heads back and forth, their ears perked up and twitching. They seemed to have forgotten about Diana and Chris as they tried to pinpoint the sound of something that was beyond Chris's hearing.

Diana tugged on Chris's sleeve.

"Come on, we can both make a run for the studio while they're distracted."

"Wait, I hear it, listen. I can almost make it out."

Diana listened and a strand of music came onto the very periphery of her ears but not the kind of music the creatures made.

"Di!" Chris yelled. "It's R.E.M. it's R.E. fucking M."

Creatures and humans alike stared up the drive as the music grew to a roar. Screaming around the last bend of the drive and finally in full sight came a large four-wheel drive muscle truck. Its roll bar blazing with a row of halogen floods and the stereo cranked as the words pelted the creatures with agonizing volume.

"It's the end of the world as we know it and I feel fine."

Chris sang along while waving his arms to attract the attention of the driver as the creatures literally fell over themselves trying to escape. They couldn't shield both their eyes and ears from the dual onslaught.

The carrion army was abandoned as the creatures madly sought escape. The one that had struck the other of its kind became so totally disoriented that it fled directly into the path of the oncoming behemoth truck. It disappeared beneath the oversized tires as well as did all the carcasses that were in the trucks way.

Chris and Diana stood awash in the brilliant glare as the vehicle stopped just feet from them. The driver door kicked open and a man older than Chris would have imagined their savior to look like yelled for them to get in over the din of the speakers.

They hurried over to the passenger side. Chris had to reach up for the door handle, then help Di climb up and in.

"Thanks." Chris yelled. "Who are you?"

"To paraphrase Rambo, 'I'm your best fucking wet dream.' My name's Bill. The editor of our local paper. I've been tracking these little beasties for a while and the trail led me here, luckily for you two from the looks of it. You guys okay?"

"Our Children." Diana put her hand on Bills arm. "Those things have our Children."

Bill felt her eyes burning into him seeking knowledge of the kids.

"It's getting late. If those things have your kids and they are still alive, there's only one place I know of where they would take them before the sun comes up. And that's not a good thing." Bill added.

"Can you turn that music down?" Diana asked. "I can hardly think."

"Sorry." Bill said reaching for the volume control. "It seems safe enough for the moment. These Creatures come from underground; they can't abide bright light or loud noise. Breaks their concentration and they can't focus to control their zombies."

"If you think you know where the kids might be, then lets go." Chris's voice sounded weak after the blaring music. "Like you say, the sun will be up soon. If they're headed back underground then we've got to reach them before they descend."

"Exactly." Bill concurred. "But if we go in blazing like I just did, then they're going to scatter the way they did now. The ones that got away will have had time to warn the others so we won't catch them off guard this time. And I'm not really sure what the distance is that they can control their dead animal buddies. They might just hide out of sight and sound of my truck and send their goons to bump us off."

"Well we've got to do something!" Diana was shaking with frustration.

"We will, Love." Chris stroked his wife's hand. "I've got an idea. Bill, would you drive across the yard to the building over there? I need to pick up a few things."

"What do you have in your studio that can help?" Di asked.

"No time to explain. Bill? Are you willing to go after those things once more?"

For the kids? Hell, yes! I haven't left a story unfinished yet." So saying, he popped the clutch and the truck shot over to the building in what felt, to Diana, like one giant leap.

"How long will you be?" Diana asked as Chris lowered himself from the truck.

"Ten maybe fifteen minutes max."

"Alright we'll be back for you by then. I need some things too."

"But…" Chris started to complain.

"No time. Be right back." She closed the door on his protest and turned to Bill. "Drive us back onto the road."

Bill didn't even attempt to argue. He wasn't about to interfere with a lion fighting for her cubs. "Tell me where to turn," was all he said.

When Chris opened the door and handed out the first case, the truck was waiting for him.

"Pile all this stuff in the back," he instructed. "I'll ride back there and hook it up as you drive us to the spot."

Bill and Di loaded everything Chris handed them, then they all climbed in as the big truck once more took to the road. They had traveled only a few short miles when Bill left the road, cut across farmland on a worn dirt path. He took what looked to be a fire trail into the woods, then stopped and shut off the engine and lights. He and Diana climbed from the cab and walked around to the tailgate. Chris was in the back furiously connecting cables to various gear.

He looked up from his labors and said "Done. Are we there?"

"Almost." Bill answered. "A few yards up that trail and through the woods will bring us to an abandoned limestone quarry. That's the place I think these little demons came up from. Their hearing is very acute so we better not take the truck any closer. Now do you care to tell us what you have in mind?"

"I think I can reproduce the vocal tones these creatures use to direct the actions of the dead. I've brought along a Synthesizer and a digital sampler that can be operated by those battery packs. I may not be able to properly combine the tones to manipulate anything into fighting back for us but I'm betting that I can confuse the creature's vibrational frequencies enough so they can't attack us either."

"Sounds close enough to a fair fight to me." Bill nodded. "I've got a high powered flashlight and a forty-five magnum under the seat. If you can stop the zombies, we can put the hurt to the creatures and hopefully get everyone, including the kids, back to Big Ethyl here and hightail it to town."

"There's just one more small problem." Chris's voice fell like lead. "I have to get a clear sample of one of the creature's voice while it's animating a corpse."

"Excuse me? Could you run that by me again?"

"I need a digital recording of the vocal pattern so I can make a looped sample and play it back through my synthesizer keyboard. What we have to do is get this wireless microphone within say ten to twelve feet of one of the creatures while its animating something. Thirty seconds of sound is probably all I'll need." Chris said, defending his idea against Bill's dumbfounded expression.

"Give me the mike." Diana extended her hand. "I'll get as close as I can."

"No, Diana, I was going to do it." Chris ignored her outreach and held the mike away.

"What? You're going to sneak within a couple of feet of something that can probably hear a mouse piss on a cotton ball at thirty feet all the while dragging all your stuff along while tweaking knobs and watching meters?" Diana's statement of reality made Chris feels stupid.

"What kind of range does this mike have?" Di asked taking the metallic wand in her hand.

"About fifty feet."

"Good." Di said. "You follow about fifty feet behind me. When you get the signal and loop it, then come in shooting and get me back out."

"Here's a headphone set." Chris placed it on Diana's head and over her ears. "It has a microphone built in. When you get in position, point the wireless at the creature's head and whisper 'go' into the headphone. I'll start recording then. If it takes, we'll come running. If not, we can try again. Make sure when you say 'go' that the voice the creature is using is animating and not just conversing with another of its kind."

"Would you like the gun or flashlight?" Bill offered.

"No thank you." Di refused. "What I do need is a few moments alone to prepare for this ordeal. I'm going into the woods a few yards ahead. When I'm ready to proceed, I'll contact you on the headset, then you can back me up until we get the recording."

Chris held her for a moment in his arms and kissed her deeply. "Be very careful, Babe. I love you."

"Love you too!" She returned. "Just do your Magick after I do mine. Take care of him Bill." She said and walked off into the darkness.

"That's one tough lady you've got there." Bill said to Chris. "Now what do I need to do?"

"You can carry the keyboard and a battery pack. I'll take the wireless controller and the sampler. You'll have to be my eyes while I focus on the sound gear. We may only get one shot at this and we've got to get it right."

Diana found a small clearing off the path and sat down to make her preparations there. A faerie ring of moss was growing by a large tree, which seemed to be the perfect choice.

She emptied the contents of the bag she and Bill had collected from Crescent's rain shed while Chris prepared his equipment. She took the moonstone from the ground where it lay and placed it in her lap. She emptied her mind and began the grounding process Crescent had taught her. She focused her awareness down into the stone and through it into the Earth beneath her. Outside awareness ceased as she became connected to the soil and followed the path of the mighty tree roots that fingered ever downward. From her lower Chakra she then projected upward through her crown. She placed a clear quartz crystal atop her head and fed her energies through it in a white light spear that penetrated and connected her to the cosmic heavens above.

She poised there in the Dagazian moment, suspended in time and space. As above, so below. She saw all aspects of her life revolving around her, connected to her being by shimmering threads of light. All things were spinning there, from her husband and children to the new washer and dryer they just purchased. She released the light from those things that no longer applied to her life as she strengthened and reaffirmed her connectedness to those that truly mattered at this point.

She lifted a gold-banded ring with a Bloodstone set. This she placed upon her left hand next to her wedding band. A large, uncut piece of raw Bloodstone was placed in her lap next to the Moonstone. She opened a small vial of Heliotrope oil that she and Crescent had prepared earlier. She then anointed the ring and the stone with the oil. Grasping the Bloodstone in her left hand she dipped her finger into the oil and drew a pentagram upon her forehead: the five points of the star representing Earth, Air, Fire, Water, and Spirit. She connected the points and encircled them upon her skin, focusing all the aspects of the elements to work in harmony with and through her.

Harmony was the perfection she was attaining through this ritual. She willed herself to become one with all of nature: the trees and the earth, the wind and starlight. She would dazzle the eye of any who attempted to perceive her, for now she was not someone passing through the land but a fully integrated part of the whole. She walked in ceremony, embracing her environment. She was as indistinguishable as one leaf amongst the Oak branches.

"Blessed Goddess, let my Will be wrought this night that I may safely turn my family and self away from this abominable situation. I call upon Tiwaz for protection and justice." She made the upward pointing spear symbol in the air with the Bloodstone. "I call upon Thurisaz for strength of arm to defeat my foe." As she traced the thorn symbol, the Bloodstone left a fiery trace in the air. "Finally I ask Ansuz for Woden's wisdom to lead us to understanding rather than conflict." She stood in one graceful, fluid motion with arms held to the sky. "An it harm none, this be my will to do. So mote it be!"

She had removed the headset while she performed her preparations. As she began to move through the brush the very limbs and thorns turned from her as she flowed like a shadow of the wind.

"Chris!" Diana's voice came strongly through his earphones. "Let's go get our kids!"

"She's moving, Bill. It's show time."

Diana crested the ridge of the old quarry and looked down into its depths. Her vision seemed sharper than before and she saw several figures clambering upon the quarried stones that were piled up like a giant's block set. She could see the pathways leading down seeming to swarm and ripple as hundreds of dead animals and insects were being forced to move down into the Earth's bowels.

She let herself down over the edge, using roots and stones for foot holds. She didn't seem to need to search for her next purchase. She let the turn of a stone or the twist of a branch guide her ever-downward progress.

A skittering movement she caught out of the corner of her eye caused her to pause when she was a little over halfway down. She released the sassafras root she was clinging to and dropped noiselessly onto a flat outcropping of limestone.

The small groundhog was scrambling up the hill trying to get out of the path of the downward moving dead. Diana leaned over, lifting it by the scruff of the neck. Gently, she sat it on the flat stone behind her. A large crack split the face of the stone she was on and she saw the downward path passed directly in front of it. She lowered herself into the crack and continued downward by bracing her back against one side and her legs on the other.

Sitting there, suspended in the crack of the rock wall, she was mere feet away from the shambling vermin. She heard the singing of the creature as it finally came along behind its cadaverous puppets. As the vocals increased she knew the thing was nearly in sight.

"Go". She spoke into the headset and extended the mike as far as she could into the pathway. The creature came into view but it was walking way too fast. She wouldn't be able to keep the mike in front of it for a full thirty seconds.

"Wait!" She called out as the creature was directly in front of the crevice. The creature stopped although it continued to sing its directions to the beasts below. Its eyes narrowed as it peered into Diana's hiding spot. If it attacked her now, she would be helpless in this position. The creature took a step toward the stone.

"Cawait!" A cry came from above her. "Cawait, Cawait." It came again. The creature yelled something upward and waved its arms. Diana saw a large crow take flight from the stone top. Another joined it, and together they spun off, cawing into the night.

The creature turned away and proceeded down the path.

"I sure hope you got what you needed, Chris." She said beneath her breath. "I'd hate to go through that again!"

She listened but heard no sounds of anything approaching along the path. Agonizingly, she extracted herself from the crevice, dropping onto the spot the creature had so recently vacated. She stuck the mike into her back pocket and proceeded down to where she could see the rest of the creatures assembling.

Moving more quietly than she ever had in her life, Diana slipped past several of the creatures along her way to the main congregation. A large pool of dark green water reflected the occasional star that broke through the cloud filled night sky. The animals were climbing into the mouth of a large opening beneath two massive limestone chunks. About thirty of the white-furred creatures stood outside this entrance.

Diana was both horrified and relieved to find Alex and Jerrica in the center of these strange apparitions. Alex was sniffing as though he had been crying while Jerrica glowered defiantly at her captors. The children appeared ragged and disheveled but they did not look as if they had been harmed.

Many of the creatures were female and Diana thought she detected the one that had touched her at the house. How long would it take for Chris and Bill to arrive down here while carrying all that gear? If their descent was detected too soon, they might not be in a position where Chris could hold on to the cliff face and play his synthesizer at the same time. She may need to create another diversion.

Her thoughts were suddenly shifted as she heard Jerrica cry out. One of the creatures took her by the arm and began forcing her toward the cavernous opening. "Jerr!" Alex cried, seeing his sister so roughly handled. He lashed out with his foot and caught the creature nearest him on its shin. Its howl of pain soon transformed into a menacing snarl as the creature reached out with a clawed hand to strike the cowering boy.

"No!" Diana screamed and flung the sharp edged Bloodstone as she rushed from behind her covering block. The creature never had time to see his opponent as the dark green stone buried itself in its forehead. The red flecks of the stone's surface seemed to shimmer as real blood burst from the fallen creature's skull.

Diana appeared like a ghost in the midst of the amazed subterranean dwellers. "So much for a diversion," she spoke into the headset. "Chris if you're on your way, you'd better hurry, the fat's in the fire and yours truly is cellulose toast."

Diana moved quickly to the side of her son. He grabbed her around the waist and buried his face in her blouse. The creatures had parted before her, seeming unwilling to indulge in one-on-one confrontation. After all, why should they, when they have an array of unstoppable zombie creatures to fight for them?

For whatever reason, the kids were being taken alive into the subterranean home of the creatures. Diana, however, seemed to be too much of an adversary to try to capture. The troll-like beast holding onto Jerrica drew her aside as the lilting voices of the subterranean dwellers lifted in unison, with the destruction of Diana being their one goal. A repugnant tide of vermin spewed from the cavern. Writhing legs, arms and wings collided and crawled over each other as insect and animal vied to be the one to bring their master's tormentor to Earth.

Diana hoped maybe they would stop with her and not take Alex as well. She pried the boy's clinging arms away and shoved him up the path from whence she came. She leaped in the opposite direction and ran to the edge of the deep green pit.

The creature's voices changed pitch and the tide of vermin turned as one and boiled toward Diana, cutting her off from the children as her heel hung over the sheer edge of the pit. Plunging into the water would be no escape, Diana knew. The animals would follow and their dead weight clinging to her would drag her to the frigid depths below. Of course, she thought, that would probably be preferable to being torn apart before her children's eyes.

She slapped a sparrow away from her eyes. Again the animating melody of the creatures changed pitch. The nauseous flow of carrion turned again, just before toppling Diana into the water and to her amazement, began flinging themselves into the murky depths.

Most of them silently disappeared to the bottom. A few floated on the surface, but none made any attempt to extricate themselves from the watery embrace.

The white creatures were furious from seeing their collected army of zombie slaves sinking out of sight. They raged at each other, seeking the cause of the disharmony that allowed this calamity to happen.

A call from the rocks above turned all eyes to the approach of Chris and Bill. Chris had strapped on his portable synth while Bill struggled behind him with a small amplifier and battery pack. The creature that first spotted them rushed the pair. Bill dropped the amp and brought up his flashlight full into the night-dweller's eyes. Blinded, it miscalculated its leap and came up short against a solid block of limestone with a bone-snapping thud.

"Looks like a stalemate." Bill said as he bent to retrieve the amp. "Walk over here to us son." Bill called to Alex. "Don't run though. We don't want them to think we're afraid."

Alex got behind the two men. He held onto his father's belt like a lifeline.

They were still several yards up the path from the cavern entrance, where the creature still had its grip upon Jerrica. The creature extended deadly claws beneath the frightened child's chin. Diana was also too far below them to be able to reach her daughter before the creature could tear her throat out.

Bill dropped the amp again and took his pistol out of his jacket pocket. "I doubt I can hit that thing without the risk of hitting the girl too! If I fire over its head, it might be frightened enough to let her go."

"Or it might scare him into killing her." Chris' voice shook with the thought of making the right choice.

"Please." Diana spoke to the creature holding her daughter and started walking toward them. "Let her go. She's just a child."

White fangs glistened as the creature snarled a warning for Diana to halt her approach. It gripped the girl's throat menacingly and Diana saw a line of blood on her daughter's pale flesh as one claw broke the skin.

She stepped back a pace and turned to Chris. "What do we do?" She looked around at the other creatures. They all seemed to be waiting for this bizarre tableau to conclude before they took any further action. The one holding Jerrica was obviously the main instigator behind the attacks. The others, although following its lead, didn't appear to be independently aggressive.

Diana saw the female creature again and held out her hands attempting to implore to her seemingly kind nature. Compassion showed in the creature's overly large eyes. It spoke a brief haunting melodic plea to the one holding Jerrica hostage. The refusal in its reply needed no translation. The young girl's eyes bulged with terror as the creature began dragging her toward the opening. "Mom, Dad?" The plea was barely audible through her tightly gripped throat.

"Bill!" Diana called. "You have to shoot it! If it goes below, we'll never see her again!"

Bill cocked the hammer and gripped the gun with both hands. The creature seemed to know what he was attempting and kept the girl between them as it neared the opening. "I can't get a shot." Bill's face was covered in sweat. "God help me, I can't do it!"

The creature had one foot into the opening. "Mommy!" Called Jerrica as she was forced along, helpless in the grasp of the creature.

The entire scene in the limestone pit took on a different hue as the final clouds departed the sky and the full moon shined down, reigning the heavens. The creatures blinked in the diffused light; the moon glow was barely tolerable to their night born eyes.

Diana gasped as a new figure entered the scene. On the stone a few feet above the cavern stood Crescent. She was bathed in the radiant glow of the moon, which was mirrored in her haloed features. Her stance was regal as her gossamer robes flowed around her like a living thing. A silver tiara was bestowed upon her brow with a Crescent moon cast in the center. She had thrown off the cloak of age and stood before them all as a timeless beauty. An ivory bow was clasped in her hand and white feathers jutted from silver shafted arrows that protruded from her quiver.

She was flanked on either side by a hound. Their coats seemed to glow with fire as the moon reflected off their sheen. The pearl of their teeth was evident as their eyes locked upon the creature holding Jerrica, for his was a scent they would never forget.

"Release the girl and go on your way." The command in her voice would brook no disagreement. "No harm shall befall you or your kin if you return to your caverns now and trouble the surface dwellers no more."

Diana saw the female lower its eyes from Crescent and begin to slowly move toward the cavern entrance. As she watched, one by one the others did the same. But Diana wasn't the only watcher. The creature that held her daughter was beyond Crescent's amity. Diana screamed as the beast lifted her daughter's feet from the ground, preparing to hurl her into the cavern's depths.

Crescent's movements were too swift for the eye to follow. In one continuous motion, two arrows were notched and fired as one. The creature stared in surprise at the twin silver shafts that protruded from its chest. With an almost gentle motion it sat the girl down on the cavern floor and released its hold.

Jerrica ran to her mother as the creature's knees began to buckle. Before it hit the ground, the two hounds launched themselves from Crescent's side and were rending the fallen creature without mercy. They knew this creature as the one who had attacked their master, Clem. They marked their vengeance into the reddened stone as they ruined its body.

Diana led Jerrica to where the men stood. They all watched as the creatures filed past and entered the opening to the world below. Chris turned to call his thanks to Crescent but she had vanished as if never having been there.

Chris dropped his keyboard and picked up his son. "It's over. Leave the gear here, Bill. We'll have enough to handle getting ourselves up out of this pit."

Bill nodded. "I'm getting too old for this shit. I think I'll turn my truck in for a nice sedan when we get back."

As they started up the path, Diana looked at Chris. "Do you think it's really over?"

"Some things never end, they merely change as we go along. I guess all we can do now is try to make things change for the better if we meet up with our furry friends again."

A lone white-coated female was the last of the creatures to enter the cave. She watched as the humans departed. She knelt down and picked up a button that had popped from Jerrica's blouse. She smiled as the last moonlight shadow of the humans disappeared over the ridge.   She placed the button into her side pouch and then followed her people into their subterranean world.

PROLOGUE

Diana had talked briefly to Crescent on the phone during the preceding days. Crescent had insisted that they come over to her house to discuss the past events in depth. As they pulled into the drive, they saw Bill's macho truck parked next to the porch. Sounder and Singer yawned, lazily wagging their tails. As the kids scratched their heads before entering the house, the dogs sniffed their clothes for the scent of their cat, Bighead.

The pungent Herbs and tea smells were welcome aromas to Diana, who had spent the last few days cleaning and disinfecting her house of carcasses.

"Bill, good to see you." Bill sat on the sofa with a cup of tea. He placed the cup on an old trunk, which served as a coffee table, and shook Chris's hand.

"Chris, Diana. This is Clem." Bill indicated the one-handed man on the other end of the sofa, who was also drinking tea.

"Forgive me if I don't shake hands." Clem said. "I'm new at this one arm stuff and I'm not quite sure how it's done."

Diana walked into the kitchen where Crescent was giving cookies to the kids. "Well, Crescent, two suitors on one couch? What will the neighbors say?" Diana raised one eyebrow in accusation.

"Why, whatever I tell them to say, of course. Tea, dear?"

Diana laughed. Crescent was unshakable.

When everyone was seated Bill began. "As best as I can put all of this together, these creatures have been around as long as man has and maybe longer. Their ability to draw their food to them and man continually encroaching on their space drove them further and further beneath the ground."

"The colony we had our little conflict with, had it pretty good for awhile. The Indians, living in this area, left sacrifices to them in the surrounding caverns. When the white man came along and disrupted these ceremonies it didn't really affect them that much because the white man had this custom of burying his dead in the ground which was just too convenient for our little friends to pass up."

"The limestone quarry brought hundreds of settlers to the area. Blasting and digging limestone was dangerous business in the days before O.S.H.A. The graveyard was right next to the quarry. Between natural death and accidents the colony of Earth dwellers did all right for themselves."

Bill took another sip of his chamomile tea and continued. "Here lately, progress was catching up to the town. People were moving away from the quarries and new graveyards were built further out of town. When the quarry our friends used as their access played out, a new mining operation was started miles from here. No one was buried in the old graveyard anymore and the dead animal population that was able to travel down the caverns was hardly sufficient to feed our friends. So they came up seeking food and found a whole New World."

"So no human was using them for ill intent after all?" Diana asked.

"No, I don't believe so." Bill answered. "What do you think Crescent?"

"I agree with Bill. No one could control such creatures for long. I think they were driven by survival. They discovered how to attack and kill with the creatures already under their control. This new technique would allow them a limitless food supply, provided the ethics of eating other sentient beings didn't offend them."

Chris entered the conversation. "So why were they trying to take the children alive? If they had killed and controlled them, they probably would have gotten underground before we caught up to them."

"Breeding stock." Bill's statement was so blunt that everyone was taken by surprise. They are, after all, quick learners. The creatures observed the way in which we confine livestock for future food supplies. Evidently they thought it a worthwhile endeavor to emulate. They may have taken other live animals down in the caverns already.

The implications stunned everyone into silence. Diana finally spoke up, breaking the silence.

"Crescent, I have to ask you." Diana was hesitant. "You told me on the phone that you were leaving to talk to your sisters. Sheriff Dawson later said you were an only child. Was he mistaken?"

"No Diana, I am an only child. The sisters I referred to were not my sisters of blood, but rather my sisters in the Craft. I needed council to find out what was happening and how to proceed."

"You mean like in a coven?" Chris asked.

"Yes, very similar. Although I primarily work as a solitary, I will do workings with others when the need is there. And I'd say there definitely was a need."

"I concur. I don't think we would have made it out alive if not for you." Bill exclaimed. "How did you know where we were?"

"Yeah!" Alex added. "And where did you learn to shoot a bow like that?"

"I was not acting alone. With my sister's help, in a ritual much like the one Diana performed for invisibility, I took on the personification of a Goddess to aid us all."

"I wasn't there." Clem broke in. "Which Goddess were you?"

"Why, my patron Deity of course." Crescent smiled. "The Goddess Diana. Queen of the hunt and the full moon."

"But to bring us back to the problem of the creatures," Bill continued, "without a current food supply they'll have no choice but to return to the surface or starve."

"Or relocate," offered Chris.

"I guess negotiations of that sort will have to be addressed by their ambassadors and ours." Crescent said to the stunned faces of the group.

"You mean try to peacefully communicate with them?" Diana said.

"I don't think it's possible". Clem spoke up.

"Of course it is possible." Crescent said. "The children already had a rudimentary vocabulary going with their friend Kratel."

"But Kratel was special." Jerrica finally spoke up. "We can never find another like him."

"Then I guess we will just have to use him." Crescent finalized.

"What?" Everyone else said at once.

"Come with me." Crescent led the way through a door in the back of the room. It was a spare bedroom and there, sitting up under the blankets, was Kratel.

His upper torso was swathed in bandages. His loin cloth and belt pouch hung over the foot post of the bed.

"Kratel!" The children tried to rush in but Crescent slowed them.

"Gently." She cautioned. "He's still recovering."

Diana was fearful as the kids approached the creature, which was like the one that nearly destroyed her whole family. But as the creature gently stroked Jerrica's hair and called Alex by name she realized that love could transcend many barriers.

"How is it that he is still alive?" Chris asked. "I saw him take a bullet in the heart."

"Kratel was found by one of the pagan folk in the community. They brought him to Celeste, one of my sisters, while I was there. He was in a state of deep coma with hardly any visible life signs. That was why one of his kind was able to control his body. The bullet had smashed its way through the left side of his chest and out the back. Fortunately for him, his race has their heart on the opposite side humans do. That knowledge helped me thwart the creature holding Jerrica hostage."

Crescent walked over and felt Kratel's head for fever.

"He lost a lot of blood and his left lung was damaged. He seems to have amazing recuperative abilities though. He regained consciousness while I nurtured him and he communicated the children's danger to me as well as the location of the entrance to their underground home. He has responded well to my ministrations. He should be back on his feet in no time."

The adults returned to the living room allowing the children a few moments with their friend.

"Bill, would you kindly give me a lift back home?" Clem asked. "I'm still a little tired from all this excitement." Clem struggled a bit with his balance as he attempted to stand. Bill started to help and then decided against it. He knew Clem did not want to be treated like an invalid, so he let the big man regain his balance alone.

"Thank you for taking care of my dogs." Clem said softly to Crescent. "They're the only family I got."

She handed him a paper bag and said. "Not any more they're not. You're welcome here anytime. I put some healing salve and some Herb tea in there for you." Crescent pointed to the bag. It'll help you get your strength back quicker."

"Crescent." Bill said as he followed Clem out the door. "You're a special woman. I'd like to come back to visit also, if I may?"

"My pies will be out of the oven by noon on Tuesday. It would be a shame if one didn't get eaten while it was hot."

"That it would, That it would." Bill tipped his hat to Diana and Chris on his way out. Clem held the door open for him, then closed it as they left.

"We better be going too, Honey." Chris said. "I'll get the kids in the car. Goodnight Crescent, thank you." Chris kissed the lady on the cheek, then turned to collect the kids.

Crescent held up an orange cat hair, which she had removed from Chris's shoulder. "Still claim you don't have a cat?"

"Everything deserves a home. Still I'm not sure if we own him or he owns us?" Diana suddenly became serious. "I can never thank you enough, Crescent." Diana hugged the woman until tears streamed down her face.

"Oh my dear one," Crescent smiled through her tears, "but how I do intend to make you try."

Edred Breedlove and Trish Breedlove

ABOUT THE AUTHOR

Ed Breedlove was born in Bedford, Indiana, and also lived in Indianapolis and Harrison, Ohio. He is a novelist, published songwriter and recording artist proficient as a guitarist and midi composer. He studied Shamanism from the Harmon Institute and the Wolf Clan of the Lakota Sioux. Ed does divination using Runes and Stones and is a Reiki II Healer.

Trish Breedlove was born in Cincinnati, Ohio. She writes poetry, ritual, how-to books and novels. Trish leads workshops on Tarot, GemStones, Chakra Healing, Sacred Dance, and Designing Herb Gardens. Trish is a Reiki Master and Wiccan Priestess.

Ed and Trish live on eight acres of Sanctuary in Southeast Indiana with their son, Kevin, 5 cats, 18 chickens and 2 dogs.

Printed in the United States
1201100004B/388-396

9 781410 765987